Tarot of the Archons

Immortal Montero Book Two

By Greg Mongrain

The characters and events portrayed in this book are fictitious. Any similarity to persons alive or dead is coincidental and not intended by the author.

Text copyright © 2016 Greg Mongrain
All Rights Reserved

Manufactured in the United States of America
10 9 8 7 6 5 4 3 2 1

For Lauren

Prologue

My greatest fear is to be caught by an unscrupulous man—or an enemy—and imprisoned. If my tormentors were to strap me to a table and decide to torture me to death twenty-four hours a day for weeks, even months, I would surely lose my sanity the way any man would. A far more terrible thought is what if nothing could drive me insane?

Sometimes, listening to the crickets, the dark smoothing away ephemeral thoughts, my mind calculates how many times I could die in a day. As long as I don't have to regenerate a limb or reskin myself after being burned, I can recover in as few as twenty seconds, certainly under a minute. Sixty times an hour, let's say, if death is instantaneous upon my regaining consciousness. One thousand four hundred and forty times a day—I get shot in the head one minute and wake up to a man who curses at me before jamming a knife into my heart. When I come to, two giggling men hold my mouth and nose closed, and when I wake up after that, a man watching me with hatred, leans over and begins slowly cutting my throat with a rusty serrated knife. Coming to and smelling gasoline, I see a man at the end of the table holding a match . . .

It made Sisyphus's punishment look like a Club Med vacation.

Yes, I have lived for more than seven centuries, appear to be a youngish thirty, and have amassed such a fortune I spend time figuring out how to lose some of it before a government begins to wonder how I could possibly have acquired assets so extensive in one lifetime. I drive expensive sports cars, go anywhere I want, do anything that amuses me. As enviable as that sounds, my nightmares are much worse than yours.

Because you can only die once.

Tsim Sha Tsui, Hong Kong
Thursday, April 9, 1949

I strode across the lobby of the Peninsula Hong Kong hotel, my shoes clicking on the floor of the magnificent foyer. Ignoring the concierge, I proceeded directly to the elevators. This place contained nice memories. I had been here twenty-one years ago when the hotel, the crown of the island, had opened. I had amazed the patrons of the Nathan bar by drinking four magnums of ice-cold Taittinger champagne in five minutes. Doing that gives one a very chilly head indeed.

The lift doors opened, and I stepped aboard.

"Have you eaten rice today, my son?" I asked the young elevator operator cordially in Mandarin.

"Yes, thank you, father," he replied politely. I nodded and faced the closing doors. As soon as the car started to rise, he began speaking rapidly in Cantonese.

"The colonel is on the ninth floor, sir, but you'll never get near him. Third houseboy Tang said he was checked five times by armed men before he was allowed into the suite to collect the laundry."

"Let me worry about them," I told him in the same language. "Take me to the twelfth. What else do you know about his setup?" The elevator passed the fifth floor.

"He always stays in this same room. He had it altered five years ago, very quietly. There is a secret door in the parlor, behind the bar. Beyond is a space just large enough for one person to be able to sit. He keeps an armed man in there most of the time."

"Nice work," I told him.

As the circle lit for the eighth floor, I pulled the Beretta out of my shoulder holster and checked the safety. The shiny new grooves circling the end of the barrel matched the threads inside the heavy Brausch silencer in my jacket pocket. I slid the gun back under my arm and re-buttoned my coat.

We passed the tenth, then the eleventh, and the elevator came to a smooth stop at twelve. The doors slid open.

"Good luck, sir."

I stepped out, turned right, and walked across a blue-and-gold carpet to the double doors at the end, keying myself into room 1202. Once inside, I closed the door and locked it. I checked both bedrooms and both bathrooms. As soon as I confirmed the suite was empty, I returned to the parlor.

A pale green carpet with a gold border stretched from wall to wall. Near the balcony doors, an oak sideboard contained tantalizing bottles of liquor. I stood next to a large, blocky executive desk with a guest chair in front and a high-backed chair behind it. It faced into the parlor, where there were three chairs around a table with a lamp, a brocade couch, and a long, low divan.

I walked past the bar and slid open the glass door leading to the balcony, stepped out into the balmy Hong Kong afternoon, and moved to the railing so I could look below.

This room lay directly above Colonel Nishiki's suite, three stories higher. His balcony jutted slightly left of mine. No others stood between these two, and none stuck out below his. Like mine, his had a small outdoor table and chairs and a brazier on which to burn fragrant sticks of incense.

I stepped back into my room and sat on the long gold-upholstered divan. I removed my watch and turned it so the back faced up, took a dime out of my pocket, inserted it into a groove carved on the watch case, and twisted clockwise a half turn. The crown popped up.

Holding the watch in my right hand, I pressed the crown down with my thumb. The case vibrated for three seconds. When it stopped, I strapped the watch, now useless, back on my wrist.

By pressing the crown, I had transmitted a high-frequency signal, and now the US Hong Kong field office was sending a coded radio transmission to the commander of the sixteenth fighter-interceptor squadron, giving them the signal to launch their wing of four F-80Cs, America's new fighter jets.

I sat cross-legged on the couch, closed my eyes, and began to meditate on the universe. I knew it would be at least thirty minutes before the jets could scramble, even though they were waiting for the order.

I had drifted light-years away when a high whine brought me back. I opened my eyes, climbed off the divan, and strode back outside. The sky remained clear. I waited. The distinctive rumble of the F-80s approached. Swinging one leg over the railing, then the other, I gripped the metal bars, let my feet slide off, and struggled down until I hung by my hands.

I desperately tried to still my swaying body before the jets arrived. I looked up. I could not see them yet, but the noise they were making would cover the sound of my landing. I let go.

The roar as the planes overflew us became earsplitting—the high whine of the turbines on top of the booming howl of raw power drowned everything else out. I dropped in the middle of this maelstrom, looking down, hoping I wouldn't hit the railing and go tumbling over into the bay. As the jets' passage washed over us, I crash-landed on the colonel's balcony.

I hit awkwardly; my left ankle snapped, and my right leg landed stiff, directly on the heel, jamming my knee up and dislocating my hip. I fell onto my side, the bolt of pain from my broken and tortured bones pushing an inaudible cry out of me.

All of this occurred in a maelstrom of sound even as the jets began to peel away, their thunder still reverberating back to us, shaking the hotel, the building's tall, flat exterior amplifying the concussive sound wave.

The people stationed at the American embassy would get a call about violating airspace by flying too close to the hotel, but they were ready for it and were prepared to say they were terribly sorry—it would never happen again.

I had just dragged myself behind the garden furniture, cursing in Korean and Japanese, when the door slid open. I stopped moving and watched through the legs of a wicker chair.

A man pushed past the curtain and took a step outside. He wore a long red smoking jacket with black lapels and black cuffs. He looked up at the retreating jets, a sneer on his face. He turned and walked back inside, leaving the door slightly ajar.

I waited, catching my breath, feeling the internal engine that repairs my injuries kick into high gear. Clenching my teeth, I popped my hip back into place. Intense pain flashed, nearly forcing a cry of agony from me. After that, a dull ache remained. I tested my ankle. It still hurt but worked fine.

Cautiously getting to my feet, I remained crouched behind the lounge chairs. On one knee, I pulled the Beretta out and took the short, precisely machined metal tube from my jacket pocket. I screwed the thick silencer onto the end of the gun. Once the muffler tightened in place, I thumbed the safety off.

With the pistol pointing along my right leg, I crept across the balcony. The afternoon sun shone on the opposite side of the building, so I did not generate a shadow that could fall on the curtains.

As I neared the crack in the door, I could hear people talking inside, speaking in Japanese.

" . . . jets are made by the fat, overfed Americans. They will never be a threat."

"Don't be so sure. The Americans may be fat, but their funding is equally substantial. It will only become more difficult to keep up with them if we fall behind early."

"Surely it's not so bad as that."

"Those jets are more advanced than anything we or our allies have, and air domination is war domination. We do not commit as much money to vital research and development as we should."

"Yes, sir."

"That's all. And keep an eye on that elevator boy."

Footsteps crossed the room. A door opened, clicked shut. I waited, heard the creak of someone sitting in a leather-covered chair. A few more moments. There were no other sounds.

I stepped through the opening, half-in and half-out, pushing the curtain back with my left hand, the gun extended, the man behind the desk already in my sights. I did not fire. He had not seen me. He was bent over, absorbed in something he was writing. I looked around cautiously. We were alone. The wet bar stood to my left. I would have to walk past it if I wanted to get closer.

The colonel had mounted his war sword on the wall behind him. I made a note of that.

I crossed the room as silently as a beam of light. When I came into his peripheral vision, he gasped, flinched back in his chair, and dropped his pen. He looked up and opened his mouth when he saw me.

"Make a sound and I will be forced to shoot you," I said softly.

He closed his mouth.

I recognized him from his pictures, but he had done well transforming himself. He looked his part: a business executive who had made his fortune in the Japanese textile industry and retired shortly before the end of the war. He had put fifty pounds on his spare frame in the last two years, changing his overall appearance drastically, and he had begun to bald. He no longer had a tan but rather the florid features of a heavy drinker. Drowning his guilt, no doubt.

His eyes gave him away. I saw the same cruel glint that had been the last thing more than three hundred civilians had seen before he beheaded them with his blade.

He and his men called it baseball. Four people at a time—men, women, children—were placed at four corners on their knees, blindfolded, hands bound behind their backs. They were the bases. The "hitter" stood in the center of them, his sword held high. If he could hack off all four heads with four strokes, it was a home run.

Colonel Nishiki and his men had become proficient at hitting home runs during the war.

His gaze was calculating as he took in my automatic pistol. I sat in the guest chair on the other side of the desk. His cigarettes sat on top. He pointed to them. I nodded.

I crossed my legs and laid the Beretta on my thigh. I straightened the crease at the knee of my pants, pulled my pack of Players out. We both lit up simultaneously. I snapped my stainless steel Zippo shut and placed it on the desk, its mirror-like exterior giving me a tiny view of the room behind me. I slid my pack in my pocket, tilted my head back, and blew smoke at the ceiling.

He shook out his match and tossed it in the ashtray. He had one book on his desk. It didn't look as if it had a title. The edge of a thick card with a gleaming gold border stuck out of the pages. He took a long puff, his hands steady. He closed his eyes momentarily. The smoke hissed out between his lips.

We locked eyes. For more than a minute we smoked and stared.

"How did you get in here?" Now that he knew I was not going to kill him outright, his voice was relaxed, even amused. The voice of a man who has an ace up his sleeve.

I continued staring at him, silently smoking.

"You have come to kill me? Why?"

I tapped the ash off my cigarette and let it fall to the carpet. A flash of irritation crossed his face. Such impertinence. I decided then to kill him as slowly as his flabby body would allow.

"I am a retired business owner. Who am I to you?"

I shook my head.

"I tell you, you have me confused with someone else, young man." He tried to appear relaxed and confident, but he still sat straight up, not leaning back. His eyes cut to the wet bar.

I could imagine his rising panic and fury at the thought that his sentry might have fallen asleep.

I continued to smoke my cigarette. When I had taken my final puff, I exhaled, opened my mouth, tossed the butt in, and swallowed.

He blinked. He hesitantly took another puff and leaned forward. As he stubbed his cigarette out, the crystal ashtray wobbled under his now shaking hand.

I picked the gun off my thigh and pointed it leisurely at him.

The man in the secret room never made a sound, and the colonel never gave anything away on his face. But I saw movement in the Zippo and knew the guard was positioning himself behind me.

"You are making a very bad mistake, my foolish friend," the colonel said. He leaned back comfortably and steepled his hands. "Would you like to tell me your name while you still can?"

I cocked the pistol.

"Stop," said a voice from behind me.

I felt the barrel of a gun touching the back of my neck. With the pistol pressed against me, the man reached over my shoulder for the Beretta. I pushed the chair back into him hard and twisted to my right, falling to the ground. As I came up on my knees, he fired. The bullet caught me in the chest, slamming me backward. I crashed into the wall next to the bathroom, slumped sideways into the doorway. My head hit the frame hard enough to cut my forehead. Warm blood seeped into my right eye.

I sat up. The shooter already loomed over me.

"Good night," he said in Japanese.

I looked into the single eye of his .45 automatic as he pulled the trigger. The bullet snapped my head back, and my whole body went rigid as the metal object plowed into my brain. I shook and consciousness left me.

I heard a buzzing in my head. Not unpleasant. A soft drone. Soothing. A white light beckons me. I feel a presence. Mama? Marguerite? I turn . . .

Crash. Return of light and form. Shiver. Back. Sounds. Alive.

"What were you doing in there while he had me covered, you fool?" The voice growled, full of menace. I heard a slap. And again.

I was twisted to the side, my body still crumpled in the doorway to the bathroom. My eyes were open. I was careful not to move them. I could feel drying blood on my forehead. My body tingled as the internal mechanism of my repair process mended my wounds. I told it not to heal the hole in my forehead. How my body knew what I meant, I did not know. I only knew I could control my repairs by thinking about them.

"Please, Colonel," the man said. Another slap.

"Don't call me that! Have you lost your mind as well as your vigilance?"

"No, sir."

Pounding footsteps. Three more men strode into the room.

"What the hell happened?" the first one said. "Sir?"

"How did this man get in here?" the colonel asked.

"I don't know."

"Then why are you standing there? Find out! Somebody is going to wish the day never happened!"

I could see their shapes out of the corner of my eye, all of them standing next to the desk.

"What do we do about him now?"

The phone rang. My gun lay on the desk in front of the guest chair.

The colonel picked up the phone. "Yes?" As he spoke, he looked at his men, waved them out, and nodded. They left the room quickly, the clicking of the door marking their exit.

"No," the colonel said into the phone. "Do not send anyone up. It was a loud champagne bottle. We are drinking mimosas. No. I forbid it. My guards will not allow your security men to enter. Do you know who I am? Correct. Now do you understand? Good. Please send up a boy with a large, empty dining cart. He is to leave it with my men. Not at all. Thank you."

He hung up the phone and stubbed out his cigarette. After a look at me, he walked around his desk and went behind the wet bar, bent down, and came up with a bottle of Wild Turkey and an ice bucket. A tumbler came next. He reached for the ice, hesitated, pulled his hand back. Grabbing the whiskey, he twisted the top, breaking the paper seal, and poured two thick fingers of the dark liquid into the tumbler. He tossed it back, downing the large shot in one gulp.

The glass rattled as he set it down, his face scrunched from the burn of the liquor. Slowly, the lines of his face relaxed. Now he added ice to the glass, poured more whiskey over the cubes, and returned to his desk.

I had four, maybe five minutes before the houseboy arrived with the cart that the colonel undoubtedly planned to use to get rid of my body. Then this room would be filled with men, and I would never get near him.

Straightening up slowly, I slid silently up the door frame until I sat up with my legs in front of me. The colonel relaxed in his chair, eyes closed, touched the cold, sweating glass to his forehead.

I stood quietly and managed to take the four steps to his desk and sit down in the guest chair without making a sound. I wiped the blood off my forehead and ordered my body to repair the wound.

The colonel lowered the glass, took a sip, and opened his eyes. I gazed into them. He made a sound—"guk!"—and coughed. His glass slipped from his fingers and fell into his lap. I heard the thump as the leaded crystal hit the carpet.

I leaned forward, retrieved my gun from his desk and set it on my thigh. I pulled my pack out, shook a cigarette from it, and picked up the Zippo. I lit the cigarette and exhaled.

"I am afraid we were rudely interrupted, Colonel," I said.

"But . . . you . . ." He looked back at the bathroom door, seeing the spatters of blood on the door frame and linoleum floor. "How . . .?" His eyes widened as he gaped at my forehead. I could feel the itching sensation as the gunshot hole closed. His complexion turned waxen and pasty.

"Have another cigarette," I said. "I guarantee you will not die of lung cancer."

He leaned forward and shakily lit another of his foul Chinese gaspers.

"What are you?" he whispered.

"A *kami*," I said, using the Japanese word for spirit, or ghost. "And I have come to collect a debt." I puffed, exhaled. "A blood debt."

"Please," he said. "You have the wrong—"

"You escaped the International Military Tribunal, but you were recognized—quite accidentally—by an attaché to US Naval Intelligence stationed here in Hong Kong." I casually flicked ash off the end of my cigarette. "You really should have stayed someplace less luxurious, Colonel. But that wouldn't do for you, would it? I am afraid your taste for elegance has left you exposed."

"And now you are here to kill me. Is that it?"

"No," I said. "I am here to make sure that the justice meted out to you, Colonel Nishiki, is sufficiently painful." I ground out my cigarette and stood, leveling the gun on his chest. "Stand up."

He rose slowly, his smoking jacket dark where he had spilled his drink, drops rolling down the satin fabric and dripping onto the floor.

"Now—"

I heard a strange sound behind me, like an electric crackle. I instinctively hunched and turned toward it.

A man stood in the middle of the room, leaning forward, his right hand extended toward me. The barbed shuriken flew halfway across the room before I saw it coming. I turned my head to the side, but one of the steel points sliced my face, slicing my cheek open. I grunted and dropped the Beretta. I stepped to the right, crouched defensively.

My mind raged in turmoil: where had this man come from? Had there been two men in the secret room? No. The room was too small for that. And that sound . . .

I felt my muscles tighten as the poison from the throwing star spread through my body. I took several gasping breaths. Curare. My lungs were shutting down.

The colonel took his military sword off the wall and drew it out of its scabbard. The steel made a low, metallic hiss as he did. "Do you play baseball, Mr. Assassin?" he asked.

I fought off the toxin but continued to pretend I was in respiratory distress, my legs shaking slightly.

The colonel walked around the desk and stood in front of me. The other man walked over next to him, a tall man dressed all in black, skintight cotton, only his mouth and eyes visible.

"On your knees," the colonel said, gesturing with the sword.

I fell to my knees, gasping, hand at my chest, eyes pleading.

"I don't know how you survived, but it must have been a freak shot," he said. "Let us see if you can reattach your head."

He lifted the blade high. As the sword whistled down in a powerful arc, I leaned back, lying flat, feeling the heels of my shoes digging into my shoulders. The blade whirled over me. I continued with my motion, flipping over, pushing up with my hands, and landing on my feet. I picked the heavy glass ashtray off the top of the desk and threw it at the colonel, hitting him in the chest. He grunted loudly and fell to his knees as the ashtray thudded to the carpet. The sword jangled as it slipped out of his hand.

The other man had a second poisoned star in his hand primed to throw. He did not. "Who are you?" he asked.

I was intrigued, but I had a job to do. If this man hesitated, fine. I dove to the carpet, curled my hand around the butt of the Beretta, and fired at him just as he threw his shuriken. My gun made a soft spitting sound and a blue hole opened up on the man's forehead. He jerked backward, falling flat. His throw went left. The barbed metal slammed into the side of the desk in front of my eyes, embedding itself in the wood.

The colonel was still reaching for his sword when I swung the barrel of my silenced gun around on him. He gave a cry of fear.

Voices in the corridor outside and footsteps pounding toward us told me I had no more time. I shot the colonel in his right hand and stood quickly. I took two steps and picked up his sword.

"Please, can't you leave me in peace?"

"Yes," I said.

He gave me an uncertain smile.

"You may have that. The peace of the grave. Perhaps then, your victims will have it, too."

He tried to fall out of the way, but I had seen men try that for centuries. I leaned to the left, brought the sword straight down, and chopped off his head. The colonel hit the carpet. His head didn't roll away, attached to his neck by a thin bridge of skin and sinew.

I dropped the blade on the floor and ran to the sliding door, jumping over the body of the tall man on the way. The door burst open behind me just as I pushed through the curtain.

"Stop!" a man shouted in Japanese. I continued onto the balcony. Two shots boomed out. A stabbing pain heated my back, and I flew forward, landing on my chest. I scrambled up, knowing I could not afford to let them catch me.

The sliding glass door crashed the rest of the way open. I jumped on top of the railing and looked down at the filthy water, boulders below the surface.

"Stop!" someone shouted again. More gunshots, too many to count. I dove forward as two bullets hit me in the back and three hit me in the rear.

As the water rushed up and I approached the rocks—knowing how much this was going to hurt—I spread my arms wide, chest out, and kept my feet together in a perfect swan dive.

Chapter 1

Present Day
Friday, January 23, 5:18 p.m.

I lay in bed with a vampire, waiting for her to wake up. The sun would set in two minutes. The room radiated warmth, softly lit by the fading rays outside the open door.

This marked the third time Aliena had stayed with me during the day. When the sun rises, vampires drop into an unconscious fugue and become as helpless as creatures can become. For that reason, they always sleep in places too difficult for mortals to access, like mountaintops, deep caves, or parts of the forest no one visited. By staying here under my supervision, Aliena had placed her life in my hands.

We were in my Malibu home, in a guest bedroom I had decorated especially for her. In addition to the huge four-poster bed and Tiffany lamps, the modifications included blacking out the one big window in the room and changing the glass to a high-security bulletproof composite that could not be broken.

The door leading to the rest of the house had a computer-controlled lock. A glass security panel on the wall next to the door served as the knob. To open the door, Aliena pressed her palm against the plate. A security scanner read her palm imprint and compared it with the examples in its memory. Once it confirmed her identity, it would lock or unlock. Once closed and locked, the door sealed the room from any possible intrusion. A matching scanning plate lay outside at shoulder height against the wall.

I was the only other person allowed access by the scanner, but I entered only if Aliena permitted it. She had not allowed it before this morning.

I reclined on my side, under the blankets. Aliena faced me, also on her side. Her thick mane of honey-colored hair spread softly on her pillow, spilling over her left cheek. Her pale complexion shone unblemished and unlined, and she looked peaceful as she slept. I stared at the sexy mole above her upper lip.

In all the time I had known her, she had never given me the location of her daytime sleeping place, so I had never before seen her wake up. I wondered if she would stretch in her sleep or if her face would twitch or if she would blink when she came to life.

She didn't do any of those things.

I watched, and one moment she slept; the next, her lustrous brown eyes opened and she looked at me. No blinking. No sleepiness.

I smiled at her, reached over, and pulled her close. Her yielding, cold, curvy body pressed against mine. I kissed her lightly on her icy lips. "Good evening," I said.

She reached one arm up and wound it around my neck. "This is nice," she murmured. "I could get used to it." She closed her eyes and snuggled against me. "Mmmm, you are so warm." Then she looked up at me suspiciously, raised the covers, and looked down at her body.

"What?" I said.

"Just checking." She lowered the blankets.

I did not like her implication, so I decided to tease her.

"Of course, any time today, I may have undressed you, played with your magnificent body for two hours, and then put your pajamas back on."

She gave me a stern look, her smooth brow now creased in a frown. "Did you?"

"No." I waited. "I played with it for three hours."

She wound her other arm around my back and crushed me to her. I howled as she cracked two vertebrae and broke three of my ribs.

"That is not funny, Sebastian," she said fiercely in my ear.

"Okay," I said, the pain of the broken bones immediate agony. "No more jokes! I promise!"

She released me. I rolled onto my back, rubbing my chest gingerly and grimacing at the stabbing, broken-glass feeling of my internal engine repairing my spinal column.

Note to self: do not tease Aliena when she wakes up. She's cranky in the early evening.

"I am so looking forward to the program at 49 tonight," she said, still on her side, now with her hand supporting her head. It relieved me to see she had gotten over my pain so quickly.

When I didn't say anything, she stroked my chest, climbed on top of me, pressed her hips into mine, leaned down, and tongued my neck. "You promised, Sebastian." She breathed against my skin, sending shivers through me that contrasted sharply with the fading pain of my injuries.

"Yes, I promised."

She smiled and hugged me—gently this time. She jumped out of bed, her Bugs Bunny pajamas swaying, walked over to the wardrobe, and opened the doors. My ribs and back ached, but they were nearly repaired so I swung my legs out of bed. I had joined Aliena just a few minutes earlier and had gotten under the covers fully dressed, except for my shoes.

"Hamilton called again yesterday," I told her, lacing a brogue. "He wants to talk to us." I work as a consultant to the LAPD, and Steve Hamilton is the detective with whom I usually work.

"He is very sweet."

"No," I said, without thinking.

She turned around. "You do not tell me no. I will not take him, but that is my decision, not yours."

I could not seem to stop making mistakes tonight. "You're right. I apologize. I did not mean to say it that way. I just meant he has a high enough profile and a real value to me as he is." I opened my mouth to add more when she laughed, a tinselly giggle.

"You may stop your analysis. I would never drink Detective Hamilton. I prefer him alive. Whenever he is near me, I can feel his desire washing over me in waves, and I find the sensation enjoyable."

"I'm sure."

She gave me a sad smile. "I wish he could let me have a small drink. I would even let him squeeze my bottom for that." Aliena did not have a bottom. She had a booty. A can.

I knew the experience of being on her bill of fare. The first night I encountered her, in 1864, I had played the role of dinner—one of those Aliena had decided to consume completely. Vampires rarely kill their "meals" since mortals would notice if too many people died of exsanguination. But Aliena was hungry that night and had taken me with the intention of draining me dry. Only my prodigious ability to replenish my blood saved me.

Hamilton had never been touched. He knew nothing of my immortal nature and remained unaware of the existence of vampires.

"He hasn't seen us in a month," I continued, "and we did run out on him last time. I know he has many questions."

"Yes," Aliena said, shucking off her pajamas. "I'm sure he does. And most of them will be questions I would rather not answer." She moved some of her clothes around. She kept the rest of her garments and personal belongings in an apartment she owned in Studio City.

Standing on her toes she reached for a towel off the top shelf of the armoire. Comfortable with her nakedness—even though she had been born in the seventeenth century, a time when nudity was nearly as bad as blasphemy—Aliena thought nothing of undressing in front of me. I loved her bare body, but her curves were ridiculously sexual, making it difficult for me to remain casual. Although she and I were dating (sort of), we had only reached the kissing and hugging stage, so the excitement of seeing her nude was tempered by the frustration of not being able to touch her.

In spite of her incredible body, her beautiful face made her unforgettable.

She padded across the room, her movements smoothly feline, her feet hardly seeming to touch the thick carpet.

"We will have to work with him again," I said, "and he's not going to forget."

She disappeared into the bathroom. "I am not so sure I want to work with him again, not after last time," she said, her voice echoing.

I could understand that. On our previous case, she had almost been raped and killed by the very serial murderer for whom Hamilton and I had been searching. Oh, and this killer had also been a sorcerer who wanted to cut Aliena's heart out so he could use it in magical rituals. It was what you'd call a traumatic experience.

The shower began running.

"He has some hard questions for me, too, you know that," I said. "I am going to do what I always do when it comes to questions about my nature."

She came back to the door with the towel wrapped around her. "Lie?"

"Of course. It makes up for all the other times when I tell the truth and it makes me look bad."

She frowned. "I've never heard you say anything that made you look bad."

"That's because you've known me for less than a hundred and fifty years."

She gave me a look. Then she removed the towel and slowly closed the door.

After her shower, dressed in jeans and a black T-shirt, Aliena flew off to get someone to eat. We agreed to meet at 49—her favorite club—at midnight.

I turned on the TV and switched to a football game replay. Five minutes later my cell buzzed. I muted the game.

"Montero."

"Sebastian, it's Hamilton."

Speak of the devil. "Yes, Steve. What can I do for you?"

"I'm over in Brentwood," he said loudly. I could hear other voices in the background, some shouting. "We've got an interesting one. I'd like you to take a look."

Brentwood sat southeast of Beverly Hills and Bel Air Estates, with pricey homes nearly as exclusive as those of its cousins.

"Of course," I said. "What's—"

"You're going to have to speak up."

I shouted, "What's so interesting?"

"Oh, nothing much. Just a dead rich man in a room locked from the inside."

"Did you say locked from the inside?" I pointed the remote, turned off the big screen.

"That's right."

"Then it's suicide," I said, disappointed.

"No. Gunshot wound to the temple."

"So? Still sounds like suicide."

"No gun." The din behind him increased. I wasn't sure I had heard him correctly.

"What?"

"So far, SID has not been able to find a gun in the room," Hamilton yelled, referring to the Scientific Investigation Division. "I've looked it over, too. There is no sign of the murder weapon

Chapter 2

Friday, January 23, 6:28 p.m.

The address Hamilton gave me was off Sunset Boulevard on Ashford. When I arrived twenty-five minutes after receiving Hamilton's call, emergency vehicles clustered around the residence and yellow tape surrounded the front yard.

I stepped out of the Maserati, slid my jacket on. A holster with a Beretta 92FS was clipped to my left hip. I had a permit to carry concealed and armed myself whenever I worked with the LAPD. The gun I usually carried was a Glock 23, but I had fired it in a compromising situation last month and decided it was time to go back to Beretta.

A crime scene at night has a surreal quality. All the police cars and other emergency vehicles had their lights flashing and their sirens off, which gave this dark tree-lined residential street the look of an alien landing strip. I wound my way through the cars, the loud buzz of the motors running and the rotating lights pulsing like the hidden machines of the Morlocks.

Neighbors stood in their yards, some drinking from mugs. A group of five teenage girls sat on the curb on the opposite side of the street, leaning forward, their arms crossed over their knees, faces pasty under the streetlight. Some people watched from lawn chairs in their front yards.

They observed the action silently and remained motionless, as if afraid to attract the attention of the person who had killed on their street tonight.

The officer securing the perimeter was a man I recognized. I flashed the ID card identifying me as a police consultant, and he held the tape up without a word. I ducked under and clamped the badge to my lapel.

I stood there for a moment looking at the house, the front facade lit up in the circular spotlights from the police cruisers. A white mansion in the neoclassical style, it had immaculately sculpted grounds and a thick, spongy lawn rising to the front porch.

Hamilton waited inside the door as I walked across the yard. When he saw me, he came out of the house and down the steps, walking quickly enough to cause his badge to flap against his jacket. He met me ten meters from the porch, holding his hand out to halt me there.

"Thanks for coming by," he said as we both stopped.

"My pleasure."

He nodded. We stared at each other for a few beats. He wore a taupe suit with an off-white shirt and a rust tie. Inexpensive but sharp. It helped that he was tall and good-looking, a cocoa-skinned man with an African American–Puerto Rican pedigree. His boyish face was made more interesting by a scar along the line of his left jaw.

"How is Aliena?" he asked.

"She's fine. I will let her know you asked."

"Why don't we all get together for dinner tonight?"

I shook my head. "Aliena is already dining with a friend."

"Tomorrow, then."

"I think she has plans." I had no idea what Aliena was doing tomorrow night, but she had made it clear *this* night that she intended to avoid Hamilton, so I dared not commit her to anything. Thinking about what she would do if I did, I pressed my hand to my chest, remembering how she woke up this evening. Hamilton saw me do it.

"Something wrong?"

"No." I lowered my hand.

He looked around, confirmed no one was within earshot, and turned back to me.

"Dammit," he said in a low voice. "The two of you have been avoiding me since we took Kanga out, and I still have some questions."

"That's one reason Aliena does not want to meet with you any time soon. She knows you will make her relive something she would rather forget."

"She was held hostage by a serial killer who just happened to be able to do magic." He looked around again, afraid his words might have been overheard, and dropped his voice. "Could she at least give me a statement?"

"I will ask."

"I could drag her into the station as a material witness. She was there when Kanga died."

I remained silent.

"What about you? Are you willing to answer some questions?"

"Of course."

"I guess that's something." He handed me a pair of nitrile exam gloves. "Come on, then."

We stopped on the porch and I signed the log before entering. While I pulled on the gloves, I nodded at the uniform standing behind the table. "Nice to see you again, Officer Kennedy." Kennedy had blonde hair and green eyes. Cute. She had been one of the responding officers on our previous case.

"You too, sir," she replied. She looked at the house, looked back at us. "I'm just glad they turned that music off."

I glanced at Hamilton.

"Oh, yeah, the music. When Kennedy first got here, a small tape recorder was playing in the study. Turned all the way up. Some kind of chanting or something. Tribal, maybe."

"Creepy is what it was," Kennedy said.

Hamilton led the way into the foyer. A huge staircase faced us, white wood with pale blue carpet, curving gracefully to the left and ending on a landing that became a hallway. We walked past it and turned down a corridor to our right, our shoes clicking on the hardwood floor.

"Vic's name is Mason Cavanaugh. Retired antiques dealer."

"Cavanaugh?"

"Yeah. Know him?"

"No, but I have shopped in his store." The two items I had purchased from Cavanaugh's included a beautiful Victorian standing mirror and a set of three Tiffany lamps. They currently decorated Aliena's room. "He acquired several of the rarest pieces I own."

"Yeah? You'll have to show me sometime. Never shopped there myself. I don't suppose they carry those inflatable football chairs?"

The hallway along which we walked stretched fifteen meters and ended in an ivory-colored wall with a beautiful stained glass window. Halfway down, a damaged doorway allowed loud voices to spill into the hall. I recognized one of the speakers as Hamilton's partner, Alfred Gonzales.

"No, you better leave that there," he said. "Our specialist might want to listen to it." From where we were, we could see the shattered door frame, its exposed wood gleaming whitely.

Hamilton and I stepped into the room. Gonzales loomed over a technician who wore a black Windbreaker with LAPD SID silk-screened in white on the front and back. The young man fitted a cassette tape into a small old-fashioned player. They looked up at us.

"Talking about anybody I know?" I asked Gonzales with a smile.

"Nobody important." Gonzales wore his usual brown suit. He looked like a nightclub bouncer who had fattened up a bit and decided to dress like an accountant. A bushy brown mustache adorned a face topped by a bad haircut. He favored short-sleeve dress shirts.

I turned to the body. Cavanaugh slouched in a wingback chair with his head tilted up. He sported a large hole in his forehead, like a third eye. The ME's people were still examining him, so Hamilton and I waited. I took my first close look at the office.

What a room! It reminded me of the secret dens I always hid in my estates, rooms that contained the notable—and valuable—artifacts I had accumulated over my lifetime.

To the left, an antique globe and a green-shaded dual library lamp stood on a Pembroke table from the late eighteenth century. I wandered over. To one side of the table stood a William IV mahogany bookcase with glassed-in shelves and gleaming brass accents. I inspected the books inside. Leather-bound first editions, including a rare three-volume set, *History of the Royal Residences of Windsor Castle* and a first edition of Milton's *Paradise Lost*. On the other side of the table, a beautiful rosewood escritoire gleamed.

Crowned with a buff ceiling, the room contained many other beautiful pieces—silk Turkish and Chinese rugs, an antique vase, and banker's lamps that softly illuminated the area. Overall, a scent of wood polish and old leather gave the room a warm, comfortable aura.

There were three paintings—two on my left and one on the back wall. All of them sat inside lit frames with glass fronts. I walked over to the nearest one and looked at it closely. A mother holding a child to her breast. I thought I recognized the style. Heart speeding up, I looked for the artist's signature. There it was.

"I knew it," I said under my breath.
Hamilton had walked up behind me. "Knew what?"
I kept my voice low. "This is a Rembrandt."
"So? He was a rich guy. Why so impressed?"
"This painting is unknown."
"Are you sure?"

"Quite sure. I have always suspected paintings from the masters ended up in private collections with no record of their existence." In fact, I knew it, as I possessed a Renoir, a de Kooning, and a book of sketches by van Gogh, all uncatalogued. I impulsively reached forward and touched the glass with a gloved hand. "I wonder where he found it. He must be a direct descendant of the original buyer. It's the only way he could have kept it quiet."

"Just out of curiosity, what would a painting like that go for?"

"Well," I said, leaning forward and looking at the signature. "This is an unknown, so once its authenticity has been established, the sky is the limit. The last painting of Rembrandt's sold for more than thirty-three million dollars."

"That's insane."

"It's not bad."

"Rich boy," he said in disgust. "What about those other two?"

I walked over to the next one. A pastel garden. I did not need to look at the signature. "Monet, also unknown."

The last exhibit hurt my heart. I began to feel an emotion with which I was unaccustomed: envy. The third painting was a rich oil of three women sitting next to a brook. One of them drew water from it while the other two watched.

"Well?" Hamilton asked quietly. "Who is it?"

"Da Vinci." I wanted to say more, but the splendor of what stood before me had robbed me of speech. It was a gorgeous example of Leonardo's work, with his angelic faces and lifelike details. And it was another painting the general public did not know existed.

I turned around and stared at the dead man sitting in the chair with his head thrown back as if he were looking at a bug on the ceiling. I looked back at the da Vinci. Why would someone want to murder this mild-mannered antiques dealer with the impossible art collection?

Chapter 3

Friday, January 23, 7:17 p.m.

Hamilton and I left the paintings and walked over to the desk.

Mason Cavanaugh sat upright in a wingback executive chair that had blood, brains, and bits of skull spattered across the dark green leather behind his head. He was a short man with a soft belly, wearing a blue silk smoking jacket with black lapels over a white dress shirt, open at the collar, and black slacks. His leather slippers still rested under the desk. His legs were crossed at the ankles. He had a full head of white hair. The only jewelry was a wedding band on his ring finger and a Patek Philippe chronograph watch on his left wrist.

Deputy ME Tasha Watanabe examined the victim's wound closely, her nose inches from his head. She had her long black hair tied in a ponytail. Clad in blue jeans, a green turtleneck sweater and a black Windbreaker with *Coroner* imprinted on the back, she also sported black Converse All Stars.

Hamilton moved behind Watanabe, looking over her shoulder, and I stood on the other side of the chair.

"Single shot through the forehead, just above the left eye," she said. "Looks like a big gun, probably a .44."

"It is," Gonzales said. "I pulled the bullet out of the padding in the chair. You can see the hole in the leather behind his head."

He was right but it was hard to identify inside the blood spatter.

"Time of death?" Hamilton asked.

"Based on lividity, less than ninety minutes ago."

"That's consistent with Mrs. Cavanaugh's statement," he said, glancing at his notebook.

I leaned over the body until my head was close to Watanabe's. I looked carefully at the bullet hole in Cavanaugh's head. The edge of the wound bulged slightly all around. I turned to her, our faces almost close enough for kissing. "Is that stippling, Tasha?"

"Yes," she said, touching the skin surrounding the ridge of the entrance hole with a white-gloved hand. "The shot was definitely close range." She stared me directly in the eyes, then leaned back and let her gaze travel up and down my body. When she finally looked back up to my face, I pretended not to notice that she had just checked me out. "The gun may have been pressed against the skin when it was fired."

I glanced at the body. "So if the vic was sitting facing forward . . ."

Gonzales grunted in surprise. "Yeah, where was the shooter? In the middle of the desk?"

"Maybe he leaned over from the side," Hamilton said, "and popped him, like this." Watanabe moved out of his way. Hamilton stood on Cavanaugh's left, facing the desk. He put his left hand on the desk and leaned forward. But he couldn't get turned around properly, not with the gun in his right hand. He could get in better position with his left hand, but it was still impossible to reach an angle that would allow him to press the barrel against the vic's forehead over the left eye. I tried it on the other side with equally negative results.

The desk was too wide and too deep for someone to reach far enough from the sides or front.

"I don't see how he did it," Hamilton said, his eyebrows crunched together.

"Maybe he jumped from the opposite side of the desk," Gonzales offered, but even as he finished, I could hear that he didn't believe his own theory. The desk was more than a meter deep.

"And then what?" I said, not challenging him but saying what we were all thinking. "Slid on his knees until he was in front of the target?"

We were quiet for a while.

"I'm ready to have my people remove the body," Watanabe said to Hamilton.

"That's fine," he told her. She gestured to two young men waiting with a gurney. While they wrestled with the body, Watanabe's assistant handed Gonzales a tablet and he signed off, handed it back.

"I'll have the autopsy results by tomorrow afternoon."

"Thanks, Tasha," Hamilton said.

She nodded at Gonzales and me and followed her people out.

I crossed my arms over my chest and looked from the desk to the chair and back again. If the shooter didn't stand on either side of Cavanaugh, then he must have been on the desk or hovering just above it, facing his target. That made no sense.

"Is this the way you found the desk?"

"Just like you see it," Gonzales said.

The chair rested on a beige Turkish silk rug. A hefty piece of furniture, it was tall with solid legs that did not have rollers. Cavanaugh would have had to pull it forward and push it back. I got down on one knee and looked closely at the rug. I could see the faint outlines of the ruts created by this back-and-forth movement. I looked to the left and right to see if the chair had been moved sideways, but I could see no tracks in the intricate tapestry to indicate that. So it was unlikely he had turned his chair to the side before the murder.

I straightened up. The SID had already dusted the desk for prints—I could see patches of remaining white powder along the front edge. The only thing on top was the tape recorder, a cheap old gray machine that looked incongruous among the breathtaking antiques of the room. It seemed odd that there was not a pen, pencil, or scrap of paper on the desk—there were no

35

in/out trays, no framed pictures, and no coaster with a cup of coffee or a snifter of brandy.

I ran my left hand along the groove between the wood and the leather on top. As I moved along the right side, I banged down on the desk with my other hand at intervals.

"What are you looking for?" Gonzales asked, watching me.

"No idea," I told him. After I rounded the corner, I stood directly in front of the desk. I leaned forward and pressed all over the leather top in the middle. I banged my hand down hard.

"Mind telling us what you're doing?" Gonzales asked.

I shrugged. "It's a big desk. I thought it might have an interior chamber or even a trapdoor leading under the house." I pounded on the front. The dull sound of solid oak came back. "I suppose not. Did you make sure all the drawers are real?"

"Yes," Hamilton answered. "When we were searching for the gun, we pulled all of them out."

"Who was the first one in the room?"

"Officer Kennedy."

"Did she hear or see anything?"

"Only the chanting on the tape and the body."

I glanced at the player. "The weird music?"

"Yeah. Come on, let's listen."

The three of us clustered around the corner of the desk. Hamilton pressed the Play button. The machine was small and cheap, but it still filled the room with a booming drumbeat and wailing voices. I found the volume control and turned it down. Even low, it played a queerly ominous sound. That's not what got my attention. It was what the voices were saying—and the language they were using.

"It's a shaman's death chant," I told them.

"You recognize that language?" Gonzales asked.

"Yes. Magistine. Middle European. A Turkish dialect. I thought it died out hundreds of years ago."

"Why?"

"Because that's when the Magistines were annihilated."

"Okay, I'll bite," Hamilton said. "Who were they?"

"A small, clannish, secretive group living in the western foothills of Turkey in the thirteenth century near a city known as Konya. The people in the towns and villages around them believed Magisty had committed itself to witchcraft, so they put the city to the sword and burned the town to the ground. The attackers even killed their animals, fearing they might be witches in disguise."

"Pretty thorough," Gonzales commented. "How do you know about all this, Montero?"

"History is a hobby of mine," I said. "The problem is that this should not be on a cassette tape. The last time anyone chanted this was more than six hundred years ago."

"Apparently not," Hamilton said. "What do you think it means?"

"It's intended as a curse. A death curse."

"Why curse the guy after he's dead?" Gonzales asked.

"The curse is not for his body," I answered. "It's for his spirit."

"Yo," Hamilton said. "He must have pissed somebody off."

I was still in shock and working hard not to show it. How could a Magistine chant possibly be on that cassette?

Though I had not participated in the extermination of the mystical society, I had witnessed it. I, too, had heard the stories of Magisty's strange reputation: scary tales of alchemy and shape-shifting that people passed around in whispers. As soon as anyone mentioned anything to do with the town, they crossed themselves and jabbed two fingers at the ground to ward off the evil eye.

I had arrived several months earlier and confirmed that the village elders were indeed skilled shamans, capable of much more than healing and communing with the spirits. These men and women used elemental sound combinations (they referred to them as the names of God) to perform miracles.

For instance, an eighty-six-year-old man cupped his hands over his mouth, closed his eyes, and whispered between his fingers. He then gestured at a tree ten meters away. Something left his hand—it caused a ripple, or wake, in the air as it rushed over the dry ground. The tree shook as if buffeted by a high wind. The branches and leaves flapped from the lowest to the highest, and I had the impression that a smaller tree would have bowed backward from the force.

The effect ceased after several seconds.

When I asked the Magistine people about these words, all I received in response were smiles. The elders guarded the secrets of the sounds with (understandably) religious fervor.

In June of 1296, a Magistine woman allegedly killed a man by looking at him "with the devil's eyes." Two weeks later, when a team of horses ran out of control down the central street of a nearby town, a man from Magisty stepped in front of the bolting creatures. Everyone watching knew he was dead—the horses were wild-eyed, spooked. But just as two tons of equine flesh were about to trample him, he made a motion with his hands and the horses seemed to float, their limbs moving leisurely, their noses only inches from the man. He petted the snouts of all the horses while slowly backing up in front of them. When the horses started moving normally again, they walked slowly.

Some of the people who witnessed the event said they saw the Magistine's lips move just before the horses slowed. Many swore they saw a wrinkle in the air that enveloped the team before it slowed.

In August of 1296, the surrounding villages decided the small town of Magisty was in league with Satan and had to be purged by fire before the turn of the century. On a humid, misty midsummer's night, the sultan of Anatolia and his elite army led a raiding militia of more than one thousand townspeople against a population of 328 men, women, and children. They attacked before dawn.

Perched high in an oak tree, I watched from a road that ran parallel to the unofficial border of Magisty. The action occurred on the other side of the low hills, so I couldn't see the invasion, but I could hear the sounds of the battle. Children's high screams of terror mingled with the outraged roars of men and the shrieks of women, like some malign symphony of chaos. Flickering orange light began to stain the sky above the town. In a few minutes, I could hear the crackling of the fire under the wailing, baleful voices. Several minutes after that, I could detect the aroma of cooking flesh. I recognized the smell for I had already been in several battles.

I climbed out of the tree and ran away then, and I did not slow down until the sounds of the dying town were drowned by distance.

It never occurred to me there would be survivors.

I looked at Gonzales. "Now what?"

"We get to the money question," Hamilton said. "How did the killer get out of this room with the door locked from the inside?"

Chapter 4

Friday, January 23, 7:48 p.m.

I looked along the upper walls near the ceiling. Two ventilation grates.

"Forget it," Gonzales said when he saw me looking. "Even if a kid was responsible, both vents taper to hoses about five inches in diameter before they reach the utility closet near the laundry room."

I looked along the baseboard. One grate—and it was too small for anything larger than a Chihuahua. Three rugs lay on the floor. "Did you look under these?" I asked, picking up a red one with a geometric pattern in tan and brown. Gonzales lumbered over to a vanilla-colored Chinese rug lying below the da Vinci and flipped it over while Hamilton inspected a light-blue one.

"Nothing here," I said, carefully replacing the runner.

"Me neither," said Hamilton. Gonzales dropped his rug without a word.

I stood in front of the William IV bookcase. Heavy, solid mahogany. Hm.

Hamilton and Gonzales joined me. "Well?" Gonzales asked.

"If there was a secret entrance to this room, it would probably be hidden behind an object that looked too heavy to move," I said.

Hamilton stepped forward and grabbed the lower ledge of the case and then leaned back. The antique did not budge. "It doesn't just *look* heavy, it's a mutha," he said.

"Maybe it has a release that opens it pneumatically or electrically. We should look for a button or lever or something somewhere."

"This isn't a Zorro movie, Montero," Gonzales said, but he began studying the right side, sliding his hand along the wood. I opened the upper glass doors and carefully removed the books. I probed the shelves and interior wood. Nothing.

Ten minutes later, we concluded the bookcase was just a solid oak antique.

"Behind one of the paintings?" I said.

"*That* we thought of," Gonzales said. Drops of perspiration dotted his forehead and upper lip. He looked around the room, his hands on his hips.

I could not see any other alternatives. Hamilton's expression showed he was equally baffled.

"How the hell did this guy get *out* of here?" Gonzales asked.

Twenty minutes later, Gonzales said good night and left, headed back to the station to start working on the case reports. I wandered around while Hamilton phoned in and gave Chief Reyes a briefing. My gaze traveled the books in the bookcase again. When I had pulled out *Paradise Lost* during my search, I had seen a marker sticking up in the middle. Of the approximately seventy volumes on the four shelves, only it had a bookmark.

The placeholder turned out to be a tarot card: the Prince of Wands, featuring a picture of Dagon as a horned sea serpent or possibly a merman brandishing a scepter.

The card dazzled the eye; more richly detailed than any I had seen, wrought in bold primary colors with a prismatic, three-dimensional depth. It seemed a bit heavy for its size. Gold leaf covered the border. Turning it over, I saw the back had a black background with a design of gold eights tipped sideways—the symbol for eternity.

Hamilton still had the phone to his ear. I replaced the book, closed the door, and looked carefully at the glass.

For a moment temptation urged me to pocket the tarot card and take it without Hamilton's knowledge. Intuition indicated it didn't belong in this room, so it might be an important clue.

I decided against keeping it. If the tarot could lead us to the killer, Hamilton needed to know. And I felt certain the Prince would prove essential.

After all, who has one tarot card?

When Hamilton hung up, I showed him the card and told him where I had found it. He took it. "What do you think it means?" he asked. He walked over to the Pembroke table and held the card under the green-shaded lamp.

"As you can see," I said, "it's the Prince of Wands. The picture is of Dagon, a shape-shifter that liked to take the form of a serpent or a great fish. That's why he has a whale's tail attached to a human torso."

"It's a tarot card, right?"

"Yes."

"Don't all tarot cards mean something?"

"Yes, but I don't know what this one means. A standard deck doesn't usually have Princes."

"There's more than one?"

"If it's a regular deck of seventy-eight cards, there should be four Princes, just as there are four of everything—not counting the trump cards. This card's suit is wands."

"Hm," he said, straightening up and turning to me. "I guess we could ask a tarot reader what it means."

"Aliena is an expert on the tarot and its symbolism. I will ask her." I held out my hand.

"We'll have to keep this," he told me.

"You don't have anyone in your department who knows as much about the occult as Aliena and Reed, you know that," I said, lowering my hand. Augustus Reed worked for my company, BioLaw. He had briefed us on a previous case, so

Hamilton knew the man's credentials. But the detective wasn't budging.

"Then we will fax you a picture."

"You know that's not good enough," I said. "My specialists will want to examine it, including x-ray and fluoroscope. We can't do that with a picture."

He looked thoughtful. "Call the chief and get clearance, if you can. I'll have SID photograph and bag it." He left the room.

I called Chief Reyes and explained what I wanted. She gave me her approval, but reluctantly. The police do not normally release any evidence recovered at a crime scene to an outside party. I knew Reyes only agreed because BioLaw operated as an accredited laboratory, meaning the district attorney could admit evidence based on our examinations and test results, and my employees could be called as expert witnesses. All BioLaw's senior specialists had written a book or treatise on their subject. Most of my forensic scientists had testified in the past, and they were used to handling evidence in important cases.

And whenever I worked a homicide, the in-depth analyses and reports related to that case arrived as fast as my people could perform them. At no charge to the police.

While waiting for Hamilton to return, I walked around the room knocking on the walls every couple of meters, listening for a hollow sound that indicated a chamber on the other side. I completed the circuit. Nothing.

Hamilton came back holding the card. It now rested in a clear plastic evidence bag.

"Did you talk to Reyes?" he asked.

"Yes." I held out my hand, and he gave me the card. I pocketed it. "Thank you. I promise to have something for you by tomorrow. Was anybody here during the shooting?"

"Just Mrs. Cavanaugh. She heard the gunshot and the freaky music. When she found the door to the office locked, she called to her husband, but he didn't answer. She swears she heard someone moving around in here, though. That's when she called 911." He stripped off his gloves, and I followed suit. I could only think of one thing to do.

"Let's ask her if her husband believed in the occult," I said.

Chapter 5

Friday, January 23, 8:21 p.m.

"We're sorry to bother you, Mrs. Cavanaugh, but we need to ask you some more questions," Hamilton said in a quiet voice. "We'll be brief."

She looked up at us with red-rimmed eyes, held a handkerchief to her mouth, and nodded. Her gray hair remained thick and still had streaks of her original brown. A soft, chubby face regarded us as we questioned her. She wore a yellow sundress that revealed strong shoulders and muscular calves.

We sat in the parlor, an airy room with French doors and three panoramic windows that would allow plenty of sunshine during the day.

"Have you noticed anything missing in the house?" Hamilton asked, taking out his notebook.

She shook her head. "I don't think so."

"Do you know if anything is missing from Mr. Cavanaugh's office?"

I had looked for any sign of a missing article, but I did not see anything signaling that one of his possessions had been stolen: no empty hooks on the walls, no surfaces with places of less dust that would have indicated something had been moved recently.

"I haven't been in there," she said. "I don't have to, do I? I wouldn't know if anything was missing anyway. I did not go in there very often. It was Mason's sanctuary, as he called it. I didn't have a key."

"If you could look at the room tomorrow or the next day . . ." He stopped as Mrs. Cavanaugh shook her head. "I understand," he said. "If you can't do it . . ."

"I don't believe I can," she said. "Is that terrible of me?"

45

"No," I said. "It's perfectly understandable." I leaned forward. "Mrs. Cavanaugh, did your husband have any enemies? Anybody who might want to harm him?"

She blew her nose daintily. "If you knew Mason, you would understand how absurd that question is. He was a quiet retired shop owner, the most even-tempered man I ever knew. I never even heard of him arguing with anybody."

I liked this woman. Even in grief she functioned well.

"Why would anyone want to kill him?" she asked.

"That's what we're going to find out," Hamilton said. "How long has he been retired?"

"Almost nine years."

"Cavanaugh's Antiques is still going strong," I said.

"Yes, Mason turned the business over to our daughter and nephew. They have done very well with it."

"What about tarot cards?" I asked.

"What?"

I held up the evidence bag with the Prince inside. "We found this in your husband's study."

She gave the card a blank stare. "I never saw it before."

"Was your husband seeking spiritual guidance of any kind?"

"What do you mean? Talking to a priest?"

"Actually," I said, "we mean, was Mr. Cavanaugh having his fortune told?"

"His fortune?"

"Yes. Might he have visited a tarot card reader?"

"No."

"Perhaps as a joke?"

"That would not be funny to Mason," she replied. "And he did not believe in witches or whatever they're called."

"Do you know anybody who *is* a believer in the occult?" Hamilton asked.

She thought about that. "We have friends who are very spiritual. I don't think any of them study witchcraft, though."

"Does your husband have a deck of tarot cards?"

"Not to my knowledge."

"Mrs. Cavanaugh, did your husband tell you about the paintings in his office?"

"What about them?"

"Did he mention where he got them, who painted them, things like that?"

"I only saw them once. I thought they were just old paintings," she said. "Mason never talked about his possessions. His treasures, he called them."

The poor dear had a big surprise on her horizon. I decided to have one of my people contact her discretely and inform her about the paintings so that she could keep them secret if she wished. Once discovered, Mrs. Cavanaugh and this home would seethe with reporters and TV camera operators. She looked like a person who would find that situation intolerable.

I had run out of questions. Hamilton looked at me. I nodded. He closed his notebook and handed Mrs. Cavanaugh one of his cards.

"If you think of anything else, please give me a call."

"Yes, of course."

"We will be in touch as soon as we know something," he said.

"Thank you."

As we left, we heard her cough. Then she began sobbing softly.

"There's something wrong with this picture," I said as Hamilton and I crossed the manicured lawn. We had decided to get a bite to eat at the Fatburger on Ventura Boulevard in Sherman Oaks.

"You noticed?" Hamilton said. "Why would anyone want to pop a retired antiques dealer? The guy isn't exactly the type to

47

be assassinated. And how did they pull off the locked room trick?"

I didn't answer, my mind picking over the facts. No secret panel in the walls. Nothing behind the paintings or the bookcase. Nothing in or under the massive desk. No chance of entering or exiting through the ventilation grates. That left the door. Somehow the killer got out . . . and locked the door from the inside while leaving the house without being observed?

We ducked under the yellow tape and crossed the street. Some of the neighbors had gone back inside their homes but most were still outside, watching and waiting—as was the Channel 5 news team.

Field reporter Virginia Sanchez had her back to us, so we dashed to the car before being spotted. As I turned the lights on, somebody ran up to her and pointed at us. She spun around and started moving in our direction even as I began a U-turn. Hamilton and I waved at her, smiling. She did not wave back. I drove off, heading for Sunset Boulevard.

"Uh-oh," Hamilton said. "She looked pissed."

"Sure did." We both knew that Sanchez felt unrepentant about slanting her stories a certain way to make us seem inept when we didn't cooperate with her. We never deliberately crossed her, though we did our best to avoid her and any other reporters while we investigated a case.

"You remember how powerful Kanga was?" Hamilton asked as I turned onto Sunset Boulevard and shifted through the gears.

"Yes," I said, tapping the paddle shifter.

"Do you think someone like that could pop into a locked room and pop out again?"

I hadn't thought of that. "I never saw him do it, but, yes, I think he could have." That theory seemed untenable when considering what Kanga had done, including the three murders he had committed, to achieve such power—all while in possession of a rare magical object that magnified the effect of every ritual he performed. The probability of two such men in LA must be astronomical.

We both watched the traffic flowing by lost in our own thoughts. I decided not to waste time trying to figure out how the murderer got out of the room while leaving it locked from the inside. That mystery we would solve by gathering more information. We needed to learn why someone wanted Mason Cavanaugh dead, especially since they hadn't been after his incredible treasures. If we were fortunate, the answer would lead to the murderer and an explanation of the locked door.

I merged with the freeway traffic and signaled my way across the lanes until I was cruising in the number one lane. I waited. Since we were talking about Kanga . . .

"Speaking of Kanga's death," he said.

"Yes?"

"You survived all those wounds when you came back from the astral plane. You had a hundred freaking holes in your jacket and pants, blood all over you, but as soon as you woke up, you started the car, ready to go."

During our last case, the detective had witnessed things I would have preferred to keep secret. So I took the Fifth—and intended to continue taking it.

"Funny thing is," Hamilton went on, "the autopsy of Kanga shows that he bled out massively before he died. From the same wounds you had, all over his body, also apparently received in the ether. You told me people didn't bring those wounds back with them, and that was why, in spite of your blood-soaked clothes, you were okay again in a few moments. Want to try again?"

I changed lanes to the right, skirting a slow-moving Saab, accelerated past, and switched back.

"I'm not sure what you want me to say, Steve." I glanced at him. "Kanga died as a result of a knife wound that slit him down the middle, just as he had done to his victims."

"Actually, he didn't, but that reminds me: did you make that cut, Sebastian?"

Hamilton knew what Kanga had done to three teenage girls, surveying the grisliest crime scenes of his career. Although admission of a crime to a police officer carried obvious risks, I decided to tell him the truth. I really did prefer telling people the truth.

"Yes."

"And rip his heart out?"

"Aliena did that."

"Really," he said, clearly impressed.

"Yes."

"Now that I think about it, I'm not surprised. There is something about that girl. Anyway, according to the ME, Kanga was already dying when that cut was made. I would have done the same thing to the bastard. He was a dead man anyway. But that's my point. He was dead from the same wounds you had because your astral bodies were in the same area. Dammit, Sebastian, stop jerking me around."

Like the Grinch, I thought up a lie, and I thought it up quick.

"He was standing right next to the Akashic Records when they exploded. I was much farther away." That much was true. "His wounds were far more severe than mine, so he brought them back with him." Not true.

"You keep telling me that," Hamilton said, "but I've done a little research and talked to a few astral travelers. And they insist that you want to avoid being hurt in the ether because it's the same as being hurt in reality."

Okay, so my lie was not so Grinch-like after all. The Grinch's lie worked. Of course, he fooled "little Cindy Lou Who, who was no more than two." I had to deceive a seasoned—and suspicious—metropolitan police detective.

I had known Hamilton would investigate these topics before he asked me questions, but I had hoped he would get conflicting stories to everything so he would not know what to believe. I continued to push that idea.

"Are you sure these experts of yours really have experience in astral travel? It is a difficult thing to do."

"I checked them out. And before you say anything, I know the experience is so personal there is no way to tell if a person is lying or not. But my *abuela* used to talk about it, too, and she told me the same thing."

His grandmother had been an accomplished Candomblé priestess with genuine powers. Hamilton knew I knew that. I had to stonewall again.

"Steve, I'm not sure what you're implying. Are you saying I *did* come back with the same wounds? And?"

"And fuck. I don't know. That's why I'm asking. There's something weird about you. You healed yourself, somehow."

"From a hundred wounds all over my body."

"I don't care how it sounds," he said. "Kanga bled out and you didn't, but you both had identical wound patterns. I was *there*, Sebastian."

"If you're asking me if I have some ability to repair myself after receiving wounds, the answer is yes. Everybody does. If you're asking me if I can repair major injuries in seconds, the answer is no."

"You remember the strange blood we recovered in Madame Leoni's back room?"

LAPD forensic specialists had collected samples of my blood on our last case, at the Leoni crime scene. An analysis of this blood showed it to be very unusual with strong regenerative properties. The identity of that person remained an official mystery with law enforcement.

And now Hamilton, making one of his intuitive leaps, had connected it to me.

"Yes?" I said, putting a puzzled look on my face at this change of topic. "I remember. What about it?"

"Stop playing dumb. The analysis of the blood of our unknown shooter indicated he might be immortal, remember? Even Preston, your own man, said it."

"Yes, he did."

"Now that I think about it," Hamilton said, "you had opportunity and motive to return to Madame Leoni's place after you dropped me off. You were the third man in that back room, weren't you?"

"No."

"The pattern is exactly the same," he said, as if talking to himself. "Our unknown shooter has massive blood loss but is able to get out of the store under his own power. And based on our analysis and yours, this man would be capable of repairing injuries very quickly. I was there—I mean here," he gestured at the car—"when you were battling Kanga in the ether. And I witnessed the same massive blood loss. But you kept going as if nothing was wrong with you. It all fits."

"It does add up," I conceded, "but it's the wrong conclusion."

"Care to take a blood test?"

"Not really."

"Is that a no?"

"Yes."

He rapped the dashboard with his knuckles. "And just when I was beginning to like you. That's not so good, Sebastian. You know I have strong probable cause here, and your refusal to cooperate, well, that makes me wonder."

"You think I'm immortal?"

"Shit, man, I don't know what to think anymore."

Bad luck. I loved Steve Hamilton like a brother, and now it seemed I would have to do one of my disappearing acts, forging a new identity in the process. Not only is that the same as attending your best friend's funeral, it is a mountain of work.

He took a deep breath, let it out.

I held mine.

"And then there's Aliena. You were right; I have not been able to find her last name. Another mystery. And why did Kanga call her a vampire?"

Though relieved the subject had turned to Aliena, her identity required deception as well.

"When Kanga took her, she tried to bite him on the neck."

"That's it, huh? Okay, when she was crying, why were her tears dark?"

"It was a side effect of the drugs he used to keep her quiescent."

"I have never heard of any drug with that side effect."

"Kanga was using concoctions he synthesized himself, as the ME's office and my specialists proved. You can't compare his formulas to those of mass-produced drugs."

"I know that," he snapped. "Don't patronize me. But come *on*, Sebastian, black tears?"

"I have heard of stranger side effects."

"Hell," he said disgustedly. "That's bullshit and you know it."

I waited, wondering if the storm had passed. It hadn't.

"What about your blood?" he said. "Why did Kanga want your blood?"

"The man was a conjurer. He used blood in his rituals all the time."

"There you go again," he said. "When you play it that dumb, you make me feel I'm right. You're not that slow. He wanted *your* blood. Not mine and not Aliena's. Why yours?"

He had built his case and backed me into a corner.

"As I also said then, I don't know all of the reasons why he wanted mine particularly." The weak, lawyer's explanation dropped from my lips, a waffle—and untrue to boot. Kanga wanted the plasma because he had learned of my immortal nature. I presumed he planned to use the blood in a ritual designed to give him everlasting life.

53

I had not intended to tell Hamilton any of that. Unfortunately, he required no explanation. The irritatingly intuitive detective was figuring it out on his own.

"It all fits," he said again. "Kanga stabs you multiple times in Madame Leoni's back room. From your blood loss, he must have given you mortal wounds. Then he discovers you survived. So he blackmails you for your immortal blood by holding Aliena hostage."

The events had happened exactly that way. He had me trapped. "All I can tell you is that you're wrong."

"Hell." He watched me. "You wouldn't tell me the truth anyway—if I was right."

His instincts remained razor-sharp. I should tell him that. Hamilton was a good man who deserved better than he was getting from me.

What was there to fear in telling him the truth? The man worked in law enforcement, so knew how to keep restricted information to himself. More importantly, he was one of the good guys. And then there was the most important reason of all: he had become a dear friend.

From centuries-long habit, I kept quiet. But this time, the effort took will and left a rancid aftertaste. Secrets could be bloated, rampaging beasts, fighting to get out. Keeping them hidden is often exquisitely painful.

Throughout our lives, we reach crossroads, unsure which path to take. Leaving Los Angeles was not an option for me. Aliena loved living here. She would not willingly relocate, and I did not plan to move away without her.

"Steve, you are a man I hold in the highest regard. If there was something unusual about me, I would tell you."

He sat back, watched the traffic. "Sure."

Despair settled hard on my shoulders. Hamilton saw all the angles, asked the questions that drove me to deceit. I had to tell him the truth soon or disappear.

Lying is acid to the soul.

I pulled into the little lot behind Fatburger.

"What were you doing tonight when I called?" he asked as we walked toward the door.

"Watching a football game."

"Really?"

"Yes. What's so unlikely about that?"

"I don't know . . . it just doesn't fit you."

"Yes, it does. I also love cartoons. The Cartoon Network is one of my programmed favorites."

"Now that *does* sound like you."

"Oh?"

"Yeah. Weird."

I held the door open. We both ordered cheeseburgers and fries with large Cokes. When they were ready, we took our trays to a table.

"This feels like a funny one," he said, taking a bite of his burger.

"Yes." I munched a few fries. "We'll need to talk to the daughter tomorrow. We should probably start at Cavanaugh's Antiques."

He nodded. "I already spoke with Amanda Cavanaugh. They open at ten. What about the tarot card?"

"I'll have Aliena look at it immediately. I have to meet her later. She's taking me to a private club."

"Is it so private you can't bring me?"

"I am afraid so. You wouldn't like it anyway." I did not bother to tell him that he also would not survive it. "I don't."

"Then why do you do it?"

"Because Aliena loves it."

"Sounds like someone is whipped."

"You wouldn't do the same for a girl you loved?"

55

He continued chewing, a thoughtful look on his face. As soon as he swallowed, he said, "Yeah, okay, you're right. If you love her, you should do stuff like that."

"I noticed you called me in on this investigation, not Reyes."

"Yeah, well. You approach these homicides from a unique angle," he said. "You're untrained, so you notice unusual things. Like that death chant." He looked me in the eye. "Also, you probably saved my life twice on our last case."

"Bey's charms saved you, but I know what you mean," I said. Geoffrey Bey was an old friend who dabbled in shamanism. He had given me several fetishized objects and I had used some of them to protect Hamilton.

"The truth is, if I had been working that case with *anybody* else, I'd be dead. Hell, if you had told me that you placed charms throughout my apartment to protect me, I would've gotten rid of them."

"Precisely why I hid them."

"Yeah, well, I owe you," he said.

"I appreciate that, but you owe me nothing. My motivation was entirely self-serving. I like working with you."

"That's it?" he laughed.

"Tell me something, Steve: if you had saved my life, would you feel I owed you a debt?"

"That's different. I'm paid to save lives."

"Fair enough. But why are you paid? Because as a society, we agree killing is wrong. Anybody in my place would have done the same thing."

"Can't you just let me thank you?" he said.

That got a laugh out of me. "Yes, sorry. You're very welcome."

We finished and bused our trays, said good night to the girl behind the counter.

I drove Hamilton to his apartment complex on Murietta Avenue. He lived so close to Fatburger, he could have walked home.

"Pick you up at nine?" I asked.

"Sounds good. Thanks for coming in on this one, Sebastian."

"It's always a pleasure to work with you, Steve, you know that."

That was the truth.

Chapter 6

Friday, January 23, 10:48 p.m.

I parked the Maserati in the garage and pressed my right hand against the glass security plate as the garage door silently descended to my right. The panel glowed red as it scanned my palm, then turned green. The door popped open, and I pushed into the house.

    Lights came on automatically. I sat down on the couch, pulled my computer close, swiped my fingertip along the biometric strip, and created a new folder. Titled "Hamilton IV," the folder would contain all the information I had on the Cavanaugh case, including the details about the locked door and the search efforts we had employed to find a way out of the room. I recorded our interview with the widow.

    In my office, I scanned the tarot card front and back, saving the pictures to a USB drive. I transferred the images to the folder. Then I pulled out the drive and tossed it on the table.

    I plucked a cigarette from a silver case and lit it, thinking a 750 ml bottle of tequila would hit the spot. Opening the kitchen cabinet where I kept bottles of liquor, I selected the Don Julio, popped the top, and drank it in a gulp. The empty fell into the plastic recycle can.

    With a pleasant lightness in my head, I opened a pair of glass doors and stepped onto the patio. Sitting on a low wall, I watched the Pacific Ocean while I puffed.

    Recording my observations of the case got me mulling it over again. And much as I tried not to let it distract me, the problem of the locked room kept buzzing around my brain. After a thorough inspection of the scene, it just did not seem possible to pull it off, yet someone had. Whoever he was, he was sharp and catching him was not going to be easy—but when we did, I would know his secret.

Ten after eleven. I needed to get going or I would be late for my date with Aliena.

11:56 p.m.

Tonight, the vampire club 49 was located in a part of East LA that was not a good area for a white boy to be caught wandering around. Not a safe place for girls, either, but in a different way. Since only vampires attended 49, whether or not its location contained violent humans had no pertinence.

The neighborhood sagged, dismal and abandoned. No streetlights worked, and no lights burned in the buildings I passed. This looked to have been a commercial street in the past: an auto repair shop sat next to a glass installer and across the street from them bulked a moving company. All the buildings had broken windows, and the front doors were either open or missing.

The address Aliena had given me led to an abandoned warehouse with a small parking lot. I cruised in, the Maserati's headlights dazzling in the dark. As I parked, I saw the small door to the right with the flashing 49 sign over it.

I killed the engine and climbed out, slipping my jacket on. For a moment I remained undecided as to whether or not I should walk in alone. I had been to the club many times now, but Aliena had always been with me. As I stood there mulling it over, a figure materialized at my side.

I turned, expecting to see Aliena. My eyes widened when I saw Marcus.

Marcus had lived more than two thousand years—and Aliena infatuated him. He dressed impeccably, and, like me, still preferred suits and ties. Tonight he wore a black silk three-button with a white shirt and an ebony ascot. He combed his brown hair backward, off his forehead. His skin had a luminous quality only the most ancient vampires achieved. Quite handsome. As always, he exuded an aura of dark power. A very imposing personality.

I bowed slightly. "Marcus."

"Sebastian," he said, smiling. "It is nice to see you. Is Aliena joining you?"

"Yes."

"Of course," he said. "Tell me the truth: you do not like our games, do you?"

"No," I said. "How did you know?"

"I have seen your expression during the bouts." He gave a soft laugh. "For one who has witnessed as much of human nature as you have, I still find your attitude inexplicable. Men are beasts. They always have been and always will be. Vampires are a higher form of life."

Marcus loved being a vampire. So did Aliena. I couldn't imagine either of them as anything else. And he was right. Vampires were amazingly civilized. They only killed occasionally when they fed, and they never killed for sport (with the exception of the bouts at 49). They rarely killed in anger. They didn't war among themselves. Indeed, the most cherished rules of their society revolved around the issue of individual privacy.

That is because vampires are loners. They rarely assemble in numbers greater than two or three. If a vampire wants to remain alone (and this is communicated simply—she stops coming to any gatherings), the others leave her alone. Any vampire breaking that rule was subject to the only punishment vampires had: death.

"Shall we wait for Aliena inside?" Marcus asked. We had adjacent seats at ringside.

"I had better stay here."

"See you inside, then."

Aliena showed up a minute later. I gave her a light kiss and we turned toward the warehouse.

"I really appreciate the sacrifice you make, Sebastian, coming to 49. I love having you with me."

"Why?" I didn't know it mattered that much to her. She always asked me to attend, but I didn't think she considered my presence that important.

"At first," she said as we neared the door, "I knew the other men would leave me alone when you were with me."

"And later?"

She squeezed my arm and turned to me. "Now I want everyone to know that you and I are together and not just for one night."

"Are you saying we're dating?"

"Don't you want to?"

"My darling," I said, raising her hand to my lips and kissing it lightly, "I have wanted you since that first night in Paris when you tried to kill me."

She laughed delightedly, hugged me, and kissed me on the cheek. "Then that's settled. You are my boyfriend."

When I had seen her that first night—the pale, ethereal beauty with the blurry speed and easy strength—I knew immediately I had met someone special (that I had been dinner at our introduction became a moot point). More than alluring, she was another immortal being.

When I found her again, I discovered she was not only beautiful, but also intelligent and interesting. In a short time, I had fallen in love with her. Normally, I would press my suit when this smitten, but I knew becoming too attached to Aliena left my heart vulnerable. She has always been friendly but has deflected my intimate advances, so I have not imagined us as a couple very often. It pained me to return to reality.

Did she love me now? I decided not to ask. It had taken me more than a century to get to the boyfriend stage, so I remained patient.

I had to admit that knowing Aliena loved it when I accompanied her, I felt better about going to the club, and as we passed through the door and under the pulsing crimson sign that read 49, my heart felt lighter than it had in centuries.

No matter how much life has disappointed you, when you are in love, nothing else seems to matter—and the world becomes beautiful again.

Chapter 7

Saturday, January 24, 12:13 a.m.

The man in the ring sported a decidedly nonathletic body, a pale, paunchy, balding business type who looked to be in his late sixties. Even from this distance I could see he had spent as much time in front of a dinner table as a work desk. His belly hung over his white satin shorts, his arms bagged under the biceps, his chest had sunken, and his red boxing gloves looked three sizes too big on the end of his skinny wrists.

A petite black woman faced him. She wore blood-red shorts with a red stripe and the wide waistband of traditional boxing trunks but featuring a shorter-than-traditional hemline. Her matching top fit snugly, and tall red boots complemented the shape of her legs. She looked to be a full hundred pounds lighter than her adversary.

Two tall stadium-style lights hooked to car batteries lit the ring brilliantly. The vampires sat in individual seats. The rows were stepped like a theater and had attached stairs. Four sets of them were arranged around the sides of the arena.

We sat at ringside. The man to my right always sat there. Young, dressed in black leather, and wearing dark Ray-Bans, he had never spoken to me. Every time I glanced his way, he smiled—with his fangs extended. Occasionally, he ran his tongue over his lips and made wet slurping sounds.

Pleasant fellow.

All four hundred or so vampires in the building could smell me and knew I was not one of them. Only my relationship with Aliena and Marcus kept them from falling on me and feasting.

"What did this poor sap do?" I asked Aliena.

"No idea." Her eyes shone brightly as she surveyed the fighters.

Marcus answered. "This swine owns a group of low-rent tenements, and he has allowed conditions to become deplorable."

"But why would he agree to fight for fifty thousand dollars?" Vampires offered the human fighters fifty large to fight to the death, conveniently leaving out that the mortal would be facing a vampire in the ring. The cash was always paid to a nominee chosen by the fighter before the bout. In case of "accidental" death. Looking at the man in the ring, I could not believe he would have taken any amount of money to participate in a death match.

"This man is a different case," Marcus said. "Special preliminary bout. We had him brought to us blindfolded. Two of the women living in these buildings are the mortal mothers of some of our brothers."

I began to see. Vampires could become highly protective of the people they had loved in life, even though they did not talk with them after being turned. They served as the ultimate guardian angels (and not noticeably different from biblical angels). Mess with a vampire's human mom, and you would die a most horrible death. For some reason, they did not consider messing with dad as bad.

Once transformed, a vampire cares for his family more than ever. Although the vampire will live an eternity, his family will not. And a vampire can never have another family like that one. No one can.

My parents had not been immortal and neither had my brother and sister. A part of me had died with each of them. They have been gone so long I can no longer clearly remember their faces. But I remember their souls, and I long to be reunited with them, that I might again hear their laughter.

The "fight" was mercifully short. The vampire boxer had barely started bobbing and weaving, playing with her lumbering opponent, when two vampires left their seats and flew through the air, landing in the ring and baring their fangs at the old man. Since no one complained, I assumed these were two of the vampires with offended relatives.

The old man stepped back, his gloved hands held out in front of him in a warding-off gesture, until he leaned against the ropes. I saw him scream something, but the crowd roared, drowning out his voice.

Aliena jumped to her feet, cheering. I stood with everyone else.

The old guy tried to slip through the ropes, but the girl caught him and tossed him into the middle of the ring. He staggered and went down on one knee, his right hand on the mat to prevent him from tipping over. He looked up, fear on his face, eyes wide.

As if on cue, the three vampires fell on him. This time I heard his shout of terror before the tumult of whistling and clapping began.

One vampire attacked his throat. Another his arm. And one bit him on the leg. The old landlord fought for a little while. Then the death spasms. Then stillness.

I leaned over to Aliena and shouted over the crowd, "Would you like to go now?" We always left after one fight, but I had a feeling it was not going to be possible tonight. My premonition proved correct.

"Oh, no, Sebastian," she said, taking my arm and kissing me on the lips. "Let's stay for a couple more. Please? It's a special night."

This is not how I wanted to spend it, but since Aliena did, I nodded. The smile she gave me made any sacrifice worthwhile.

"Yay!" When we sat back down, she dropped in my lap, put her right arm around my shoulders, and started playing with my hair. I wrapped my arms around her. "Isn't this nice?" she said in my ear.

The second fighter was a white boy, a gang banger, as his Eighth Street tattoos attested. He fought well—better than many professional boxers I had seen. Not that it mattered. He ended up flat on his back, his head pushed to the side as his vampire opponent drained him of life.

A young Chinese man entered the ring. Tattoos covered his arms, but he had no obvious gang affiliation. Tall and well muscled, he had broad shoulders and solid legs. He wore his hair in a ponytail, and he paced in his corner, giving his small female opponent a deadly stare.

"Let's get ready to driiiiinnnnnk uuuuuuuuuup," bellowed the little black vampire emcee. He had black-and-gray hair that stuck up a full meter. "Tonight's main event! In the red corner fighting for the 'hood, wearing red shorts with red trim, is Lourdes *"El Tiburón"* Cardoza!" The petite Spanish girl held her hands up and bowed to all four sides of the ring, applause washing over her.

"Have we seen her before?" I asked Aliena over the crowd's roar.

"I don't think you have," she shouted, not looking at me.

I turned back to the emcee.

"And her opponent, in the blue corner, fighting for the mainland, wearing white shorts with blue trim, is Gary "Screw" Yu!" Boos and hisses followed his introduction.

The announcer scrambled through the ropes.

When the bell rang, the vampire met Yu in the middle of the ring, where he landed a hard combination, staggering the girl. Three more good punches to the head had Lourdes backpedaling, trying to get out of the way. The crowd surged onto its feet, howling. Aliena leaped out of my lap, jumping up and down.

Lourdes bounced into the ropes, trapped.

Yu came in quickly. He led with a left and followed with a right to Lourdes' nose that had all his weight behind it. Her head snapped back. She straightened up, and he crossed with his left, a perfect punch on her right ear, knocking her sideways. She fell.

He kicked her in the side, then in the head. This was no time for chivalry. This was a fight to the death. He pulled his leg back for another kick to her face, but as his foot flew toward her, she slipped away and his leg shot up, tipping him over. Before he could fall, Lourdes righted him with her gloved hands. She began punching him feebly on the chest, her gloved fists hardly tapping him. He backed up anyway, a look of bewilderment on his face.

Lourdes did not have a scratch after the beating he had given her.

Yu threw a straight right. She dodged and the glove flashed past her head. Lourdes twisted with cobra speed and struck at the inside of his wrist. When she latched onto him, he yelled.

"Get off me, bitch! Get the fuck OFF!" He punched her on the back of the head and tried to pull his arm away from her. The movement jerked her head down, but she hung on.

Yu looked into the crowd, perhaps thinking someone would help him. The vampires on that side of the ring bared their teeth at him. His face drained of color.

"Holy SHIT!" He went berserk, punching and kicking Lourdes, screaming like a madman, trying to wrench his arm free. No matter what he did, she remained fastened to him, slowly draining his essence. The eeriest part was the way her arms flapped limply at her sides as he shook her. The floppy body and securely fastened mouth gave the impression of a giant leech.

When he tried to drag her through the ropes, she squatted and threw a lightning fast thudding punch to his groin. When she straightened up, Yu drooped, hanging awkwardly, his right arm up at a weird angle, his mouth a big O of agony before he passed out. Lourdes dragged him back to the middle of the ring as if he were a trampled doll, his wrist still clasped in her mouth.

About a minute later he stirred sluggishly. He still hung partially off the mat, at a slant to Lourdes's right. He struggled to gain his feet. When he got up, he started pleading with her.

"Please, lady, please stop. I can't feel my arm anymore," he said, sobbing. The crowd whistled and shouts of *boohoo* and *mommy* resonated through the warehouse.

When Lourdes didn't answer, he began yanking on his arm again, but his legs sagged. Tears flowed down his face, and he moaned, "No, no, no," a frightened chant.

Yu punched her—it glanced off her head. His knees shook. He blinked rapidly several times. He put his free hand on her shoulder, trying to hang on with the thick red glove. When he began to sink to the floor, the glove slipped and dragged along Lourdes's back.

The young man went down slowly, twisting in front of his vampire opponent, his right arm pointing up as she held his wrist fast in her mouth. His left hand drooped to the mat.

"Please," he said, looking dully up at her. I only saw his lips move. The crowd roared. Yu's body had turned pale white with a horribly drained look, and his smooth, vital skin pouched, lacking elasticity. His gaze drifted to Lourdes's knees. Then his eyes stared into the middle distance, and his body sagged. Lourdes took a last drink and opened her mouth. Yu's arm and upper torso fell limply to the canvas. The inside of his right wrist was mangled bloody meat.

Lourdes clasped her hands over her head and shook them. The crowd responded with catcalls, whistles, and shouts of "Lour-DES!" and "Marry me!"

My taste for 49's entertainment had ebbed to an all-time low. When Aliena turned to me laughing and clapping, I smiled and started clapping, too. She had seen my face, though. She picked up her jacket.

"Thank you for staying with me," she said, kissing me on the cheek. "Let's go."

We said good night to Marcus and walked out of the warehouse as the emcee introduced the next fighters.

We heard low voices as we crossed the parking lot. Four men had grouped around my car, one sitting on the hood and the other three leaning against it. Hispanic and by the look of them, 8th Street gang.

"Yo, yo, yo," said the man sitting on the hood. "Check this out, dawgs." He threw his cigarette on the ground and exhaled his smoke slowly while folding his arms across his chest. He looked at Aliena. "Damn, man, this car and that *mamacita*, you got it made."

"Fuck yeah he does, Sammy," said the man on his left.

I could feel Aliena's glee at this serendipitous encounter. After the brutality of 49's entertainment, she lusted for a kill. I hoped to defuse the situation with a calm voice, but I would need more than that to keep these kids from becoming her next meal.

"Don't lean on the car, please," I said. "Your jeans have metal studs that could scratch the clear coat."

"Damn, *ese*, you talk like a *big* dawg," Sammy said. "Okay. We'll get off your ride."

He leaned forward and slid off the Maserati's hood with his arms still crossed. I could hear the slight scrape of the rivets on his back pockets as he scratched the paint. The other three stood up straight as Sammy's feet hit the ground.

"We were thinking you should share with us," Sammy said. "Maybe you could let us take the car for a spin?" He smiled broadly, and his friends tittered.

"You're not covered by my insurance," I told him.

"If I smash it up a little, I promise to pay for it. Come on, let me have the keys."

"No."

"Ah, man, don't say no. Give them to me."

I shook my head.

He shrugged. "If that's how you want it." He pulled out a Sig Sauer P226 and fired two shots at my front passenger tire. They both hit the mark. The car sagged as the tire went limp.

"Damn, that's too bad," Sammy said to laughter. "I don't think they have the auto club out here, bro."

"Eighth Street must be profitable," I said. "That's an expensive piece you're carrying."

"Yeah, well, I didn't pay retail." He slid his gun back into his pants and ogled Aliena. "Mm-*hmmm*. Girl, you have got it going *on*," he said.

Aliena stood hands on hips, her short leather jacket pulled open, her taut t-shirt bulging through the opening.

"I like you, too," Aliena told him. "Chubby and full of blood."

Sammy stopped smiling. "What'd you say, bitch?"

She opened her mouth to reply.

"Aliena, please don't say it again."

The four bangers moved closer to us.

"Listen," I said, "I have about four hundred in cash on me. That's a hundred dollars a man. Take it, and we'll just walk away."

"No, we will not," Aliena said.

"Aliena, please." Holding my left hand up to show it was empty, I slid my right into my pants pocket and slowly brought out the money. The bills were clasped in solid gold. "The clip is worth three thousand. Do we have a deal?"

Sammy took the cash, looked at it, slid it into his jacket pocket. "Okay, you paid your toll, bitch. Now get your stupid white ass out of here. We still got to collect from the lady."

I stayed where I was. "Take my advice. Leave with what you have. You've made a killing tonight."

"I will make a killing," Aliena said, voice edged.

"No, Aliena."

Sammy leaned forward and squeezed Aliena's breast. She stood there, letting him do it. I knew that was trouble. I never saw her move, but suddenly Sammy flinched back, holding his hand up to his chest.

"*¡Carajo!*" He grunted in pain. He massaged his right side and his eyes squinted, murderous. Aliena had either punched him or pinched his nipple. I took a quick look around. The street remained deserted.

"Aliena, let's just go. Fly us out of here."

"No."

I looked at these men barring our path, all of them in their early twenties. Children who did not recognize the dark entities they faced. If they had known, they would have stepped away from my car and watched us pass by like the angels of death we were.

But they didn't know.

"Look," I said, holding my hands up, "we do not want any trouble. You have my money. You—"

"Shut up, just shut the fuck up!" Sammy pulled his gun again and pointed it at me. "You had your chance, bitch. Permission to cross has just been revoked."

As his finger tightened on the trigger, I twisted left and brought my right hand up. The shot still caught me on the edge of the shoulder, but I was able to knock Sammy's hand high so he couldn't shoot me again.

After that, I didn't have to do a thing. Aliena blurred as she disarmed the other three men and knocked them to the ground. In a blink, she had already pulled Sammy up and now held him in the air, ready to sink her teeth into his neck. He choked, his throat squeezed by Aliena's hand. His feet hung a meter above the ground, kicking feebly.

I grabbed her hair and pulled hard.

"NO! No, Aliena!"

She turned muddy eyes on me. "Take your hand out of my hair, Sebastian," she said. Her voice was low and raspy, and a menacing rumble came from the lupine face staring at me.

I carefully disengaged my hand.

She continued holding Sammy aloft, her rock-hard hand jammed under his jaw. Her mouth opened wide, and with her eyes glowing red and her canines shining whitely as lethal fangs, she hissed in Sammy's face, shaking him as if he were a puppy.

He let out a gargled moan of terror.

The other three men had stood up. Now they backed away from us. They could see Aliena's face and knew they no longer wanted to be anywhere near her. Their reaction was an instinctive one, born from millennia of evolution. When a man sees a lion in his path, his whole being surges with a desire to get away from it. So it was with these three. They ran into the night, leaving their leader—and their guns—behind.

"Aliena."

She finally lowered the struggling Sammy to the ground. When she let him go and stood back, he sank to his knees, heaving and moaning. Then he leaned forward and threw up.

I laughed. "Good lord, Sammy boy, you can't even hold on to your groceries." I stepped around the mess, grabbed him by the collar, and jerked. He flopped onto his back. I reached into his jacket pocket and retrieved my money clip. I took the four hundreds out and tossed them on his chest.

"Sorry about the trouble," I said. I felt the knitting of my skin and finally glanced at my shoulder. The bullet had ripped the edge of my overcoat. "Sammy, you little pestilence—I like this coat." I don't think he understood me. He had curled into the fetal position, eyes wide with shock.

Perfectly natural after his encounter with us.

I pulled my cell and called Hector, one of my special problem solvers, and told him to locate the Gran Turismo by GPS and bring it in tonight. I hung up and looked at the silver glow of the car in the moonlight.

"Now could you fly us back to my place?"

She pulled me close and latched onto my throat, lifting us up and away, drinking me as she whirled into the air and steered us toward the ocean. I automatically reached for her hips as she went horizontal.

She pulled her mouth away.

"Are you grabbing my derrière, Sebastian?"

"You know I am." I squeezed. "Unbelievably curvy. Even Hamilton has commented on it more than once."

"Yes. He calls it my booty." She licked blood from the corner of her mouth.

"You know, Aliena, just because you can hear us from far away does not mean you should listen to us. It's a violation of our privacy."

"Not if you know I'm listening."

"Only I know you can do it," I said. "Hamilton does not. And I don't always know when you are there."

"A technicality. Besides, it's much more fun when you and he do not know, of course it is! And it is a harmless conceit." She squeezed me hard. "You are not to spoil that. I forbid you to tell him that I can hear you from a long distance."

"Very well," I said as she continued to python me, "I know a woman's love of eavesdropping and gossip, especially when you get to hear people talking about you. I can understand why you would place a high value on it. I would do nothing to ruin it."

She stopped squashing me and prepared to fasten her mouth onto my throat again.

"Of course," I said, "I still think it's a violation of privacy, and you—"

She bit into me much harder than usual and I yelped. I tightened my arms around her back, watching the twinkling lights of the cars on the freeway below us, as Aliena, slurping my blood, flew us toward the sea and home.

Chapter 8

Saturday, January 24, 1:51 a.m.

We landed on my balcony. Aliena had finished drinking me minutes ago, but my legs were still shaky from blood loss. She pressed her hand to the security plate to open the sliding doors, her other hand resting on my shoulder.

"Are you okay now, Sebastian?"

"Yes," I said.

She headed for the living room. I moved unsteadily into the kitchen, opened the freezer, and pulled out two bottles of ice-cold Stolichnaya.

Whenever Aliena drank from me—or any time I lost a great deal of blood—the eternal engine in my body began operating, replenishing what I had lost. Since this vital ingredient consisted mostly of water, the replacement procedure was incomplete and left me dehydrated.

I drank one bottle of vodka before the fridge door closed. I tossed that bottle in the recycle can and stood still for a moment, letting the warmth spread through me.

I reached into the refrigerator again and drank two liters of water and one of orange juice.

Carrying a second bottle of vodka, I walked into the living room and lit a cigarette. Aliena held her nose and pointed to the patio.

"Yes, okay." I went outside, sat on the white wall. The surf boomed distantly on Malibu beach while I watched Aliena.

Her hands flew over her laptop's keyboard. She was probably shopping or scheduling banking transactions. A financial wiz as well as an authority on the occult, her investment portfolio performed better than most. She had left the computer on once after heading for her lair, and I had seen her account with Goldman Sachs, probably one of the many places she kept her wealth. Her balance exceeded $140 million. She had registered the account in the name of Aliena Turner, one of her pseudonyms. She told me that the introduction of online trading was the best stock market innovation for vampires, eliminating the need for human intermediaries, thus improving the bottom line.

It also removed what had been one of the biggest threats to the vampire community. With vampires opening so many accounts (they are avid investors and love the world financial markets), the threat of exposure existed in every transaction involving one of their human partners. Online trading allowed investors to schedule transactions in advance and complete them while the vampire slept, eliminating the need for an associate who could move around in the daylight.

I finished my cigarette and stubbed it out, drank the rest of the vodka. I tossed the bottle into the recycle can and walked back inside.

Now for the tarot card. I pulled it out of my jacket and flopped down next to Aliena. I laid my head on her shoulder. "Whatcha doin'?" I asked, looking at the computer screen.

"Playing."

"Oh, boy. I remember," I said, recognizing the virtual world through which she traveled. "*World of Witchcraft*, isn't it?"

"Warcraft," she said, her fingers tapping the keyboard lightly. "I have been using it to keep in contact with friends around the world."

"That's the one." I remembered because the last time she had started playing, she had remained on my computer until nearly sunrise. "I have something for you to look at." I lifted my head.

"What is it?" she asked.

"A tarot card."

"Um. What kind of tarot card?" She was in a battle now, her voice faint and uninterested.

"That's what I was hoping you could tell me. We recovered it at a murder scene. Just the one card. We could not find the rest of the deck."

"That's nice," she said.

"Very." I would have to wait until she decided to take a break. I held the card up. It struck me that even through the plastic bag the picture had that mesmerizing, three-dimensional look. I became aware that Aliena had stopped typing.

"Where did you get that?" she asked in a whisper.

I turned to her, surprised. "What's the matter?" It sounded like her game character was being killed, but she didn't seem aware of it. She reached out and took the card.

"I don't believe it," she said. She set the laptop on the table with *World of Warcraft* still running.

"Well? Are you going to tell me?" I was getting excited. The card obviously meant something to her. I couldn't believe my luck. I had known she would be able to tell me about the card in a general way, but I had not expected this reaction.

"Where did you get this?" she asked again. It was also obvious she hadn't heard a word I had said up to now.

"At a murder scene. Just that card. No others."

She nodded. She broke the seal on the bag.

"Aliena! You know better than that! You can't just open an evid—"

She gave me her do-not-mess-with-me look. She did not use it often.

"Naturally," I said, "if it's something you must do . . ."

She dipped her hand into the bag and took the card out. She couldn't taint the card in any way that mattered, but protocol required documentation every single time someone opened an evidence bag. My techs would not like logging the bag in its current condition.

She held the card up and scrutinized it. I waited, knowing she would tell me when she was ready.

"Who was murdered?" she asked. "You have a name?"

"Yes. Cavanaugh. Mason Cavanaugh."

She shook her head. I waited for more, but she had fallen to staring at the card again.

I stood and was moving around the table so I could step outside when her voice stopped me.

"We need to meet with Marcus."

That I did not want to hear. I knew Marcus wanted Aliena the way I wanted her. And he was a suave, dynamic, darkly charming man. However, this was a murder investigation. It was no concern of his.

"Why?" I said, irritated. "He doesn't have anything to do with this."

"Yes, he does." She said it matter-of-factly, her voice level.

"How? I thought you were the tarot expert."

"I am. This is more than a tarot card."

Now we were getting somewhere. "What else is it?"

"I—I do not think I can tell you. Not now. Please let me talk to Marcus first."

Being patient was one thing, but in a murder case, gathering information quickly was critical to success, and she knew that. If she possessed significant information, she should tell me. We had worked together on many cases. Just the two of us. Marcus had worked with us on our last case, and I hadn't been too keen on it.

"It has to be tonight," I said. "I'm going to arrange for my people to examine the card right now. I already promised Hamilton and Reyes that you would give us the benefit of your experience," I said, pressing her.

"I can tell you that the Prince of Wands, in a tarot reading, means something unexpected is coming."

"Thank you. What about the part you need to discuss with Marcus?"

"I can't, Sebastian."

"This is hardly the way to start a romantic relationship," I said, half to myself.

Her eyes widened in surprise. "What does this have to do with us? Are you saying you would not want to be with me if I didn't tell you?"

"No," I said. "No, of course not." I returned to the couch and sat next to her. I took her hands in mine. "But one of the most important ways to show love is by trusting each other. Even with our secrets. Please look at it from my point of view. You tell me Marcus knows of this, but you can't tell me. I do not know what to think of that."

"It is not something I am truly keeping from you. I will tell you as soon as I see Marcus, no matter what he says. I promise." She stopped, looked at me with pleading eyes. "Please, Sebastian, let me talk to him first. He will need to know about this anyway. You must trust me," she ended triumphantly.

"Oh, very well. But you can't take the card."

"Yes," she said, "the card." She turned it over, looked at the pattern of infinity signs on the back, and then turned it to the face side. "Can you describe where you found it?"

"In a mansion owned by an antiques dealer. No known enemies, very low-key. Shot in his study from what appears to be an unlikely direction. The room was locked from the inside, and we could not find a gun. I found the card in that room, stuck in a copy of *Paradise Lost* in his book cabinet."

"As if it had been hidden?"

"Not exactly. Why would anyone want to hide it?"

"To prevent it from being discovered."

"Obviously. But why? What's so special about this card?"

She shook her head.

"Can't you talk to Marcus now?" I said. My watch read 2:30. Sunrise was at 6:56, just more than four hours away.

"I think so." She handed the card to me, took her phone out, and dialed. "Hello Marcus . . . Yes, I might be able to do that . . . No, we will not . . . You know very well why. Please listen for a moment. Sebastian has recovered one of the archons . . . Yes, I'm sure. I am looking at it . . . The Prince of Wands . . . At a murder scene . . . I know . . . At Sebastian's place . . . Yes, I will." She disconnected.

"And?"

"He wants to meet with me immediately."

"Is he coming here?"

"No. I am going to him."

I did not care for the way she said that. "You may not take the card," I reminded her.

"I know."

She stood up and walked to the patio. "When will you be back?" I asked, following her.

"Before sunrise," she said over her shoulder. She turned and waited for me near the wall. I went to her and took her in my arms.

"Try to come back sooner than that," I said.

She kissed the tip of my nose. "I will. May I spend the day here again?"

I squeezed her, my immortal blood singing. "Of course, my darling. Any time you like."

When we released each other, she rose into the sky, fading quickly against the star-filled black.

Chapter 9

Saturday, January 24, 3:01 a.m.

I called Augustus Reed, my company's expert on the occult. An Aussie I found in Argentina, Reed had been studying with a Candomblée priest at the time, learning how to conjure potent magic.

He worked at night and rode the waves at Manhattan Beach during the day. The late schedule proved convenient since he and Aliena occasionally worked together.

"Hi Sebastian."

"Auggie, please dispatch a messenger to my home. I'm going to send you a tarot card. You and the lab take a look at it and get back to me right away. And send the messenger back here with the card as soon as you're done. Make your analyses quick—we can do a more thorough inspection later today. LAPD protocols. Aliena broke the seal on the evidence bag, so gloss that, would you?"

"Not a problem. I'll take care of it before I forward it to the lab. I'll have a driver there double-quick."

We disconnected.

I leaned back and steepled my fingers under my chin, wondering what Aliena and Marcus were doing right now. They obviously knew something about this card. One of the archons, she had told him. The common definition of the noun is leader, or sovereign. Did she mean the Prince specifically?

She had also said "one of," so I knew there were at least two cards. She had recognized the Prince immediately, and Marcus had been so intrigued by her news, he had asked her to come to him that moment.

How did they know about these cards? I asked myself if there was an obvious answer.

If more than one archon existed, perhaps there were many more. If so, why not a full deck of seventy-eight cards? And since Aliena and Marcus knew what this card was, they must have seen cards like this before.

They might even be cardholders.

The messenger arrived thirty minutes later. I met him as he finished his U-turn in my gravel drive. The van pulled up in front of the house, and the driver rolled down the window as I approached. He was a college intern currently working the night shift.

"For Mr. Reed's eyes only," I told him as I handed him the sealed manila envelope containing the evidence bag.

"Yes, sir," he said, stifling a yawn. "He already told me."

"Off you go," I said, stepping back. He hit the accelerator and sped down the driveway.

4:06 a.m.

My computer played a short jingle, letting me know someone wanted a video conference. I tapped the mouse and accepted the invitation. Reed came on-screen.

He didn't wear glasses these days, and with his dark tan, sandy hair, and light-blue polo shirt, he looked like a kid who crewed his college team or maybe worked as a Venice Beach lifeguard.

"What have you got?" I asked him.

"I don't know how you do it, but you certainly become involved with some of the strangest artifacts in history."

"Oh? You know what this card is?" It seemed everybody knew but me. "How common is this knowledge?"

"Highly uncommon. I haven't come across references to them very often and then only in very ancient texts. The stories are vague but interesting."

I lit another cigarette while he continued.

"The lab dates the card at about two thousand one hundred years old."

I coughed slightly. "You said . . ."

"You heard right. This card has been around for more than two millennia."

Older than Christ? "How can that be? I did not see any signs of extreme age about it." There had been no creases, no deterioration of the paper used. The colors still shone vibrant, and the gold border gleamed with a rich luster. "It's impossible."

"You can talk to Preston if you like," he said, "but he gets the same reports I do. Anyway, that's it for the lab report, except for the fluoroscope pictures, which I'll get to in a moment. Now, according to my research, this card is part of a deck called the Tarot of the Archons, which was created by the Gods. And they made the major arcana cards special somehow."

Of the seventy-eight cards in the tarot, twenty-two made up the major arcana—the cards that represented the original trumps. Today's modern deck of playing cards does not include them.

"What was significant about them?" I asked.

"That's just it," Reed said. "Nobody knows. There are a few strange references to disappearances that apparently had something to do with the cards and a couple of bizarre stories about travel to the stars. Although the deck was called the Tarot of the Archons, the major arcana cards became known as star cards. No idea why. Until now, I thought they were a myth."

"Hold on, Auggie, the messenger is here." I ran outside, collected the card, and hurried back in. I tossed the bag on the coffee table next to my laptop and sat down on the couch again. I thought back to the last thing he had said. "These references to disappearances," I said. "What did the cards do? Were they the cause?"

He gave a frustrated sigh. "It's hard to understand, but from what I could find, the stories don't say. The magical spell placed on the cards, according to one author, "did imbue them with portals to distant places." And in the same group of anecdotes, there was a story that seemed to be related."

"Oh?"

"Yes. It was about one of the star cards being the cause of a nobleman's death in 845."

"Caused his death how?"

"It doesn't say. Only that the man was never seen again "when he was shewn the card.""

That sounded ominous.

"What about the tarot I sent you?" I asked. "Can you tell me anything about it?"

"A little." He tapped his keyboard and my screen filled with a picture of the Prince. He certainly was an ugly heir to the wand throne. "First of all, the Prince does not usually appear in the most popular tarot decks today."

"I know."

"This Prince is Dagon, a shape-shifter, also known as a phoenix. In a tarot reading, he usually refers to all that is unpredictable or unexpected. Although the phoenix must die a fiery death in order to be reborn, this card is not always interpreted as a bad card, depending on the other cards in the spread."

That made sense. One of the main themes of the tarot revolved around the circle of existence, the endless cycle of birth, death, and resurrection.

"Now, you see the border?" He enlarged the corner. The dim luster of the card's encircling band filled the screen. "It's gold, but it's magnetically charged, as if it's generating a weak field."

"Magnetically charged? Is there anything in the history of the cards that indicates they could be using a magnetic field?"

"For what?" he asked. "Traveling to the stars?" He removed the magnified image and his face came back onscreen.

"Well?"

"If we assume the stories have some basis in fact, I think these cards may have to do with teleportation."

"Teleportation? Do your sources say how the cards do it?"

"No, of course not. That would be too easy. But one of the stories I read said that every time one of the archons traveled through a card, her "visage did remain" on it."

That piece of information sounded like a non sequitur. "I am not sure I understand the significance of that fact, Auggie."

"You will. Check this out," he said. "This is what the Prince of Wands looks like under a fluoroscope."

He tapped his computer, brought up the card again. I could still see the details of the Prince, but they were faint. Superimposed over Dagon were a man's face and two objects not visible to the naked eye.

"Any idea what we're looking at?"

"No idea," he replied. "Here, I cleaned it up before I tried to identify him . . . there he is. If my texts are accurate, this is the last man to journey through this card."

He had long, black hair and coal-black eyes. His face was flat with a squashed nose and a shovel chin, and he was not smiling. He wore a dark shirt with a low collar, had a three-day beard, and sported a tattoo on the left side of his neck. I recognized it.

This man was a Magistine.

So, we had a Magistine death chant in the murdered man's room, and now a man from Magisty appears on a card recovered at the crime scene. Did he have something to do with Cavanaugh's death? Was he the killer?

"Could you send me a copy of that?"

"Sure." I could hear him tapping his keys while I looked at the picture, memorizing the man's face. "It's on the way."

"What do you think those other two things are?"

"Looks like a clock and a doorway."

"Yes," I said, "that's what I see, too."

"Where did you say you found this?"

"At the Cavanaugh murder scene. It was marking a place in a first edition of *Paradise Lost*."

"Hm," he said. "God vs. Satan."

"Yes. I need to get back to work."

"Don't you ever sleep?"

"Bye Auggie."

Chapter 10

Saturday, January 24, 6:29 a.m.

I paced on the patio, smoking a cigarette and drinking vodka, wondering when Aliena would come back. I realized I had killed the Stoli bottle. I tossed it in the green recycle trash container. Sunrise would come in less than half an hour. Although I had asked her to come back early, she still had not returned.

This situation irritated me. She knew something about these archon cards, knew I wanted the information, and had decided to spend the entire night with Marcus rather than hurry back to me. It hurt that she had given so much of our first night as an official couple to him. At this rate, she would arrive just minutes before she lost consciousness, which meant she would not be able to answer a single question I had. That meant I would have nothing for Hamilton later this morning.

I looked at my watch, cursed, and took a final puff of my cigarette. As I turned to extinguish it in the ashtray, I saw Aliena standing in the corner watching me.

"Is it safe for me to return?" she asked.

It embarrassed me that she had heard my profanity and mortified me that she had correctly surmised I was angry at her lateness. I had never meant to say anything to her about it. I was not her keeper and knew that's how she expected me to treat her, however much I might dislike her nights out.

"Of course it's safe," I said with a laugh. I held my arms out to her. She shook her head.

"Just because you are my boyfriend does not mean I suddenly approve of your smoking. You stink."

She walked past me and into the house carrying a book. I followed and pressed the button that closed the patio doors before crossing the living room to the hall that led to her bedroom.

As soon as I walked through her door, I headed directly to the bathroom so I could wash my hands and brush my teeth. Aliena began removing her clothes. She had tossed her Bugs Bunny pajamas and the book she had been carrying onto the bed. The volume was actually an old leather-bound journal.

I snapped on the light, took the toothpaste out of the left-hand drawer, and grabbed my toothbrush (mine was the blue one—hers was pink). I squeezed the aqua gel onto the bristles when Aliena walked in and plucked her toothbrush out of the cup. She held it out to me. I squeezed a small glob of gel onto it.

"Thank you," she said, and turned the water on. She put her brush under the flow for a moment and started brushing. I capped the toothpaste and dunked my gel under the water before turning the tap off.

We watched each other while we brushed. We finished at the same time and took turns rinsing our brushes and gargling with mouthwash. She had gone through the same routine the night before.

"Why do you brush your teeth before you go to bed?" I asked.

She looked at me, eyebrows raised in surprise. "Do you know what my mouth would taste like in the evening if I let that residual blood decay while I was sleeping? Un-unh, not me. I have sensitive taste buds."

"I understand," I said. I could also imagine what her breath would smell like if she didn't brush. *Caramba.*

I followed her to bed. Before she climbed under the covers, she picked up the journal. I looked at my watch. It was 6:52. Four minutes.

"Can you tell me anything about the archon card before you go to sleep?" I said, sitting on the edge of the bed. "How do you and Marcus know about them?"

She looked at me with that wide-eyed innocence I found so shattering. It was impossible to resist, for I could tell she was not deceiving me. She pressed the journal against her chest, both arms crossed over it. Now she held it out to me.

"What is this?" I noticed a place had been marked about a third of the way in with a slip of perfumed paper.

"You said we should trust each other with our secrets. This is one of my diaries."

I looked up at her, shocked. "You're letting me read your diary?"

She nodded.

I examined it. Like the books in Cavanaugh's library, it appeared to be a hundred years old, at least.

"It will answer some of your questions. Even some you have wanted to ask me but have not," she said with a furtive smile. "For now, know that the tarot card you have recovered is powerful. And dangerous. Be careful until I am with you again tonight."

"Can you at least tell me how you know anything about it at all?"

"I knew you would ask." She opened the drawer on her nightstand, took something out, and showed it to me. The Moon. With brilliant colors and the now familiar gold border. But this was a major arcana card. One of Reed's star cards.

"How long have you had that?"

"You will see the exact date it was given to me in my diary, but it was more than fifty years ago." She put the card back in the drawer.

"That's certainly an old deck," I said. A tarot deck lay next to her Moon, the cards well worn.

"Yes, it's old," she said, touching it gently. She continued gazing at it for a few moments. I waited for her to say more. Instead, she closed the drawer, yawned, and scrunched down under her blankets.

I leaned over and gave her a quick kiss on the cheek. "Thank you for telling me. May I come in again at sunset to be with you when you wake up?"

"I would like that."

I had started to rise when her arms encircled my neck, and she pulled me back down. I set the book aside as our faces drew closer.

"Oh, no you don't," she whispered. Our mouths came together, and we kissed wonderfully for almost a minute, her lips and tongue full of passionate promise and ardent desire, her hand a soft claw in my hair. Suddenly everything that had irritated me earlier faded to a ghostly echo.

Her grip on me loosened, and her arms fell onto the bedspread.

I pulled away and ran my hand through her thick mane of honey hair. After tucking her arms under the blankets, I kissed her mole, picked up the journal, and stood. After turning off the lights and closing the door, I pressed my hand against the wall plate, heard the security bolts slide into place.

I grabbed a big bottle of orange juice out of the refrigerator and took it and Aliena's diary onto the patio with me.

I plopped down onto one of the white plastic chairs and drew another toward me so I could put my feet up. Then I opened the journal in my lap and began to read at the place she had marked.

April 26, 1865

Dear Diary,

Happy Birthday to me! Celebrated my 170th today. I have been a vampire for 150 years.

Have I told you, Diary, that I love being a vampire?

Guess who I saw again tonight? The immortal I drank from last year. He waited for me at my favorite coffee house, Chez Gauthier. I do not know how he found me. I was tempted to taste him again, but I left before he could accost me. His blood is delicious, but I already have my own immortal.

"What?" I said aloud. What did she mean by that? I shifted more comfortably in my chair and continued reading, interest soaring.

Marcus asked me to join him for the evening, saying he would treat me to dinner and the theatre in New Orleans. I was tempted. I know several boutiques in the French Quarter, and I dearly wanted to buy some special clothes for the weekend. When I asked him how we would get there, he told me he had a secret way. I do not know what he meant by that.

I knew I could not go, though. I told him I was honored but I had already made plans. Marcus is very handsome, but I love another.

I thought it would be interesting to have my fortune told this birthday. Within the small Egyptian community in the nearby forest of Argonne, there lives a woman people say has the ancestral gift of second sight. I visited her two nights ago and told her what I wanted and when. I had fed only minutes before seeing her and kept the meeting brief. She did not realize what I was.

Tonight will be different. She will certainly be able to discern that I am a vampire. I am still undecided as to how I will handle that exposure. Ah, well, why worry? I will make the decision when the time comes.

Oh, boy.

I flew to the gypsy camp late, gliding under a bloated moon that gave enough light to see the wagons clearly among the trees below.

When I climbed the four wooden steps outside the door and entered Maman Djeserit's wagon, she rose from her table to greet me. I stayed near the door for a moment looking about. The feeble light of two hanging lamps provided the only illumination, but I could easily see into every corner. We were alone.

Most of Maman's possessions were of poor quality. Carpets with frayed edges covered parts of the floor. A small table with two chairs at the back and a bunk on my right. A battered chest of drawers. A pair of shoes. Strewn throughout were knickknacks and clothes, pictures, boxes, and even several books.

The place had a warm aura, as if it were a sanctuary, a place where anyone would be safe.

The old gypsy wore a modest white chemise and reed slippers. She had a mottled complexion, giving her face a patched look, as if two colors of skin had been used to create her. She looked old, with gray hair and bad teeth, but her eyes shone bright and alert.

I stepped into the light, where she could see me clearly.

She had been saying, "Welcome, my dear," but now she stopped and her greeting abruptly came to a halt. Her face paled. I could smell the change in her, the sudden sour fear sweat. We stood frozen like figures in a diorama.

I held my right hand up, palm out. The old gypsy woman hesitated still. I remained unmoving. Thus reassured, she approached me slowly, her eyes wide. I lowered my hand.

Her blood exuded a delectable bouquet, her fear a tangy spice. Maman Djeserit's curiosity overwhelmed her trepidation. She continued coming to me. I stood still.

She held up her right hand to touch my face, stopped, and looked into my eyes. "May I?"

I inclined my head slightly. Her nearness caused me to salivate.

She ran her fingertips lightly along my cheek. The smell of her was sweetly intoxicating, and her proximity racked me with delicious hunger pangs. I inhaled her succulent aroma. I could feel my fangs extending, anticipating the rip of her soft throat tissue, the spurt of her salty hot blood on my tongue. I turned my head in her direction.

She jerked her hand back and took three stumbling steps away from me, banging the backs of her knees on the low chest of drawers before sitting down hard. "Please," she said, holding her hand to her throat.

I fought down my thirst. "Do not fear," I told her. My fangs retracted. "I am here to learn, as I promised. Only that. You must excuse me, I have not yet dined this evening, and your nearness reminded me of that."

She nodded, but I could sense her continued anxiety. She stood and moved behind the little table, gesturing me to the chair opposite with a shaking hand. I removed my long overcoat and set it on the wooden chest. I walked to the table and sat in the chair she had indicated.

She took a deep breath. "Now, Your Highness, we begin." She handed me the deck of cards. "You must shuffle the cards for several minutes so that they become infused with your energy."

I slowly began melding the cards over and over, mixing them up as thoroughly as I could. When I had done so, she took the deck and set it on the table. She never took her eyes off me.

"Did you wish to ask the cards a question, or did you want a general reading?"

"A general reading, please."

She nodded and began turning the cards over. She arranged them carefully and revealed them slowly, muttering after the fourth card and continuing to talk under her breath until she had laid out the last card, the tenth. She touched the cards in the middle, the first two she had revealed, and looked up at me.

"It is your birthday," she said. "Many happy returns."

That impressed me. "Thank you. How did you know?"

"The cards told me."

"Can you tell me how?"

"Yes, but it would take some time. It involves many things, including the position of the cards and their relationship to one another. And you must have a feel for it."

"A feel for what?"

"For the mana. The universal force. It is what helps you see, helps you know. Otherwise you cannot hear what the cards are saying."

Her description of a universal force intrigued me. I had never heard of such a thing before. "I would like you to teach me. Perhaps we could arrange lessons?"

"It would be an honor," she said. Her eyes glinted as she looked up. "What does Your Highness want, exactly?"

"Everything you know." I took five gold coins out of my pocket. "Please accept this as proof of my commitment." I set them on the table next to the crystal ball. Solid gold, they gleamed in the lamplight, looking like mellow butter.

Maman Djeserit picked them up.

"They are beautiful, Mistress," she said, her hand trembling. The coins were worth more than all the wagons in her village. I knew she would be cheated and receive only a fraction of their value when she sold them, but even that would be a princely sum.

"Please, go on with my reading," I told her.

"Yes," she said, and I felt her fear dwindle even more, caught the aroma of her excitement. She peered at the cards again. "I see you with a dark-haired man. He is holding you in his arms. He is a special man," she said, fingering the Lovers card.

That could not be. François had blond hair, a little darker than my own. We were in love. I wanted him to be my first. I felt a luscious chill whenever I looked in his face or thought of his kisses.

Now I was becoming jealous.

"What do you mean, a special man?" I asked her.

Her brow furrowed, and she continued tapping the card with her fingers. "He is not a normal man. He is not like you, but he is not like me, either."

That sounded like François. He was immortal, but he was not a vampire. He did not have dark hair, though.

"Are you sure he does not have light hair like mine?" I asked her.

"I can see him very clearly, highness. He has dark hair and the aura of a peaceful tiger."

That did not sound like François, who was a painter, sensitive and emotional. He was younger than I, barely one hundred. The other vampires terrified him. He never attended the games at 49. I asked the others to leave him alone and so far they had, except for Rachella, who has "met" us a couple of times at Le Monde's. I do not like her, Diary. It is not because she is beautiful and sexy and older than I am. It is something in her eyes, as if she is always playing a joke on me. I think she secretly hates me and wishes to do me ill.

"Do you know how this man is different from us?"

She closed her eyes. Her hand rested on the Lovers. I could see every line in her face, the deeply etched ones around her eyes and mouth and the fine ones under her ears. That odd discoloration of her skin gave her an eerie visage, as if I were looking at the head of a patchwork doll.

"He is a warrior who does not fall," she said. "He walks on the graves of friends and foes alike. There is blood on his hands, but it is the blood of his times, for he is a peaceful man. He looks to the horizon and sees eternity." Her eyes opened and she smiled. "And he loves you very much."

"I do not know a dark-haired man such as you describe."

She frowned. "It is possible he is merely an acquaintance now, but the cards are never wrong. You have met this man at least once."

At least once. Could she mean . . . good lord, she meant this man Montero. He was dark-haired and immortal. And the way he moved and spoke that night on the roof when I tried to drain him of blood indicated a bold, decisive personality that had acquired its tenor from experience, not boastfulness.

I was not as impressed with this prognostication. It seemed farfetched considering my relationship with François—in fact, I was going to ask him tonight to come away with me so we could spend a weekend together. I had already dreamed about it many times, feeling shivers when the images became too clear in my mind. Because this weekend, I would do anything he liked. And I wanted to make love to him.

I lit another cigarette.

She swept the cards with her gaze. Then she caught her breath and gave a small cry.

"Highness!" She pointed to a card. It was the eighth one she had turned over. The Tower. "Something terrible is happening to you, even as we speak." She looked again at the Lovers. "Someone has done a dreadful thing to you."

"What?" I asked her. "What is this? What are you talking about?"

She looked at me, and her eyes were filled with fear again, but not of me this time—her fear was for *me. "Your dearest love . . . a woman with green eyes . . . a woman like you . . . she is taking him . . ."*

I heard no more, already out of the gypsy camp and high above the trees, leaving my coat behind. Rachella had green eyes. She was taking François? But she could not. The other vampires would slaughter her for such a violation of my rights. Unless . . .

Unless he agreed to go with her. If he went of his own free will, then she could do whatever she wanted with him.

I could not believe it. François was terrified of other vampires. Of course, I was a vampire, and he loved me, so he was not frightened of all of us. And Rachella was beautiful and sexy—and promiscuous. Could he have been tempted to go with her if she promised she would give him . . . ? I could not finish that thought.

I arrived at his little villa and pushed the back door open, not bothering with the handle. The frame splintered with a sharp crack. I strode into the living room.

"François?" I called. I looked in his bedroom and his bathroom, my breath coming in short gasps. His home was empty. All of his possessions were in their usual places and there were no signs of a struggle.

That's when I became aware of an odor. I sniffed.

Perfume.

I stopped, set her diary on the table, and ground my cigarette out in the ashtray. Rachella had accosted me outside 49 a few weeks ago and had promised me an unforgettable night. She had been sultry, playful, but she had not pressed me when I said no. It had seemed like an accidental meeting at the time, but now I was not so sure. I realized she had probably planned it.

A chill went through me. I had thought she only wanted a drink of wonderful Sebastian. It's possible she may have been hunting for much more than that.

I picked up the journal and the orange juice and took them to the kitchen.

Aliena had warned me about Rachella, saying she liked to take an immortal and keep him prisoner for decades, draining him repeatedly. When she tired of him, she invited her friends over for a final drink. I can withstand two, maybe three vampires trying to suck my life away. But four is too many. My blood cannot replenish itself fast enough to replace that amount when the loss is so fast.

She must have been talking about François when she told me the story. Oh my God. Rachella had killed an immortal—who had also happened to be the love of Aliena's life.

I set the diary on the counter and put the juice back in the refrigerator. After opening the freezer, I pulled out a bottle of vodka, unscrewed the cap, and drank half of it, wincing at the cold head. Picking up the journal, I walked back into the living room and sat on the couch, the bottle still in my hand. I set the book on the coffee table and lit another cigarette with one hand.

Thinking about the way immortal blood replenished itself gave me a bad feeling about Aliena's diary story. Had Rachella killed François immediately? If not, what did they do together when she was not feeding from him?

I took a swig of vodka, set the bottle on the table, and picked up the evidence pack. I put my cigarette in my mouth and took the Prince of Wands out of the plastic.

I was holding the card, looking at it but not seeing it, remembering Aliena's warning that it was dangerous, when I realized the picture had changed. It was no longer the Prince. A man looked out of the card's border, a red-haired man with strange gray eyes that looked like holes in the universe. The card pulsed, lighting up the gold border from top to bottom, and sending out shock waves that seemed to distort the air around me. It pulsed again, causing more ripples, and quivered in my hand.

It began to grow larger.

And before I knew what was happening, the man reached out of the card and seized me by the neck.

Chapter 11

Saturday, January 24, 7:32 a.m.

My first reaction, other than choking, was to reach for the wrist attached to the hand throttling me. Surprised or not, I needed to do something fast—this man's grip was crushing my throat.

The card was no longer in my hand, and I could not see it. My attacker stood in front of me, and now he looped a punch at my face with his left hand balled into a fist. I jerked my head aside, but his knuckles connected and a heavy gold ring on his third finger banged into my temple, stunning me. My cigarette fell out of my mouth into my lap. I straightened up, grabbed the cigarette with my right hand, and pressed the hot end of it against the inside of his wrist. He howled and let go of me.

I gasped in air, punched him in the stomach with a short, jabbing blow, then stood and pushed him backward, against the coffee table. He staggered and fell, crashing down on his back, flattening the piece of furniture.

Even on his back, he was dangerous. His right foot came up, and he delivered a ferocious, crushing kick to my family jewels.

Immortal I may be, but my gems are as sensitive as the next man's. I am not immune to pain. I feel the same thing any human feels at first. I just don't experience it as long. But something like this . . . my breath whistled out of me and I fell over like a tree, my knees pointed at each other, my hands gripping my groin, my eyes bulging out of their sockets. After I hit the carpet, I couldn't breathe or move.

He got to his feet. He walked over to me, drew his foot back, and kicked me hard enough to mash my nose against my face. My head whipped back, snapped, fell forward. A great gout of blood spattered onto the carpet, and I lost consciousness.

When I came to, my face hurt so badly I did not want to open my eyes. I thought he might have kicked me hard enough to blind me temporarily. I wondered how long I had been out and whether or not my guest had left yet.

I heard a movement. It was partially behind me, in the direction of the bedrooms. No! What if he was going after Aliena? I calmed down. The intruder would need plastic explosives to get past the reinforced door.

I turned my head slightly so I was looking in the direction of the sound and opened my eyes to slits.

The man who had come out of the card stood next to the foyer table going through my mail, looking at each envelope briefly, and then tossing it on the floor.

He was not the same man Reed and I had seen superimposed on the card earlier. Did that mean anything? Reed thought it significant. And if the fluoroscope of the card now showed a different face—my red-haired attacker's face—then we would know he was right about the last traveler to move through the card leaving his image upon it. I would have to ask Aliena when she woke up. That was just one of many questions. Reed had told me the cards were used for teleportation, but it had only been a theory then. I wished Aliena had confirmed it so I could have been prepared for this man.

My body healed rapidly. I could already open my eyes, although I kept them narrowed to slits. The pain in my groin was harder to ignore.

After ransacking my mail, the man put his hands on his hips and slowly swung around, surveying the whole room, his eyebrows knotted. He appeared perplexed.

Since he was obviously not after Aliena and he wasn't setting my place on fire, I continued playing dead. Maybe I would learn something if he thought I was unconscious. *Take out your phone and call someone.* That would be perfect.

Instead, he strode in my direction. I closed my eyes. He stepped over me and I heard the whisper of his clothes that told me he was bending down, picking something off the floor. The Prince of Wands.

I could not let him take the card. How would I explain its loss to Hamilton and Chief Reyes? I had personally guaranteed the safety of this piece of evidence.

My body had fully healed, ready for action again. I hated that I could not see my assailant before attacking him. It meant I would have to roll away from him before standing to give myself some room. If only he would step over me again.

He did. Good man. He held a card in his right hand. I swirled silently up and rushed at his back.

He heard or felt me coming at the last second and tensed as I slammed into him. I drove him against the wall next to the front door. We hit it so hard that I bounced off. As he righted himself, I lunged.

I chopped him on the side of the neck with my right hand, missed with a straight left that he dodged, connected with a thumping right to his kidney. He gasped in pain. I threw the left again, but he blocked it and feinted, then dove right, tumbling on his shoulder and popping back up. Before I could reach him, he held up the tarot card.

"*Benuto venzon,*" he said. The card pulsed twice and swelled. He leaned forward, and the card pulled him in. He disappeared in an instant. The card shrank in midair and faded to nothing right in front of my eyes. It went with a tiny flash and an electric crackle.

When I looked down, I did not understand. The Prince of Wands lay on the carpet where the man had been standing. So he had used a different card to escape. Did that mean he did not know how to make the Prince work? Was his other card one of Reed's star cards? It seemed likely. But why did he leave this card behind?

I picked it up and set it on the club chair, then headed for Aliena's room. I was sure the intruder hadn't gotten back here, but I still wanted to see for myself. Her door clicked open when I pressed my hand against the security plate.

She still reclined in bed, her blonde hair gleaming in the darkness. The air had the faintest smell of her. I crossed the room, leaned over, and kissed her ice-cold lips. A little blood showed on her mouth when I leaned back. I had forgotten about my injuries. Watching her curiously, I wondered if her body could tell it was there. Apparently so. Her tongue poked out, and the blood disappeared. It must have been an involuntary reaction, for I knew she was unconscious, not sleeping. A vampire could not wake during the day. But her body obviously never let food get away.

Aliena represented an efficient life-form, beautiful and deadly—a great white shark. I pulled the covers up a bit, ran my hand through that mane of lustrous hair. Aliena would not have a single physical weakness if it weren't for this daytime vulnerability. There is just one way to kill a vampire: expose her to the sun.

I straightened up and walked out, locked the door, and returned to the living room.

Aliena's diary and my computer lay where they had fallen when my red-haired guest crushed the coffee table. Setting them on the couch, I grabbed the evidence bag, replaced the tarot card, and put it next to the computer.

The mess took me a few minutes to clean up. Afterward, I shaved and showered, then looked in my closet at the casual clothes Aliena had helped me pick. Today seemed like the day to try them instead of my usual suit and tie.

I threw on indigo denim carpenter's pants (blue jeans) with a black leather belt, casual black shoes, and a white long-sleeve shirt that I left untucked. After I secured my holster, I picked a black cotton blazer.

The remains of the coffee table were beyond repair. I called Hector.

"*Buenos días,*" I said. "Hector, I need you to bring a truck by and take a broken coffee table out of my living room," I said in Spanish.

"Will do," he said. Hector did not ask questions. He handled all of my personal crises and took care of my vehicles. One of the best drivers in the world, he also handled special transportation runs.

"*Gracias.*"

As I disconnected, my mind clicked. Now I knew where I had heard the sound the tarot card had made. And I finally solved the mystery of how that man in black tights had appeared in Colonel Nishiki's hotel room more than sixty years ago.

Chapter 12

Saturday, January 24, 9:10 a.m.

I pulled into the parking lot at the Van Nuys police station and slid my new car into a space. I had come from BioLaw, having dropped off the tarot card with the lab and instructing them to take another picture of it under the fluoroscope. I also told Preston to get Pitbull into the lab pronto, and have him stand guard. Wherever that card went, I wanted Pitbull, an ex-Marine who worked for BioLaw, covering it with a gun.

The new car was a concept model I had talked Ford into selling me, a sleek black coupe that had arrived just this morning. Ford had named it 49. I couldn't wait to show it to Aliena.

The blacktop of the parking lot shimmered with heat. The temperature already stood at eighty-six degrees. In January. A light wool suit would have been far more comfortable than denim jeans.

I still hadn't decided what to tell Hamilton concerning this morning's incident with the tarot card.

I pushed through the doors into cool air conditioning, checked in with the officer behind the desk, and took the stairs up to the detectives' squad room on the third floor. There were only three detectives in; Hamilton was one of them. I walked over and sat in the chair next to his desk.

"Morning," I said.

He had on a light tan shirt, blue tie with tan lozenges on it, and a heather-brown suit.

"Morning," he said. "I'm just finishing up last night's report on the Cav—what the?" He stopped. "You're not wearing a suit. And jeans! What's up?"

"Nothing's up," I said, my voice a little cross.

He laughed. "Aliena."

"What do you mean?"

"You're doing it for Aliena. Is it because she's younger than you?"

"Hardly." Although I was four hundred years older, it didn't show.

"Casual looks good on you," he said, turning back to his computer. "At least you know how to pick the right clothes."

I felt much better. It was amazing how well compliments worked. Are we really the insecure babies the gentler sex often portrays us to be? I decided not to ask Aliena that question.

He closed the file and started the shutdown routine on his computer. "Ready?" He stood. "Let's go."

We took the elevator down, crossed the lobby to the doors, and pushed out, heading across the parking lot.

"Is this a new one?" he asked as we approached my car.

"Yes," I told him. "Just got it today."

"It looks slick but what is it?"

"It's a Ford 49. It's a concept car."

"That figures. I suppose it's one of a kind?"

"You know, I'm not sure," I told him. "I'll have to check."

He opened the door. "Crazy interior."

The seats were two-tone black and dark-orange, a bit loud, but I loved them. Anything different and unusual appealed to me. We strapped ourselves in, and I backed out of the space, headed for the Sylmar Avenue onramp.

"What's Aliena doing today?"

"Probably just lying around."

"Where does she live?"

I didn't say anything. He sighed loudly.

"What is the big deal?" he asked, sounding irritated. "Why all the mystery about her?"

"No mystery. She's a busy person and rarely feels like socializing."

"What do you mean? She's always nice to me. Sometimes, it even looks like she's giving me the eye."

The same way an epicure looks at *caneton à l'orange* with champagne. "Yes, I know."

"What? Jealous?"

I turned to him and smiled. I couldn't help it. "Not a bit. She and I are dating now. Officially."

"Does that mean she doesn't work our cases anymore?"

"I'm sure she will come in with us, but Aliena does what she wants, when she wants. And right now, she does not want to be grilled by you about the Kanga case. I can almost guarantee that unless you give me your promise about that and allow me to pass it on, you won't get to talk to her this year." Probably not even this century.

"What the hell? Is she some kind of princess?"

"Yes," I said. "Some kind."

"Shit." He peered at me. "So you two are dating now, huh? What's that booty feel like?"

"That is hardly a proper question, *mi amigo*."

"Come *on* Sebastian. I haven't had sex in two months. What's it like to get busy with that outrageous bod?"

"I'm your partner, not your sex chat girl. You'll have to get Mr. Johnson his entertainment somewhere else."

"So you haven't gotten down with her yet." He said it flat—not a question. It irked me that he was right for the wrong reason. A gentleman never discusses the intimate details of his relationships with women.

I glanced over at him. "Do you really consider two months a long time to go without sex?"

"Are you kidding? Don't you?"

"Hardly. I don't even consider two years a long time. It is not like having a job."

"I could never last two years, never," he said, shaking his head. "I couldn't last one. And why should I? There are honeys all over the place, and when they like what they see, I give them what they want. What's wrong with that?"

"Nothing at all."

"Women enjoy sex as much as men, probably more. And girls like being warm at night." He dropped his voice, half talking to himself. "People just want to be needed. It makes them feel safe."

Hamilton understood people very well.

"I agree." I turned left. "But Aliena is more than you could handle."

He snorted. "Now you're talkin' out your ass."

"Find yourself a nice girl."

"Thanks, Dad."

9:28 a.m.

I pulled into the parking lot and stopped in front of the store.

Cavanaugh's Fine Antiques was located in an upscale strip mall on Sepulveda, just off the boulevard. It shared a parking lot with a jeweler, a dentist, a Greek restaurant, and a small theater. Displayed in the big picture window was the Closed sign.

"Are we early?"

"No," he said. "They're expecting us. They don't open until ten, so we'll have about thirty minutes to ask questions."

"Good."

We walked up, and he knocked on the door. He pulled his shield out and clipped it to his lapel. I did the same with my ID.

A woman's face appeared in the window. She looked at us briefly. I heard the locks turn and then the door opened.

"Detective Hamilton?" she said.

"Yes. Are you Miss Cavanaugh?"

"Karen. Won't you come in?" She pulled the door back for us, and we stepped inside.

I estimated Karen Cavanaugh to be in her late twenties. Pretty. She closed and locked the door and gestured to a couch and three chairs arranged like a living room. Hamilton and I chose two of the chairs, and she sat on the couch facing us.

"This is my associate, Sebastian Montero," Hamilton said. I inclined my head in her direction.

"You look familiar," she said to me. "Have you ever shopped here?"

"Yes," I said, surprised. "I don't remember you." And that did not seem possible.

Karen Cavanaugh had thick chestnut hair pulled back into a ponytail and light hazel eyes. Light makeup, barely there, complexion rosy. She wore a man's long-sleeve chambray work shirt tucked into loose khaki pants with a wide brown belt and white tennis shoes. A small Cartier watch was her only jewelry. In spite of the masculine clothes, she looked like an all-American girl, the one boys wish lived in the house next to theirs.

"I was doing an inventory that day," she said, sounding exhausted. "You probably didn't see me."

"You have an incredible memory." The last time I had been here was a little more than a year ago to buy the Tiffany lamp now in Aliena's bedroom.

"I never forget a face."

"That must serve you well as a shop owner."

"My father says . . . I mean used to say, it was my greatest business asset." Her eyes de-focused for a moment, and I could see the depth of her grief, then she looked at me and said, "How can I help you?"

Hamilton had his notebook on his lap and his pen in his hand. "Do you know of anyone who would want to hurt your father?"

"No. It still doesn't seem . . . no, I can't think of anyone."

"Did he have a deck of tarot cards?" I asked.

"Sorry?"

"We found a tarot card in your father's study," Hamilton said. "Any idea how it got there?"

She shook her head. "A tarot card?"

"Yes," I said. "It was placed in one of his books."

"I don't understand it. My father did not believe in the occult."

"So he would not have gone to someone for a tarot reading?"

"I can't imagine it," she said. "Why would he do that?"

"It's not important," Hamilton said. "According to your mother, your father retired some years ago and turned the business over to you."

"Yes, and my cousin, who handles the financial side of the business."

"Is he here now?"

"No. His work does not require him to meet with customers, so he does not need to come in every day."

"What do you do?" I asked.

"I work with our clients and help them find exactly what they are looking for, even if I have to send them to another store. And I handle exports and imports for our customers and us. I am the face of the business."

With a face like that, I thought, it certainly made sense to have her out front. Probably men stopped by more than once just to talk to her.

"We have many repeat customers," she said, as if reading my mind. "Most of them go back a ways and want to work with father, but many of our customers come back to see me."

"Has anybody asked for your father recently?" I said.

She thought about it. "Yes. You know . . . come with me." She stood and led us across the store to the counter. She went behind it and started tapping on a keyboard.

A wooden container the size and shape of a cigar box and covered with multicolored stickers sat to my right on the counter.

"How do you process items from other countries?" I asked.

"Everything we import passes through our inspection staff before we sign for it," she told us.

"What about this one?" I put my hand on the sealed parcel sitting on the counter. "It doesn't look like it's been opened."

"That's the package I was going to tell you about. It's one of my dad's items. We don't open those."

Hamilton glanced at me, back to Karen.

"Do you know what's in it?" he asked.

"I can check the manifest but that will only give us a general description."

"Could you check it, please?"

"Give me a moment." She began tapping her keyboard. After a minute or so, she said, "Okay, that package is listed as an archaic game."

"That's it?" Hamilton asked.

"I told you it would be incomplete. Only the bill of lading will have the exact description."

"What kind of game is it?" I asked.

"I don't know. It doesn't say."

"Where's the bill of lading?"

"It's attached to the box inside a plastic sleeve."

Hamilton and I looked. On top of the package was a small red plastic bag with the words *Bill of Lading* printed on it.

"You are not allowed to open that," Karen said. "Only my father or the buyer may do that."

"But . . . do you know who the buyer is?"

Her eyebrows crinkled. "No. My dad didn't tell us."

"So what will you do with it?"

"We will hold it until someone claims it."

"But you don't know who the right person is," Hamilton pointed out.

109

"If someone comes in and asks for an ancient game, I think I can feel confident they are the intended customer. We haven't advertised it."

I laughed. "I see why your father felt comfortable turning the business over to you."

"Thank you, Mr. Montero."

"How long will you wait?" I asked.

"Thirty days. After that, we are legally required to return it to its origin. Unopened."

Hamilton made a soft snort of disappointment. "That figures. What is its origin?"

"Let's see," she said, tapping the keys again. "From Shibin el-Kom, Egypt."

"What was that?" Hamilton asked.

"Shibin el-Kom," I told him, spelling it out. "It's a city."

"Hm." He finished writing and looked up at Karen. "When someone picks this box up, will they have to present identification? Is any money owed?"

"Yes, they will need to sign for it, so we ask for ID, but no money is due."

"So they walk in, ask for the item, sign for it, and you hand it over?" I asked.

"That's it. It's already passed through customs and it's already paid for. What else should there be?"

"Nothing." I started looking along the upper walls of the store. "I just wanted to see the procedure clearly in my mind."

"What are you looking for?"

"Ah," I said. "That. Does it work?"

She looked up. Pointing toward the checkout counter was a video surveillance camera.

"Yes, of course. We have many valuable items."

"We'll get a look at this person at least."

Hamilton put his notebook away and pulled out a card, handed it to Karen. "If you can think of anything else, please give me a call. And if you could call me when the person picking up that game is in the store . . ."

She smiled, slid the card into her shirt pocket. "Sure, I can do that." She picked up the box and set it behind the counter. "Is there anything else I can help you with?"

"No, that's it," Hamilton told her.

"Actually," I said, "I'd like to take a look at your coffee tables."

Chapter 13

Saturday, January 24, 10:27 a.m.

After arranging the delivery of my new coffee table with Karen Cavanaugh, I joined Hamilton outside and we walked to the car.

"What happened to your old coffee table?"

"I had a guest last night. He fell on it."

"Really. What were the two of you drinking?"

"It wasn't like that. I sort of bumped into him, and he stumbled. He landed on it pretty hard."

We climbed into the 49. I headed toward the Van Nuys station.

"It looks like the tarot card is a dead end," he said. He took his phone out and started tapping the keys. "It was just a book marker. Cavanaugh probably didn't even know what he had."

"He knew," I said. "Antiques were his business. That tarot card is old and valuable, part of a very special deck."

"Did you get this from Aliena?"

"No. Reed. He said the deck is more than two thousand years old and . . ."

"Oh, no. And what?"

"Well, it also appears the cards are magical."

"Magical," he said, barely audible.

"According to Reed, the cards are a means for traveling."

"I assume you mean without a car or plane or anything like that."

"Yes. Just the card."

He tapped his knuckles against his window. "Why did I have to call you in? Everything is magical to you and your staff. Don't you guys ever work normal cases?"

"All the time. But sometimes we get lucky and find an interesting one like this." I turned left on Ventura Boulevard.

"Do you have any proof the card is magical?" he asked.

I decided to tell him. Since the cards had nothing to do with my immortality, I couldn't think of a good reason not to.

"The man I told you about—the one I said fell on my coffee table?"

"Yeah?"

"He didn't come in through the front door, and I didn't invite him."

For a moment he just sat there. Then he got it. "For God's sake, are you saying he came through that tarot card?"

"Right into my lap. And he tried to strangle me. I was barely able to beat him off."

He exhaled loudly. "Are you some sort of magnet for this kind of thing, Montero?"

Once again, I invoked my Fifth Amendment right.

"What did he look like?"

"Redheaded man with strange gray eyes. Square jaw. About an inch shorter than you but heavier. He was wearing a brown leather jacket and khaki pants. The one time I grappled with him, he felt like he was all muscle. Moved like it, too."

"You couldn't hold him?"

"No, sorry. He got away from me."

"I suppose he used the card to escape?"

"Yes and no. He used *a* card but not the one we found in Cavanaugh's study. I still have that."

"Great." We were both silent for a while. At least he seemed to be accepting my story. After our last case, I should have anticipated that. "So there is more than one of these cards?"

"It may be that there is a whole deck."

"Are you saying there could be seventy-something of these travel cards out there?"

"Yes. Seventy-eight."

"Even better." He did not sound happy. "How the hell am I supposed to report this?"

"Don't," I advised.

"I need you to tell me that. Of course I'm not going to pass on anything about tarot cards that help people travel around. How does that work, by the way?"

"Not sure. I have the lab doing a thorough analysis now, and Reed is trying to find everything he can about this particular deck."

He started tapping his phone again. "If somebody can come out of that card, I better get an officer over there to keep an eye on it."

"No," I said. "I have Pitbull guarding the card and my people if anything happens."

He put his phone away. "You have an employee named Pitbull?"

"Yes. He insists."

"What's his real name?"

"Carmen."

"Jeez. Why in God's name would his parents name him that? What the hell were they thinking about?"

"They're Italian. Carmen is a normal name for a man."

"Whatever. I see why he changed it. I would have, too, and quick before I got my ass kicked."

"I can imagine."

"But not Pitbull. That's almost as bad."

"He's very good. Ex-marine."

I turned right on Burbank. Hamilton shook his head.

"How do you get these people? Is it just money?"

"And the medical and dental plans."

"Hm. What do we have here?" he said, sitting up and pointing to the right. "Pull over, Sebastian."

I parallel parked in front of a small house with a sign on the lawn that read:

114

Psychic Readings with Angella

Palm Tarot Crystal Ball Hypnosis Healer

Past Life Regression Predictions Spiritual Cleansing

Available for Parties
Please ring bell

    We stepped out of the car and walked up the path to the door.

    "Looks like she does it all," Hamilton said, reading the sign before stepping onto the porch. I stood behind him, to his left.

    I did not look forward to this. Nearly all these "psychics" were nothing of the sort. They possessed no talent other than clever imaginations combined with atmospheric suggestion. I expected Angella would take us to a dim room lit only by candles. She would have a crystal ball and a deck of cards on a table covered with runic symbols, including a pentagram in the center. The chairs would be small and puffy, for women. And I would have to sit through an obvious charade without falling asleep.

    "You have a picture of Cavanaugh?" I asked.

    "Yes."

    "Let's just show it to her and get out of here. Most of these people are fakes."

    The door opened and a middle-aged woman stood there, a smile on her face. She wore a pale-yellow short-sleeve blouse, gray wool pants, and black shoes with medium heels. She had brown shoulder-length hair and hazel eyes.

"I have met many charlatans in my time as well," she said to us. "Please, come in. I have been expecting you."

As she turned to lead us in, Hamilton looked at me questioningly. I rolled my eyes.

"You just met me, Mr. Montero," Angella said, her back to us. "That is not very polite."

I looked for a mirror but couldn't see one. Lucky guess? Too risky. If she were wrong, her credibility would be destroyed before we even sat down. And how did she know my name? She would have had to call the Van Nuys station to get that. Which begged the question: how did she know we were coming?

She led us into a bright, cheerful room with a sea foam carpet, flowers, and pictures on the walls. She did have a table with a crystal ball, a deck of tarot cards, and what looked like a white stone amulet, but it was a normal table with no designs on it, surrounded by sturdy, high-backed wooden chairs.

Angella gestured us to them and sat in the one against the wall.

"What did you mean, you were expecting us?" Hamilton asked as we sat down.

She patted her crystal ball. "I saw you here."

"Exactly what did you see?" I asked.

"I saw the three of us talking as we are now, in this room. I saw a policeman's badge. I saw both of your faces."

"How did you know my name?"

"I saw that in the crystal, too, as well as your name, Detective Hamilton," she said, looking at him. "I saw one other, too. Not in this room but with you somewhere else. A very big man. I think he is also a policeman."

It sounded like Gonzales.

"What about him?"

Her face changed, and she looked at us with sadness. "I am sorry, but he is going to die violently. Very soon."

"You really shouldn't say things like that," Hamilton said. "Police officers are superstitious."

"I am telling you what I saw. What you do with the information is up to you."

"Do you see anything about his death?" I asked.

"Yes. He is in a hallway. He is lying on his back, and he is bleeding. You are crouched over him."

"Me?"

"Yes. That is all I see of him."

"You don't see who killed him?" Hamilton asked. "I mean, will kill . . . I mean . . . hell, you know what I mean."

"I only see him and Mr. Montero."

"How come you don't know his name?" I asked.

"The crystal did not show me his name."

Hamilton produced a picture. "Ever see this man?"

She looked at it. "Mr. Cavanaugh."

"So he was a customer?"

"No."

"I suppose you saw him in your crystal ball, too," I said.

"No," she replied, taking no offense at my sarcastic question, "I saw him in the *Times*. Poor man."

"Are you saying you never saw him before that?" Hamilton asked.

"Yes, that is what I'm saying."

I showed her a color picture of the Prince card. "What about this?" I asked.

"Wow." She took the page from me. "That certainly is a lovely card."

"Have you seen it before?" Hamilton asked.

Angella handed the picture back to me. "No, but it is beautiful."

"And you've never seen a card like it?"

"No. Is that what you're looking for?"

I resisted the urge to say, *Don't you know?* Hamilton turned to me, and I shook my head.

"Okay, thank you for your cooperation," he told Angella.

"You have an interesting aura, Mr. Montero," she said. "May I see your palm?"

"Sure," I answered, holding my right hand up, palm out.

"Oh, no." She patted the chair next to hers. "Come sit here. I can't read you from that far away."

With a sigh, I stood and walked over to her, sat in the seat indicated. She turned in her chair to face me and took my hand in hers, running the fingertips of her right hand over my palm.

"Now, let's see . . . your lifeline says—" She stopped. "This can't be right." She looked up at me.

Staring into her eyes, I realized I had made a terrible error. This woman could really see. And now she was reading me in front of Hamilton. The Fates only knew what she would say. I resisted an urge to jerk my hand back.

She glanced at Hamilton, back at my palm. "You will live a long time," she said, and I knew she was being discreet for my benefit. I wondered how much she could discern. "You have a strong heart line and a long, thick love line," she said, running the tip of her index finger horizontally along my palm. "Extremely substantial."

Hamilton made a sound.

"Ah, your heart line . . . you are in love right now." She closed her eyes and held my hand tightly in both of hers. "She is a beautiful girl, and she is—" she looked up at me, a question in her eyes. Finally she said, "Your girl is very special. A child of the moon." She released my hand. "I would love to do a more thorough reading sometime. No charge." She inspected my face closely. "The story on your palm is fascinating."

"Perhaps I will do that."

The three of us stood. Angella walked us to the door. "When you come back," she said to me, "bring your girlfriend. I would love to meet her."

"I will try," I said.

I was worried now. If Angella could know our names, determine my unique nature, and know that Aliena was different without ever meeting her, why shouldn't her prognostication about Gonzales's death be equally correct?

Chapter 14

Saturday, January 24, 12:17 p.m.

After we were in the car, Hamilton said, "Well that was a waste. We still have no clue if this tarot card has any bearing on the case."

"The man who attacked me this morning seemed determined to take it, and I think he was willing to kill me to get it."

"Then why didn't he shoot you?"

"I don't know."

"Because it seems obvious now that's what he did to Cavanaugh. The card was probably sitting on the vic's desk."

"I agree about the method, but I don't know if the man who attacked me is our shooter."

"You said he tried to kill you."

"No, I said he would have killed me if that's what it took to get the card. But as soon as he thought he had knocked me out, he stopped."

"Who else could it be?"

"It depends. We should check in with Preston." I was eager to see if the fluoroscope picture showed the same long-haired man. If it did, then the man who attacked me might be our killer. But if it showed my attacker's face, then he was probably not the man who killed Cavanaugh.

We stopped at Fuddruckers for lunch. As soon as we had finished ordering, I asked Hamilton about Gonzales.

"What else is he working on?"

"He's still working our case but when you're in, he knows he can spend more time checking backgrounds and supervising door-to-door efforts to find witnesses."

"In other words, he doesn't like working with me."

"Yes," he said. "Alfred does not like you at all."

"I've always been cordial, and he's always been rude, right from the beginning."

"So was I, if you'll recall." He shrugged. "We knew who you were. To check your background was automatic. Can you imagine how we felt when we were told to work a homicide with a rich young man who had no law enforcement background of any kind?"

"Yes, I know. But you were never as bad as Alfred. And you at least gave me a chance."

"Uh, well, not really. We knew one of us had to work closely with you, but the other could stay in the background."

"Don't tell me you lost the flip?"

The waiter brought our food.

"Two out of three, actually."

"Too bad."

"Yeah, well . . . ," he said, eyeing his plate. "There are benefits."

"I guess. It still bothers me, Steve, really. Angella told us she saw him dying." I munched a couple of fries.

"She also said you were crouching over him as he bled out."

"So I will be there when whatever happens to him happens. So what? I obviously don't stop it."

"Jeez, Sebastian, you're talking like we already know it's going to happen."

"She was right about everything else."

"Oh? Are you saying she's for real now?"

"As a matter of fact, yes."

121

"I don't know that it is a matter of fact," he said. He ate a couple of fries. "But I can't explain how she knew our names. I mean, we just stopped there out of the blue."

"Exactly. And she knew I was making a face at you when her back was turned."

"Educated guess," he said, sounding not at all convinced. "She heard you say you thought she was a fake."

"No." I shook my head. "Too risky."

"Yeah, okay, I can't figure that one, either. That doesn't mean she's not just a clever illusionist with a bag of tricks."

"Knowing our names was no illusion."

"No."

"Let's keep an eye on Gonzales, okay? For the fun of it."

"Why not?" he said. "But if it goes down like this lady said, I'm never going anywhere near her again—and I'm going to pray she never sees me in her crystal ball."

1:28 p.m.

I turned off Moorpark onto Camellia Avenue, where BioLaw Industries, my research facility and forensics laboratory, was located. It was a three-story white brick building with the ubiquitous palm trees in front. Hamilton and I walked through the reflective glass doors and into the marble-floored foyer.

We took the stairs to the second floor, where the offices and laboratories were located, and headed straight for Preston.

A genius, Dexter Preston ran the company. An expert in multiple disciplines, including computers (hardware and software), forensics, and chemistry, he had a flair for business management. I handed over the reins to him three years ago, when he was twenty-three. I have never regretted it. His mania for perfection exceeded my own.

He was also as big as a house. I had racked my brain for ways to get him deflated, but I had come up with nothing. As long as he could run BioLaw, Preston had everything he wanted.

Hamilton and I walked into his office to find him adrift in paper printouts and old pizza boxes. I sat down in one of the guest chairs. Hamilton had to pick up a pizza box before he could sit. He looked around.

"Where should I . . . ?" He looked at Preston.

"That one still has a few slices left," Preston said, holding out his hand. "I'll take it." Hamilton handed it to him, and he set it somewhere behind his desk. He picked up a soiled napkin and wiped his fingers on it. "Okay, let me show you what we've got."

He tapped his keyboard. A twenty-seven-inch monitor faced us, the display linked to Preston's computer. The first thing that came up was a regular picture of the card with the Prince of Wands. Under it was a graph.

"We estimate the card's age at about 2,100 years old."

"It doesn't seem possible," Hamilton said.

"If the deck is magical," Preston said, "normal wear and tear would have no effect. We've examined the card every way possible, but we did not find anything unusual except the fluoroscope picture and the magnetic field."

He punched a few keys on his computer and we could see the image with the superimposed face.

"Notice anything?" he asked.

"Well, well," I said. "It looks like Reed was right." The image was now of the gray-eyed, redheaded man who had come through the star card in my living room.

"Right about what?" Hamilton said.

"When we 'scoped this yesterday," Preston said, "there was a different man's face on this card."

"This is the guy who attacked me," I told him, pointing at the monitor. "But he wasn't on the card earlier this morning."

"Who was?"

We looked at Preston. He tapped up the other picture, put it alongside the first. The sallow-skinned long-haired man looked out of the screen. I wanted to tell them this man was a Magistine. The tattoo proved it, but I could not think of a good explanation for how I knew it.

"So we got a scary-looking white boy and a freaky-looking white boy with light eyes," Hamilton said. He pointed at the Magistine. "What is that on the side of his neck?"

"A tattoo," Preston replied.

"That's brilliant," Hamilton said. "I mean—"

"You mean does the design indicate its origin or meaning," Preston interrupted. "We have already extrapolated what the image would look like flat." Two more taps. Our monitor showed the design up close.

"I don't recognize it," Hamilton said. "It's not gang related."

"And I could not find a match in any database on the Internet," Preston told him.

"Then it's unique," Hamilton said.

"By the way, Sebastian, you never did tell me the whole story about this attack," Preston said. He and Hamilton looked at me expectantly. I ran through the story, leaving out that he kicked me in the face, saying I played dead when he hit me hard. I was sure neither of them detected my fabrication.

"You say this dude was strangling you at first?" Preston asked.

"Yes."

"And he only hit you hard enough to stun you, but when you played dead, he accepted it."

Okay, so Preston had noticed. After all, the guy was a genius.

"Yeah, I was wondering about that, too," Hamilton said. "Most people can tell when they've hit someone hard enough to knock him unconscious."

Okay, so they both had noticed.

124

"He did hit me hard enough," I said. "On the back of the head. It knocked me to the floor and really did stun me."

"I guess," Hamilton said. Preston looked unconvinced. He opened his mouth when the fire alarm started clanging in great whoops. I stood. The tarot card. I looked at Preston. He had not moved. He knew, too.

"The card?" Hamilton said.

We ran out of the office, turning right and bolting down the hallway toward Laboratory One. We heard a gunshot, a big, booming one. A man bumped into the door frame of the lab, facing inside.

The shooter was tall and heavily muscled: our long-haired suspect. He still looked into the room, and now he raised the gun.

"No!" I shouted before he fired again. At the sound of my voice, he spun out the door, then pointed the gun at Hamilton and me and started shooting. The report had the echoing rumble of a .44 Magnum.

Hamilton and I were still in the atrium that separated the offices from the labs. We dove for cover, he to the right and I to the left. Before I could get horizontal, I took a slug in the stomach.

I hit the ground and slid to the wall. When I stopped, I clasped my hand over the wound. My eyes watered with the tearing pain. I could see Hamilton across the small expanse of the hallway opening.

"Sebastian? Are you hit?"

I shook my head. I could feel blood against my hand and knew it must be seeping into my white shirt. I had a serious problem.

How was I going to hide this?

Chapter 15

Saturday, January 24, 3:07 p.m.

"LAPD!" Hamilton shouted. He glanced quickly around the corner. "Shit, Sebastian, he's not there!"

"He may be in the lab," I said. "Call out for Pitbull."

"Hey Pitbull!" he yelled. "You back there? Can you hear me?"

"Yeah!" came the reply. "He's gone. Somebody call an ambulance."

Hamilton looked at me and I nodded. He got up and hustled down the hallway. I stood, too, and quickly buttoned my jacket before following him. The bleeding had stopped, but the damage had been done. We turned into the lab.

Two of my science techs crouched on either side of Pitbull, cinching a slim belt around the upper part of his left thigh. He sat on the floor, blood seeping through his pants. It looked like he'd been shot just above the knee.

I walked over to them, holding my bloody hand close to my leg. Hamilton called for an emergency medical team.

I got down on one knee next to Pit. He stood six feet tall, but he looked shorter because he was so broad from east to west. Thick neck. Biceps that stretched the sleeves of his red polo shirt. Thighs like freeway girders under his black cargo pants.

"How is it?"

"Not bad," he said, clenching his teeth. "I think it missed the bone. The bleeding is stopped. Kathy and Mike did a good job." He looked up at me, his eyes apologetic. "He got the card. I saw him pop out, but I was so amazed at first that I didn't shoot. He did. Good shot, too; hardly aimed and popped me on the first try. I went down and never got a clean shot at him. He grabbed the card, then he turned at the door. He was about to fire at Kathy because she hit the fire alarm. But hearing your voice stopped him. Then these guys got the tourniquet on me."

"Pretty quick work, you two," I said to them. "Thanks."

They smiled the way kids do when a teacher or other adult compliments them.

I looked back and forth between them, and they looked at each other. Pitbull watched them, nodding. As soon as they were distracted, and with Hamilton still behind me, I put my right hand unnoticed on the bloody pants leg below the wound and pulled it up gently.

"Are you sure you stopped the bleeding?" I asked, making sure everyone saw me gripping his soaking pants leg.

"My leg is already starting to feel numb."

"Okay," I said, pulling my bloody hand back. I unbuttoned my jacket and wiped my hand over my shirt, rejoicing at my luck. I was sorry Pit was shot, but . . . I stood and turned to Hamilton.

He pocketed his phone. "EMTs are on the way, and I called for backup to surround the building," he said, looking at the bloody patch on the front of my shirt. I was sure he would not be able to see the bullet hole in all the mess. "Jesus, Sebastian, that's a lot of blood. You sure you're not hit?"

"I think I would know, chief. Come on."

We pulled our guns, ran back into the hallway, and started for the door that led to the stairs.

Hamilton got there first and stood on the left side of the door. I stopped on the right, and he nodded at me. I switched my gun to my left hand and turned the doorknob. I pushed it wide open and stepped through and to the left, pointing the gun down the stairway. Hamilton came in right behind me.

I looked quickly up: nothing. As the door swung closed, we pounded down the steps.

We only had one floor to the lobby, so in no time, Hamilton sprinted the short distance to the utility door that led out of the stairwell.

"Try not to freak my people!" I shouted at him. We had a Fresh Grill restaurant in the lobby, and BioLaw employees might be seated at tables with a view of the area.

He hit the metal bar and jogged through, his gun down by his side. I buttoned my coat before I stepped out.

There was no one in the lobby but the security guard. Sirens approached. Hamilton and I proceeded outside to meet the approaching squad cars. He turned to me.

"The third floor?"

I nodded and went back to the stairwell. I started up, my gun at the ready. After passing the second floor, I sprinted up the last two small stairways and stood outside on the landing for a moment.

The third floor contained spare bedrooms for overnight employees or guests, an executive office, a master suite, and Preston's group of rooms. I did not think our long-haired assailant would be here. He could use his card to escape at any time, couldn't he?

I opened the door and walked in, making as much noise as I could. I started with my office and proceeded down the hallway, checking each room and bath. They were all immaculately clean and completely devoid of fugitives. I only had Preston's suite left. I wondered what his rooms looked like. Probably a mess, like his office.

I pushed inside, holding the Beretta up. I quickly confirmed there was no one in the living area. I checked the bedroom and the bathroom. No one. Preston's rooms were neat and clean, almost excessively so.

I went back to my office suite, into the bedroom, took off my jacket, and removed my holster. The bloody shirt went into the hamper in the bathroom. I would have to come back and retrieve it later. When I stood in front of the mirror, I saw a little blood on my stomach. I rubbed it off. My pants had no stains. I washed my hands and returned to the bedroom. A sliding door revealed a closet, and I changed into a clean shirt.

My jacket and holster on again, I walked back into the hallway. I looked along the ceiling. No one could escape from this floor. I looked at the stairway on this end of the building. Nothing. The only other way out was the elevator.

Halfway down the stairs, I thought of something. I hurried the rest of the way and joined Hamilton on the sidewalk. EMTs went past with a gurney.

"Anything?" Hamilton asked when he saw me.

"No. But we should search the third floor."

"Didn't you do that already?"

"I looked for our shooter. Now we need to look and see if he left the tarot card."

Gonzales had come in an unmarked car and now stood with us.

"Why would he leave the card behind?" he asked.

I shrugged. "No idea. I only know it's been left behind before, so this guy may have left it, too."

"He comes in here with a gun," Gonzales began, "shoots one of your armed employees, takes this card, and now you're saying he hid it on the third floor? Why would he do that? What the hell is this about?" He looked from me to Hamilton. "Steve?"

"We're not sure what it's about," he told Gonzales. "But Sebastian is probably right about searching the third floor."

"You want us here for that?" Gonzales asked, indicating himself and the other two uniforms.

Hamilton looked at me. I didn't say anything. If he didn't want them to hunt for the card, it just meant I would have to do it myself.

"It's okay," Hamilton told him. "We can handle it. Everybody can get back to what they were doing. Thanks, bro."

"Sure." Gonzales walked off without another word. The two black-and-whites drove away.

"I appreciate you keeping your visitor to yourself," Hamilton said to me as we turned to head back inside.

"I did not want you to get kidded to death by your fellow officers. They might say you're working on the X-Files."

"Too late."

"I think it's a shame we can't tell Gonzales the truth. He believes in the occult, you said."

"Believing in it and seeing it are two different things. I know. Besides, nothing will happen while he's around."

I smiled.

"I know it and you know it," he said. "And then there we'll be, two crackpots looking for a *chupacabra*."

We stepped into the elevator, and he hit the button for the third floor.

Hamilton found the card hidden among the extra towels in one of the guest rooms. "Why?" he asked. "Why does no one take this card with him? Is it cursed or something?"

"I have an idea. Reed and Preston said the card has a magnetic field, right?"

"Yeah. So?"

"If all of the cards have a magnetic field, maybe it's not possible to take one through the other."

"What if those guys have one of those star cards?" Hamilton asked. "Didn't you say they were different?"

"Yes, it's possible you need one of the major cards to travel through the minor cards. It's all speculation at this point. We'll have to wait until Reed comes up with more for us."

"I thought Aliena was an expert on this."

"She is. I will ask her, too."

"I would like to sit in on that."

"Yes, I know." I could not see how to avoid it. I was cleared to participate in homicide investigations, but Hamilton always took the lead, rightly so. And this subject had to do with a current case. "Let me talk to her."

"If she knows something important . . ."

"She has an obligation to inform you, I know. I'm positive she will be cooperative, I would just like to prepare her."

"Little princess," he said under his breath.

"I know, I know." I had confessed to myself that Aliena's aloofness was one of the things that endeared her to me and drove me crazy at the same time. It was the same with her unfailingly independent attitude. I admired that; on the other hand, I wished she needed me more. This reminded me that she was sleeping at my place unattended. "I have to get back," I told Hamilton.

"Okay," he said. "Just drop me at the station." He held the card up. "Do you want this back?"

"I would like to show it to Aliena." And Marcus.

He handed it to me. "Keep me advised."

"I will. Did you want to get together later?"

"Sounds good," he said. "You can take me to dinner. Can you bring Aliena?"

"I will ask her to join us, but . . ."

"Little princess."

After I left Hamilton at the Van Nuys station, I sped home to check on Aliena. She looked peaceful under the blankets.

I sat on the couch, opened the Hamilton IV file on my computer, and updated it with today's interviews and events. I closed the folder, leaned back. I had a couple of hours before Aliena woke, so I took the opportunity to read some more of her diary. I carried it onto the patio and picked up where I had left off.

Chapter 16

Saturday, January 24, 4:38 p.m.

April 28, 1865

I spoke with Marcus tonight about getting François away from Rachella.

"I am sorry, Aliena," he said when I told him that I suspected Rachella of kidnapping my beloved. "Many people—including me—saw them together at Gauthier, *and he did not look like he was being coerced in any way."*

"Marcus, please, you must help me." I was near to pleading with him. I have never done that in my life but the thought of Rachella and François together, perhaps even . . . it was too painful to endure.

"I do not know how to help you. Even if he is immortal, he is a human. We have no rules that protect them. Our rules are only to protect us, chiefly from discovery, as you are aware."

"What about my rights?"

"Are you saying this man is your possession? That he agreed you should make all his choices for him?"

"You know he did not."

"In that case, if he chooses to be with Rachella . . ."

"But I don't think he does. He wants to be with me, only I will not—"

He watched me impassively.

"I do not think François realized what he was getting into. He has been frustrated, and I—" Even I did not believe what I was saying. My mind kept crying out, Why would he go anywhere with Rachella? Was it only because *I would not make love to him and she would? Oh, God, no!*

"I am sorry," Marcus said gently. His compassion brought home the truth of the situation. François was gone. Rachella had tempted him, and he had succumbed. Had he been so uncommitted all along? Was I not enough for him?

I felt as if my feet weren't on the ground anymore. Everything became fuzzy. My eyelids fluttered. I saw Marcus start toward me. At the last moment, I knew I was fainting. Instead of worrying, I thought how blessed that would be, so that I could no longer feel this all-consuming grief.

"My poor darling." I gazed at the sky for several minutes, stood and stretched, looked at the ocean. I understood now why it had taken her so long to warm up to me and why she has been so reluctant to let anyone get too close. Her chastity had become a symbol of her dedication to true love. Virginity was apparently her penance for failing with François.

I sat down and continued reading.

August 27, 1865

Hello again, Diary. I have spent the last four months looking at the world from the tops of mountains. Cold and snowy, every one of them. I tried to empty myself of the pain and think only of the icy flakes turning the shoulders of my coat damp, but it was very difficult.

Marcus is here in Marseille, and he asked me to dinner last night. I accepted. I think he knows I am not interested in him sexually but still wants to try to convince me I am wrong. Other men have tried to do that in the past but never one so handsome.

"If she calls him handsome one more time . . ." I stopped, realizing I was being jealous of events that had occurred more than a century ago. Even for me, that wasn't exactly yesterday.

I asked what he had meant when he said he could take us to New Orleans in a moment. He showed me a tarot card, the Ace of Swords. It was an unusually colorful specimen with beautiful artwork and a gold border.

"This is part of a very special deck," he told me. "With a card like this, I can see through the other cards. If I know where a particular card is, I can use it to observe people without them knowing."

"How can the cards do that?"

"Only the four Aces can look through the cards. I planted a card in Rachella's bedroom many years ago. Would you like to see?"

"I don't understand what you mean."

"I was in that room, and I put one of the cards on her wall. The minors blend in with their surroundings. If a person with a star card is close, it will become visible, but Rachella knows nothing of the cards."

"Why would you want to watch Rachella's bedroom?" I asked him, smiling. "And why were you in there all those years ago?"

"Why indeed? Would you like to look or not?"

I thought about it. If the card did what he said, and I did not like what I saw, I could stop watching. And I would know if Marcus was telling the truth about its powers. And if he was, I wanted to know everything. Rachella seemed as good a choice as any if I were going to use a tarot card to spy on someone.

Oh, Diary, how I regret my next words.

"Yes. I would. Let's see if Rachella is in."

He held the card to his face and spoke so softly I could not discern the words. Then he positioned the Ace in front of him, facing me. I saw the gold strip encircling the card shine briefly and then a second time. He let it go. It floated in the air, where it began to grow, and then I could see a small room with a bed and a chair within its borders. I stood closer, my mind filled with wonder.

Two oil lamps burned in the small chamber, giving the place an inviting glow. I peered at the scene. I could see every detail clearly, as if I were looking through a window.

Rachella and François came in, laughing and holding hands. He twirled her around and then took her in his arms. They kissed. Did I need to see any more?

A perverse desire to watch them held me in front of the card.

As they broke the kiss, he closed the door, returned to her, and undid the fastenings of her dress. She let it fall to the floor. He bent to her breasts; she held him there with both hands, her head thrown back. After a moment she straightened and so did he.

"Aliena." There was concern in Marcus's voice. I shook my head, unable to look away from the scene playing out on the Ace.

Rachella removed François's clothes, doing it slowly and kissing his body along the way. I watched with fascinated dread, a part of me screaming I would never forget this, and another part, more defiant than the first, wanting to see how François loved a woman.

She pushed him backward onto the bed. She lay on top of him, and they began kissing again. Seeing his arms around her shoulders and seeing her hand stray to his hardness, I felt my heart start screaming at me to stop looking. I felt dizzy again. I did not want to faint, but I could not look away.

"Aliena?"

I ignored him.

They rolled around on the bed, their limbs leisurely intermingled, their mouths busy. They finally ended up with him on his back and her on top of him again. Rachella lowered herself, and François's eyes fluttered in ecstasy. She began a rhythmic motion. She leaned down and kissed him on the neck. His knees stiffened and his toes pointed as she bit into him. Then

135

his body relaxed, and Rachella continued to churn her hips as she drank.

    I finally turned away. "I have seen enough," I said in a whisper.

    Marcus spoke the words, and the card resumed its normal size and appearance. He plucked it out of the air and tucked it into his coat. He watched me. "I am sorry. I did not know . . ."

    "Of course you didn't. How could you?"

    "Aliena?" He peered at me closely. "Are you feeling well? You look pale, even for a vampire." His laugh sounded uncertain.

    I felt sick to my stomach, something I had never felt as a vampire. My head buzzed, and the images of François and Rachella intertwined on the bed continued to play in my mind.

    "Come," Marcus said, wrapping his arm around my shoulders. "Let's get you in the fresh air." He took me across the room, nearly carrying me. I felt foolish.

    "I am capable of walking," I told him. I still felt dizzy.

    "I know you are," he said as we stepped onto his patio. "It is a beautiful night. We needed to come out and look at the stars. The atmosphere in there had become stifling."

    I squeezed his arm thankfully. The cool of his backyard stopped my head aching, and my stomach settled down. After a few moments of looking at the constellations, Marcus took his arm away and moved over a few paces.

    "There we are," he said. "You look much better."

    "Thank you." My voice still sounded a little weak. I tried to stop myself, but I couldn't. "Why? Why did he go with her, Marcus? Why would he leave me and do . . . that . . ."

    "I do not know. Truly. I have always thought you far more beautiful and exciting than Rachella."

    "Thank you," I said, but I would not have cared for any other man to say it but François. How could that possibly be? After what I had witnessed only moments before? Somehow, *seeing him with another woman made me sick with desire for him.*

I looked up at the stars. I could feel Marcus watching me.

The scene that had played out on the Ace was branded on my mind. I pictured François with tortuous clarity as Rachella eased herself onto him and his eyes closed with obvious pleasure. The way his toes pointed for a couple of moments when she bit into his throat. The sight of Rachella as she smoothly gyrated on top while drinking his blood.

I had to stop. I would go mad if I could not get these images out of my head. This was a new ache, and I found myself recoiling from the finality of the situation. When I remembered him with her, my jealousy felt like a force too massive for my body to contain.

I could not tell what part hurt the most. Never drinking François's blood again, smelling his sweet smell, feeling his arms around me, tasting the delicious hot drink that was his essence? Or was it that I now knew I would never make love to him?

"*The best thing to do is to get away, far away,*" *Marcus said.* "*Let time do its work. I have a way to travel halfway around the world in an instant. We will arrive at our destination at sunset and return shortly after the sun has set here.*"

In spite of my heartache, I was curious. "*How?*"

He held up another tarot card. This one was from the major arcana. The Hanged Man. In spite of its apparently negative meaning, it was a favorable card in most forecasting spreads.

"*This is another very special card from the same deck as the Ace. Only twenty-two exist.*"

"*How does it help you travel?*"

"*I tell it a place and when I say the words that activate it, we can step through it. It is a portal to another part of the world.*"

"*You're serious?*"

"Yes."

"How did you get it? Where did you find it?"

"The deck was constructed thousands of years ago. A traveler from the stars gave the deck the power to teleport people from one place to another as easily as walking through a door. I don't know about the story, but the cards certainly exist."

"You can travel anywhere?"

"No." He replaced the card in his pocket. *"Only where a minor card is located. And you must know the 'sound address,' the word that takes you to a specific portal."*

"Like the one you left in Rachella's room?"

"Yes."

"Is that the only way one can travel? Through the minor cards?"

"Yes." He held out his hand. *"Let me show you how it works."*

He took me into his bedroom and showed me the Four of Swords on the floor. It had been invisible before he held the Hanged Man close to it.

"This is where we will return tomorrow. We can spend some time traveling around the world."

I left with Marcus that night.

I looked farther down the page. The next entry was nearly eighteen years later.

I glanced at my watch. It was 5:06. Sunset in fourteen minutes. I marked my place, took her journal into the house, and locked it inside a small strongbox I kept bolted under the floor. Next to the journal lay a Beretta 92SB with a full clip. The rest of the contents were some of the valuable pieces I had acquired during my lifetime, including both of my marriage certificates and a stick that had once been a magic wand for my little brother, James.

138

I brushed my teeth, pressed my hand against the glass plate to Aliena's room, and climbed under the covers, waiting for her to wake up.

Chapter 17

Saturday, January 24, 5:20 p.m.

When Aliena awoke, she rolled to me and smiled. I circled her waist with my arm and pulled her to me.

"Mmmm," she said as her long body molded against mine. "I wonder how I went without this for so long."

"I don't know," I said, nuzzling her neck. "I'm just glad you finally decided to stay." I licked an earlobe.

She reached up and ran her fingers through my hair, gripped it in her fist and pulled me close.

We stared into each other's eyes, our noses nearly touching. Her lips parted. I slid my hand below the small of her back and pressed her to me. Our mouths met and my hand slid lower, caressing the silky skin of her curvy bottom.

She murmured softly as I pushed her onto her back and pressed against her with my hips, desire rising, tongue insistent. Her arms tightened around my neck and suddenly the world existed beneath that comforter as Aliena and I melted together.

Our tongues fencing, I explored her body with my hand, palming the firm mounds beneath her top and pushing her pajama bottoms past her knees. My hands began searching in earnest when she broke the kiss and set her hand on my wrist. I groaned in frustration, kissing her neck.

"Ohhh," she sighed, "oh, Sebastian, no, we have to stop, I . . ." Then she turned her head and her mouth was at my neck and I felt her teeth.

"Sweetheart," I said, breathing hard, "my darling, don't stop . . ." I slid my palm between her legs and she parted them, panting against my neck, but she kept her hand on my wrist and stopped me from going too high.

I lowered my head to her breasts, pushing her top back down over them. I squeezed my lips over a nipple through the thin fabric, feeling it moisten from my tongue.

"Oh, Sebastiannnnn . . ." Her voice was hoarse and yearning, but she resisted the feeling, still holding my wrist.

With tremendous willpower, I brought myself back from the brink. I pulled her onto her side and pressed her to me, ran my hand over the bare smoothness of her derriere, kissed her hard on the lips.

"Aliena . . ."

She looked at my mouth, raised her brown eyes to mine. "I know."

We disentangled, and I climbed out of bed, standing a bit crookedly while my ardor cooled. Aliena pushed the blankets back, revealing her partially covered body. I stared at her, a starving man beholding the cornucopia.

"Sebastian, behave yourself," she said shyly. I turned away. Any more of this, and I would need a cold shower.

"I'll wait for you in the living room."

"Yes," she said. "That's a good idea."

She joined me twenty minutes later, wearing blue jeans, black boots, a pink blouse, and a sapphire-blue medium-length velvet coat with a standing collar.

I wore a black T-shirt and jeans, with a black leather jacket she had picked out for me. I decided now was as good a time as any to ask her about a briefing on the Tarot of the Archons.

"I'm having dinner with Hamilton later, and we were hoping you would join us."

She narrowed her eyes, so I added hastily, "Nothing about Kanga. He just wants to ask what you know about the card I showed you this morning. The Prince of Wands."

The fierce look left her face. "Oh, yes, that." She ran a hand through her hair. "I suppose I have to talk to him sooner or later. I am not so sure about a restaurant."

"In a public place, he will be forced to question you with greater restraint," I said.

A small smile appeared. "You think he would try to intimidate me?"

"No, I suppose not. But I do know that while eating and drinking, people generally relax. It would be easier for him, and he does need to know about these cards as much as I do."

"He won't think it strange when I do not eat or drink?"

"Maybe. Do you really care?"

"No."

"Do you know what these cards can do?"

Something in my voice must have given me away, because her eyes widened. "Oh, no," she said. "Did someone use the card last night?"

"Someone certainly did," I said. "He used it until he had me by the throat."

She put her hand on my arm. "Sebastian, I am sorry. What happened?"

I told her about the fight and about the second man who had appeared at BioLaw, the man who had been the first to show up on the Prince of Wands under the fluoroscope. "Does an invisible imprint remain on the card? A picture of the last person who traveled through it?"

"Yes."

I nodded. "I had better stop there, or you'll end up repeating everything. Let me call Hamilton and arrange to meet him."

8:18 p.m.

We took the Ford coupe. When I told Aliena it was a 49, she said she wanted one.

"I don't know if there is another," I told her.

"Then I want this one."

"This one is already mine."

"You won't let me have it?" She sounded both teasing and hurt.

I smiled. "Maybe. Do you always get what you want?"

"Not always." She looked out her window then turned back to me. "Almost always."

"You really are a princess."

"Thank you."

Hamilton said he had a yearning for baby back ribs and knew a good place in Tarzana, just north of Sherman Oaks.

"Fantastic," he promised.

We met him at Monteleone's West on Ventura Boulevard. He was already there, sitting at a table, when we arrived. A waiter led us to our seats. Aliena sat across from him, and I sat on his left.

Hamilton and I each ordered a rack of ribs with seasoned french fries.

"And bring us a pitcher of Heineken, please," Hamilton told the waiter. "You look nice," he said to Aliena.

She did. The severe military-style cut of her blue velvet jacket seemed to emphasize her curves, and the color was perfect for her pale skin and blonde hair. "Thank you." She did not order anything to eat.

"You like raw food?" Hamilton asked. That's what I had told him on our last case, when he questioned me about her.

"Love it."

"So you're really not going to eat anything here?"

"I really am not," she replied, sounding amused.

"What about your water?" he said, nodding at the icy, sweating glass. "Or does it have to be bottled?"

"I like my drinks hot."

The waiter had returned with the beer, and Hamilton filled my glass, then his.

"Well, you don't know what you're missing," he said before he took a long chug.

Aliena stared at a young man walking by. I turned toward her. "Now, darling, we can get you a snack later," I whispered. She gave me a very naughty smile.

Setting the Prince of Wands on the table, I asked Hamilton, "Did you circulate the pictures of those two men on the card?"

"Yeah. But so far, zippo. Gonzales is heading that team."

"How unexpected."

"Do you know what the card means?" he asked Aliena.

"If this card is turned up in a spread, it usually means a change or an upheaval is coming. It's not a good card to see during a reading about one's future, but every card has to be evaluated against the others."

I slid the card back into my pocket. The waiter brought our ribs. Hamilton and I started getting outside of them. I set the card back on the table.

"Have you ever seen one like that before?" Hamilton asked.

"Yes," said Aliena.

"Exactly like that one?" he asked incredulously. "You know what the card can, uh, do?"

"Yes. I know all about this deck. It is the Deck of the Cosmos. The Tarot of the Archons."

Hamilton shot me a suspicious look. I held up my sauce-covered hands.

"I just found out tonight."

"Yeah, okay." He wiped his fingers on a napkin and took another drink of beer, his eyes never leaving Aliena's. "How do you know so much about the cards?"

"A friend showed them to me a long time ago and told me what they could do."

"Who was that?"

"I cannot tell you."

"Not even if I ask nicely?" he said, giving her a suave smile. I was sure he had used that smile to get past many a woman's defenses. It was a good smile. It had no effect on Aliena.

"Not even if you arrest me," she said. "You do not need his name."

"Hm. What about you? What's your last name?"

"Why?"

"I'm a cop. I ask everybody what their name is. Besides, we work together. It's not a strange request."

I said, "Yes, but she has already indica—"

Aliena shook her head. "That's okay, Sebastian. If he must know, my last name is Turner."

"There," he said to me. "What was all the mystery about?" He looked back at her. "Can you tell me where you live?"

"I live with Sebastian."

I felt a flush of pure pleasure hearing her say those words.

"Where did you live before that?"

"Why?"

He shook his head. "Fine." He didn't look satisfied, but he couldn't pursue it now without seeming nosy. "Can all the cards do what that one does?" he said, pointing to the Prince.

"No. All of the minor cards can serve as destination portals, except the Aces."

"What do they do?" Hamilton asked.

"An Ace allows a holder to see what is beyond the doorway of any minor card. The person must know the syllables to activate the planted card, but if she does, it's like looking through a window."

Hamilton was obviously intrigued. "What, in real time?"

"Yes. You can watch what is happening wherever the portal card happens to be, but . . ."

"But what?"

"If the card is in a book or a box, or is pointing straight up, you may not be able to see anything useful."

I remembered what Aliena had written about Marcus's cards. He had planted the card on Rachella's wall so it faced everything in the room, but he placed the one in his home on the floor, giving a view of a blank ceiling.

"Yeah, now I was thinking about that," Hamilton said. "What if that long-haired guy had tried to travel through this card while it was in Cavanaugh's bookcase? Would he have been crushed?"

"Of course not. He would come out of the card just outside the case, box, or any other place that did not have sufficient room for a human-size traveler. But he would not have that view through an Ace."

"Does the portal card stay where it was in such a case?" I asked.

"Yes."

Aliena watched us as we gnawed on our barbecued bones.

"Do you know where the deck came from?" Hamilton asked, wiping his chin off.

"Only what I was told. And he was not sure, either. The deck's powers were bestowed by someone from the stars."

"An alien? Is that what you're saying?"

"I am not saying anything," Aliena replied. "I am passing on the only story I know concerning the origins of the deck."

"The star cards are the cards of the major arcana?" I asked.

She nodded. "You must have a major card to travel. And the major cards are individually owned."

"How many?"

"Twenty-two."

"Do you know anybody who has one?" Hamilton asked.

"Yes."

"Is this another name you can't tell me?"

"I am afraid so."

"It could become important, Aliena," he said.

"I know. Sebastian showed me the pictures of the two men." She tapped the Prince. "I have never seen either one of them."

"Okay, I guess that's something. Anything else?"

"I also know why these men left the card behind."

"And?" Hamilton had his sauce-coated hands poised over his plate.

I hastily wiped my hands and picked up the Prince, sliding it into my jacket pocket as the waiter walked up with the check. I handed him a credit card. He gestured at a kitchen helper and had our table cleared. When he left, Aliena continued.

"Minor cards cannot travel through other minor cards. They must be physically taken to a location and planted."

"Where are these cards?" Hamilton asked.

"All over the world. The only way to find one is to hold a star card close to it."

"That would reduce the chance of accidental discovery to almost nothing," I said.

"Both of these men must have intended to take this card with them," Hamilton said.

"Yes, but out the front door." I thought about it. "And when that wasn't possible, they were forced to exit through their star cards and couldn't take the Prince with them."

"That fits. Well, we know why the card has been left behind, but we don't know why these men are after it, or whether or not it has anything to do with Cavanaugh's murder."

We both looked at Aliena.

"It's possible someone used a star card to get into the room," she said.

Hamilton did not respond. We had already come to that conclusion. I wondered about the cards scattered all over the world. That reminded me of the imported package containing the ancient game.

"You know," I said, "we might want to put a man outside Cavanaugh's Antiques. Maybe we could even get a picture of everyone coming out."

"I can set that up," Hamilton nodded. "We won't get it until tomorrow, but I'll have someone there by the time they open in the morning. Good idea, Sebastian."

"Only kind I have," I said.

They both had short comments for that. Not complimentary at all, I thought.

11:48 p.m.

After we returned from dinner, Aliena and I sat on the patio for a couple of hours, talking about the star cards. She showed me her Moon card again.

"What if it appears in a reading?" I asked.

"The Moon is one of the most feared cards in the tarot," she said with a devilish smile. "If revealed, it means—"

My cell rang. "Montero."

"It's Hamilton."

"Hey, Steve. You're burning the midnight oil."

"Not by choice. Got a call about a burglary an hour ago."

"Burglary? What's that got to do with you?"

"Nothing. Until I heard the responding officer give the location."

Uh-oh. "And that was . . ."

"Cavanaugh's Antiques."

I swore under my breath. "We should have watched it all night. Is anything missing?"

"Karen Cavanaugh is on her way to check the inventory, but I've already had a chance to look around for myself."

"And our package?"

"Nowhere to be found," he said. "The son of a bitch grabbed it right from under our noses."

Chapter 18

Sunday, January 25, 12:01 a.m.

"Have you determined the method of entry?" I asked.

"Looks like a pry bar against the front door. He set off the alarm, but the dude was gone by the time we got here."

"So he knew what he was after."

"It sure looks that way," said Hamilton. "Unless Ms. Cavanaugh moved it someplace else."

"I doubt it," I said. "She set it behind the counter so she would have it when someone called for it. I assume that's where you looked?"

"There and everywhere else. It's not here."

"What about the surveillance tape?"

"We're still checking it." His voice turned furious. "Want to bet we never see his face?"

"No. Did you want me to come there?"

"Why bother. There's nothing to see. I just thought you should know."

"I appreciate it."

"If I learn anything more, I'll call you."

"Thanks." We disconnected.

Aliena had heard both sides of the conversation. "Do you think the box contained archons?" she asked.

"I don't know, but I think it's likely. Will Marcus talk to me?"

"He said he would," she told me. "I did not press him. He will contact you when he is ready." She tilted her head to the side. "As a matter of fact . . ."

A voice from the corner of the patio said, "I am ready now." Marcus emerged from the shadows. He wore a dark suit and a sky-blue tie lay against a white shirt.

"How long have you been there?" Aliena said.

"I have only just arrived." He walked over to us, kissed Aliena's proffered hand, and sat on the wall with me, to my left. Aliena sat in a patio chair facing us.

"We think a parcel containing archons was stolen tonight," I told him.

"Witnesses?"

"None. Aliena has told me you also possess a star card."

"Yes, I told her she could. I also have two minor cards from that deck, including one of the Aces."

"Can anyone travel through your minor card?"

"As long as they have a star card and know the proper sound. I have changed the password many times, and I have only given it out once."

"Do you know where the deck came from? Who created it?" He had told Aliena he did not know. I found it hard to believe. Marcus was more than two thousand years old, just like the cards.

He stood, paced to the end of the patio, turned, and came back. He remained standing. I felt certain he would tell us something important, but I never expected him to say what he did.

"I was there when the Tarot of the Archons was created."

Aliena sat up. "That's not what you told me," she said accusingly. "You told me you didn't know!"

Marcus looked abashed. "I have never told anyone before this." He looked at her keenly. "Claudius was there, too."

Aliena's face revealed a tragic mask of betrayal. I could see the hurt in her eyes as she absorbed this information. Claudius was her sire and mentor, and Marcus a trusted friend. And neither one of them had confided in her.

"I'm sorry," he said. "Secrecy is of the greatest importance. If knowledge of the cards became general, we would have a very serious security problem. Some of the cards are owned by vampires and . . . ," he trailed off.

"And?" I prompted.

"And other immortals."

"What?" It was my turn to look stunned. "You have known of the existence of immortals like me and never bothered to tell me?" I did not realize I had stood and was poised in front of Marcus in a very aggressive posture.

He gazed at me calmly. "It was not my place to betray their existence. I am not certain I should have done so now. I have told them nothing of you."

I finally backed off a step, exhaled loudly, and returned to the wall. I sat down. "You might have said something before this." I looked accusingly at Aliena. She would not meet my gaze.

"Yes," Marcus said. "I might have, but I did not have a reason before now."

I nodded. Marcus and I stared at each other. I knew he was jealous of my relationship with Aliena, but I had never before considered him untrustworthy. Putting my anger aside, I knew it was not fair to do so now. He had not lied to me in keeping the knowledge of other immortals confidential. And although he knew the information was of great interest to me, it was not necessary for my survival, so he had certainly not betrayed me or placed me in danger by keeping it to himself.

"If it is any consolation, Sebastian, you should know that not all immortals are like you," he said.

This was turning out to be a night of revelation. "What do you mean?"

"There are other . . . creatures . . . that are naturally immortal—the way vampires are. Please," he said, holding up a hand as I started to speak, "do not ask, I beg you. You would place me in a compromising position. I promise you will learn more as we investigate this. For now, you must be patient."

Patience is usually not a problem for one who is immortal, but it took extraordinary effort to push these questions to the back of my mind.

"Very well," I said. I looked at Aliena. She seemed as unhappy as I felt. I shook myself mentally. This represented information, nothing more, nothing less. That I didn't know it yesterday was moot. I knew it now, and I could put the data to good use.

"Do you know where Claudius is?" Aliena asked Marcus in an arctic voice.

"He is here in LA. I summoned him through the cards. He agrees we may have a crisis if one of the star cards has fallen into the hands of unscrupulous people. We must have a care as we move forward."

"Can Claudius help us?" I asked. I had never met him. I was intensely curious to meet a vampire older than Marcus—and the sire of Aliena.

"Not directly," he said. "Claudius shuns mortal concerns, but as this relates to the cards, he will make inquiries." He gave me a small smile. "I doubt you will meet him, Sebastian. He rarely communes with non-vampires. He considers humans to be a lower life-form."

"That is your opinion, too, is it not?" I was reminded that Marcus could interpret the smallest change on a person's face and that if I wanted my thoughts to remain private, I had to keep my expression impassive. He had known I wanted to meet Claudius because my eyes had widened a fraction when he mentioned the name. It was too small and too fast for mortals to detect, but Marcus read it easily.

"I do believe we are a higher form of intelligence, yes, but I acknowledge that it is mostly due to our longevity. Nevertheless, mortals are grasping, lying, brittle little beings rarely concerned with anything but their own comfort."

"That is a slanted depiction."

"Is it? Look at the state of the world today. Would you say humans have progressed from the fifteenth century? Forget technology. I mean man and his 'civilization'."

I thought about that. I compared the brutal personalities of five hundred years ago to the people of today. "Not individually, no, but conditions are certainly better."

"That's technology." He looked at Aliena.

"No, I don't think so, either," she said.

"No." Marcus's smile was tight-jawed and grim. "Man is still as wicked, childish, and selfish as ever, serving only his narrow needs and trampling on the rights of others to get what he wants."

"Not everybody is like that."

"You are right."

My mind still reeled from the knowledge there were others like me that were cardholders. I could not contain my curiosity. "About these other immortals, Marcus . . ."

"I know you have many questions. But let's start with the deck. Do you know how the cards work?"

"I think so, yes."

He nodded. "Good. Although we do not know where all the star cards are or who holds them, we know they are still out there. No cards from this deck can be destroyed."

"So someone has possession of them."

"That may not matter," Aliena said. "If the card was not properly assigned, it's possible the current holder does not know how to use it. Cards could be sitting in attics or at the bottom of trunks, their powers unknown to their current owner."

"Of the twenty-two star cards, how many do you know are currently in action?" I asked.

Neither Aliena nor Marcus spoke.

"Well?"

"Fourteen," Marcus said. "Although I am sure five of those are not being used."

"Which five?"

"The World card was kept by the Woman of the Stars, the person who imbued the deck with its teleportation powers."

"How did she do that?" I wished Reed were here. I would have to compose a report for him and Preston before morning, bringing them up-to-date on the cards.

"That, no one knows. She was not from this planet."

Aliena leaned forward. "What planet was she from?"

"She told us its name but not where it was."

"If the star cards are not limited by the distance between the portals . . . ," I said.

"Incredible." Aliena's voice sounded awed. "If we knew the code for a portal on her planet, we could travel across the galaxy, perhaps even the universe."

It boggled the mind.

"What about the other four?" I asked.

"They are in safekeeping," Marcus answered, "possessed by four cardholders who will decide when to confer them."

"Very well. Now we know there are two men who traveled through the Prince," I said. "Are they working together?"

"Good question."

Aliena said, "It's possible they are working against each other."

Marcus and I waited.

"The first thing the man traveling through the Prince did was start strangling you, right?" she said. I nodded.

"Why would he do that? You have nothing to do with the cards, and you don't know why someone killed Cavanaugh. Also, when you travel, you can't see what's on the other side of the card until a moment before you emerge, so he must have already decided to attack whoever was on the other side of the card before he began."

"Unless he had an Ace," Marcus reminded her. "Then he could have taken a look before activating the portal."

That made me think of a question, but I would have to wait to ask it.

"Yes," Aliena said. "If he did not have an Ace but thought the killer was on the other side of the card, his first action might be to subdue that person."

"That makes sense," I said. "It also explains why he looked confused when he was inspecting my place. If the Aces are windows, what special ability do the Princes have?"

Neither answered me. Aliena averted her gaze.

"I do have the card," I reminded them, directing my comments at Marcus. "And you know very well I mean no harm to vampires, would never endanger you in any way."

"I know," he said. "But there is more to the card than what it does. Much more."

"You could use my computer to type out the details."

"I could." He didn't move. "The special value of the Prince is that the traveler has the ability to set his return time in advance. Any travelers who step through the portal while the clock is active will be returned to their origin at the designated time. Even those who do not have a card."

"That's nice," I said. "All of these cards are pretty powerful."

"They are," he agreed. "As for the men who seem to be after it, do you have pictures of them?"

"Yes. We have the images they left on the Prince. Come inside."

We walked into the living room. I picked up my laptop and set it on the dining room table. The three of us stood around it. I opened the file with the two pictures taken from the card. Marcus looked at them closely and then shook his head.

"I don't recognize either man. However, the tattoo on the neck of this one," he pointed to the long-haired man who had 'broken into' BioLaw, "looks familiar."

"It's a Magistine tattoo," I told him.

"Magistine?"

"Yes, that's right. From an old village in the foothills of western Turkey." I decided to stop there and see how much more Marcus knew. But he was as careful as I was.

"Do you know anything else about them?"

"Yes. A great deal more." I stopped again and watched him.

He smiled. "You have no reason to withhold information from me, Sebastian. I know the Magistines were sorcerers practicing soundcraft and that their village was destroyed." He looked back at the picture. "I never believed all of them had been killed."

"Soundcraft? You know about their powers?"

"Yes. And I did not need evidence to tell me they were still among us. They were too powerful to be wiped out. Curious to find one in Los Angeles. Something must have drawn him here."

"Cavanaugh?"

He shrugged. "The name means nothing to me. He was not a cardholder, unless he had one of the lost cards."

I had not even thought of that. I assumed the killer had planted the Prince there somehow and had entered through it to kill Cavanaugh. If Cavanaugh was the cardholder, how did the killer know the card was there? And why would Cavanaugh leave it sitting on his desk if he knew that someone could pop out of it at any time? Did he want to be killed? There was something wrong here, and I could not fathom what it was.

"What do we know about Cavanaugh's background, Sebastian?" Aliena asked.

"So far, uninteresting. Nothing that has a bearing on this case. You know," I said, remembering Aliena's diary, "we may want to start over at the crime scene. He had a bookcase filled with books. What if one of them is his journal?"

"Do you have any reason to believe he would have kept one?" Marcus asked.

"No," I said. "But we did not search the crime scene for something like that."

"What is it you hope to find?" Aliena asked.

"Anything that will tell us why somebody wanted to kill him."

Chapter 19

Sunday, January 25, 3:09 a.m.

After Marcus left, I wondered about everything he had said. He had offered no more information on the other immortals. Since he knew, it was likely Aliena was also aware of who they were. I couldn't decide whether or not to question her about it. I did want to know about Marcus, though. "Is he telling us everything he knows?"

"I doubt it," she said. "And, Sebastian, you may never catch these two."

"Because Marcus and Claudius will get to them first?"

"It is a possibility."

Yes. The question was whether they were going to kill these fellows immediately, or did they intend to determine whether the men should be executed at all.

She went into her room and came back with her laptop. "Yours is so old," she complained. Bringing her computer here sounded like she was moving in, which was fine with me. "What is your police password?" she asked.

"It's TK492MRT09238THX113814."

"Thank you."

She accessed the Internet, went to the LAPD database, and entered my ID and password. Then she began searching through the files on the Cavanaugh case.

I wandered into the kitchen and pulled a bottle of ice-cold vodka out of the freezer. I drained half of it in a gulp. I went back to the living room and sat on the couch next to her.

"Do you know of any other immortals?" I asked her as casually as I could.

Her hands froze over her keyboard. "Sebastian . . ."

"Darling," I said, "you know how much this means to me. I have searched for centuries and never found someone like me."

She put her icy hand on my cheek. "I know. And it pains me to keep this from you, but I have no more right than Marcus to divulge their identities. I have always given you the same confidentiality."

"I would not mind if you confided my identity to another immortal, as long as you told me about it."

"There. You have a condition already. And what if they also have conditions?"

I glared at her. No effect.

"Besides," she said, kissing me, "I don't know of any immortals like you."

"Thank you for that." I asked the next question uppermost in my mind. "Have you traveled through your card?"

"Yes, of course," she said, still looking at her screen and tapping the keys.

"And you have had it for more than fifty years?"

"Yes."

"I see." I did not say anything about her withholding this information from me for half a century. "Do you have any minor cards?"

"Yes," she said.

I waited. Nothing. "You are making me ask?"

She tapped the Enter key twice and turned to me. "Sorry, sweetheart, I wanted to get that finished. I also have the Princess of Cups, the two of Swords, and the four of . . . Sebastian? What are you doing?" She started giggling.

I got up on my knees and turned toward her. She leaned back as I straddled her thighs. I rested my hands on the back of the couch on either side of her and leaned down. As she tilted her head up, I took her jaw in my right hand. I kissed her mouth, her nose, her eyes (softly), and returned to her lips.

"Wow," she said when I finally leaned back. "If that was for something I did, tell me, so I can do more of it."

"You called me sweetheart."

She reached for the front of my shirt, grabbed a handful of it, and pulled me down to her. "You're going to get a lot more than that," she breathed, and our mouths were together again.

With my right hand, I began exploring her body. She did not stop me when I cupped a heavy breast and slid my palm over it. I let my hand drift lower. When I set it on her thigh, she slid her arm from around my neck and rested her hand on my bicep. I recognized that as a signal not to go any further.

I raised my hand and plunged it into her golden hair. Her arm slid back up, around my neck.

We kissed like that for a deliriously long time.

6:46 a.m.

Aliena and I held hands on the patio, watching the ocean. The sky had started to lighten.

"Time for bed," I said.

She reached out to me. I scooped her up, carried her inside, and took her to her room. I set her on her feet and held her close. She was colder than usual.

"You did not eat tonight," I said, scolding.

"I do not have to eat every day, you know that. Even a week is not painful."

"I know. I am concerned for your comfort."

She kissed me on the nose. "That is very sweet, Sebastian."

"You still have six minutes," I told her.

She changed into her pajamas, slid into bed, and pulled the covers up. "You're right. Come over here, then." She smiled at me with her vampire teeth. It was a disturbing sight. She looked predatory, and her eyes had a red glint, giving her the appearance of a hungry wolf.

"Since you are the one falling asleep," I said, climbing on the bed, "I should be on top."

"Mm hmm."

I positioned myself so my head was a little higher than hers. Her freezing hands clasped my head and shoulder. She pulled me to her, sinking her fangs into the soft skin of my throat. It always felt as if I had been stabbed at first—an intense, sharp pain—but as she drained me, the ache began to fade and the experience grew sensual.

Until I lost consciousness.

When I came to, my head lay on Aliena's chest and she was stroking my hair. She must have gotten out of bed while I was out—she smelled of toothpaste.

"Sebastian?"

I lifted my head. I could hear the roar of blood as my internal engine replenished my stock and sent it coursing through my body. I leaned over and kissed her. Her complexion was rosy and her hand on my scalp was warm. She pulled me close.

"Thank you," she said when we broke apart. "You are soooo delicious." She smiled and then yawned, a jaw-cracking one. Her eyes looked sleepy. "You have always taken care of me, haven't you?" She closed her eyes and sighed as she fell into her daily fugue.

"Not always," I whispered, caressing her rosy cheek. "But from now on."

I tucked her hands under the comforter, kissed her forehead, stood, and left, sealing the door on my way out.

I glanced at my watch. It was 7:05. I had arranged to pick Hamilton up at nine.

Aliena's drink had left me wobbly and as thirsty as a desert cactus. I opened the refrigerator, grabbed a glass pitcher of ice-cold orange juice, and drained it. I took another full bottle onto the patio and set it on the table. I went back inside and knelt in front of the fireplace. I pulled up the square of carpet and opened the safe, extracting Aliena's diary.

Chapter 20

Sunday, January 25, 7:07 a.m.

June 2, 1884

I am sorry, Diary, that I have been gone so long.

I'll say. The previous journal entry was nearly two decades earlier. I thought about that. It did not mean she hadn't written in her diary for eighteen years. She told me this was one of her diaries. Naturally, I thought that meant she would write in them in consecutive, unbroken years. Knowing her love of secrecy convinced me she probably switched back and forth between diaries, perhaps even randomly. In order to get the journal entries in chronological order, you would need all of them.

I have spent these last years sitting on the beaches from Nice to Saint-Tropez watching the ocean. I found new places to sleep. I discarded some of my clothes and jewelry the first year and felt much better. Three years after François left, I decided I wanted to live again.
I no longer have any interest in men.

Great. And all this happened to her just after she met me. Thanks, Franky.

I began studying with the old gypsy fortune-teller. It had been a long time since I had last seen her, but I could not forget about her. Her abilities astounded me. I had to learn more. I appeared on her doorstep the day I decided I no longer ached for François.

"Highness," she said. The heat-smell gushed from her, filling my nostrils. "I have awaited your return."

I confirmed there was no one else in the room. I noticed my coat hanging on a hook above her traveling trunk.

She saw my look. "I have kept it for you since you left it. I knew you would return."

"Because the cards told you?"

She nodded.

"I no longer want that garment. You may give it away." I did not tell her to destroy it. Coats were valuable.

Tonight Maman Djeserit wore loose-fitting, coarse pants and a billowing tunic. She had on her reed sandals. I dismissed the sweet scent of her blood. It was easier tonight because I had fed lustily on three victims (no, Diary, I did not kill any of them this time).

Only one of her lamps burned with light, but even in the dimness, I could see the patchwork skin of her face and the keen black eyes. She lit a second lamp and came close to me. She was not so fearful, her curiosity overriding her anxiety. She looked at my face and held up her hand again. When she hesitated, I nodded.

As she had done the last time we met, she slid her fingertips along my left cheek. She stood in front of me and gazed at me with something akin to wonder.

"You look human. And your skin is warm. Is this because you have fed tonight?"

"Yes."

She lowered her hand. "It is remarkable. You could move among us, unknown for what you are."

"I have and I do."

She nodded. She walked back to her table and sat down. "Where would you like to begin?"

I sat down opposite her. "At the beginning," I told her. "Assume I know nothing at all."

After that session, I saw Maman Djeserit nearly every night. She was an extraordinary woman with the gift of true sight. I warned the other vampires to leave her alone. After what Rachella had done, I was prepared to kill one of my own if my requests were ignored this time.

I learned rapidly. For me, the sessions were nearly one long apprenticeship with breaks only for eating and other minor necessities. I do not sleep the way I did when I was a mortal girl. When I wake up, it seems as if only a moment has passed since the sunrise. I close my eyes, I open them, and it is sunset the next day. It was very disorienting at first, but my mentor, Claudius, explained to me that we do not experience the sense of time the way we did when we slept as mortals.

I had not permitted Maman to do a reading of me since that first night.

She never asked me about François, but I knew she could see the pain in my face. It is a bearable pain, now, but I think it will be with me for the rest of time. I cannot ever remember feeling so desolate. The old gypsy woman filled the void for me. She was a demanding instructor, forcing me to concentrate.

"Yes, yes," she would say after I did a reading, "that is obvious but what do the cards say *to you?"*

"I am not certain what you mean, Maman."

"You cannot think your way through the tarot. You must feel it. All of your interpretations are good, and you have learned much, but you still only see a tiny bit of what the cards are trying to tell you."

"But I don't know how to do that."

"You must relax. You are so tense, so alert. To let the spirits in, you must let your guard down. It is as much a declaration of trust as it is a use of power."

I practiced doing it her way, and I was able to see a little more by meditating before a reading, but I never had interpretations as complete as Maman's.

Over the next thirteen years, she became a treasured aunt to me and taught me everything she knew about the tarot. Unfortunately, she could not teach me everything she could see or hear.

"No, mistress," *she would say when I read the cards,* "you must see beyond the card, even beyond the delicate balance of the spread."

"But what is there beyond that, Maman?"

Those wise old eyes would close and she would smile, as if she knew a secret no one else did. "Life is beyond that, child. The light and the strength. The knowledge."

I am still not sure what she was talking about. But I knew she did see something others did not, heard sounds no one else could.

She was the most important member of her village, a trusted midwife and a cherished fortune-teller. There was no one who had not asked her a question about a child or listened to her advice about planning for the winter.

"What do you see?" *I would ask her sometimes when she was sitting in front of a tarot spread, her eyes closed, her fingers tapping the cards.*

"Pictures behind my eyes," *she would say so softly only my vampiric hearing allowed me to discern the words.* "Stories and songs. They talk to me."

If attending a reading for another, I would eat as fully as possible before coming to Maman's wagon so as not to frighten the members of her village. I saw her tell women what their true loves looked like and men when to plant their wheat. I saw her cure boils. She made poultices for rheumatism and teas for impotence. She read the cards and told her people their fortunes.

She knew where to find healing herbs and when to pick them. Sometimes, she would walk at twilight into the forest, and I would follow her, the tops of the trees golden in the gloaming, the forest floor dark and soft. I shadowed her from above.

167

After thirty minutes or so, her slow footsteps would stop. She would look around and then approach a bush or a stand of grasses. She would sink to her knees, lean forward, pick here and there, lean back, inspect her harvest, and tuck it into her bag.

I watched her three or four times a week. I liked being with her when she did not know I was there—at least, I do not think she knew I was there. She never gave a sign that she was aware of my presence.

I followed Maman because it soothed me to be close to her. She had a calmness about her, a palpable serenity, that drew people to her.

One August night, I watched her from a tall tree as she moved through a tiny clearing, her herbs tucked safely into a bag on her hip. She was heading back to the gypsy camp, walking slowly toward me, when three men jumped from behind the bushes in front of her, blocking her way.

I had been squatting on my haunches on a high branch, but now I stood up. The first man got to her and knocked her down. I leaned forward and became the wind. By the time his friends joined him at her side, I was there.

And I was not happy.

Chapter 21

From Aliena's Diary:

Two of them faced me. One had his back to me. I hooked my right hand into a claw and ripped his throat out. The hot spurt of blood from his jetting jugular sprayed onto the faces of his accomplices. They staggered back, making noises of fear and disgust.

I looked down. Maman was moving, sitting up.
"Maman?"

She looked up, nodded. I helped her to her feet and turned to the two men now standing very still in the small clearing.

The moon shone brightly that night and they could see me clearly as I strode toward them. My fangs poked out, my eyes fire. My long coat swished along the backs of my ankles. I retracted my fighting nails.

They moaned and fumbled under their cheap tunics. One finally pulled a small wooden crucifix out and held it toward me, hand trembling.

I laughed. As I reached out to crush it—and his hand along with it—Maman spoke.

"No, Highness," she said. "Please do not hurt them."

I stopped. Her shuffling footsteps approached until she stood at my side. Both of the men were making small breathy sounds and the air reeked of their urine. The one with the crucifix looked paralyzed with terror. Maman placed her hand on my forearm. She turned to the men.

"Go back to your home. Stay out of this part of the forest. If you return, I will not prevent this spirit from taking your lives. Go now. Go."

They walked away, stumbling, looking over their shoulders at us; then they broke out running. I turned to Maman.

"Are you hurt?" I asked her, sweeping her quickly with my gaze. I brushed some grass off her arm and picked a small leaf out of her hair.

"No, my child," she said. She brushed at her rough pants then straightened up. She looked at me slyly. "It was fortunate you happened to be here."

"Yes, it was. You should not walk so late. You are too old to be alone."

"Am I? Alone, I mean. I know I am old."

I smiled. "Not tonight, at least. I was coming to see you."

"Yes, of course. Well, as long as you are with me, let me lean on you the rest of the way home."

I slid my arm around her back as she pressed against me.

"Oh!" she said. "You are very cold."

I hesitated. "Do you wish me to release you?"

"No, dear, I did not mean that. You have not yet eaten tonight. I should have let you have one of those men."

I laughed. Strange. Her blood smelled as wonderful as ever but it no longer touched my hunger. As she snuggled against me, I wondered at the soft feel of her skin and the warmth she radiated. I had never felt closer to anyone since my parents had died.

We walked quietly through the chirping forest, and she continued teaching me about her craft—how to read the cards and how to tap into the forces that surround and permeate us all.

"They are outside of me?"

"Yes and no. You can use the power of the things around you. But your spirit causes it to happen."

"And I cannot let it in yet because I cannot achieve your state of relaxation?"

"You have allowed it to enter you," she said. "You do that much spontaneously. To go deeper and experience more, you must surrender yourself to the forces of nature."

I wondered if I could ever surrender to anything. "And this is how you see the future?"

"I do not know how it works, mistress. I simply become an empty vessel and allow these outside forces to fill me. I know it is difficult for most, but it has always been natural for me, even when I was very young."

We arrived at her village. As we walked through, many people greeted her and bowed to her as we passed. Many also bowed to me.

"Why are they paying me any mind?" I asked Maman.

"They know you are my student."

"Is that all they know?"

"It is all that I have told them. That one's ready for a husband," she said, nodding at a girl of sixteen or so who was helping her mother get a fire started for dinner. "Look at those hips. A good breeder. She could have many fine children. And I know just the man for her."

The way she said that made me suspicious. "You don't tell modified fortunes in order to be a matchmaker, do you?"

"What if I did, my dear?" She chuckled. "Sometimes it is not necessary to consult the spirits to know what is best for certain people."

I helped her up the steps to her wagon. Once inside, she lit a lamp with a tremulous hand. She shuffled to her bed, sat on it, and shook off her loose sandals. I sat next to her.

As I stared at her with my preternatural sight, the signs of old age showed clearly. Her gray hair had become thin and wispy, the skin underneath covered with brown spots. Her elbows and knees were knobby, and the patchwork skin of her face had become heavily lined. She did not know her exact age. I estimated her to be ninety, perhaps a bit older.

She laid down and let out a long sigh. I pulled the soft, thick blanket I had brought her many years ago up to her chest. Looking at her face and seeing the diminutive shape of her body *under the covers, I realized I did not want her to die. I did not want anything at all to happen to her.*

But she was mortal.

I leaned over and kissed her cheek. "I will put out the lamp," I whispered to her.

"Thank you, my child," she said tiredly, her voice already a sleepy murmur. "You're always a good daughter . . ." Her voice trailed off.

I stood, blew out the light, and went out to search for dinner.

That was the last time I saw her. I traveled in the East for several weeks with Marcus and seven others. By the time I returned, she had gone.

When I found her wagon dark and empty, I looked around, still smelling her presence. But it was very faint, like the faded scent of a cut flower. Her reed sandals lay beside her bed in their usual place. The thick blanket was gone.

I left her wagon and turned into the village. I listened carefully as I walked down a crude path and found another wagon like Maman's just a short distance away. Voices came from inside. I purposely allowed my boots to sound on the wooden steps before I entered through the open door.

It was a couple with a small boy. The woman held a baby. They were thin and brown and young. They both froze and stared at me with wide eyes.

"I am a friend of Maman Djeserit," I told them. "I wish to know what has become of her. She is not at home."

"Yes," said the man. "Maman said you would come. She gave my wife the beautiful blanket that was your gift to her." He looked at it. I followed his gaze and saw it was on top of a small bed. He turned back to me, a fearful expression on his face. I realized how I must look to them, a pale, golden-haired devil wearing a long, black coat.

"I am sorry, mademoiselle," he said in a shaking voice, "but Maman has passed on."

I had known, but I went numb when he said the words aloud. We all stood there for several long moments. I tried to think what to do next and could not. I stared at the rough floor of the wagon, my mind a cavity filling with despair. It seemed impossible she could be gone.

He walked to a travel chest, opened it, pulled out Maman's deck of tarot cards and a small package, and brought them over, clearly not comfortable being close to me.

"She asked us to give you these." He held them out, and I took them.

I looked at the old cards, their surfaces smoothed by years of Maman's touch. I slid the deck into my jacket pocket and began opening the package. Before I pulled the paper away, I knew what it was. My eyes filled with blood tears as I beheld the gold coins I had given her that first night as payment for my lessons. She had kept them. All these years, when she could have sold them and made her life more comfortable, she had kept all five of them.

"I have everything I want," she always used to tell me. I never believed her. Until now. After she was gone.

The young couple watched me apprehensively. The man spoke again.

"Maman made me promise to tell you that she loved you very much," he said. "She called you her daughter." He paused. "We all knew you were very special to her. I am sorry."

I could only nod dumbly. I swiped at my eyes. I think I thanked them. I don't remember it or leaving the gypsy village. I only remember the wind of my flight away from the village, those first moments in the air when I knew what was in my future, a future I needed no cards to discern. I could already see the great chasm, the yawning emptiness that stretched before me, a future without that wonderful old woman.

An empty forest.

As I flew, I stared at the beautiful gold coins, remembering Marcus's warning about becoming attached to mortals.

"They die," he had said. "That's all. And it hurts when they go."

Oh, God, how right he was. I wanted to scream at the stars and demand Maman's return, crying that I wasn't here when she died, I wasn't ready, it was so unfair, I hadn't had the opportunity to say good-bye to her!

The only thing I learned from the cold heavens was that she was gone. Forever.

Although Marcus had disapproved of my relationship with Maman, he knew how much I loved her. And when he saw the depth of my sorrow at her passing, he sympathized with my pain and helped me through the grieving period.

She left us three years ago, Diary. Incredibly, losing her hurts more than François's betrayal. I dearly want her back.

Marcus was right: the only way to keep this pain from engulfing me again was to never love a mortal. Perhaps it was safest to love no one at all.

"Good lord," I said aloud, closing the journal. I stood up and moved to the low white wall surrounding the patio, smoking and watching the surf.

It had never occurred to me that Aliena might have lost someone during her vampire lifetime. She was so aloof and independent; I never dreamed that she had allowed a mortal get close to her. It was clear now why she always maintained such a detached air. She lost her parents when she was fifteen; at twenty, her mortality was turned to immortal night by a monster; she endured the loss of François. And then, just thirteen years later, the old woman of whom she was so fond passed away.

I knew the grief she must have suffered. I have lost many loved ones. When my last child died, the pain was so bad that I vowed never to have children again or love a mortal. I have allowed only Aliena to get close to me in the last two centuries. I am thankful she is immortal. Unless she goes away, I will not have to endure life without her.

We were more alike than I had known. We both had watched time do its destructive work to someone we loved. That was a significant experience to share. It had become habit with me to shun even ordinary friendship, and so it was with Aliena. Friends become too important, too cherished, and if mortal, they are gone too soon.

And the pain of their passing echoes forever.

I glanced at Aliena's diary sitting closed on the table. She was allowing me to peer behind the curtain and see the delicate center of her being, now not so cold and assessing, but vulnerable and capable of deep love. She was giving herself to me. After reading her life's experiences, I understood what a gigantic step that must be for her.

In spite of all that, we were together. I was thrilled to have the responsibility of taking care of her. She could not be in better hands. She was my adored one, the girl I had cherished for more than a century.

Unfortunately, I still had one problem. I did not know if Aliena was in love with me.

Chapter 22

Sunday, January 25, 9:02 a.m.

Hamilton stood outside the station when I drove up. He opened the door, a manila file in his hand.

"Where to?" I asked him as he buckled his seat belt.

"Let's start with the last customers to interact with Cavanaugh. Spent some time with Karen last night putting together a list of the people who made special purchases from her father." He tapped the folder. "This is everything records could dig up on these people."

"How far back did you take the purchases?"

"Six months," he said. "And we have a whopping two people."

"At least we can check this angle quickly. What's the plan?"

"Simple. We interview them, ostensibly about their furniture acquisition from Cavanaugh's, and try to find out if they know anything about him that might help us find his murderer. Who knows? Maybe one of them bought an expensive piece of furniture and thought Cavanaugh charged an exorbitant amount."

"So they killed him?"

"It would not be the first time money prompted a murder."

I did not laugh, though the theory was thinner than a magazine model. I could tell Hamilton didn't believe it, either. But it was necessary to run down every lead.

"Who's our first stop?"

"Jason Parmalee," he said, glancing down at the folder he had opened on his lap. "Did a short stint in the army," he said slowly, reading, "and was honorably discharged after two years. No explanation." He flipped through more pages. "Made his living as an insurance agent for one of the big companies, pulling down six figures a year. The bling came from a series of shrewd investments. He's sixty-two now, retired for ten years and living in Beverly Hills."

"The American dream."

"Yeah," he said. He turned to the next page. "Hm. This Parmalee guy is sort of a weirdo."

"Uh-oh. Weird how?"

"You know, Sebastian, I wish I had that calm demeanor down pat like you. You didn't even sound mildly worried when you asked me that."

"You still knew, so I guess I wasn't as casual as I thought."

"Your act is perfect. I just know you better."

Yes, I thought. And I was getting to know him very well. I liked being with him and looked forward to any time we could get together. He was important to me, and I cared what happened to him.

That was not good for me.

On another note, I have often wondered how the brain computes the timing for such decisions. For instance, was it ever late? Was Hamilton actually a close friend a week ago, and I just didn't think of it? Or is it only real if I *do* think of it? Recognizing for the first time that a song is my favorite is the same. I hear it and suddenly know it's my favorite song—but I wonder if it was really my favorite song a couple of days earlier.

What can I say? You have to think about *something* when you're a sleepless immortal.

"This Parmalee likes to be called colonel, or sir," he told me.

"I thought you said he was only in the army for two years."

"He was."

"You can't make colonel that fast."

"He didn't. Let's just humor him," Hamilton continued. "We only want to ask about the piece he purchased and see if he knows anything about Cavanaugh's death, which is a long shot."

"Fine, colonel, sir," I said.

"Don't be a dick in there and screw with this guy."

"Did you just say something about a dick and screwing this guy?"

Out of the corner of my eye, I saw his head swivel toward me. "Sebastian?"

"Yes?"

"Remind me to kill you later."

"Will do."

We had to identify ourselves on video before the security gates opened, and we were admitted to the grounds. The estate was considerable, with a Japanese garden near the front of the house and horse stables and what looked like a firing range in back.

Parmalee answered the door. He was dressed in green army dress slacks, black riding boots, a tan dress shirt with a black tie, and a red-and-black plaid hunting jacket, unbuttoned.

"Good morning, sir," Hamilton said.

"Ah. Please come in, lieutenant," he said as we stepped across the threshold. The old boy gave me an eye like that of a milk cow before it raises its tail and lets go. "You must be the consultant."

"Yes," I replied. "Sir."

"Well, come in anyway," he said. He was clean shaven with a mop of gray hair and drooping hazel eyes. Under his jacket on his right hip was a black holster containing an army-issue .45 automatic.

He led us down a thickly carpeted hallway to a room that was clearly his favorite. It was filled with military memorabilia: a torn, smoke-scorched American flag, pictures of generals (including Eisenhower and MacArthur), rifles and other weapons—some going back three hundred years—and what looked like a functional brass cannon. I noticed that Parmalee was not in any of the photographs.

He waved us to leather chairs in the middle of the room. "Please sit," he said, walking to a sideboard. He mixed himself a stiffish highball. "As the two of you are on duty," he said, and tipped the glass toward us before draining half of it. "Now, what can I do for you gentlemen?" he asked, freshening his drink.

"It's just routine, Colonel. We're backtracking some of Mr. Cavanaugh's movements before he was killed. You are aware of his death?"

"No." He looked shocked. "I have a radio, but I don't watch TV."

"No newspaper?" Hamilton asked.

"No. I am not much of a reader." He took another long drink. "Unless it's about war, of course."

"When was the last time you saw Mr. Cavanaugh?"

"Oh, I haven't seen him in years," he said. "Not much in common, you know. You say he was killed? How?"

"We haven't released that, so I am not at liberty to tell you, sir. You understand." I had to admit, Hamilton was playing the colonel like an old video game.

Parmalee nodded sagely. "Of course, lieutenant." He began construction on a new drink, building on the icy bones of the first.

"You purchased an antique armoire two months ago. Do you remember that, Colonel?"

"Armoire? Two months?" He stirred his new drink slowly with a clear swizzle stick, his face slack as he tried to remember. Animation returned to his features. "Oh, yes. For my daughter's room. She's moving back in with us next month."

"Yes, sir. Do you remember your meeting with him? Where were the two of you?"

"Where?" the colonel said, sipping his drink. "He said . . . let me see . . ."

"Did you meet him at his store?" I said.

His face cleared. "Yes, that's what he said. He couldn't accompany his delivery men out here, and he wanted my signature before he transferred ownership."

"Your signature? How much did the armoire cost?" I asked. He looked at me as if I were a puppy that had peed on his rug. "Er, Colonel."

"If that has any bearing on this investigation," he said, "you may as well know it cost $214,000. I had been searching for such a piece for years. Mr. Cavanaugh knew that and attended an auction where he purchased it for me."

"Do you know where that auction was held?" I asked. "Colonel?"

He looked at me, squinting. "You know, you sound a little like a punk. One of those smart-mouthed know-it-alls who burn flags and call us veterans baby killers."

"No, sir," I said, shaking my head. "I meant no disrespect, Colonel, I assure you. If I have offended you in some way, I apologize." I bowed my head slightly. I hoped he would accept my apology and that the use of his rank had softened him. If not, Hamilton really was going to kill me.

"Well, that's not all bad, then," Parmalee said grudgingly. "I don't think you'd make it in this man's army, though."

"No," Hamilton agreed. "He wouldn't fit in any army."

"And he sure hasn't seen the red pageant of war." The colonel laughed. He talked about war as if it were a romantic encounter. He and Hamilton smiled.

I smiled with them. "No, sir, I don't have your experience."

I saw in my mind's eye the bloody battlefields in England and France and Germany and all of Europe, remembering how I fought men while stumbling over the bodies of the dead, the smell-of-fear sweat so thick it nauseated; personally killing two of my own men for bridling at my orders and putting my absolute authority in question; walking through the carnage with the other survivors, helping the wounded when they could be helped, and dispatching those who could not be.

War is never romantic and battles are never epic. They are grinding encounters of fear and violence. Most men do not die bravely. All I remember are screams and eyes when I killed a man.

The colonel's face had grown flushed. "We've become a nation of fat pussies," he said. "A little magnetic storm from the sun knocks out our satellites and a couple of power plants and look what happens. Take away our toys, and we talk about how hard life is. No fortitude—that's how to describe American youth today. Thank God they didn't have to win the big one."

"What big one?" Hamilton asked.

"The big war, of course. World War II."

"No offense," I said, "but you don't look old enough to have served when they fought that war."

"What has that got to do with it? I can't appreciate what they accomplished and see what kind of people it took to get that job done? I've studied this stuff, you know." He made a sweeping gesture at his bookcase. I had noticed it when we walked in, but I had not given it much thought. The spine of every volume looked brand new. It didn't look as if Parmalee had ever opened those books. "Are you saying I have to have been there to appreciate the courage it took to beat the Nazis?"

"Of course not," I replied. "Everybody in the world today should be thankful for what we, er, they did. I just think today's young people have a reputation they don't deserve, as happened in the fifties and sixties when parents hated rock and roll. Now it's computers and iPods. If anyone threatened America's peace, I think our young people would fight as hard as anyone in history has ever fought."

"Pussies," Parmalee said, obviously unconvinced. "If the chips were down, they'd fold like lawn furniture."

"Right," Hamilton said. "Could we get back to the meeting with Cavanaugh, sir? So you met him at his store. Did you see him?"

"Yes, lieutenant," he replied. He began mixing another bracer. He was going to be so braced by the time we left, he would need a nap. "I signed his form and shook his hand."

"Is that all?"

Parmalee nodded.

"Okay," Hamilton said, standing. I followed. "We can see ourselves—"

"Wait a minute," Parmalee said, "there was one other thing. I was watching the men prepare my armoire for delivery—they never take enough care and when they scratch it, they deny that, of course, and—"

"Please, Mr. Parmalee," Hamilton said.

Parmalee stiffened. "Colonel. Colonel Parmalee."

"Of course," Hamilton said. "Colonel Parmalee."

"Um, let's see . . ."

"You said you saw something while you were watching the delivery men?" I said.

"Yes, that's right. Don't know how I got off the subject. Anyway, I saw this punk arguing with him near the back of the store."

"Arguing with Mr. Cavanaugh?"

"Yes."

"Could you describe this man?" Hamilton asked.

"Oh, yes," Parmalee said, taking a long pull off his glass. "I've seen his type many times before. A no-account. A punk. The kind of man that doesn't respect the unif—"

"Colonel, could you tell us what this man looked like?"

"Big. Long, black hair. Black leather and blue jeans. Silver jewelry. Like I said, a loser. Oh, and a tattoo on his neck."

Hamilton reached into his jacket pocket and produced the picture of the first man we had seen on the Prince card. "Is this him?" he asked, holding the picture out.

Parmalee squinted at it. "That's the bugger. Look at him," he said. "Didn't I tell you he was a punk?"

Chapter 23

Sunday, January 25, 10:11 a.m.

We thanked Parmalee and left.

"Nice," I told Hamilton. "I never thought we'd get something that useful from these interviews."

"Neither did I. So Cavanaugh knew our shooter," Hamilton said as we drove off the colonel's grounds.

"If he is the shooter," I reminded him. "We don't know that for sure. But if he is, the bullet that killed Cavanaugh should match the slug Pitbull took."

"You saw the gun that guy was firing at us. A .44, same as the gun that iced the vic." He pulled his phone out and dialed a number. "I'll still have ballistics check it out."

After his call he said, "What did Parmalee call this guy again? I've heard the word before. Oh, yeah. What does it mean to call a person a bugger?"

"A bugger. Well, a bugger is a man who does unto other men."

"Okay, you can stop now."

"Yes." I turned onto the freeway. "There was a time when calling a man a bugger could get you into a fight or even a duel."

"Anybody calls me that, and I'll kick his ass. We'll see who the damn bugger is then."

"Are you against homosexuality?"

"No, of course not. It was just a joke. As long as no one is harmed and everyone wants to participate, nobody should be able to tell you who you can get down with. Or what you can do. I know I wouldn't want anyone deciding that for me. I'm all for protecting the public, but the public can stay the hell out of my bedroom."

"Eloquently stated," I said.

184

"Fuckin' A."

We decided to postpone our second interview and instead stopped at Cavanaugh's Antiques. We had already planned to track the package that had been stolen back to its point of origin to see if we could determine who had sent it. Now we were also hoping that Karen would recognize the picture of our Magistine and be able to tell us something about him.

I pulled into the lot and parked in front of the store. A black-and-white occupied the space next to ours. The debris from the night before had been cleared, and the store was open for business.

We walked through the front door, hearing the tinkle of the business bell. Karen Cavanaugh was talking to a customer. When she saw us, she excused herself and came over.

"Have the two of you discovered who killed my father?" she asked. Circles stood out under her eyes.

"No. Ms. Cavanaugh," I said. "We need to trace the package that was stolen and see if we can determine who sent it."

"Way ahead of you," she said. "That package was forwarded by an attorney. It was part of an estate."

"Whose estate?" I asked.

"It didn't say. It does have the attorney's contact information, though."

Hamilton handed her his notebook. "Could you write it down for us?"

"Certainly."

We waited while she did that. When she came back and handed Hamilton his notebook, she said, "I assume you're pursuing this angle because you still have no idea who killed my father."

"Please," Hamilton said, "you must be patient. This sort of investigation can take time."

"I read that the longer a case remains open, the less likely it is to be solved."

He didn't say anything to that and neither did I. She was right, statistically speaking.

"I'm sorry," she said, closing her eyes and rubbing them. "I know you're doing everything you can."

"We'll find him," Hamilton told her. He pulled the picture out. "Do you recognize this man?"

She took the picture. "Yes. He came into the store about two months ago and again last week, both times to talk to Dad." She handed the photo back.

"Do you know who he is?" I asked.

"No. My father never introduced us."

"Do you know what he wanted with your father?"

"No." She bit her lower lip. "Don't tell me this man may have killed my dad. I don't know anything about him."

"Karen," I said, "there was no reason for you to give this man a second thought."

She nodded wearily. "I know."

"He didn't buy anything?" Hamilton asked.

"Not to my knowledge."

Hamilton made a note and put his pad and pen away.

"How is your mother?" I asked.

"Not good. My dad was her whole life."

"I'm sorry."

The three of us stood there. We all looked at the ground as if an exciting drama was being played out there. Hamilton finally spoke.

"Well, we had better be going," he said.

"You will let me know when you have something."

"Of course."

10:30 a.m.

Our next stop was the crime scene. LAPD had not cleared the room yet, but we needed permission to enter. Hamilton had made an appointment with the widow for eleven o'clock.

"What are we looking for?" Hamilton asked as I sped up the on-ramp to the freeway. "We searched that room thoroughly, remember? The desk, the bookcase, under the rugs—even the heating vents."

"There were three places we didn't look."

"Three?" He was silent for a moment. "Oh, no, don't tell me you want to take those paintings out of their frames."

"We're talking about a man's life."

"I don't think we're authorized to do that, Sebastian."

"I thought anything to do with your investigation was permissible as long as it was legal."

"Yeah, okay. Do you know anything about that kind of frame? Can we open it and put it back together in a way that is undetectable?"

"Yes."

"You're sure?"

"Quite sure. In fact, I can show you before we do anything and if you don't think it can be done, you can still decide not to open them."

"And you will accept that?"

"Of course."

He turned to me and I could sense his suspicion at my acquiescence. "Then what? You'd break in and check for yourself later?"

"Something like that," I admitted.

"You know you couldn't take that chance. I'd be waiting. You know that, so you wouldn't be fool enough to try. If you did, we'd have you locked up before morning."

"Oh, you wouldn't catch me."

"Bull*shit*," he said, no longer sounding amused. "You always say things like that, but nothing in your background indicates any special skills. It's just smack talk with nothing to back it up."

I did not pursue it. If I said, "You can believe what you want," it would still sound as if I was claiming I could do all these things. "If we don't find anything in or on the paintings, the only other place we have not searched thoroughly is the bookcase."

"We checked the bookcase."

"Not every book."

He blew his breath out. "What do you expect to find?"

"I have no idea."

"Don't tell me, let me guess: we'll know it when we see it."

No idiot he.

Chapter 24

Sunday, January 25, 11:02 a.m.

The Cavanaugh home looked very different in the daylight. Sunshine washed Ashford Avenue this morning and the tops of the trees looked like pistachio ice cream bulging out of graham cracker cones. As we drove along, I thought about archons and Magistines and using portal cards to appear in a person's room to murder him. Such imaginings seemed incongruous in a neighborhood like this.

"Pretty," Hamilton commented as he looked around.

"It is that."

I parked in front of the house. A few moments after we rang the bell, a maid answered.

"LAPD," Hamilton said, showing her his badge. "We have an appointment."

She stepped back, pulling the door with her.

"Thank you," he said

We turned toward the long hallway to the study. As we walked down the corridor, I noticed the splintered door had been removed. When we entered, I looked around. It was not inside.

"Where's the door?"

"We took it. Forensics is having a look."

"Good idea."

We wandered over to the first painting on the left, the Rembrandt. I lifted the right side so I could see the wall behind it and looked for a hook. There it was three-quarters of the way up.

I moved in front and spread my arms, gripped the sides, and grunted as I lifted the heavy frame.

"Are you sure you don't need help?" Hamilton asked.

"I'm sure."

I stepped back, but the wire remained stuck on the hook. I moved forward and lifted a little higher. This time the painting came free.

"Set it over here."

I carried it to where he was standing, set it down gently with the glass front facing us, and leaned it carefully against the desk. I stood back, staring. Even if there had been no signature, I would have known it was a Rembrandt by the distinctive use of light and shadow. I would have been willing to stand there admiring it for a long time if Hamilton hadn't brought me back to reality.

"Well, are we going to open it or not?"

"Hm? Oh, right. We'll have to turn it around to do that."

"Then why did you set it . . ." He stepped in front of me, picked up the frame, and turned it so the back faced us. After he leaned it against the desk, he inspected the rear of the frame. On the right side was a recessed gold key. Above it was a red button. Hamilton pushed the red button. The narrow end of the key popped up. He put his fingertip underneath it and lifted it out of its groove.

On the other side of the frame was a keyhole. Hamilton inserted the key and turned it clockwise. We heard a small click. He pulled and the backing began to swing open.

"That was simple."

"And no one will be able to tell we unlocked it," I said.

He opened the frame until the inside of the case was completely exposed. It was about five centimeters deep. We both leaned forward.

I scanned the interior. I could see nothing but the back of the canvas. Hamilton ran his fingers along the inside edge. I did the same on the right.

"No lever, no button, and it's not thick enough for a secret panel," he said. "Anything?"

"No. This side is smooth."

"Should we pull the canvas out?"

"I don't see why," I said. "We would have seen anything unusual through the glass if something was in front of the painting."

We replaced the Rembrandt and repeated the procedure with the Monet. Nothing. I had removed the da Vinci and set it down carefully when Hamilton, seeing the back, said, "We've got a difference here."

I turned the frame around and saw what he was talking about.

"Where's the key?" he said. "Why is this one different?"

I went down on one knee to scan the backing. Hamilton joined me.

"What are you doing?" Mrs. Cavanaugh stood in the doorway. I felt as if she had caught us stealing her silver set.

"Mrs. Cavanaugh," I said, "we have reason to believe your husband left something behind that will explain why he was murdered."

It sounded weak and I waited for her to tell us to leave the painting alone and get out of her house. Instead she nodded and said, "That sounds like Mason," held a handkerchief to her nose, and walked back down the hallway.

"She's really going through it, isn't she?" Hamilton said with compassion.

"Karen said he was her whole life."

"Yeah. Losing someone you love is one of the worst feelings there is."

"So I've heard. What's this?" I said. I had been searching the outside of the frame, running my hand along it, when I felt a small groove under my fingertips.

Hamilton came over, and we peered at it. It was an almost invisible notch along the right side of the frame.

"Looks like a lever." He scraped it with his fingernail. When that didn't work, he got his nail under it at an awkward angle and jerked. There was a snap, but it wasn't the groove in the frame. "*¡Carajo!*, mutha humpah," he said, shaking his hand.

"Break a nail?"

"Screw you, Sebastian." He stepped away looking at his finger. I leaned down, looked at the groove, and ran my hand over it to feel how far it protruded. Almost not at all.

I got my thumbnail under it anyway and jammed it down and out. The splinter of wood poked all the way under my nail and I saw blood welling, but the lever popped out. I looked at Hamilton, who could see the back.

"Well? Is your pinkie good enough for you to take a look and see if I opened it?"

He had his finger in his mouth, but now he gave me the finger. He checked the frame and pulled the backing.

"Yeah, that's got it."

As soon as he touched the frame, a piece of paper fluttered to the carpet. He picked it up and unfolded it.

"That's great. That's just great," he said. He handed it to me.

Numbers covered the page. All of them had dashes between two- and three-digit numerals. No, not all of them. There were two figures with a dash between them, a space, two numbers separated by a dash, a space, as, 43-169 120-71 376-197. Parsed that way suggested the use of sentences.

"Code," Hamilton said. He sounded unhappy.

I shared his pessimistic attitude. The numbers could refer to anything, although the dual number coupling—and the other contents of Cavanaugh's study—suggested a book, directing the decoder to specific words on indicated pages. That did not help much. The key might be George Orwell's *1984*, or the illustrated version of the *Kama Sutra*.

The more I looked around, the more my eye fell on the bookcase, and the surer I became that the code *was* a book, with the first number in each pairing representing the page, and the second corresponding to the word, counting from the top left. Composing a letter would be laborious, and decoding it would be time-consuming even with the key—but it was unbreakable, unless someone discovered the code book.

There were about sixty or seventy volumes. Would he keep the code right here? Why not? The message was hidden.

"You have an idea?" Hamilton asked.

"I was thinking this code looks like it could be from a manuscript." I explained my interpretation of the double numbers. He looked at the bookcase, too.

"You think Cavanaugh kept the key here?"

"I don't see why not. It's still pretty safe."

"Maybe it's not even a book."

"There's only one way to find out."

"Yeah." He got on the phone, told them what he wanted. "I'm going to have them delivered to your place," he told me, closing his phone. "We can go through them there. I'll clear it with Mrs. Cavanaugh."

"Sounds good."

"You have beer in the house?"

"Yes. Ice-cold."

He looked at the bookcase with an expression of loathing. "Why couldn't he hide his message in a *Playboy* collection?"

Hamilton and I each had a copy of the coded message. We had eaten first, stopping at Fatburger for something to go. Now we were sitting on the floor of my living room with the books stacked all around us and frosty beers close by.

"This is going to be a bitch," he said, picking up a book.

"It shouldn't be too bad. You'll be able to tell in a couple of words whether or not you're building a coherent sentence."

"I suppose."

I didn't say anything about how this might be a complete waste of time. He knew it.

I started with *Paradise Lost*. It only took me five minutes to determine it was not the right book. Ten more books and I shifted onto my back. Ten more and I sat up again.

We took a break after a couple of hours and stood on the patio. I smoked two cigarettes while Hamilton told me everything he had read on lung cancer. We went back inside and flopped down on the carpet again.

I picked up the folio of Dante's *The Divine Comedy*, where I had found the tarot card. No good. Neither were the next twenty. Hamilton was on his left side and I was on my right—our butts were sore from sitting.

I tossed *Wuthering Heights* away and picked up a hardback copy of *The Tomorrow File*. Published in 1975. That did not fit with the rest of the books. I turned it over. A futuristic thriller. I scanned it. Using its pages, the first three words of the code were "a rank amateur." I continued. "A rank amateur holds the key."

"I think I have it," I said to Hamilton.

"Really?"

"I think so. The first line reads, 'A rank amateur holds the key'."

His eyes lit up. "That sounds like the real deal. What's the rest of it say?"

"Better give me an hour or so."

He stood and stretched. "Thank God that's over with," he said. He took his beer onto the patio while I scribbled and searched. He walked between the patio and the kitchen three more times before I finished.

I joined him on the deck after grabbing a beer. "Okay," I said. I handed him the sheet. "There it is."

He took it and read it aloud.

> A rank amateur holds the key.
> No one knows it's there but me.
> To locate, explore the ancient tray.

> Find it before someone takes it away.
> It is a door to other places.
> Watch out or you will see enemy faces.
> Don't let them retrieve it before you do.
> For if they win, we are all through.

"Does that make any sense to you?" he asked.

"No, except it's obvious he's talking about one of our tarot cards and where he hid it."

"Yeah, I got that too. Who's 'them'?"

"The enemy, I guess."

"That's brilliant. Anything else?"

I shrugged. "We don't know enough yet. Who's the rank amateur?"

"You tell me, and we'll both know," he said. "It's useless to us, then."

"For now, yes."

He exhaled, stuffed the paper into his jacket pocket. "Well, what's the next move?"

"More background." We were stuck. There was nothing else to follow up. If we didn't find something soon, the whole thing—whatever it was—might be over before we figured it out. I felt good about one thing: we had proved that Cavanaugh knew what was going on around him. Whatever he left behind should be useful. If he hid a card for us, I wondered where it might lead.

Perhaps to an inescapable trap?

"Can you take me back to the station?" Hamilton asked. "I should file some reports."

"Sure."

We barely spoke on the drive back, each of us lost in our own thoughts. I had just pulled into the Van Nuys PD parking lot when we saw him.

"Is that—"

"Yes, it is," I said, equally astonished.

Standing on the sidewalk in front of the doors leading to the police station was the red-haired man who had attacked me through the Prince of Wands.

Chapter 25

Sunday, January 25, 4:29 p.m.

Hamilton was out of the car before I came to a complete stop. "Put your hands up!" he shouted, drawing his pistol and covering the man. "You're under arrest!" I stopped next to them, jumped out.

The man raised his hands. "What are you arresting me for?"

"Breaking and entering, assault, attempted murder. How's that for starters?"

The man looked at me, his hands now flat on top of his head. "Are you pressing charges, Mr. Montero?" Those strange gray eyes watched me.

He had attacked me, kicked me in the face, and escaped through a magical tarot card, but now he was clearly confident that I would not seek retribution. I put my hand on Hamilton's shoulder.

"Put it away, Steve," I said. "He came here voluntarily."

He lowered his gun but kept his eyes on our mystery man. "Are you sure? Christ, Sebastian, the guy already tried to choke you to death."

"That was a mistake," the man said. "I thought you were someone else." He lowered his hands, leaving his shock of red hair pressed down from being squashed.

"Would you mind coming inside and talking to us?" I asked him.

"That's why I'm here."

Hamilton holstered his piece. "Let's go, then." He led the way into the station, the slanting rays of the setting sun filling the lobby.

"Okay, let's hear it."

We were seated around a rectangular table in an interview room. Hamilton sat at the head, and my attacker and I sat on opposite sides. A tape recorder captured our conversation.

"First of all, I would like to apologize to Mr. Montero for assaulting him in his home. I made a grievous error."

"Think nothing of it," I said. He was still looking at me with some puzzlement in his eyes. I knew he was wondering why I showed no signs of a broken nose.

"Why don't we start with your name?" Hamilton asked. The man was consistent.

"Erol Diacos," he said, spelling it.

"And exactly what were you looking for when you, uh, traveled to Mr. Montero's house?"

"A man."

"Who?"

"A criminal."

"What's his name?"

"I can't reveal that just yet," Diacos said.

Hamilton threw up his hands. "Of course not. Why did I even ask? Look. You tell me this man is a criminal, you apparently know who he is, and yet you won't reveal it to a sworn officer of the law. You know that's obstruction?"

"And possibly even an accessory after the fact," Diacos said, smiling.

"That's right." Hamilton said this last in a descending voice. "Listen, smart guy, I don't need you to build my case for me. Maybe twenty-four hours in the tank will change your mind about your buddy's name."

I saw the subtle change in Diacos's face. I realized Hamilton had just insulted him, and he was going to launch himself over the table. I was getting ready for it when I saw his muscles relax. "Do not call that man my buddy, detective. And you could not hold me for very long."

"Oh, we'll take any cards you may have before we incarcerate you," I said.

"I know."

It was my turn to be puzzled. "Then how do you think you'll escape?"

"I am not at liberty to tell—"

"Christ!" Hamilton shouted. "The next person who says that gets a mouthful of my right shoe!"

There was a knock on the door, and Gonzales stuck his head in. "Got the report from ballistics. Pitbull was shot with the same gun that popped Cavanaugh, a .44 mag." He ducked back out.

"So we know our shooter is the same man we saw at BioLaw," Hamilton said.

"Yes." I focused on Diacos. "And you state you know this man but are unwilling to give us his name. So what *can* you tell us? You did come here to tell us something?"

"Yes. The two of you are in very great danger. The forces around you now are in conflict and it would be unwise to be in the middle of that."

"Are you warning us?" Hamilton said.

"If that will motivate you to stay out of the way, you may take it like that."

"We may take it like that?" Hamilton looked at me and laughed. "Get this guy." He stood and leaned toward Diacos. "You're not auditioning for a comedy routine here, so you can save the funny remarks. If I don't get answers to questions—real answers—you will be a guest of the city of Los Angeles for the next few days."

"I do have more information for you," Diacos replied, seemingly unperturbed, "but it will not answer all of your questions."

Hamilton glanced at me. I shrugged. He sat back down. The tape recorder popped as it came to the end of the first side.

Hamilton was reaching for it when Diacos said, "Don't turn that back on, please."

"What? Of course I'm going to tape you."

"Steve," I said, "let it go. I'm sure Mr. Diacos will feel more at liberty to share sensitive information with us if we don't record it."

Diacos inclined his head in my direction.

Hamilton pulled his hand back. "Fine." He pointed at Diacos. "But if you say that sentence again, well, you've been warned."

"Fair enough. I am a descendant of an ancient dead culture. I am currently attempting to stop a plot constructed by members of an evil faction of this same society."

"With all of you people running around," Hamilton said, "it does not sound like a dead culture to me."

"Our ancestral home is gone, burned to the ground in a heinous act of genocide. Our teachings, our documents, *our past*, were erased in an afternoon. And the people for whom I am searching are part of the group that brought the neighboring towns down on my ancestors."

"And what was the name of your town?" I asked, knowing the answer.

"Magisty."

Chapter 26

Sunday, January 25, 5:06 p.m.

"Magisty?" Hamilton looked at me. "Isn't that the one you told us was wiped out hundreds of years ago?"

"Yes," I answered.

Diacos and I stared at each other. He had pale skin with high cheekbones and a sculpted nose. His gray eyes startled. A smattering of freckles crossed the top of his nose and cheeks, but they were hard to see as he had a mild sunburn. He was the same height as me, but his shoulders were wider. I already knew how strong a fighter he was and that he was probably in awesome physical condition. He sat erect, and I noticed he kept his hands in his lap, even when talking. The overall effect gave him an air of sophisticated elegance, in spite of that unruly red hair.

"So you're saying these other people are also from Magisty?" Hamilton asked him.

"Their ancestors were, yes."

"Do you know the whole story? Everybody today thinks you people are extinct."

"I doubt that. However, we are a tiny group of survivors. Our forebears happened to be traveling far away when our village was destroyed."

"How many people was this?" I asked.

"Four couples."

After five hundred years, that could have mushroomed into a big family picnic. Let's say each couple had two children. And then their kids had two . . .

"And how many exist today?"

"Less than a hundred."

"Why so few?" I asked.

"Not everybody worried about carrying on the tradition."

I understood that. I had kept few mementos from my travels and did my best to live my life as if I had no past.

"How many people are involved in Cavanaugh's death?" Hamilton asked.

"Two."

"Exactly? How do you know?"

"Because I have been trying to catch them for most of my adult life."

"And what will you do when you catch them?" I asked.

He glanced at Hamilton. "I would prefer not to say."

"Buddy, that was close," Hamilton said. "Do you know where they are now?"

"No."

"Then what's your next step?" I asked.

"Actually, I wanted to talk to you alone, Mr. Montero, but I did not think it wise to come through the card again. I didn't think you would give me a chance to explain."

Hamilton made a derisive sound. "I would have popped a cap in your ass on general principles."

"Yes." Diacos continued looking at me.

"Where did you want to go?" I asked him.

"Your place."

I turned to Hamilton. I could see he did not like this. But he knew that if I could get something out of Diacos, it would be worth it if it helped us solve the case. For all his threats, he knew he couldn't hold the man legally if I was not pressing charges.

"Fine," he said. "Give me a call later?"

"You got it," I told him.

Diacos and I did not talk much on the drive. I learned his parents still lived in Turkey. He was unmarried but had a girlfriend in Istanbul.

I pulled into my private drive and parked the car in the garage.

I made a lot of noise as I was opening the back door, letting Aliena know we were coming. Vampires don't oversleep and it had been half an hour since sunset. I did not want to walk in on her unannounced.

I led the way, threw my keys on the foyer table, and got us both a bottle of water. Aliena was nowhere in sight, so I concluded she must have gone out. Crossing the living room, I noted that Hector had replaced my broken table with the one I had purchased from Karen Cavanaugh. I pressed the button that opened the patio doors.

"Now then, Mr. Diacos," I said, turning, "what can—"

He stood next to a club chair, his feet slightly apart. He pointed a Sig Sauer 9 millimeter. "Who are you, really?"

"Do you think you can get answers from me by threatening me with a gun?"

"My friend, I had better or I will give you a new meaning for pain."

"I seriously doubt that."

"Why isn't your face bruised? How come you don't have a broken nose?"

"Not sure what you mean."

He thumbed the safety off.

"I will give you one more chance. How is it you show no signs of my having kicked you in the face yesterday?"

"Sorry. I am not at liberty to disclose that."

He shot me in the right leg and popped one into my left as well, both shots just above the knees. I went down hard, gasping at the immediate pain. The water bottles fell from my hands and rolled away.

"Wrong answer," he said. "The next one you get in the chest. And after that, one in the head. Answer my question."

"Okay," I said. "I'm from Jupiter and sort of like Superman when I'm on this planet."

The next shot pierced a lung. My body sagged.

"Try, try again," he said.

It was hard to talk now, but I forced it out. "Okay. I'm the last survivor of Teotihuacan, and I have magical vodka from the Gods."

As promised, the next shot was to my temple. My head jerked, and I landed on my back, turned to the side, my eyes staring at the north corner of my patio.

A familiar smell. What was that from? It was something good, I knew, but I couldn't quite catch hold of it. James? Momma?

Something smacked my face.

"Hey, Montero, you in there? You can get up now."

I lay still. I could tell Diacos loomed over me, apparently smoking one of my special cigarettes. He poked me in the stomach. "Come out to play, Sebastian."

What the hell? There was no doubt about it. He knew about me. I opened my eyes.

"Turkish tobacco," he said approvingly. "It's like being home." He held his hand out. I took it and he pulled me up. He stared at my wounds as they began to close. "Amazing. Sorry about that, but I had to know."

"I understand," I said. I turned quickly and kneed him in his secret sack. He made a very soft whistling sound before crash-landing in front of my fireplace. I picked up his dropped cigarette and crushed it in the ashtray.

"Thank you for not hitting my new table," I told him. I leaned over, patted him down, pulled his wallet and a tarot card out of his inside jacket pocket. The Emperor. A star card. His pistol was in a shoulder holster. Relieving him of it, I set it with the wallet and the archon on the coffee table. "I have to change. You owe me for the shirt and trousers." The patch of blood near the patio window caught my eye. "You have made a mess of my carpet. I'd like to talk to you about that. Would you mind staying for a while?"

I took his wheezing as agreement.

I ran upstairs and changed quickly into a white shirt and a dark blue pair of slacks and took the jacket off the hangar. Walking downstairs, I tossed it over the arm of the couch and got a bottle of vodka out of the freezer. As I set it on the table, I plucked a cigarette from the silver case and lit it. I took a puff, looked at the feebly moving pile of clothes on the carpet, leaned back on the couch, and exhaled.

He grunted a few times.

While waiting for him to recover, I unscrewed the bottle's cap, took a long drink, puffed a couple of times, took another long swig.

Groaning sounds now. That was good. It would only be a couple of minutes more. I finished the vodka and relaxed into my two-minute buzz.

I was leaning forward to stub out my cigarette when he sat up slowly.

"That wasn't fair," he said, his voice hoarse. "I didn't hurt you as much."

"Mr. Diacos. You are lucky you are not dead. In fact, I am still not certain that I will allow you to leave."

"Why not?"

"Who do you think you are, sir? You come into my home and shoot me four times?"

"I knew it wouldn't hurt you."

"Did you now? And did it occur to you that once I realized you knew my secret, I might decide the safest course would be to eliminate you?"

He had struggled to his knees. He stood shakily and limped to the chair in front of the fireplace, sitting down on it gingerly. "I thought of that, yes."

"And?"

"And I decided you would not kill so indiscriminately. It would go against your ethics."

"Don't be so sure."

"According to you, I am betting my life on it." He looked at the empty vodka bottle. "Is there more where that came from?"

I watched him for a moment, then went to the kitchen and got another bottle after tossing the old one in the recycle can. I unscrewed the cap as I was walking back, and handed Diacos the bottle.

"*Teşekkür ederim*," he said, and took a long drink.

"*Bur şey degil*," I told him. You're welcome.

He took another sip and set the bottle on the table. He touched his crotch tentatively. "Don't ever do that again. I thought I was a lifetime soprano."

"No promises. And that was a payback for yesterday." I nodded at him. "We're alone."

"Very well." He looked at his wallet and tarot card. "How much do you know about the cards?"

"Not much. I had never seen one before Cavanaugh's murder."

He nodded. "I hold a star card from the Tarot of the Archons." He gestured at the card and his effects with his eyebrows raised. I nodded, and he replaced them in his pockets, slid his gun into the holster. "My father passed it on to me, just as his father had given it to him. That was when I learned more about the background of my people. And the existence of our enemies."

"You said you know who killed Cavanaugh."

"I do."

I powered my computer and called up the file of the first man's face on the Prince. I turned the display to Diacos. "Is this him?"

"Yes. Detrit Bork."

"You said there were two of them."

"This man is muscle only. The other is the truly dangerous one. It is her I seek."

"Her?"

He was about to answer when we heard the click of the front door. Aliena walked in. Her gaze fell immediately on the blood patch, and she looked sharply at Diacos, then at me.

"So," she said. "You have found one of them."

Chapter 27

Sunday, January 25, 6:11 p.m.

Both Diacos and I had risen as soon as Aliena entered. She closed the door softly and walked over to us.

"Actually, he found me," I told her. "Aliena, Erol Diacos."

"Charmed," Diacos said, kissing her hand. He looked at her closely. "I have seen your picture. A portal imprint my grandfather saved. He thought you the most beautiful woman he had ever seen." Now his forehead creased as his eyes narrowed. "But that was more than a hundred years ago. You are another immortal?"

Aliena had eaten, so she appeared human. She did not answer his question, only stared at him. I suspected she was deciding whether or not to kill Diacos for knowing her secret. I turned out to be wrong about that.

"You are a star card holder?" she asked.

He nodded.

"How many other cardholders do you know?"

"How many do you know?"

She crossed her arms over her chest and leaned on one hip. She had that look on her face. *Now* I knew she was deciding whether or not to kill him.

Diacos glanced at me. "Since you have a friend who is a cardholder, you must know all about the Deck of the Cosmos."

"No, I don't."

He nodded. "Good. She shouldn't tell you anything. It is nobody else's business."

"A man has been killed."

"True. And I will exact retribution on his behalf."

"Sorry. I can't leave this up to you. The question is do we work together or independently?"

He considered. He glanced at Aliena. "Together," he said. "But I will direct the action."

"Under very strict guidance," said a voice from the patio. Marcus walked into the room. He nodded at me, smiled at Aliena. The smile vanished as he turned to Diacos. "How do we know you're not one of the villains?"

"Actually, there is no way to know that."

"Exactly. If we work together, we will choose our direction together."

"That is hardly what I meant."

"I know. I am offering nothing else."

Diacos turned to me.

"I am afraid I agree with Marcus," I told him. "I've known you for two hours. And nobody in this room is used to following any directions but their own."

He nodded. "Will you consider my suggestions very seriously? I know more about this than you do."

"Of course we will," Aliena said.

We were all standing in my living room, and I wanted a cigarette. I turned on my outdoor light and gestured at the patio. "Let's talk out here."

They all moved outside. I lit a cigarette and joined them. Aliena sat in a chair facing the ocean. Marcus stood to her left, Diacos to her right. I walked between them and sat on the wall facing her.

"The more I learn about these cards, the less I want one."

"Unfortunately, you have one," Diacos said. "It's not a star card, but it is valuable. And others will try to take it from you."

"Why?"

He looked at Aliena and Marcus before answering. "It is one of four cards—all the Princes are the same—that cannot be planted but is rather a free-floating card."

"What's the advantage to that?" I asked. Marcus hadn't told me that.

"Normally, there isn't one. For one thing, they don't disappear. But they can do something the other cards cannot."

"I already figured that part out." Marcus had told me earlier. Would Diacos have the same story?

"Yes, of course. The Prince cards can be set to take you back to your point of origin in a specified period of time."

"How?"

"If you know the right words, you activate a timer. Nobody is sure what the time limit is. When the time is up, you come back to your original location immediately."

"No matter where you are?"

"Correct."

"What if you don't have the card with you?" I asked.

"That doesn't matter. You can't travel with a minor anyway. And in the case of the Prince, you would want it to remain in a safe place."

"I don't understand. If you can't travel through the Prince, how does it identify the people it's supposed to bring back?"

"Before journeying, you touch a star card to it after setting the timer. The Prince will return anyone who steps through the portal."

"Yes, of course." My annoyance stemmed from the natural pique one might experience when recognizing that everyone in his group knows something he does not. I felt like an outsider whenever these infernal cards became the focus of our investigation.

"He has identified the Magistine in our Prince picture," I told the two vampires, then turned back to Diacos. "Do you know anything else about this Mr. Bork?"

"Yes. Sociopath. Extremely dangerous. But he does not possess a high level of sound control. He's a bit dim—Salomé only uses him for violence. If we could get close enough to him, we could kill him. But that's the trick. Anybody who gets too close to this man ends up dead."

I took a final drag off my cigarette, stood, and crushed it in the ashtray. I walked back to the wall but remained standing.

"Who is Salomé?" Aliena asked.

"The Queen of a Magistine coven," Diacos answered. "Two people from her ancestral group survived the massacre. She and your long-haired man, Mr. Bork, are their descendants."

"You think Bork killed Cavanaugh?" I asked.

"Yes."

"Was he after the Prince of Wands?"

"That and the box Cavanaugh was holding in his store."

"How did Salomé know?" Aliena asked.

"She has powers taught to her by her family, just as my family taught me. She is a formidable enemy."

"Do you know what was in the box?" I asked.

"Of course. Archons. Salomé had Bork break in and steal them."

I had already theorized that as the most likely answer.

"This is my first time meeting a vampire," he said to Marcus. "It is an honor." Although Diacos could not tell Aliena was a vampire, Marcus had not eaten so could not hide the preternatural sheen of his perfect, unblemished skin.

"It will not be an honor if I decide to kill you," Marcus told him.

"You don't worry me," Diacos said. "You cannot harm me."

Marcus raised an eyebrow. "Indeed? You are a normal mortal. How would you stop me from taking you?" As he said this, he began to walk toward the Magistine.

Diacos spoke a word, too low for me to hear.

I was the closest to him and suddenly felt a blast of extreme heat. I instinctively recoiled from it and stepped to my left a couple of paces until it was cool again.

Marcus apparently felt it, too. He stopped approximately the same distance I had been from Diacos, so I knew it was hot where he was. He closed his eyes and lifted his arm in front of him. He jerked his hand back. He opened his eyes and retreated slowly, a small smile on his face. He inclined his head. "Very impressive."

I knew that if Marcus ever decided to kill him, he would use his vampiric speed to get close. Diacos would never see him coming and would be dead before he identified his killer. I also understood why the vampire was keeping that fact to himself.

"Merely a social bubble," Diacos said. "No living creature will move toward intense heat, not even the largest predators. And if anything stayed close to me for more than a few seconds, it would suffer the same injuries as if it had caught on fire."

"How do you produce this heat?" Aliena asked.

"Focused articulation. I tap into the energy around me. Some call this energy mana. Others simply call it the life force. It exists everywhere, all around us, even in that rock." He pointed at a pebble on the patio. "If you know the proper sounds and how to say them, you can manipulate these forces to great advantage. Most people cannot learn it because it takes complete relaxation combined with concentration. It's a sort of nonchalant deliberation, as illogical as that sounds."

I glanced at Aliena. I could see the reaction on her face. Diacos's description of his procedure sounded similar to what Maman said she did in order to "hear" the tarot cards.

"Do you become an empty vessel to do this?" I asked.

"Something like that," Diacos replied. "You know of this?"

"A little. I know the forces can be used for many different things. I also know achieving the proper mental state to use that energy takes years of practice and dedication, even if one has a natural aptitude for it."

"Many years."

"What about your tattoo?" Marcus asked.

"It is on the back of my head and cannot be seen as long as I have hair."

Considering he was a Magistine, that seemed like a good idea.

"Do you know of any other Magistines?" I asked.

"Forgive me, but for the time being, I cannot disclose some information. If events should transpire that convince me you need to know, I will tell you."

"I do not like that arrangement," Marcus said.

"I assure you, sir, that the number of Magistines in circulation is not relevant to this matter. There are only two other people involved in this."

"And what is 'this'?" Aliena asked.

"I believe it is their plan to resurrect eleven men and women who were massacred five centuries ago."

"With the two of them, that makes thirteen," she said.

"Yes."

"Is that significant?" I asked.

"A coven is thirteen," Aliena answered, "with a queen at its head. The number is sacred because it relates to the thirteen lunar cycles each year."

"And women have always been associated with the moon," Diacos added.

She nodded. "It is the symbol of the Great Goddess. The Queen is also the thirteenth card of her suit in a tarot deck."

I was still confused. "What do they want with the cards? How does that help them revive their people?" I looked from Marcus to Aliena. Marcus looked distant. Aliena remained silent also. Diacos answered.

"Card combinations," he said. "Having certain archons together gives them specific powers. Very formidable powers."

I should have thought of that. Still, this time I was irritated with Aliena and, to a lesser degree, Marcus. If they did not want to tell me such things before this case, I understood. To withhold it from me now was not very helpful. I was beginning to like Erol Diacos. Strange, considering the circumstances of our first meeting.

"Do you know which cards they need to accomplish this?" I asked him.

"I think so," he said. "The seven cards are the Empress, which is Salomé's card, and she also has the Fool. The Sun, the Four of Pentacles, and the Nine of Cups were in the box stolen from Cavanaugh's by Bork. The last two are the Queen of Swords and the Six of Cups. And if I am right, these last are the only two cards left that they need to acquire."

Two cards. Then the world would have a coven of dangerous Magistines scouring the earth for more archons, combining them, and gaining greater and greater powers over the years.

And with Cavanaugh's murder, they had proven they would kill anyone who stood in their way.

"Do you have a plan for stopping them?"

"Not really," he said. "It is essential we think of something, though. Salomé is from a family that is very bad news. They dabbled in soundcraft in ways they should not have, and other people became fearful of them. And Salomé is not known for her kindness. She would be the worst person to have the power these cards could give."

"And she is nearly there," Aliena said.

"Yes."

"You three are all cardholders," I said. "What about combining the major and minor cards you have?"

Diacos shook his head. "I suppose it's possible we possess a magical combination but extremely unlikely."

Marcus watched Diacos with a smile on his face. It appeared he had warmed to the Magistine. Still, he did not volunteer which cards he held. Neither did Diacos or Aliena.

"Do you have any suggestions on how to proceed?" I asked Diacos.

"There is someone we need to question," he replied.

"Who?"

"Kismet."

I heard a startled inhale from Aliena. Marcus nodded.

Diacos said to Aliena, "You know her? How?" Aliena watched him silently.

"It appears I am the only one who doesn't know anything," I said. Again.

"She's a seer."

I glanced at Aliena. She looked at the floor and unless my eyes were deceiving me, she was blushing.

I turned to Marcus and raised my eyebrows.

"I have met her," he said. "She is very youthful and has . . . a bubbly personality."

Aliena gave him a nasty look.

"I can call her now," Diacos said. "We should be able to meet with her right away. She loves evening visitors."

"Would somebody just answer the question," I asked, weary of the unspoken something. "What else?"

Marcus said, "She's a mermaid."

That caught me off guard. The only thing I could ask was the one interesting fact I had read about merpeople. "Does that mean she's immortal?"

"Yes," Marcus said.

"Which star card does she hold?"

Aliena answered that one, in a low voice. "The Lovers."

Chapter 28

Sunday, January 25, 9:51 p.m.

I prepared for my first journey through a star card. Aliena and Diacos wanted to arrive at Kismet's home in as short a time as possible and traveling through a star card made the journey instantaneous. And, they assured me, it was safer than any other mode of transportation.

"What if you walk into a dangerous situation?" I asked.

"Technically," Diacos said, "that would happen upon reaching the destination and therefore would not be part of the journey."

"You're right. That is a technicality."

We had decided to use the Prince as our return portal. Diacos knew how to activate it.

"Do you know how to set the timer as well?" Aliena asked.

"Yes."

"What do you think?" she said, including me in the conversation with a flick of her eyes. "For our purposes, does fifteen minutes sound like a reasonable amount of time?"

"Are we in a hurry?"

She didn't answer.

"Fifteen sounds fine to me," Diacos said.

"Okay," I said. I turned to Marcus. "Would you remain here until we get back?"

"Certainly."

"Then let's see what a mermaid looks like."

I traveled with Aliena. Before we left, I remembered she had not told me the meaning of the Moon card.

"The Moon represents the Great Goddess—and this was long before anyone had the idea of a male supreme being. Even after Christianity began to spread, women prayed not to God but to the moon when they wanted something."

"Is it a good card or a bad one to see in a reading?" I asked.

"It has always been feared because of the two dogs on the card."

"Why?"

"The dogs are howling, and people believed that dogs could see the approach of the Grim Reaper."

"Are you saying your card is a portent of death?"

"Yes."

"And you love that, don't you?" I said. "If we are traveling to Kismet's place, that means you both know how to activate one of her portal cards."

"That's right," Diacos said.

"Are you ready?" Aliena asked him.

"Yes."

He held the Prince to his lips and spoke. The gold border lit up and stayed on. Diacos touched his star card to it and so did Aliena. The card returned to its normal appearance and he set it on the ground.

"The Prince now recognizes our cards," Aliena told me, "and will return anyone to this spot who steps through them."

Diacos nodded. He held his Emperor card to his mouth and in a moment it began to expand. When it was tall enough, he stepped through, and the portal closed behind him.

Moments after Diacos disappeared with a crackle, Aliena held her card close and uttered a sound too low for me to hear. The gold border pulsed twice, and the moon began to move away from the dogs. Now it was as big as a doorway.

"Come, Sebastian," Aliena said, holding out her hand. I took it, and we stepped through.

If you have ever been in a very hot place, some buildings will have a strong fan over the entrance that activates when the door is opened. Whether coming or going, you pass through a barrier of air blasting from above. It is an effective way to keep bugs out and air conditioning in.

That is what it felt like to travel through a star card: an intense downdraft accompanied by a hurricane-like whoosh and a flash of icy coldness.

I kept my eyes open and watched carefully as I stepped into the void, but the journey was so fast, I only had an afterimage on my retina before we were emerging in a large vestibule. The image was clear, though. It was the black emptiness of space with the stars in the background. I believe that for a microsecond, our bodies *had* been in space during our jaunt.

Kismet's house (I learned later she calls it a hydro mansion) was beautifully lit, with colorful bulbs in recessed fixtures that caused the water to glow. I looked around for the portal card on this end. It lay on the floor, flush with the surface. Planted. Since two major cards were near, the portal shone, visible to all: the Seven of Cups.

"I welcome you," Kismet said. Her voice came from the left. We could not see her. "Please remove your shoes before coming in."

I stood on tile made of pastel seashells that formed an ocean mosaic of a whale's fluke above moonlit water. This foyer led to one of the most elegant rooms I have ever beheld. I looked around as I unlaced my shoes.

The decor was eighteenth-century French rococo, with standing sculptures, large looking glasses, and original Chippendale furniture. The ceiling had gracefully curved corners and soared at least five meters above our heads. A chandelier sparkled above an oak dining set. White walls with gold trim and gold-upholstered overstuffed chairs completed the appearance of an eighteenth-century European drawing room. Jade-green velvet drapes were pulled back from the tall picture windows, and I could see twinkling city lights below in the distance.

The floor consisted of clear glass with sapphire-blue water rippling beneath it. The furniture seemed to float above the waves.

There were several places in the room where there was no floor but rather running water. Near the far windows, the wall did not continue into the water. It was obvious that one need only dive under the surface briefly to come up in the pool outside the house.

In the opposite direction, there were three shimmering liquid channels that led to the rest of the house. The place had an enchanted aura and to find a mermaid amid such decoration seemed perfectly natural.

As if on cue, Kismet appeared, swimming in one of the channels. She looked normal from this angle, although she was swimming noticeably upright, with her entire torso above the surface. She raised an arm to Diacos in greeting. Then she gave a small cry.

"Allie!"

Four long padded lounge chairs sat on either side of the waterway. Kismet sped toward a red velvet one on our side. With a powerful move, she lifted out of the water in a very nonhuman way and slid onto the long chair. She had used too much speed, though, and shot across the upholstered surface. As she crested the back of the chair, her eyes widened.

"Uh-oh," she said. She went over the top and off, and she would have hit the floor hard, but Aliena moved there quickly. She caught the mermaid and set her on the lounge.

"You should be more careful."

"I just got excited," Kismet said in a girlish voice. She twisted so she was facing us. "Oh, I must look a sight." She patted her hair and then stopped with her hand on her head. She stared at Aliena, a smile of delight on her face. She didn't appear to notice I was there, so I got a long look at this magnificent creature.

She reclined on the overstuffed chair and was wearing a tiny pink string bikini. Turned sideways to us, her curves were easy to see. Her bare skin looked café au lait and silky smooth. She had long, wavy black hair that tumbled over her shoulders to the tops of her breasts. Her eyes were mesmerizing, large and blue-gray, exotically slanted.

Her tan thighs slowly melded to buttery golden scales at the knees. The fluke of her tail was the same shape as a whale's. It hung over the edge of the chair, in the water, swaying forward and back slowly.

Aliena and the mermaid still faced each other. Kismet's lips parted and she put her arm around Aliena's neck. To my astonishment, Aliena leaned down and they kissed lingeringly. Her hand brushed Kismet's hair as the mermaid's arm tightened on her. I heard a splash as Kismet's fluke flipped up and down.

What the?

When they broke apart, Kismet said, "I have missed you, Allie. So much."

Aliena nodded and straightened up. I felt a bolt of jealousy when I saw her lips glistening.

The two of them stared at each other for a few more moments. I've been around for a long time, and I recognized the look they shared, difficult as it was for me to believe. These two had been lovers in the past. The gorgeous vampire and the stunning mermaid? My mind conjured an extraordinarily erotic image of the two of them together. Then I deduced the meaning of what I had just heard Kismet say in the tone she had used.

This breathtaking creature was still in love with Aliena.

Chapter 29

Sunday, January 25, 10:12 p.m.

"Kismet," Aliena said, reaching back and pulling me forward by the arm. "This is Sebastian."

Those slanted blue-gray eyes focused on me, and I felt the irresistible magnetism she exuded. She projected sexuality but much more: she was the most feminine woman I had ever met. Seeing her up close made it easy to believe that she would be attractive to women as well as to men. She had a vulnerable innocence that contradicted a body made for sinful pleasures. It was a powerfully attractive combination.

The Lovers certainly seemed the appropriate card for her.

"A pleasure," she said, holding out her hand. I kissed her knuckles. When I straightened up, she studied me—the way a general surveys the field before a skirmish. "So you are the one."

"The one what?"

"That Aliena has chosen."

"I certainly hope so," I said.

The exotic eyes blazed briefly with hot jealousy. The depth of her passion and the strength of her love impressed me. She and Aliena had had more than a casual affair.

Then her gaze was off me, and her attention shifted to Diacos. He stepped toward her.

"You look wonderful, as you always do," he said. She smiled at him and raised her hand. He took it, bowed, and kissed her. I noticed her skin gleamed very dark against his. Apparently immortal women didn't worry about wrinkles from deep, natural tans. I never have.

"Did you say you wanted a reading, Erol?" Kismet's voice sounded distracted. She continued to glance at Aliena and I knew she wished they could be alone.

"Yes."

"Hm? Oh, of course. Please," she said, gesturing. A couch and a chair were right behind us, so the three of us sat.

"You said you wanted me to find something for you. What are you looking for?"

Diacos leaned back and crossed his legs. "Who, actually. I would like to know where to find Detrit Bork."

"Bork?" The mermaid's fluke twitched in the water. "What do you want with that fiend?"

"We would like to call on him. Unannounced."

Diacos watched her with glittering eyes. I knew he was a very strong fighter, but the man who had appeared at BioLaw had been huge.

Kismet's fluke swished languidly in the water. There was something in her expression as she gazed at Diacos that I could not decipher. "Anybody close to Bork when he doesn't want them there ends up dead or missing," she said.

"Yes, I know."

Another mermaid appeared from the back of the house, swimming toward us in the main channel. She held a tray with drinks, and with red hair and green eyes she was as beautiful as Kismet. Diacos stood immediately and went to her.

"Hello Echo, nice to see you." He leaned over and accepted the proffered tray. "May I call on you later tonight?"

Echo looked at Diacos with interest. "I have told you no three times, yet you continue to ask me. Why?"

"I keep hoping you will change your mind and agree."

Echo looked puzzled. "But I will not change. You are a nice man, but you are not attractive to me." She spoke as if to a slow but well-meaning child.

Diacos straightened up. "I see."

"Now," Echo said, turning her gaze to me, "if you looked like this man, I would certainly accept." She stared into my eyes, her torso bobbing in the water, a lascivious smile on her face. I saw the fluke of her tail break the water behind her. She wiggled it seductively when she saw me look at it.

"Echo," Kismet said, "this is Sebastian, Aliena's boyfriend."

The smile turned off and the fluke submerged. "Oh. Hi, Aliena."

"Hello, Echo."

"Nice to see you," the mermaid said, and she immediately turned and swam away.

Aliena did not reply, looking stiffly at Echo's retreating back. She turned on me angrily.

"What?" I said.

"You encourage it. Somehow."

"You're imagining things," I said.

Her eyes had not yet softened, and she added, "If you *are* doing something irresistible to women, stop it."

"I'm not, but I will try to rein in my natural charm."

Diacos came back and set the tray on a low table. We each took a cool, dripping glass, with the exception of Aliena. It did not have a familiar taste but it was tart and sweet. Kismet saw my face.

"It's sharkade. My own recipe."

"Delicious."

"You look well, Kiz," Aliena said, and the mermaid turned to her.

"It is so nice to hear your voice again, Allie." She took a sip from her glass, spilled some onto her chest. "Oh, Triton's beard," she said, brushing at the drops. "You would think I was just out of the shell."

"Do you think you can locate Bork for us?" Diacos asked.

"I still think it's unwise."

"I would place only myself in danger, but Aliena and Sebastian are determined to accompany me."

"Is that true?"

"Yes," I said. "He is wanted for murder by the LA police."

She stared at Aliena adoringly. "Do you know about this man Bork?"

"Yes."

"He is one of the most violent men in history. He has powerful weapons, including the kind that can hurt even you."

"I am quite capable of bringing my own violence to the party," Aliena said. "If this man Bork hurts anyone important to me, I will make him suffer. Kiz, we really do need to find him quickly."

"Very well. I never could talk you out of something once you had made up your mind."

I knew about that, too.

Kismet set her glass on the table, too close to the edge. It began to tumble off, but Aliena caught it before it could fall.

"Oh! Thank you, dear."

Now I had the answer to the question about why the relationship between Aliena and Kismet worked. In spite of her abundant female qualities, Aliena represented the traditionally male side of a couple: independent, aggressive, aloof. Kismet not only represented the female side, she was the embodiment of it.

Both were alluring in their own way, but my choice would always be a strong woman like Aliena. Girly women—no matter how beautiful—usually end up boring me. Although, I had to admit that a weekend with Kismet would be unforgettable.. Hm. And since she and Aliena had already been lovers, maybe the three of us . . . I decided uttering such a suggestion would probably end in broken bones.

Kismet slid back into the water and swam to the other side. She wore a thong, and her naked, sun-browned behind jutted above the water, spectacular. Aliena saw me looking and elbowed me in the ribs.

The mermaid pulled a small bag out of an ornate wooden chest of drawers and began to swim back with it. The bag slipped out of her hand and disappeared under the surf quickly. She put her hands on her hips as she looked into the water.

"Oh, for Triton's sake! Now I have to get my hair wet," she said, clearly unhappy. She dove down and came up with the bag.

Using her powerful tail to lift her onto the lounge again, she came up in a spray of water. She judged her speed correctly this time. She set the bag on the table with our drinks and ran her hands through her hair.

"I must look just awful," she said. Hardly. Her wet skin glistened with health and the drops flowing off her body were hypnotic. Her pink bikini had become transparent in strategic places, and her unconscious sexuality filled the room. I noticed her tail went from gold to pink to purple and back to gold as she moved it in the lit water. I wondered what it would feel like to run my hand over it.

She pulled the top of the bag open and shook the contents into her hand. About twenty-five or thirty multicolored miniseashells spilled onto her palm, glinting in the soft light.

She made a fist and held it out to Diacos.

"Give them your energy and think about Bork."

He leaned over the glass table and clasped both hands over Kismet's closed one. They shut their eyes for a moment. Then Diacos removed his hands and sat back.

Kismet glanced at the shells in her hand. She tossed them into the air. She threw them so high, I was sure they would not stay on the table when they came down. With a clatter, they landed like metal snowflakes and not one fell to the floor.

Kismet passed her right hand, palm down, over the shells, her eyes lidded. She made a low, enchanting musical sound and drew her hand back. Now she looked at the arrangement before her.

She reached out and touched her fingertip to a blue shell that had come to rest in the middle of the table. That shell and six others around it began blinking, rising off the table.

"You have an unknown enemy," Kismet said.

Why did that have to be the first thing she saw? This reading was not starting out so great. Our known enemies seemed formidable enough. Why couldn't the shells say we had an unknown friend?

These seven levitating shells, apparently having completed their task, floated away from the table and into their bag.

Kismet extended her finger toward a yellow shell that sat by itself, partially hanging over the edge. When she touched it, the shell lifted into the air, began shaking violently, and exploded into tiny particles. The pieces floated for a few seconds, then pulled together as if magnetically attracted and reconstituted themselves into a single shell. The repaired piece floated into the bag.

"What does that mean?" I asked. Nobody needed to tell me it was bad. I got that part.

Kismet searched our faces. "It means one of you will die. Very soon."

The four of us sat motionless for a few moments, lit from below by the shimmering blue water under the floor.

"You don't know which of us it is to be?" Diacos asked.

"No, I can't see that."

I didn't look at Diacos, but I thought he was the most likely candidate of the three of us. That did not make me feel any better, since I was not absolutely sure I was right. I took Aliena's hand and she squeezed it.

Kismet looked at another grouping of shells to her left. She leaned forward and pressed a purple one near the middle. At once ten shells lifted off the table, blinking rapidly, and began to spin counterclockwise.

Aliena said, "Doesn't that mean we will be successful at our task?"

"Yes," Kismet answered, with a reluctant note in her voice. "You should have become my apprentice, Allie—you're so in tune with nature."

"Thank you," Aliena said quietly, and the two of them shared a lover's look. It was obvious Aliena still cherished Kismet. For some reason, though, she had been the one to end the sexual side of the relationship, I felt sure. It seemed clear to me Kismet had not wanted the separation and still wanted Aliena back.

"What about Bork?" Diacos said.

Kismet scanned the remaining shells. "Here we are." She tapped a blue shell, and it rose into the air, blinking slowly and appearing to tremble. "You do not need to look for him. He will come to you. He will take one of us hostage."

"What?" Diacos was clearly incredulous. "Us?"

The mermaid shivered. "Yes, I am included in the prediction."

"Why would he do that?" Diacos asked her.

"You have something he wants."

This entire reading made me uneasy. First, Angella's portent of death for Gonzales, now Kismet's announcement that another death was coming as well, this time possibly Aliena's or mine. I began to agree with Hamilton: the best thing to do with seers is to avoid them.

The blue shell returned to the bag. All the other shells began to levitate.

The mermaid leaned back. "That's all there is," she said. The remaining shells floated back into the bag, and the top cinched tight.

"We had better prepare to leave." I glanced at my watch. "We have less than a minute."

"So soon?" Kismet said.

"We have set the return timer on a Prince card," Aliena told her. Kismet held her hand out and Aliena clasped it.

"Please don't go," Kismet said. "I sense something terrible is going to befall you. Stay with me, where you will be safe."

Though they had been past lovers, I would have endorsed this idea—anything to keep Aliena out of harm's way. But Aliena does what she wants, and I was not surprised by her answer.

"Dear Kismet," she said, stroking the mermaid's lush mane of hair. "I can take care of myself. You know that."

"You can be killed. If something happened to you, I—I don't know what I'd do."

"You needn't worry about that. If I get in trouble, Sebastian will be there to help me."

The lovely blue-gray eyes swiveled to me, now fierce and penetrating. "You are responsible for her." I noticed her fluke had ceased twitching. "If she dies while she is with you, I shall curse you for all eternity."

"Kismet!"

"Perhaps you are wrong about a death," I said.

"I am never wrong about death. You have been warned."

Aliena kissed her hand and released it.

"When will you come back?" Kismet asked.

"Soon. I promise."

"I shall count the moments." She reached over for her glass of sharkade and knocked it over. It fell on the table with a loud clatter and spilled onto the floor.

"Triton's beard!"

Diacos suddenly disappeared. I looked away from the spilled drink to our shoes. It did not seem we were going to be able to get them in time. I was right.

I heard the blast of air and felt the chill of the ether; then we were back in my living room.

"Exactly fifteen minutes," Marcus said. "Very reliable."

"But we lost our shoes," I pointed out.

Aliena's card pulsed. She held it up, laughed. "Yes, thank you, Kismet," she said. The Moon card expanded slightly and our shoes dropped out of it, thudding on the carpet.

At that moment, an unearthly scream filled the room, and Aliena shouted, "no!"

She held her card to her mouth and it began to expand. I stepped to her side and took her hand.

"What?"

"It was Bork," she said. "He was grabbing Kismet! Sebastian, we have to help her!"

When the card was barely large enough, the two of us dove into its inky void.

Chapter 30

Sunday, January 25, 10:17 p.m.

We hit the tiled floor on our stomachs. I felt a brief pressure, as if someone was on top of me, then it was gone. I scrambled up. Marcus stood at my side.

"I followed you through," he said.

Aliena had already dashed about the glass floor, shouting Kismet's name. Marcus and I followed. Diacos appeared and he started calling her name, too.

"Kiz!"

We heard a crash from the back of the house, and the four of us rushed through the archway leading out of the drawing room. There was a twinkling waterway on our right.

"Kismet!"

"Allie! Help!"

Marcus and Aliena disappeared. I saw a blur of color moving toward what looked like a bedroom door. Diacos and I brought up the rear, well behind.

When we entered the room, before I could take in everything I was seeing, a thumping sound that pressed my eardrums shook the house. Then Marcus was twisting backward in front of us, sailing over the bed and crashing into the wall. He fell limply.

Bork hulked near a chest of drawers, holding Kismet aloft by her tail with his left hand. This was a big man. The mermaid twisted and fought, but Bork maintained his grip on her. The outer edge of Kismet's entire body lit blue-white for a moment. It blazed again just seconds later. I could feel the hair on the back of my neck stand up both times she did it. It was obviously a powerful defense mechanism, but Bork shook it off—though he grunted loudly each time she electrocuted him.

He brandished something white in his right hand that looked like a tube of toothpaste.

Aliena closed in on him, moving in a serpentine fashion to make it more difficult for Bork to aim his weapon at her. He pointed the tube and again my eardrums felt as if the atmosphere had temporarily thickened to flannel. The concussion missed Aliena, and then she was grappling for possession of Kismet.

Diacos's lips moved, and he gestured toward Bork. The air in front of him rippled, shot across the room. Bork cried out, letting go of Kismet. She dropped into Aliena's arms, and the two of them were out of the room so fast they may have met themselves coming in.

Bork fired his weapon again. Diacos stood right next to me, and we both were caught in a blast that flung us backward out of the room as if we had been swatted by an invisible giant foam hand.

I went heels over head and made a forced landing against the dining table, crashing into it back first and feeling excruciating pain as I broke my tailbone. Diacos continued past me on his end-over-end flight and landed in the pool.

I struggled to my feet, knocking over a chair, and sped back into the bedroom, letting out an angry bellow as my body repaired itself.

Bork had gone.

Marcus sat up, a dazed look on his face. I went to him, got a hand under his arm, and pulled him until he was standing. He leaned on me for a moment. I took the opportunity to inspect Kismet's bedroom.

The one window faced a beautiful mountain panorama. Her bed was as big and fluffy as any I had seen in a woman's room, though with a ramp at the foot that extended into the channel of water. A bedside lamp sitting on an antique night table glowed. An open book lay spine up next to it.

I felt Marcus gather himself.

"Where?"

"He's gone," I told him. "Come on."

We ran into the living room. I vaulted the chair I had knocked over and skidded to a halt. I saw I did not need to hurry.

Diacos lay on one of Kismet's padded lounges, a shallow gash in his forehead. Aliena sat on one side and Kismet the other, both bent over him.

"We're fine," I said. Marcus laughed.

Aliena turned and was in my arms before I knew she had moved.

"Thank God, Sebastian," she said, holding me tight. I could see Kismet over her shoulder and recognized the aggrieved expression on the mermaid's face.

"He's gone, sweetheart." I stroked Aliena's hair. "We're okay now."

"Yes." Her voice was muffled by my shoulder. She leaned back and looked up at me, her disheveled blonde hair enhancing her beauty. "We heard his card activate."

"Ah." I kissed her nose. "I was probably flying through the air and missed it."

She laid her head on my chest. "I was more scared for you and Kismet than for myself."

"I know the feeling."

"Well, I don't."

She said this so frankly, I laughed. "You have probably never had loved ones in danger. Especially since there are so few of them. Ouch!"

"You really do ask for it, Sebastian," she said.

We walked to Kismet and Diacos. He struggled up, a small towel pressed to his head.

"Well?" I asked.

"I'm fine," he said, swinging his legs off the lounge and standing up. "Barely a scratch." He set the towel on the table next to the lounge.

Kismet slid back into the water and was about to push herself onto the lounge when Echo appeared plainly terrified from the back of the house. I had forgotten all about her.

"Echo!" Kismet went to her quickly and hugged the shaken mermaid.

"What happened?" Echo's gaze darted all over the place, and her shoulders shook. "What was that terrible sound?"

"It's okay," Kismet said, although she trembled, too. She maneuvered Echo back to us and then jumped onto the lounge Diacos had vacated.

Aliena knelt next to her. "How are you, dear?"

"My heart is still going pitter-patter, but I am not hurt." She stroked Aliena's hair. "Thank you for coming so fast." She looked up. "All of you."

"Kiz, do you know why Bork would want you?" Aliena asked.

"No," the mermaid wailed. She looked terrified. "I was not aware he even knew of my existence. Why should he?"

"What about Salomé?" Marcus asked.

"I never even heard of her," she said, her golden fluke splashing in the pool.

Diacos watched her with his arms crossed over his chest. I could not read his expression, but he looked like he did not believe her.

"There must be some reason for him to try and grab you so boldly," I said.

"I don't know what it is." Kismet started sobbing.

Aliena took her hand. "Don't worry. We will protect you."

"How?"

"We are going after these people, of course. I promise they will never bother you again while I am alive."

"You should stay," Kismet said, gripping Aliena's forearm. "You personally, to make sure."

"Kiz, I have to help Sebastian and Erol."

"I'm afraid to be here alone now," she said. Echo began crying, too, and added her agreement.

Aliena looked up at me. "What do you think?"

I was trying to come up with something. Kismet was right. She and Echo weren't safe here now, not by themselves. A guard? I looked at Diacos.

"Anything?"

He shook his head. "Not unless I stay here myself. And I believe it's more important to stop Salomé and Bork than to . . ." He stopped. There was a ghastly silence. He had really put his foot in it even though I knew what he had said was probably true.

"Than to protect me?" Kismet said, her lower lip trembling. "Is that what you were going to say?"

"I am sorry it came out that way," Diacos said, bowing his head. "But, yes, I think the threat from Salomé is that bad. In order to stop it, I would risk the life of anyone in this room."

"I knew I was right not to put you in charge," Marcus said.

Monday, January 26, 3:18 a.m.

Aliena and I relaxed at home now, spooning in front of the fireplace, lying on a huge, fluffy blue comforter, with a pile of logs blazing behind the glass grate, spilling sputtering light over our cozy crib.

Marcus had remained at Kismet's and would stay for the night, but we still had no plan for protecting the mermaids after sunup. Diacos had gone home for some sleep and agreed to return at sunrise if we had no other options.

"Is Kismet telling the truth when she says she knows nothing about this?" I asked.

"Yes."

"It looked like Diacos did not trust her. Is it possible she really does know Bork and Salomé?"

"You are well aware I have no way of knowing that."

"How do you feel about it?"

"The same as ever. Kismet is incapable of deception—not because she's not intelligent enough, but because to her it would be the same as rolling in the mud. I don't know how else to explain it."

"You explain it very well." I was the spoon in back, and I used that strategic position to kiss her ear. She pressed against me. "You know," I said, teasing her, "if Kismet's tail were not all one piece, she might even be as desirable as you."

"Oh, Kismet's tail is not all one piece."

"What?"

"Although uncomfortable, she can spread her legs and separate her fluke. In fact, she likes to open her legs and then close her tail around her lover. I—Sebastian, it is a wonderful feeling." She rolled onto her back and looked up at me. "She would hold me in her arms that way, sometimes for a whole night."

"Did she let you drink from her?"

"Yes."

I felt something.

"And we would talk and kiss and . . . do other things."

"Are you embarrassed about it?" I stared at her hair spread over the pale-blue blanket, ran my fingers through it.

"Almost no one knows of my affair with Kismet."

I pulled her blonde mane playfully. "That's no answer."

"No," she said, sliding her hand along the outside of my arm. "I am not embarrassed, though it was awkward to be in a room with a past lover and a future . . ." She looked in my eyes. "And hopefully a future lover," she said, touching my face.

With the warm fire and the intimate setting, this had unexpectedly become the most erotic conversation in which I had ever participated. Hearing the person who has captured my heart describe me as a future lover made my whole body tingle, and for a moment we could feel each other's presence acutely. Gazing down at Aliena, I sensed windows had opened inside of us and allowed our souls to join in the open air.

"We did many intimate things I think are too personal to describe," she continued. "We loved each other, and we still do."

"I understand. She does not seem happy about the separation."

"No, she is not. That makes me sad because she is the sweetest person I have ever known and one of the most beautiful souls I have ever met. Don't you think she's special, Sebastian?"

"Yes," I said, smiling down at her. On her back, with her tousled golden hair spread out on the blanket, Aliena was a vision, her breathtaking beauty angelic.

"Oh, when she and I were together," she said in a faraway voice that told me she was looking at pictures in her mind, "some of the nights in the warm water with her wrapped around me, the lights off and the stars above us, having no plans but to be in each other's arms . . . those are such wonderful memories . . ." She focused on me and said in a different voice, "Am I making you jealous?"

"A little."

She tugged at the front of my shirt and pulled me down until our lips were together. Then she gave me a head-spinning kiss. We parted.

"Good," she said, smiling up at me, running the tip of her tongue along her upper lip just below her mole. "I am truly not telling you this to make you feel jealous, but if you are in love with me, you should feel something." She stopped smiling and touched my shoulder. "I am sorry I did not have time to tell you about Kismet before we met her."

"I know, sweetheart," I said. "Besides, you would never tease me . . ."

She giggled.

"And I really am interested in your relationship with her. It is obvious you loved each other a great deal."

"Yes," Aliena said quietly. "That is true."

"What happened?" I asked. Sometimes when I had asked that question in reference to an event from her past she had remained silent, and after a while we pretended I had said nothing. But she had given me her diary. I sensed this time she wanted to share with me, and I was sure I knew why: Aliena always kept her feelings reined in, and she had probably never told anyone how she felt about the lovely mermaid. This was her chance to let it out and share it with someone else.

"Kismet does not like to travel much," she began, "not even through the cards. And she always wanted me to stay with her. I loved her and her beautiful home, but I am an explorer. One reason I have always liked being with you is that you know that about me and accept it. Although," she said, "I am sure sometimes you don't like it any more than Kismet did."

I laughed, letting her know she was right. She turned her head to the side and looked at the fire. The shadows of its flickering flames danced across her profile, and I stared at the familiar silhouette that had made my heart ache with desire for more than a century.

"She was actually the one who broke it off," she said. "When I told her I could not stop traveling."

I understood. "But when she said that, she was really trying to pressure you into agreeing with her."

She turned away from the fireplace and looked back up at me. "Yes."

"And when that didn't work, she told you she still loved you as much as before and said she did not care now if you wanted to travel."

"Yes."

"But everything was different after that quarrel."

"Yes, everything was different."

"Do you know why you do not want to be with her now?"

"That is not really an accurate statement," she said, giving me a sidelong look. "She and I have been . . . friends for a long time."

"I guessed that." I put my hand on her thigh and stroked it through her jeans. "Are you saying you still desire her intimately?"

"Yes." She sighed. "But the way you touch me . . . oh, it feels so different, and the part of my body you're touching becomes . . ." She stopped and I could sense her warm desire radiating up at me. "It feels nice."

"Ah," I said as she laid her hand on mine. "Are you picturing anything?"

She laughed. "You can be so funny, Sebastian."

"Does it trouble you? That you can't tell Kismet how you really feel?"

"Yes and I truly miss her, but I do not think she will ever be able to set aside her strong feelings for me. And I feel as if I am torturing her any time I act as friendly as I feel, since I know it is not as friendly as she would like."

"I understand that problem, truly."

She gave me a look. "I'm sure you do."

I tensed for a moment, expecting a pinch. Three, two, one. I relaxed. "About this future love scene between you and me . . ."

"Yes?" she said, with the giggle in her voice I so adored.

"You do realize I'm an older man?"

"Um hmm," she said. She pulled me down on my side next to her and set her hand very high up on my thigh. I began to unbutton her blouse. She did not stop me. "I want to let you do everything and show me how to love you," she whispered in my ear, torturing me.

I groaned. "You do know you are making me crazy with desire for you?"

"I certainly hope so." She pulled me against her and blew softly in my ear, making my body shiver with a delicious intensity. Then our mouths were together, and I became unaware of the passage of time.

Chapter 31

Monday, January 26, 7:02 a.m.

After I tucked Aliena into bed, I showered and shaved. I decided to wear casual clothes again. As long as I could wear a jacket, I was not uncomfortable in them.

Aliena had signaled her approval of my relaxed look earlier by grabbing the back of my jeans.

"Nice ass," she said.

"Okay, you got me. Crudity does sound strange coming from your lips."

"Strange how?"

"Exciting strange." This time she pinched my rear.

"Don't you ever think of anything else?"

"Like what?"

I dressed, grabbed the keys to the Maserati (Hector had brought it home an hour ago, with a new tire in place of the one Sammy had punctured with bullets), and started for the Van Nuys Police Department. I knew Hamilton would be in early but not too early.

I wondered how I could tell him everything that had happened since Diacos and I left him yesterday: Diacos's heat shield, Bork's attempted kidnapping of a mermaid, his concussive sound gun, and the card combination we were trying to stop Salomé and Bork from acquiring. That was for starters.

I still had not made up my mind whether I could tell him about mermaids in general when I pulled into the lot.

It was barely eight o'clock, so many detectives were still working on laptops and drinking coffee, preparing to hit the streets. I nodded at a couple of them and headed to Hamilton's desk, sat down in the guest chair. He sat typing at his computer.

"One more sec," he said. He tapped his mouse, logged out of the system. "No need to sit, Sebastian," he said, "we've got something." We stood and started walking out.

"Well?"

"Somebody called with a lead on Bork's whereabouts."

"You're kidding." Excellent, if genuine. It would be nice to take him out of the equation now. That reminded me that I needed to get to Kismet's place later and make sure she and Echo were safe—although something told me Bork would not be coming back for them. "Somebody identified him?"

"Uh-huh. He's staying in a Van Nuys hotel, if our witness is right."

As we climbed aboard the elevator, I said, "He's a big man." I was remembering how he had held Kismet aloft with one hand. "Hard to make a mistake."

"You know that happens all the time."

"Who's our witness?"

"The manager of the place. An officer showed her the picture we have, and she positively ID'd him as a tenant who moved in a week ago."

"Sounds like our guy all right."

His phone rang.

"Yes? That's great. Okay, but you'd better wait for us to back you up, Alfred. This man is extremely dangerous." He closed his phone.

We got into my car and headed out of the lot. The address he gave me was on Sepulveda. We arrived five minutes later at the Voyager Motor Inn. As I pulled in, I recognized the unmarked car Gonzales usually drove.

"Alfred's already here," Hamilton commented.

I took the space next to his car. We had just closed the Maserati's doors when we heard shots: two booming reports that sounded like a .44 Magnum.

Bork's gun.

"Shit!" Hamilton sprinted for the lobby doors, his hand under his jacket. He pulled his gun out just as I got the Beretta in my hand. He turned down the short, stone-trimmed walkway and burst through the doors with me right behind him.

We darted across a lobby with a multicolored carpet and functional furniture. A middle-aged woman cowered behind the front desk.

"Call 911!" Hamilton shouted at her. "Tell them to get their asses down here!"

Another booming shot followed by three that were not so loud.

"Upstairs!" I said.

Hamilton slammed into the stairwell door and rushed through. We took the steps two at a time.

"What do you think?" he said as we approached the landing.

"One more floor."

We kept going up, vaulting two more sets of steps. Hamilton made the third floor landing and yanked the door open, stepping into the hall. I covered him from the doorway; then joined him in the corridor.

Another shot. To our right. Then we heard Gonzales.

"LAPD, *pendejo*! Drop your weapon!"

We sprinted down the hallway. The smell in this part of the building stung the nostrils. It was noxious, a combination of stale urine and sweaty bodies. Windows made up the right wall. I glanced down at the deserted courtyard, saw the swimming pool covered with dead leaves.

"Alfred!" Hamilton shouted as we approached the corner, giving him a heads-up that we were coming. We went around it, and Gonzales was there, down on a knee, pointing his gun at a door halfway down the hall and to our left. I glanced at it, saw a muzzle flash.

"Get down!" Gonzales said, capping two more rounds. One hit the room number on the door, launching it crazily into the air.

Suddenly the door swung open. Bork stepped out, holding his piece with two hands. He started firing.

"Watch it!" I yelled as I dove to the right. I hit the wall and heard a loud zing go past me. Bork fired again and bits of wall plaster rained down. Gonzales was in my way, and I couldn't get a clear shot.

"He's bolting!" Gonzales shouted as Bork turned and ran. "Steve, get down to the lobby. Don't let him get out of here!" Then he dashed down the hallway, moving his enormous bulk quickly.

Hamilton turned to me. "You stay with him," he said, hustling back to the stairwell.

I sprinted along the stinking hallway, closing on Gonzales. As he neared the corner, I shouted, "Wait!"

He didn't. He leaned left and turned into the new hallway at speed. I heard the boom of Bork's .44. Again. My heart filled my throat as I heard no answer from Gonzales's 9 millimeter.

I rushed around the corner, oblivious of my safety, my piece up. Gonzales was down. I saw muzzle flashes from the stairwell door. I did not try to get out of the way. I raised my gun and fired three times. I felt a burning sensation along the left side of my neck as a bullet grazed me. My shots were accurate, however, and the door slammed shut.

I turned to Gonzales. He lay on his back. One in the stomach and one in the chest. He was going fast. I knelt next to him, setting my gun down. I pulled my cell and hit speed dial, pressed my left hand against Gonzales's bloody stomach.

"Officer down," I said when dispatch answered. "We need EMTs on the double. Voyager motel on Sepulveda." She started to ask a question, but I snapped the phone shut and dropped it next to my gun.

"How is it?" Gonzales asked me.

My gaze met his. His eyes filled with tears.

"That fuck," he said weakly. "He killed me."

"Don't talk, Alfred."

"Why do I have to die with you, Montero?" His voice was barely a whisper. "I don't even like you." He coughed and blood colored his lips.

"Shhh. You're not going to die," I lied. Blood poured from his wounds and the necessary equipment to help him survive was not going to get here in time.

"That son of a bitch," he said, barely audible. Then he gasped. He stared at my neck. I had forgotten about the bullet that had scraped me. I hadn't been aware of the itching feeling until I saw him look at the injury. I knew he could see it closing.

He raised his stare to my eyes. "What are you? Are you Jesus?"

"No."

His eyes scrunched closed. "You listen to me, Sebastian." I couldn't remember him ever calling me by my first name. "I'm all my family has. They'll never make it without me."

"They won't have to," I said. I had both hands over the stomach wound, pressing down, but blood still seeped between my fingers.

"Listen to me," he said, his voice weakening. "All that money you have . . . Sebastian . . . promise me . . ."

"I promise you I will take care of them. Your wife and children will want for nothing."

Tears rolled down both sides of his face, running into his ears.

"Hold on, Alfred," I said. "Fight to stay alive, man! Don't let go!"

His eyes glazed over. "Tell my girls . . ." His head lolled to the side, and he looked through the roof as if he were contemplating the infinite.

I took my hands off his stomach and leaned back.

I was sitting on my heels with my bloody hands in my lap, staring sadly at the downed officer, when I heard pounding footsteps and looked up to see Hamilton running toward me. When he saw Gonzales down and unmoving, his face filled with superstitious fear.

"No!" He knelt next to his partner, shouldering me aside. He grabbed the lapels of Gonzales's jacket and shook him. "Alfred, no! Goddammit, no!" He felt for a pulse on the neck.

He turned to me furious now. "Fuck! It's you, Sebastian." He was up, dragging me to my feet, holding handfuls of my jacket. He pushed me against the wall, tears in his eyes. "What the fuck is it with you?" He pulled and shoved, ramming me back. "Why?" He slammed me again. "Why did this have to happen?"

He finally released me and stepped back unsteadily. He put his hand over his eyes, wiped the tears out of them, and looked down at his partner.

"Ah, God. Alfred, no."

Chapter 32

Monday, January 26, 9:24 a.m.

I spied a maid's trolley at the other end of the hall. I walked to it, took four paper towels, and wiped the blood off my hands. I moved back to the body, picked up my phone and gun, and stood next to Hamilton.

"Did Bork get away?" I asked quietly.

"Yes, he got past us. He never came out the front or back, so he probably used one of those damn tarot cards to escape." He fell silent, staring at Gonzales's body with a bleak look on his face.

The stairwell door opened and three emergency medical technicians hustled down the hall and set up next to us. As the lead man put his hand on Gonzales's neck, he looked up at me. I shook my head.

He turned to the other two. "Tell them to bring up a gurney." One of them ran off.

We looked at the fallen officer. Hamilton and I stood as still as a jury until they had him on the stretcher and wheeled him toward the elevator. We remained in that rank hallway with the stained carpet and dirty walls until the doors closed and they were gone.

"I'm going to get that fucker," Hamilton said in a low, intense voice. "If it's the last thing I do, Sebastian, I swear I am going to pop that son of a bitch."

He looked at me, his eyes hard in the hot light streaming through the windows. I nodded.

We returned to the station. Once inside, we could feel the electricity in the air. The building buzzed with off-duty cops.

Heads swiveled and eyes fixed on us as we walked to the elevator. Some of the stares directed at me looked hostile.

We boarded and ascended in silence.

Chief Reyes collared us as soon as the doors slid open. She led us to her office, where we gave her a thorough verbal debrief. I had to surrender my weapon because I had fired it during the encounter. Throughout our report, Reyes stared at me miserably, anguish in her eyes at the loss of her officer.

"What about Bork?"

"We're on him," Hamilton said grimly. "We'll find the bastard."

"Be sure you do," she said. "I want his ass fast." She nodded at us in dismissal. We rose to leave. As we filed out, Reyes said, "Sebastian."

I turned. She stared at me. I nodded.

Her unspoken message came through clearly: Don't fail me.

We walked to Hamilton's desk and sat down. The other detectives cast surreptitious glances our way.

"Well?" Hamilton asked. "Any ideas on how to track this Bork?"

I told him about the attempted kidnapping of Kismet last night. In case Bork returned.

"Who is this Kismet?"

"One of Aliena's friends. She's a seer."

"Uh-oh."

"Yes. Diacos wanted to consult with her."

"Wait a minute," Hamilton said slowly. "Kismet has one of these tarot cards, doesn't she?"

"Yes," I said, impressed. "Nice one."

"Save it. Is that why Bork tried to kidnap her?"

"Not sure."

"What about this card combination Diacos is looking for?"

"We're not really looking for it. We are trying to prevent it from occurring."

"Well, what card is Kismet? I assume it's a star card?"

"Yes. The Lovers."

"Is the Lovers one that this . . . what was her name?"

"Salomé."

"Yeah, Salomé. She doesn't need Kismet's card?"

"No."

"What's her motive for sending Bork to take her, then?"

I had been thinking about that, too. If Salomé did not need the Lovers as part of their planned resurrection rite, why try to kidnap Kismet? It made me uneasy when I couldn't ascribe a motive to someone's behavior.

"I can't think of a reason," I admitted.

"You don't think he will come back."

"No."

"Why?"

"I think the entire thing was a ruse."

"A ruse? Why?"

"To draw us out and determine our power. To better know the forces aligned against them." I did not mention that I had no idea how Bork knew we were together at Kismet's in the first place.

"Draw you from where? How did she know where you were?"

"I don't know."

"Shit. This just keeps getting better."

Another nagging worry persisted: what were the consequences if Salomé and Bork put the cards together but did not do the ceremony properly? I knew enough about the occult to realize that would probably lead to a violent, uncontrolled discharge of energy. I mentioned it to Hamilton.

"That sounds fine," he said. He hadn't heard the question. He sounded a little dulled now, and I knew the death of Gonzales weighed on him.

I grieved for the fallen detective, too, but . . . would Diacos know the consequences of a mistake with the combination? I gave his number to Hamilton, who dialed it and put the call on speaker.

"'Lo?"

"I am sorry if I woke you, Erol," I said. "It's Sebastian. I have Hamilton with me."

"Okay. Don't worry about waking me," he said in a rough voice. "What's up?"

"This card combination Salomé is putting together . . . you said there was a ceremony that had to be performed in order to activate the power of the cards, is that right?"

"Yes. The cards are triggered by sound. For this purpose, it is necessary to chant a song that the cards recognize."

"How does Salomé know which chant to use?"

"I don't know. It is possible it's a family secret passed down through the generations."

"It would help a great deal if we knew where she got the information. Perhaps it's also available to us."

"I doubt it," Diacos said.

"What would happen if she chanted the wrong song?"

"In that case, the power in the cards would be released out of control. Anything nearby would be vaporized."

Hamilton and I exchanged a glance.

"Are you with Kismet and Echo?" I asked.

"Yes. The scenery here is excellent."

"I know," I said, picturing the two mermaids.

"Could you tell Aliena to be here around 5:30? I have some errands to run."

"I'm not sure Aliena will be the one to guard the women tonight. I can't relieve you until midnight, but I promise to send someone by 5:30. By the way, I don't know where the house is." And I could not use a card to get there.

"Do you know how to get to Pacific Palisades?"

"Yes." That wasn't too far from my place. Diacos gave us an address on Miami Way, and Hamilton wrote it down. "Good luck getting some sleep," I said to Diacos.

"Thanks," he replied through a yawn. We disconnected.

"Could you dispatch a couple of officers to that address and have them keep an eye on the house?" I asked Hamilton.

"You think it's that serious?"

"Bork was there last night."

"Yes, you're right." Hamilton picked up his phone and started dialing. "It would be too much to hope that Bork would be killed by the card combination."

"We'll get him no matter what," I said.

"I would prefer that. I want him in my hands." He began speaking into the phone, arranging a guard detail for the mermaids.

Based on his last statement, it did not sound like he was thinking of arresting Bork. When someone kills your partner, you have to do something about it. And if you know who the shooter is, vengeance can become personal.

I did not mind that. For me, vengeance had been personal for seven centuries.

Chapter 33

Monday, January 26, 11:02 a.m.

"Where to?" We were in the parking lot approaching my car. I knew what he had to do now, and it was the worst duty an officer could draw.

"Drop me at the Gonzales home." We climbed in and strapped on our seat belts. "I'll probably be there until six or so."

"You want me to come in with you?"

"No, that would probably do more harm than good."

His words smarted, though I knew they were true. I could only guess how Gonzales had described me to his wife and family.

We did not talk for the rest of the drive, and when we arrived at the house, he climbed out without a word.

I decided to use this free time to check on Aliena and read a little more of her diary. I would have spent the time tracking Bork, but his star card made him untraceable. He and I searched for the same thing, however. I could only hope that my path intersected his—or Salomé's—at the right time.

I had already decided Bork should die. About Salomé I was not sure. Based on Diacos's description, though, I felt any confrontation with her would lead to the death of someone. And now with Gonzales's murder a fact, Kismet's prediction of the demise of Diacos, Aliena, or me made me anxious about a future rushing at us so fast that we were reduced to reacting instead of planning. It gave me a horrible feeling of predestination, as if a great tsunami had already produced a gigantic tidal wave bound for our shores—one that would crush us when it made landfall.

As soon as I arrived home, I pulled Aliena's diary out of the safe and palmed my way into her room, flipping the light switch. The cool air carried Aliena's scent as I crossed the carpet and sat on the bed next to her. I stroked her hair and then leaned down and kissed her softly on the lips.

Rising, I went to her vanity, hoisted the chair, and set it next to the foot of the bed. After I sat down, I kicked my shoes off and put my stocking feet up on the comforter.

I opened the diary where I had left off.

Friday, March 13, 1953

Last night, after sharing someone for dinner, Marcus bequeathed a star card to me. The Moon. He said it fit me perfectly.

"You certainly look the part of the Great Goddess."

He pronounced the sound to activate it and showed me how to reset it.

I considered my new possession, thrilled. With this card, I could pop into Rachella's room in a moment. I could travel to another continent as easily as stepping through a door. Now that I owned one, I thought about the power of the Tarot of the Archons very differently. Their potential overwhelmed with possibilities.

"Why give it to me?"

"I have been holding it too long," he said. "And I prefer to keep the cards in the hands of our kind."

I believe vampires are superior to humans, but Marcus is a true elitist. He shuns contact with mortals, seeing them only as vessels of blood. He has commented many times that if he were to become human again, he would commit suicide. When I think of my mortal life, I see his point. I love being a vampire (have I told you that before, Diary?) and would never want to be the weak, helpless thing I was when I was mortal. I would probably take my own life, too, if I were human again.

I stopped and looked up at Aliena. Would I love her as much if she were mortal? For one thing, I have known her for more than a century, so if she were mortal, I would already have watched her die. Yes, her immortality was the logical reason I was willing to commit my heart after two hundred years.

My love for her did not come from the intellectual part of my brain—my feelings toward Aliena had always been passionate and automatic, with a depth that gave me cause to worry. If anything happened to her or if she made it clear that it was over between us, I do not know what I would do.

I continued gazing at her. Her pale face was so perfect, so blemish-free it almost looked as if she were wearing a mask, A Sleeping Beauty who I could wake with a kiss. I smiled, considering myself lucky that I could kiss her when she did wake up.

"Where shall I travel the first time?" I asked Marcus. "I don't know the sounds for any of the portal cards."

"We have a primer with all of the sounds known to our kind. It is only available to vampires with a star card, which is why I am responsible for issuing them."

"I see."

"For now, I can give you the sound that activates the portal in the floor of my bedroom. It is crotellian.*"*

"What about the card in Rachella's bedroom?"

He looked astonished. "You would want to know that?"

"Yes."

"Without an Ace you can only travel there, not look at the room first and determine whether or not people will observe you appearing out of the ether. I need your oath that you will never reveal anything about the cards, including traveling in front of non-cardholders, especially mortals."

"If I don't have an Ace, how can I be sure about my destination?"

"You cannot. That rule applies to me, not you, since I do possess an Ace. And it is possible someone will observe you emerging from a portal, since you are going in blind. We would not hold you accountable for that. It happens once in a while. We are not so lenient when entering a card in view of non-cardholders. To do that, it must be a matter of life or sunshine."

"I understand."

"The card in Rachella's room is one of my minors, as I mentioned before. The Nine of Wands. Susurration is the sound to activate it."

I held the Moon up. It was a stunning card as were all the archons. The face superimposed on the lunar surface, however, was austere. This card nearly always meant catastrophe when it turned up in a reading.

I liked that.

"Does the Moon come with any minors?"

He smiled. "As a matter of fact . . ." He produced three cards from his jacket pocket and handed them to me. The Princess of Cups, Four of Pentacles, and Two of Swords. "When you touch your major against them, they will accept a new password for travel. All three of these cards can be planted."

"They will disappear if I do that?"

"Yes."

"What if someone with a star card finds one?"

"Any cardholder can reset the password by touching his major to it. If that occurs, you will not be able to travel through it. Any attempt to do so will deposit you at your starting point."

"Do you know the other cardholders?"

"Some. Not all. We keep our identities carefully masked. We dare not allow the breath of a rumor that such a deck as the Tarot of the Archons exists."

"Are you saying you won't tell me who the others are?"

"That is what I am saying."

I pouted. "There is nothing I can do to earn your trust?"

"When you phrase it like that, I can think of several things," he said. "I would rather not bargain for them, however."

I lowered my gaze. His frank adoration sometimes made me uncomfortable.

Me, too.

Although he jealously protected the identity of each cardholder, Marcus did say another vampire possessed an archon. I wondered who it was.

I thought about the card in Rachella's wall and toyed with the idea of putting a portal card in Sebastian's bedroom. I automatically pictured him making love to a woman. My heart raced and my throat constricted. I found I did not like the idea of Sebastian with someone else. The emotion surprised me with its force. I cared for him more than I had admitted to myself. I wondered if I was falling in love with him.

No. Not another immortal. Not after François.

"Damn you, Franky."

"There is one cardholder to whom I can introduce you," Marcus said. "She is unique. You will like her."

I doubted that. I disliked most women. "What is her name?"

"Kismet."

Chapter 34

Monday, January 26, 12:18 p.m.

I closed the diary and set it on the comforter, stood, and then sat on the bed next to her. I ran my fingertips through her hair as I gazed at her serene face. So vulnerable now, so powerful when awake. I leaned down and kissed her cold forehead.

I replaced the chair and picked up the diary. After I locked the door on my way out, I put the journal back in the safe. I lit a cigarette and wandered onto the patio. A chill wind knifed through my light cotton shirt.

Why did Aliena's star card have to come from Marcus? I did not like that. Inviting her into an elite group of which he was a part was another tie that bound her to him. And this was a group that excluded all others, even from being aware of its existence. Aliena had kept this from me for sixty years. A secret world she shared with Marcus.

I finished my cigarette, stubbed it out. This was no time to be pessimistic. Aliena was sleeping in my bedroom, not with Marcus. And in her diary she wrote that she did not love him.

I went back into the house. The thing to do was find Bork. I pulled my cell out, dialed Diacos's number.

"Hey, Sebastian."

"Erol, Bork shot and killed an LAPD officer this mor—"

"Dammit, Sebastian! I told you the man was a maniac! Why did you tell them? His death is your fault!" He stopped. I heard him take a deep breath. "No, I can't say that. Bork is insane. But Sebastian, I couldn't have been any clearer about how dangerous this man is."

"Dangerous or not, Bork had a warrant out for his arrest. The police don't ignore that, and they certainly know how to prepare for dangerous apprehensions."

"Oh? Did you send in a SWAT team?"

I didn't say anything. He was right. We should have sent a team in. But I know Gonzales would never have waited for them to arrive, just as he had not waited for Hamilton and me.

"Sorry," he said. "But this is why I wanted to handle the problem alone. Failure means death for anyone attempting to thwart Salomé's plans. And Bork is the instrument."

"I want to find him," I said.

"So do I."

"You don't have any ideas?"

"One or two, but . . ."

"But what?"

"They're risky. Well, maybe not for you."

"What are you thinking of?"

"Unauthorized travel. Through the cards."

"How unauthorized?"

"I know the passwords for several portal cards that belong to others."

"I suppose these were passed down through your family?"

"Most of them. Two I discovered on my own."

"Who owns them?"

"Well, if there is nothing on the other side, I would rather not say anything about the cards' planters."

Secrecy again. This case was so full of secrets I was amazed I knew anything at all. Diacos and his family secrets, Aliena and Marcus with their star cards.

"I don't know if I would like to travel anywhere without having some idea where I am going to come out," I told him.

"I understand. I would not send you to a place I know is inherently dangerous."

"Are you still with the mermaids?"

"Yes, of course."

"Give me twenty. I will have to use an automobile to get there."

Kismet's home in Pacific Palisades looked stunning from the street. I pulled up to the curb and admired the exterior architecture for a few moments. It was reminiscent of a Frank Lloyd Wright design with its flat, horizontal lines.

An unmarked police car with two men in it sat on the other side of the street.

I ascended a short flight of steps and walked under a balcony to the front door. There was no handle and no knob for a bell. There was a small recessed speaker to my right. I was preparing to inspect it when I heard Kismet's voice.

"Hi, Sebastian, come in. Please remember to remove your shoes."

The device clicked, and the door popped open a fraction. I pushed my way in. After closing the door, I removed my shoes and held them as I walked across that marvelous glass floor.

Kismet and Echo were wading in the pool. They waved and I returned it. Diacos sat in front of a coffee table, bent over and writing. As I approached, he straightened up, folded the paper, put it and his pen in his pocket. Undoubtedly more of his family secrets.

I set my shoes on the floor and sat in the chair on the other side of the table with my back to the pool.

"What's your plan?"

"Simple," Diacos said. "Now that Bork has been flushed into the open, he won't feel comfortable in a strange place."

"That makes sense. And I'm guessing you know where his favorite hideouts are."

"Some. And remember, not just where they are. All of them contain a minor card."

"And it is your idea we travel through these portals and . . .?"

"Hopefully find Bork, of course."

I thought about that. It seemed incredibly thin. "Do you have an Ace?"

"No," he said. "I wish I did." He took the Emperor out of his pocket and set it on the table. "Do you have the Prince of Wands with you?"

I took it out of my jacket pocket and placed it next to his. "Why do we need that?"

"Well, we don't, but . . . it's hard to explain and will probably seem foolish . . ."

"You would prefer I traveled through the Prince on my way back?" I asked.

"Actually, as long as I touch my card to it, it can serve as a portal both ways."

"That's convenient," I commented.

"Very convenient," he said. "A minor card can also serve as an invitation—preset to take someone to a specific spot."

I nodded. I didn't want to think Aliena purposely kept these facts from me, but secrecy becomes ingrained. Divesting yourself becomes difficult to do, even with people you trust. And secrecy seemed to be the watchword for anyone owning a card from the Tarot of the Archons.

"And all you need to know is the sound," I said. "Care to share it with me?"

He looked paralyzed. I shook my head. "Never mind. I realize why you would want as few people to know as possible." To be honest, this continued to irritate me. I felt like the student who had failed to study for the test.

"Let me prime this for you." He held the Prince to his mouth and began speaking in a voice too low for me to hear.

"Where is the Prince going to send me this time?" I asked when he had finished.

"To the Borks' ancestral dungeons in Istanbul."

"Dungeons?"

"They have a complex underground tunnel system beneath a castle that has been in the Bork family for four centuries. They use some of the rooms down there to 'detain' people."

"Even today?"

"Oh, yes."

"Some of your family?" I guessed. It was a simple deduction and explained how the minor cards got there. I was seeing a pattern. Diacos was fixated on his family's history.

He shook his head. "Not now. But a Diacos ancestor was one who was captured. They held him for five years. Five wasted years—and a long time for a family to hope and pray for his release." His eyes were slightly narrowed now, his jaw partially clenched, and I knew if I took his pulse, it would be higher than normal. Although he gave nothing away in his voice, he was clearly incensed.

"How do you know this? Your father told you?"

"Yes, but it's all written down. I can trace my ancestry back to the fourteenth century."

"It would make a great book."

"Yes," he said, with a loud laugh. "It probably would, but I guarantee those pages will never see the light of day."

"I understand. So you think Bork might be in Istanbul?"

"It's a start."

Before I knew of the cards, I would have said that was impossible since I had seen Bork this morning. However, that conclusion was based on the distance between Los Angeles and Istanbul—a measurement that had no meaning to the cards.

"How do you want to do this?"

"Well, because of your unique nature . . ."

"You want me to travel there first and give you the all-clear signal."

"Sebastian, you make conversation easy."

"I know."

"As soon as I touch my card to the border of the Prince, you have fifteen seconds to enter the portal."

"How long before the card brings me back automatically?"

"Five minutes. That should be plenty of time to determine the safety of a location. Also, I don't have to wait very long to know the answer."

"Good thinking."

"Are you ready?"

I put my shoes on and stood. "Yes."

He picked up the Emperor, and I took the Prince of Wands. He touched his card to mine, and the gold border pulsed twice. The portal began to expand. I let go of the card.

"Good luck," Diacos said.

I stepped into the dark doorway.

Chapter 35

Monday, January 26, 1:12 p.m.

The whoosh of the overhead hurricane pounded down on me, I felt that brief flash of cold, and saw the afterimage of a star field.

Light returned. I looked around. Nice. Just like my friend Rothman's dungeon back in the sixteenth century, with wall sconces and rounded ceiling edges.

Five minutes. I started my watch's chronograph.

I stood at a junction. A hallway stretched in front of me and there was another to my right. There was no sign of the portal card, and since I did not have a star card, I could not make it reveal itself to me.

Now I had to choose between two options. I held my breath in the hope a sound would tell me which way to go. Nothing. The tunnel to my right sloped upward. I turned that way.

Torches burned at intervals of twenty meters and only lit a small area beneath them. Most of the time I stepped through cool darkness. After a hundred meters, the light in front of me revealed an opening underneath it. A heavy barred gate was pushed back against the wall next to it. Silent as fog, I positioned myself to the right of the doorway.

No sound came from within, and there was no light. I still went down on my knees before peering around the corner. The room was dark, but the flickering flames above the entrance showed me that it was empty.

I was standing up when I heard the distinctive sizzle of a star card. Before I could turn around, something hit me on the arm. Bork moved into the light pointing a strange-looking gun at me. I tried to retreat into the chamber, but my body did not respond to my thoughts. I looked down at my arm. A large dart protruded from the sleeve of my jacket.

I just had time to observe it before the rock tunnel landed on my head.

When I came to, I was still groggy. My body was very slowly fighting off the effects of the drug Bork had shot into me. I had been deposited in a chair. I tried to stand but couldn't. It had nothing to do with weakness of the legs, though. Metal wire bound me to the chair, wound around my chest many times. The same wire pinned my arms and legs.

Someone—probably Bork or Salomé—had put a blue transparent bracelet on me next to my watch. Runic symbols stood out boldly in red. I recognized the characters.

Magistine.

Looking around, I could see I was in one of Bork's dungeon cells. This one was lit with a torch. A cot on my left. The barred door remained open.

I could see my watch. Four fifty-one. I had been unconscious for about ten minutes. Whatever he used on me, it was more effective than anything I had encountered before. Even a bullet to the head only knocked me out for sixty seconds or so.

Then I remembered. The Prince. It should have brought me back to Kismet's by now. What happened?

I heard heavy footsteps approaching. Bork sauntered in. He held the knockout gun. When he saw I was still tied down securely, he pocketed it and stood directly in front of me. The huge man wore creased dark gray work pants with black military boots. His khaki T-shirt was stained with sweat. I noticed he had the eyes of a cow.

"You're lucky I'm tied down," I told him, almost sick with hatred. "You killed a good man today, and, somehow, I am going to make you pay for that."

He acted as if he hadn't heard me. "Where is the Prince of Wands?" he asked.

Incredible. He and Salomé were looking for the card I had taken from Cavanaugh's at the beginning of this case. The one that started it all. Since the card was presently at Kismet's place being guarded by Diacos, it was safe.

"You know, I think I left it at the police station."

He slapped me hard enough to twist my neck around and rock my head onto my right shoulder. The pain was immediate, a hot iron bar running from the bottom of my scalp to the middle of my back. As I returned to an upright position, I waited for the pain to ebb. Bork watched me, a grin on his oafish face. After a minute, I could still feel the hot imprint of his palm on my cheek.

I looked again at my bindings. The metal rope appeared unusually light and apparently tied as easily as a shoestring. I had never seen anything like it. And the bracelet. I could decipher the message if I could see the whole thing. I had already translated the part facing me, about half of the circumference. It read, " . . . live to eternity's end . . ." I was bound so tightly, I could not even raise my hand to shake it and spin it around so I could read the rest.

The ache in my neck became more acute. My face still burned from the slap. Those were sensations alien to me. For some reason, my eternal engine remained silent.

"Where is the Prince of Wands?" Bork repeated.

"Why does Salomé want it?" It was not one of the cards Diacos had named in the combination.

"You are not here to ask questions. I see you need another reminder."

He punched me on the same side of the head. I felt excruciating pain when my head snapped over. As I straightened up this time, the left side of my face radiated agony. My eye began to swell shut. The fire down my neck and back flared as if fueled with kerosene. The pain was so intense, I nearly cried out.

"You tell me what I want to know, and I will stop hurting you."

"I hid it under your armpit," I said through gritted teeth. "You're getting it all wet."

He actually looked down for a second. When he looked up, his cheeks shone ruby. He bent his knees and punched me in the stomach, driving all the air out of me. I saw he was going to give me another, but there was no way to lean forward or twist to lessen the impact of it. He rammed his fist into me a second time. The legs of the chair scraped the floor as the blow caused me to scoot back.

I couldn't breathe. My solar plexus burned and I had lost the ability to inhale. Spots appeared before my eyes. He was drawing his fist back again when a voice stopped him.

"That's enough, Detrit. We have the Prince now."

As Bork moved to the side, I could see who stood in the doorway.

Erol Diacos.

Chapter 36

Monday, January 26, 5:07 p.m.

I stared at him in astonishment. I wanted to say something, but I was incapacitated, struggling to draw a breath, temporarily overwhelmed by the misery of Bork's beating.

Did this mean all three of them—Diacos, Bork, and Salomé—were working together? That didn't make sense. However, it did explain why the Prince had not brought me back to Kismet's house. Diacos had never set the timer. I marveled at how easily he had manipulated me.

He strode into the chamber carrying a wicker chair and a glass of water with ice cubes floating in it. He set the chair down, sat in it, took a drink, set the glass on the ground, then leaned back and looked me over.

"Wow. Sebastian, you're a mess."

I still couldn't talk.

"When I was in your house earlier," he began, "there was one room that was locked. It had a square glass plate next to it."

I remained silent. I remembered something. Kismet had prophesied we had an unknown enemy in our midst. I never suspected it was Diacos. I was still having trouble believing it. The mermaid had also predicted one of us would die. I did not want to think about that part of it—not now, with my immortal powers subdued.

"What's in there? Why is that room locked?" When I did not respond, he smiled. "You know less about yourself than I do." He took a wickedly pointed knife with a translucent blue handle out of his jacket pocket. It was the same color as my bracelet. I just had time to see how long it was when he stabbed me in the shoulder with it, twisting the blade before jerking it out.

The sharp pain was huge, agonizing. I clenched my jaws—I thought I would throw up from the intensity of the miserable, screaming ache. I bore it silently.

Thirty seconds later, there was no doubt about it. I felt no itch. I was not healing.

"Only now," Diacos said softly, "when you are about to die, do you learn of the dangerous tools that can defeat your unique nature." He held the knife up and gazed at the blood on the blade. "There are many specially designed weapons that can kill immortals. Do you know who invented them?"

"Not sure," I said through clenched teeth, "but I'll bet he was a bad Magistine."

A slap rocked my head back. I tasted blood.

"Keep a civil tongue in your head when you talk about my people."

"Your people?" I spat at him. It fell short. "You mean the demented faction that caused the genocide of your ancestors?"

Another slap, more blood in my mouth.

"You had better be more respectful than that, outsider. I am going to use this on you," he said, brandishing the knife, "but I can kill you quick or slow. What is in that room?"

"A Bigfoot," I said. "He eats a lot, but he's quiet."

"As long as you are wearing that bracelet, Sebastian, everything I do to you will be painful beyond your experience. I believe I mentioned that once before, in your living room?"

I knew he was right. The powerful signals radiating from the stab wound were excruciating. I had never felt the lasting effects of physical damage before this.

He shook his head. "You aren't going to tell me, are you?"

"Why should I? You held out on me," I said, trying a weak joke. "I suppose you also withheld the real card combination." Though still shocked that Diacos was an enemy, that did not stop me from putting a few things together. "How were you going to dispose of Marcus?"

He twirled the knife. "This works on any immortal. And the heat shield I produced for the three of you on your patio is not the limit of my powers." The corners of his mouth tightened. "I try to be polite, he threatens me, and when I make him back off, everyone acts like it's some sort of joke. When I pin him down, we'll see how funny he thinks a sunrise is."

Bork leaned on the wall, a nasty smile on his lips. "Have you ever seen that before, Erol?"

"No, not yet."

"You'll enjoy it. They scream like frightened babies when they feel those first rays. We caught one eight years ago and staked her to a fence. The sun started at the top of her body. When her hair caught fire, and she wailed like a child, I nearly pissed myself it was so good. Killing vampires is better than killing immortals." They both gave a hearty chuckle.

"Now, Sebastian, let's get back to the last few minutes of your life. What is Aliena?"

"What do you mean?"

He nonchalantly jabbed the damned knife into me again, lower on the left side this time, just below my ribcage. The agony bloomed like an unfolding flower, spreading until I thought I could not stand any more. Diacos twisted the blade out savagely and a moan escaped my lips.

Blood poured from the new wound, drenching the front of my shirt. My teeth clenched tight, and I could feel my neck muscles drawn so taut I was sure they would snap like overloaded rubber bands. Then my entire body sagged, and I rattled a despairing exhale.

I fought to stay awake. I was afraid if I grayed out, I would never wake up. My head slumped forward. My existence dwindled to a tiny point of throbbing red light. I felt him grab my hair and yank up. I looked at his unruly red mane and then into his light eyes.

"Wrong answer," he said. "I saw how she moved at Kismet's. That sort of speed is not normal, even if she is immortal. What sort of being is she?"

"The tooth fairy." So he still did not realize Aliena was a vampire. All he had seen was her speed. "She leaves coins all over the room."

He released my hair, and I fought to keep my head up. I was thinking about his threat to expose Marcus to the sun. If he could do that, he would probably do the same thing to Aliena if he discovered she was a vampire. The thought of him and Bork laughing while she screamed galvanized me. I would never let that happen as long as I could draw breath.

Diacos took a sip of water and held the enchanted knife in front of his face again, looking at my essence congealing on the blade as if fascinated by it. "No matter what I kill, the blood always looks the same."

Sweat coated my body. The left side of my torso was a combination of severe misery and numb distress. I could feel my life draining away, spilling out of the cuts, but I forced myself to concentrate on my interrogator, shoving the pain to a back corner of my mind.

"Do you know which cards Aliena holds?" Diacos asked.

"Yes."

"Are you going to tell me?"

"What do you think?"

"This is not parlor talk, Sebastian. This is your end. Cooperate, and I will kill you without making you suffer. Or think of Aliena. You do care for her, don't you? If you tell me and I don't want any of those cards, I won't kill her."

"I thought you had all the cards."

"For this combination we need one more, and I know where it is. But there are many combinations possible. I want to know what she and Marcus are holding for future reference."

My left eye had swollen shut, and my entire body felt like a stabbed stubbed toe, but I still managed a derisive laugh. "Then you would want the cards they hold anyway, wouldn't you? So you don't have to go looking for them later."

He laughed, picked up the glass, and held it to his mouth. "You're right," he said over the rim. "And Marcus must die in a blaze of fire. But I don't have to torture Aliena. I could just take her cards. Tell me what they are."

I stared at him.

"Sebastian? Don't you believe me? That I would only take her cards and leave her alone?"

"No."

"Ah, well. What can I say? I like torturing others. And even if Aliena has the most useless cards in the deck, I am going to enjoy cutting that magnificent body of hers until she screams for the release of death."

"Better than sex," Bork said huskily.

I turned to the big man. "Sex with what? A rhinoceros?"

He started toward me. Diacos waved him away.

"Not now, Detrit. Save yourself for Echo and Kismet."

"What do you mean by that?" I asked.

He took another sip of water and set the glass down. "Oh, did I forget to tell you? I hooked them."

Bork clapped his hands and Diacos bowed.

"After you walked into my trap, I asked the women to come out of the pool. Kismet, that silly airhead, jumped out immediately. But not Echo."

"Why did you want them out of the water?"

"I could not get in the pool if I wanted to capture them. As soon as I did anything they did not like, they could electrocute me. Even Detrit couldn't withstand the combined power of two mermaids especially in the water."

"But Echo did not obey you."

"No. And now that you had gone, I was not in a patient mood. It was necessary to show her who was in charge. I stunned her with a sound, and she went belly up like a fish. Kismet started to scream, so I had to shut her up as well. I hate screaming women. I stunned her hard." He laughed.

I watched his face through a red haze of hatred.

"She fell off her lounge and flopped on the floor before she went out. Echo had floated to my side of the pool, so I pulled her onto a lounge. I wanted to console her as I slipped the bracelet on her arm. The lovely thing was having a bad dream."

"Must have been about you."

His gray eyes changed. He leaned forward, raised the knife, and brought it down with savage force on my left thigh. It penetrated all the way to the handle. He twisted the blade and wrenched it out.

I strained against the bonds, my entire body tensed, my jaw cramping with the effort of keeping my scream of pain behind my lips. I remained in that frozen position, my world blind fire. Slowly, purpose returned. But everything was overlaid with the pulsing misery of my wounds.

When my muscles relaxed, my head drooped forward again. I looked at my blood-soaked lap while my sweat dropped on it like rain, and I wondered how much longer I had.

"Hey, Sebastian," Diacos crooned, "I'm up here. Or can't you make it?"

Creakily, I raised my head so I could gaze into his detestable face.

Diacos produced a card from his inside jacket pocket. It was not his Emperor star card. It was the Ace of Wands.

"So you do have one," I muttered. The liar. I nearly laughed at that thought. Liar? It was far too weak a description for the man.

"Of course. It is a critical card. I planted a minor in Kismet's house the day before yesterday. I knew she would find it eventually but not before I accomplished my task."

"Why Kismet?"

He grinned at me. "I like to keep an eye on her. I spy whenever I can. I leave cards all over the place." He and Bork laughed. "Since your Aliena is a past lover of hers, I decided to send Bork in an attempt to take her."

"Why?"

"As a bargaining chip. I intended to barter the little airhead's life for Aliena's cards."

"So Bork got there sooner than you expected and Aliena saw him."

"Yes, our timing was off. But it actually worked out well. Detrit and I still had preparations to make, and Marcus was out of the picture, watching the women. That only left you and Aliena. As it turned out, I needn't have worried. You two went to your house after that and made out on the floor in front of the fireplace."

I detested everything about this man. His entire existence for the last two days had been a fraud. People capable of deception that fine deserve my special attention. That is, if I can catch them. Diacos's deceit had been so good, he had caught me instead.

"You left a minor at my house?" I asked.

"Uh-huh. It's embedded in the fireplace, below the mantel. I put it there after I shot you in the head. You were out for nearly a minute. I didn't shoot you to prove you were immortal, you fool. I already knew that."

I cursed my overconfident stupidity. I hadn't even asked myself why he had done it or tried to fathom his motive. I was getting lazy.

"You and Aliena gave us a tender show. Detrit and I were watching closely when you unsnapped the front of her bra. Magnificent tits."

He and Bork guffawed. All I could think was that I had to kill these men.

I turned to Bork. The thought of that pig watching me undress Aliena made me sick with revulsion. I felt a surge of adrenaline. I looked back at Diacos. The gray eyes studied me dispassionately.

"Want to see something, Sebastian?" He held the Ace in front of his mouth. Then he leaned forward and positioned it in front of me. The gold border pulsed twice. He let it go as the card began to expand.

"How are Kismet and Echo doing?" he asked.

I watched as the scene stretched out and the room came into sharp focus. Kismet's living room. I could see the pool.

The two mermaids hung from the ceiling by their tails, upside down. Their arms reached limply for the clear floor and the sparkling water below it. They were not moving.

"What did you do to them?"

"Oh, I didn't kill them. Yet. They are merely unconscious."

"What about when they wake up?"

"Do you see their bracelets?"

I looked again. Both women had a translucent blue ring around one forearm. They looked the same as the one I wore.

"I can cause them serious pain if they so much as blink in a way that displeases me." He reached for the Ace, his lips moving. The card shrunk in his hand, and he replaced it in his jacket.

I was beginning to reason a few things out. "You allowed Bork to track your card."

"Yes."

So that's how he knew where we were. It did not explain how he knew the sound for the portal on her end. That meant . . .

"How is it you know the sound for the minor at Kismet's house?" I asked.

"I have known Kismet for a long time. When I met Echo a few years ago, I wanted her even more than I wanted Kismet. Mermaids are irresistible to men, you know." His face clouded with anger. "Echo doesn't remember that first meeting at all. The conceited bitch. But somehow, that made me want her even more. I just could not get over how beautiful she was. Don't you think she's beautiful, Sebastian?"

I did not say anything.

"Pulling her out of the pool was nice. My hands were slipping all over that magnificent body." He smiled at me.

"You really are a creepy little man, aren't you?"

The smile disappeared, and he leaned forward, fury in his eyes. He slashed at my face. I felt the icy track of the blade as it sped across my cheek.

"Aliena was right," he said. "You really do ask for it."

I loathed him saying her name. I felt blood flowing onto my neck. "What about Salomé?"

He and Bork laughed.

"She doesn't exist?" I guessed. Warm blood flowed over my chin. Consciousness flickered. I felt strange, as if I were participating in the conversation, yet viewing it from afar at the same time.

"Oh, she exists," he said, "but she is hardly a threat. She's my older sister."

"But . . . then why portray her as the enemy?"

"Because she is," he said. "From the moment I learned of our family's past, I knew what needed to be done. But my sister didn't agree. She turned her back on our legacy."

"I see," I said, my voice weak. In spite of my determination to stay alive, I was fading. I could feel it. "Does she have a card you need?"

"Yes. Her personal star card. The Empress. The last one." He and Bork looked at each other and laughed again. "And the best part is we will have to kill her to get it."

Chapter 37

Monday, January 26, 5:37 p.m.

Sitting on that chair, blood seeping from four knife wounds, I could not think of any way to stop Diacos and Bork from completing their mission. I shook my head at his last words. "You really are a bastard, aren't you?"

"To some, yes. But I do not shirk from my responsibility. Someone must reestablish our society and make it viable again."

"And for that you want to raise eleven people from the dead?"

"Yes. You look like you're about done, Sebastian," Diacos said. Bork sniggered. "You will finally meet the God that created you."

"You believe in God? What about 'thou shalt not kill'?"

His eyebrows rose in surprise. "Good lord, you are slow, aren't you? He didn't mean *us*. He meant the senseless animals that form the lower base of our society. They kill indiscriminately, for no purpose. But we need to kill sometimes; of course we do if we want to advance a dream."

"Sounds more like a nightmare to me."

"It is. For you."

His head jerked up. Bork stopped leaning on the rock wall and looked down the passage. We all heard it.

Someone had activated a star card outside the cell.

Diacos stood. He wiped the cursed blade on his pants and put it back in his pocket. Bork had in his hand the same toothpaste tube–shaped weapon he had used at Kismet's house.

"See anything?" Diacos asked him.

"No." Bork faced left. Now he turned and looked the other way. "There's nobody here."

My heart beat heavily in my chest, and my vision blurred. I shook my head, trying to concentrate.

"We heard the card," Diacos said, his hands empty. He apparently did not need a weapon. So he had been telling the truth when he said Bork was not as skilled at soundcraft. "Someone is out there. We'll have to search for them." He turned to me, patted the top of my head. "You will wait for us, won't you, Sebastian?" he said with a smile. "If you die before we get back, have a good trip."

Bork was clearly more nervous than his partner was. "C'mon, Erol, let's do this."

"Yes, okay." Diacos moved to his side. "Which way?"

Bork pointed left. "It sounded like it came from that direction," he said.

They left the cell and started down the tunnel.

My head fell again. I labored to get a breath. My heartbeat became uneven. I still bled from the stab to my leg. The seat of my chair dripped blood.

I heard a shout. No way to tell who it was. The sound of Bork's stun gun boomed down the hall, and I felt the change in air pressure. More shouts. The sound of a star card. A second thumping shot from the stun gun. Another star card activating.

Silence.

I waited, staring at the bracelet that was killing me. How could this happen? I had to go to my death without even knowing the inscription on the instrument of my demise.

I took a rattling breath. My heart beat very fast now, and I could feel the blackness rolling over me like a cloud blocking the sun. Before I closed my eyes and lost consciousness, I wondered if God would be a man or a woman.

Haze of red. Sounds? Roaring in my ears. Not outside. Inside. I blinked. Too bright. Keep eyes closed. Snuggle into the darkness. Stay here, away from the pain.

"Sebastian?"

I opened my eyes. Above me was the most beautiful face I had ever seen. Not only was God a woman, she was gorgeous. In spite of her angelic appearance, the light surrounding her hurt, so I closed my eyes.

I was so tired and so happy to be here away from that horror on Earth. No more liars, no more greed, no more death. A huge weight fell from me, a burden I had not even realized I carried.

Now that I lived in Heaven, I wanted to lie here quietly and let the peace of paradise flow into me.

"Sebastian? Are you okay? Oh, Sebastian."

I became embarrassed. It didn't seem right that God should pay so much attention to me, even if I were one of her special creations. What if the others could see and hear us? I felt like the teacher's pet.

"His breathing is much easier," another female voice said. I heard a splash of water and felt the touch of a warm hand against my neck. "Pulse is normal. He will be joining us again shortly."

Again? What did she mean by that? Had I been in Heaven before?

When I opened my eyes this time, I did not understand what I was seeing. This looked like Kismet's house, not Heaven. A terrible suspicion overcame me: I was still on Earth. With the liars and rapists and murderers. I was not with God and her angels.

Tears seeped out of my eyes. I felt the curse of humanity settle onto my shoulders once more. *No,* I thought, *I want to stay in Heaven. Please don't send me back here—let me come away from this madness.*

A face appeared above me. It was God's face. No, now I recognized her. Aliena. I could feel the tears rolling into my ears.

"It's okay," she said, leaning down and kissing me, "you're going to be fine."

I opened my mouth but nothing came out. What do you say when you've returned to the cauldron? More tears flowed.

"Please don't cry, Sebastian," Aliena said, stroking my hair. "You're with me now. You're safe." I shook my head miserably. I loved Aliena more than my own life, but how could I possibly explain to her my sorrow at leaving Heaven?

It was simply too much for my spirit to endure. I closed my eyes. As I fell back into the darkness, I prayed that I would wake up in paradise again.

Chapter 38

Monday, January 26, 6:06 p.m.

When I came to, I knew my location. I felt the ghost of my emotions when I believed I had made it to Nirvana but pushed them aside quickly. They were the most joyous feelings I had ever had, and I did not want to depress myself with the knowledge that I really might live forever and never go to Heaven.

For the first time I envied all the mortals who had died while I continued to walk the earth. It occurred to me that death was one of the more attractive features of being human. After all, who truly wanted to stay on this capricious plane of existence forever? Not I.

I mentally checked my body. Everything worked, and I had no pain. I opened my eyes. Aliena stood there, face filled with worry.

"Are you with me?" she asked anxiously.

I nodded.

"Oh, Sebastian." She laid her head on my chest. "When I saw you on that chair, it didn't look like you were . . . oh, my dearest. I was so scared."

I put my arms around her and hugged her to me. As sad as I was to return to this existence, I knew I was blessed to have such a wonderful companion as Aliena to accompany me through life. This trial was hard enough *with* love. It would be nearly unbearable without it.

The recent past filtered to my consciousness. I raised my arm and looked at my watch. Ten after six. What had the time been the last I looked? About a quarter to, I remembered. Twenty-five minutes ago. Was that before or after Diacos worked on me? I was not sure.

"It was Diacos," I said. "He and Bork are working together."

Aliena rose, smiling. "I realized that."

"What do you mean?"

"When I woke up tonight and you weren't there, my suspicions about him were confirmed."

"You suspected him before this? Why didn't you tell me?" I sat up.

"Because it was mostly a feeling. I wanted to be sure."

"And now you are?"

"Yes. For one thing, I could not think of anyone else who could keep you away from me at sunset." She stroked my cheek, and I smiled. "I was terrified when I realized he might have you."

I looked around. A picture of the mermaids hanging upside down popped into my head. "What about Echo and Kismet?"

"The poor dears are in their beds now, asleep."

"How did you find out Diacos had stunned them?"

"Marcus came to check on them after sunset and found them hanging from the ceiling. He called me, and I came immediately. They were badly shaken, but they told me where you had gone and helped me with you when I got back. But there was not much we could do. I don't understand how, but your injuries began to fade as soon as I removed that ugly bracelet from your arm."

"Do you have it?"

She nodded. "I knew you would want to keep it. The ones that were on Kiz and Echo were the same, so we have three."

"How did you know? What convinced you it was Diacos?"

"From the first moment I met him, I wanted to kill him. I hated the familiar way he spoke to me when we were still strangers. Inexcusable effrontery."

I remembered her expression. "So you disliked him," I said, smiling. "How does that make him a suspect?"

The finger and thumb of her right hand twitched, and I knew she wanted to pinch me. I was sure it was only because I had almost died that she stayed her hand.

"It does not. However, I started looking for reasons to doubt him. And I found several."

"Such as?"

"In an encrypted file on the Internet, I discovered the real combination of archons required to bring back the dead."

I was impressed. "So you knew the combination Diacos gave us was no good."

"Yes."

"Do you know the real combination?"

"Of course. You would not want to see that spread when predicting your future," Aliena said.

"Diacos has the Prince now. Anything else?"

"For someone who claimed not to have a Prince card, he handled it too surely. He knew how to activate it and set the timer. I was convinced it was his."

"That long ago? You should have told me," I said. I could not help a little anger creeping into my voice. "Everything about these damn archon cards is too secretive for safety."

She looked at the ground. "Yes," she said. "That is exactly what I was thinking before we found you. I should have put you on your guard."

I knew she meant it, so I wanted to change the subject. I looked down at my clothes, sticky with blood, then up at Aliena. She watched me. "Does this make you hungry?" I asked, gesturing at the blood on my shirt.

She looked revolted. "Not at all. I hate cold things."

I cupped her chin, lifted her gaze to mine. "I love cold things," I said. "Very much."

She took my hand in her freezing one. "Are you sure?"

"You know I am. Do you think I have been joking for a hundred years?"

She turned my hand up, kissed me on the palm.

"I have a million more questions," I told her, standing. "But let's talk about it on the way home. You had to carry me," I said, noting the stains on her shoulders and front. "We both need to change."

"We can't leave Kismet and Echo alone. We don't know where Diacos or Bork are. Let's wait for Marcus, okay?"

"Have you called him?"

"Yes. He should be here soon."

We heard the now familiar crackle. In the vestibule, Kismet's portal card flashed twice, then a 'hole' opened in the air and expanded. When it was as tall as a doorway, Marcus appeared and stepped out of it. The rip closed behind him. He nodded at us, took his shoes off, and came into the living room on stocking feet. He looked me over.

"Sebastian, you're a mess. What happened?"

"I don't always play well with others."

Before I stepped into the 49, I took everything out of my pockets and removed all my clothes. I stowed them in the trunk. On the drive back to my house, I called Hamilton, told him I had been unavoidably detained, and suggested we meet at his place.

As I fastened my seat belt, Aliena gave my naked body a long, languorous look.

She told me more about her investigation into Cavanaugh's past. She discovered that he had been well aware of his Magistine roots—a family tradition for five centuries. Though he knew Bork and Diacos were members of a different faction of Magistine society, and one that was antagonistic to his, he had no aspirations within the ancient culture, so he did not think they would bother him.

Unfortunately, through his antique purchases he became the owner of a star card—the previous owner conferred it to him—and Diacos discovered the fact.

"Bork must have accosted Cavanaugh at his store and offered to buy the card," she said. "It's possible he and Diacos thought Cavanaugh had no idea of the card's power. They also did not realize that Cavanaugh knew their ancestry and was now determined to thwart them."

That made sense. Cavanaugh had acquired the archons in the box I had seen at his store. His broker in Istanbul had been murdered three hours after the transaction was complete. When Cavanaugh learned of the solicitor's death, he knew his enemies would trace the cards to him.

"What about the cards that were stolen from his store? Do you know who they came from?"

"I can't find that," she said. "Yet."

"It sounds like Cavanaugh was getting in over his head."

"I don't think he expected to live through this," Aliena said. "Remember in your report you pointed out that there was nothing at all on top of Cavanaugh's desk but that tape recorder when you found him."

Her thoroughness impressed me, even if she could speed read faster than anyone I've ever seen. "He was cleaning up his affairs?"

"He sounds like he was a tidy man in every way. That's why he hid his star card in a safe place."

"Which card does he have?"

"Unknown."

"But who bequeathed it to him? Who was the previous owner?"

"I have not been able to find her," Aliena said, and she sounded piqued. "Cavanaugh left nothing behind indicating her identity."

"How do you know it's a her?"

"I assume only a very intelligent person could hold and use an archon properly."

"Hm. So we don't know why the previous owner gave Cavanaugh the card."

"No. We don't know the relationship between the cardholder and our antiques dealer. We also don't know the circumstances leading to Cavanaugh's acquisition of the card. If he did not leave a hint, it's unlikely we'll ever locate the previous cardholder. Star card holders are difficult to find anyway. If she decided to put effort into it, she could disappear."

"Sounds familiar."

Aliena did report one puzzling discovery: nowhere in any file relating to Diacos, Bork, or Cavanaugh, had she found the name Salomé.

"He told me she's his sister. I am not sure we should believe that in light of the evidence. He lied about everything else."

I turned into my drive and parked next to the T-bird. We got out, and Aliena pressed her hand to the security glass and went inside. The door to the house popped open. I took the clothes out of the 49's trunk and threw them into one of the trash cans in my garage. Hector would dispose of the garments anonymously, burning them.

I walked inside, past the front door, and climbed the stairs. As I gained the landing, I felt a puff of air. Then an arctic hand grabbed my behind.

"Nice," Aliena said. She pulled me into my room and turned me toward her. She had taken off her clothes. Her gaze traveled from my shoulders to my toes. She had her icy fingertips on my chest. Now she stroked my skin. "You have a lovely warm body," she said. Her hands strayed lower. "Mm, nice abs."

"Aliena." I raised my hands and rested them on her bare hips. Her flesh radiated coolness, so soft, and my longing became acute, like an ocean wave washing over me. With an effort, I kept myself still.

She stood on her toes and kissed me lightly, her bare breasts brushing my chest. "I know. Soon."

Seeing her without clothes was one thing, but having her rub my chest while we were both naked was too much for me. In a moment or two I would not be able to stop myself. Not with the bed this close.

"I need a cold shower."

Chapter 39

Monday, January 26, 7:34 p.m.

Aliena and I stood in front of the fireplace both clean and warm. Well, I was warm and Aliena was less frosty. We both wore jeans. Hers looked better. IMO.

She held her star card, waving it near the mantle. After a few seconds an archon, embedded in the brick, began to glow. The Six of Wands. Aliena picked it out and touched the Moon to it. The gold border pulsed once, and she held it to her mouth and whispered briefly. It pulsed one more time. She put it back below the hearth. As soon as it touched the rock, it disappeared.

"I have reset it so Diacos can no longer travel through it or use it as a window with an Ace."

"Good."

"The password is *existential*."

"I don't know what good that will do me without a star card or an Ace."

"Yes, but I can keep an eye on you—even pop in whenever I feel like it."

"Why would you want to keep an eye on me?"

"Oh, many reasons."

The bracelet Aliena had removed from my arm—the one Diacos and Bork used to torture me—now rested in my safe. The entire Magistine inscription read, "No one can live to eternity's end."

"Now that he has the Prince, how many of the cards does he have?" I asked her.

"The way he tortured you convinces me he has all seven of them."

"When will he begin the ceremony?" I knew it would not be long.

"There is no special time. I would guess after nightfall."
"Where?"
"He will return to Turkey."
"To be close to the original bodies?"
"Yes."
"We need to meet with Hamilton." We could never get to Turkey in time. Hamilton would be able to contact the nearest law enforcement agency, but I could not picture any police officers capturing Diacos and Bork.
"Do not say I saved you," she pleaded. "I do not want to have to answer his questions again."
"Not to worry," I said, hugging her and kissing the tip of her nose. "I will give him an edited report. You were never anywhere."
"Good. Because I need to come with you."
"Why?"
"I have more information," she said, a twinkle in her eye.
"What is it?"
She gave me her naughty smile. "When we see Hamilton."
"Then let's go now."
We climbed into the 49 and started for the Valley.

On the drive, I called Hamilton to confirm we would be there soon.
"How about dinner?" he asked.
"Don't you ever think about anything else?" I asked.
"After that and sex, what else is important?" His voice came out of the 49's speakers.
I glanced at Aliena. "Love is nice."
"I suppose. If you can get it. I still need at least twenty minutes to finish this report. If you really cared, you would stop for a pizza or something."
"Pizza?"

"Yeah. You have to drive past the Round Table on Ventura anyway. I can call it in and you can pick it up."

"Call it in," I said.

"Good man." We disconnected.

The interior of my car reeked of pepperoni, burned cheese, and onions by the time we turned on Murietta. I found it mouth-watering. Aliena did not.

"Oh," she said, holding her nose and rolling her window down. "Disgusting."

"I thought you liked warm meat."

"Not when it's dead."

I laughed and couldn't stop for a few moments. When I could finally speak again, I said, "You know . . ." I looked at her, a smile on my face. I wanted to tell her how happy I was whenever we were together. She watched me. I felt that irresistible adoration for her again. "I love when you're with me," I said. I suspected she was tired of listening to me tell her how much I loved her, but I couldn't help it.

She reached over and touched my hand. "I love being with you. Do you think I sleep at any man's house?" she said, pretending to be offended.

"No, I know you don't," I said. "I can't tell you how much that means to me."

"To me, too."

My feelings were so strong for Aliena that if she ever decided to leave, I knew I would suffer as I had when Karina and Monique, my two wives, had died. I never wanted to go through that again, so I continued to mute my happiness with Aliena, even though our relationship was becoming what I have wanted all along.

Reading her diary made me aware of her reasons for not wanting to be in a romantic relationship. The perfidy of François rankled still. And he was an immortal. I did not yet know if I had broken through those barriers.

When we arrived at Hamilton's building, he buzzed us in and was waiting at his door when we walked up. He took the pizza box.

"Fantastic. You do hook me up, Sebastian. Hi, Aliena."

"Hello."

"Did either of you want a piece?" he asked as he took the box into the kitchen. He was not wearing a jacket, but he still had his holster on his hip.

"Yes, I'll take a couple," I said.

He looked at Aliena and said, "Oh, that's right, you're only into natural food. What do you eat, anyway?"

"Things you would not like."

I listened, a bit apprehensive. Aliena was unpredictable in these situations. She might tell Hamilton the truth—and show him her fangs to prove it—to see how he would handle it. Since killing him would probably be necessary in that scenario, I hoped she remembered her promise to leave him alone.

"Come on. Give me an example."

"I like food with hair on it."

"Uhh. Never mind. I'll stick to pizza."

Aliena and I sat on the couch. Hamilton sat on the adjacent chair after handing me my plate.

"You have anything on Bork?" he asked.

"Sort of."

"Sort of? What does that mean?"

I finished chewing and swallowed. "Well, we don't know where he is. But we do know he's working with Diacos, not Salomé."

He stopped with a slice of pizza halfway to his mouth. "Diacos? But I thought . . . hell, that never occurred to me."

"Me, either."

"Do you know where he is now?"

"No."

"How did you find this out?"

I decided to say nothing about my capture. Instead, I let Aliena describe her reasoning. Hamilton nodded throughout.

"I never liked that mutha," he said when she was finished.

"I did not, either," Aliena said.

"Is that it?" He looked at me. "Anything else?"

I shook my head. I could see the dissatisfaction on his face. He knew we were withholding something. "Aliena said she has information for us." We both looked at her.

"I will tell you where we need to go," she said.

"Go? What do you mean?" Hamilton asked.

"There is someone we need to visit." She had a coy look on her face.

"Who?"

"You had better call him first and arrange it."

When she gave me the phone number and told us whose it was, Hamilton and I stared at each other in disbelief. She said no more. I pulled my cell out, dialed. The man on the other end agreed to meet with us in thirty minutes.

I hung up. "Well?" I said to Aliena. "Could you at least give us a hint?"

"It's from the poem you found in Cavanaugh's painting."

"I forgot all about that thing," Hamilton said. He frowned. "When did you see that?"

"Yesterday."

"Where? And where did you get his phone number?"

"In the case file. Online."

"Online? Christ, Sebastian. I can't believe you would write that password down and then give it to an unauthorized person."

"I am not unauthorized, and he did not write it down," Aliena said. "I memorized it."

"That code is twenty-one characters long, a mixture of numbers and letters. I suppose you also memorized it the first time you read it."

"The first time I heard it, actually."

He looked at me, back to her. "You two," he said, shaking his head. "You guys don't make any sense. You have a trick memory," he said, gesturing at Aliena, "and there are other things about you that can only be described as mysterious." He tossed a crust onto his plate, wiped his fingers on a napkin. "And you," he said, focusing on me, "seem to recover from wounds that would kill another man. What's next on your agenda? Going to take me to another dimension? I would not be surprised."

Aliena looked innocent, and I did my best to mimic her.

"So you found what you were looking for in the case evidence?" he asked her. "How did that poem go again?"

She recited it:

> A rank amateur holds the key.
> No one knows it's there but me.
> To locate, explore the ancient tray.
> Find it before someone takes it away.
> It is a door to other places.
> Watch out or you will see enemy faces.
> Don't let them retrieve it before you do.
> For if they win, we are all through.

"When I saw the poem," Aliena continued, "I had just finished reading your report on him. That helped me put the pieces together."

"You put it together." He shook his head again. "What the hell are you doing working with me? You could be doing anything you wanted—like traveling around the world."

"Done it," Aliena said.

"Go on an archaeology dig, then."

"We have been on several," I said.

"What about a cruise? You love the water, I know that."

"I have been on many cruises, and Aliena does not like traveling that way."

"How about climbing a mountain?"

"Done it," we answered together.

"Hot air balloons? Parasailing? Base jumping?"

"Done it, done it, done it," Aliena said as I nodded agreement. "I base jump all the time. I'm part of a club."

So hilarious. Not.

He gave up. "Fine, you two have done everything. I know when I'm licked. It still doesn't explain why you are doing this."

"To protect and serve," Aliena said.

"That's great. Another comedian. Well, are you ever going to spill that hint for us and tell us why we're meeting this man?"

Aliena said, "He is the rank amateur."

Chapter 40

Monday, January 26, 8:34 p.m.

The three of us piled into the Ford coupe and headed for Beverly Hills. After I merged onto the freeway, I reviewed the case facts in my mind. How could Aliena possibly have come to the conclusion that this man was the one mentioned in Cavanaugh's verse? I knew who it was now, and I still couldn't figure it out.

She had read the poem. And she had studied the reports the police prepared on him. What could she have seen? Other than the poem and the things we had all observed numerous times, where could the piece of the puzzle come from?

When the light finally went on in my head, I smiled broadly and looked at her in the mirror.

"You're so smart, Sebastian," she said, leaning forward and kissing me on the shoulder.

"You, too. Now that I know who our man is, it's obvious the poem is about him."

"Well, I guess I'm the odd man out, intelligence-wise," Hamilton said. "Someone want to tell me?"

Aliena nodded at me, so I explained.

"Remember the first time we questioned him? What did you tell me before we arrived?"

He thought about it. "What, his money? How he made it? Wait. The part about wanting to be called colonel?" He laughed out loud. "Rank. Of course. He cared about his rank. And amateur, because he was not even a real soldier and had never actually made colonel. I'm still not sure I get the connection. Why are we going there?"

This part I had figured out. "In the poem, Cavanaugh wrote about the ancient tray. He told us that's where we would find the hidden archon."

"Where's that?"

"What was the only connection Parmalee had with Cavanaugh? The reason we visited in the first place?"

"He had just purchased an antique . . . okay, I get it." We were quiet for a few moments. "Does this mean Parmalee is a cardholder?"

"I don't know," I said. "Cavanaugh meant to hide it, not put it in safekeeping. I doubt Parmalee even knows it's there. What do you think?" I asked Aliena in the mirror.

"I am sure our rank amateur has no idea a star card resides in his armoire. Whether he is a cardholder or not, I cannot say. I shall be watching him carefully."

"This is getting exciting," Hamilton said, rubbing his hands together. "It's like hunting for buried treasure. We're on our way to find a hidden magical tarot card." He stopped. "Um, what do we do then?"

Monday, January 26, 7:49 p.m.

When we cruised to a stop in front of the Parmalee estate, lights burned in the downstairs windows. We had to submit to the security camera. The colonel answered the door as before.

"Come in, come in," he said. When he saw Aliena, his eyes narrowed with a sharp look completely unlike anything I had seen when Hamilton and I had first questioned him.

He led us into the room with the military memorabilia. Hamilton and I followed him as far as the center and stopped. Aliena remained near the door, her right arm resting on the brass cannon.

Parmalee walked behind his bar and began mixing a drink. "What can I do for you, Mr. Montero?"

"Why did you finger Detrit Bork for us, sir?"

There it was again. That assessing look that didn't fit with his hail-fellow-well-met routine. Then his eyes unfocused again.

"Berk? Finger Berk? I don't know what you mean."

"Bork, Colonel," Hamilton said. "You ID'd him for us the last time we were here."

"The man you called a punk," I reminded him.

"Are you accusing me of something deceitful?" He pretended to be outraged. "I am an officer and a gen—"

"Save it," Hamilton said. "We have a little poem about you. Cavanaugh left it for us."

Now he definitely assessed the situation. I realized if he went for a star card right now, he could escape. He must have been thinking the same thing, because he reached inside his jacket.

"Hold it!" Hamilton shouted, moving toward him.

A blur between us. Aliena appeared in front of Parmalee, holding his wrist. In her other hand was an archon. She released him and walked over to us, showing us the card.

"Nice," I said. "The Star. Where did you get it?"

He took a long drink, draining his glass, but he still looked at Aliena. He began to mix another.

Hamilton followed his look. "Where the hell did you come from?" he asked her.

"I was standing behind the two of you."

"No," Parmalee said, "you were not."

Aliena ignored him and changed the subject. "Where is the armoire you bought from Mr. Cavanaugh's store?"

He stared at us, drinking. I noticed Aliena no longer stood behind us. I turned back to Parmalee.

"Well?" Hamilton said. "It's not like you could hide something that big, even in a house this size."

Parmalee stared past us. "What is she, anyway?" he asked in a husky voice.

Aliena stood behind us again. Hamilton turned. "What do you mean?" he asked the colonel.

"She disappeared a moment ago and then reappeared behind you."

"Save your crazy delusions for the psychiatrist. We're not buying it. Where is the armoire?"

"It's in the bedroom down the hall to the left," Aliena said.

"Now how the hell do you know that?" Hamilton asked.

"Hadn't you noticed?" she said with a gleaming smile. "I know everything."

We walked to the bedroom, Aliena leading the way. As soon as we passed through the door, I saw the large ornate cabinet against the back wall.

"There it is," Parmalee said. He stopped just inside the door and crossed his arms over his chest.

"It is beautiful," Aliena said. She pulled on the brass handles and opened both doors wide. There were only six hangers in it, all holding military jackets. The right side had four sliding trays from the bottom to the top. She pulled out the lowest one. Empty.

"What are we looking at?" Hamilton asked.

"You will see."

I glanced at the colonel. He looked puzzled. I don't think he knew what Aliena was doing.

She took Parmalee's star card and slowly waved it around. A tarot card appeared on the bottom, glowing brightly. The gold border pulsed like a heartbeat. The Chariot.

"You wouldn't happen to know the sound that activates it?" I asked her. She giggled. I couldn't believe it. She did know. "Okay, how do you know *that*?"

"It's in the poem," she said, leaning toward the card. I saw her lips move, and she plucked the card out of the oak. Once she had pulled it free, no indentation remained in the wood.

I glanced at Parmalee.

"A star card was right here?" He looked stunned. "How? Why?"

"It was the perfect hiding place," Aliena said, sliding the Chariot into her jacket pocket. "Why would you search your own house for something you didn't know you had?"

"How did he know I was a cardholder?"

"I'm sure he didn't know," I said. "He referred to you as the rank amateur—not anything to do with the cards. He may have simply wanted to put the armoire in a safe place where his enemies wouldn't think to look. Even you didn't realize what you had."

His face shone red. Being labeled a rank amateur did not sit well with the colonel. He also looked confused.

"Where are the other cards you have collected?" Hamilton asked him.

"What do you mean?"

"Let's start with the ones stolen from Cavanaugh's store."

He looked blankly at Hamilton. "I didn't do that."

"We know," I said. "Bork did. But it was at your command. That's why we asked you your reason for giving him up."

He looked at all three of us, his face genuinely puzzled. "I did not know the man in your picture, if that's who you mean."

"Then why put us onto him?" Hamilton asked.

"I heard part of his conversation with Mr. Cavanaugh. They said *star card* and *archons*." He shrugged. "I thought it would be a good idea to get them in trouble. For all I knew, they were trying to find me and take my cards."

I could see he was telling us the truth. He hadn't known Bork or Diacos and was not trying to put a card combination together. There was still something missing.

"Aliena, is the Chariot one of the cards in the combination?"

"No."

"I didn't think so."

"What?" Hamilton said. "Care to tell me what you're thinking?"

"The colonel might be the rank amateur, but he is not the instigator of the search for archons."

"That does not seem possible, Sebastian," Aliena said.

"Have you had your star card all your life?" I asked Parmalee.

He stood there. I was sure I was right.

Since he didn't have the other cards, did that mean Bork had them? I could not see Diacos trusting him that far. So where were they?

"Do you know a man named Erol Diacos?" I asked.

"No."

I believed him. I turned to Hamilton. "We need to continue our search."

"Then why did he think it was such a big deal when Aliena found that card? It sure sounded like he wanted it."

"Of course he did," Aliena told him. "Every card in the Tarot of the Archons is valuable."

"Then why did Cavanaugh hide that damn thing? If it's not part of this combination?"

Aliena answered, which was good since I had no idea.

"He wanted it to lead us somewhere."

"Just anybody?" Hamilton said.

"Whoever solved the riddle of his poem, yes. Another reason the Chariot is coveted is that there are other powerful combinations that do require this card."

"That figures," Hamilton said.

"Since I am not the one you're looking for," Parmalee said, "may I have my card back?"

"Where did you get it?" I asked him again.

"Damn you," he said. "You have no right to know that." We waited. He finally said, "My father gave it to me."

298

"Do you have any minor cards here?"

He did not answer. The star cards were most valuable when a cardholder could travel to a place of safety. No place was safer than home.

"We could search your house and grounds," Aliena said. "As long as I have my card, they will reveal themselves."

"And if you force us to look for them, we will take them and your star card," I said. It was an abominable threat. I actually had no intention of taking any of his cards.

He looked furious. "You have no right to do that. The cards are mine. They have been in my family for centuries."

"How many?"

He stared at me with unconcealed hatred. "I have three."

"Which three?" Aliena asked.

"The Queen of Wands, the Four of Pentacles and the Prince of Cups."

"Are they here in the house?" Hamilton said.

"Two are. One of them is in the stable."

I nodded at Aliena and she gave the star back to Parmalee.

"Is that a good idea?" Hamilton asked.

"It's none of your damned business," Parmalee said, clearly enraged at having to negotiate for his family heirloom. He put it in his pocket. "I want you out of my house."

"He's right," I said. "Let's go."

Parmalee ushered us to the door and saw that we left. "And don't come back!" He slammed the door.

"What I don't understand," Hamilton said when we were back in the car, "is why Cavanaugh used a poem. Why couldn't he just tell us? Did he think his message was too easy to find?"

"I'm sure that's the main reason," I said. "But the cards are based on sound, and according to Diacos the resurrection ceremony requires a song. A poem is like a song. Hm." There was something there. I could sense the edge of it but couldn't get my mind around all of it. I was missing something. This case centered on the cards, and they were activated by sounds. It seemed there should be more attached to that idea, but I was coming up blank.

"What about this card we just found?" Hamilton asked.

I waited for Aliena.

"It's obvious, isn't it?" she said. "Someone has to travel through it."

"How can we go anywhere? Don't we need to know the sound for the destination card?" I asked.

"This card has been preset for a journey. That is why it continues to pulse whenever another star card is near." She held the Moon close to it, and the gold border on the Chariot began a metronomic strobe.

"So we don't have to know the destination card's sound?" I asked.

"Correct. More importantly, the Chariot is a star card and has been preset as an invitation. That way, the card's owner can have someone visit her or meet her while keeping the sound of the card to herself."

"That makes sense," said Hamilton. "I wouldn't tell anybody my codes."

"Does the card stay here?" I said.

"No, it returns to its owner."

"Can you guess where it might take us?" Hamilton asked.

The interior of my car grew quiet as we thought about it. Did the destination have something to do with the resurrection combination? Or was it a trap—maybe Cavanaugh believed Bork and Diacos would find it first?

"I can't think of anywhere," Hamilton said.

"No," Aliena said.

I added my agreement. The only sounds in the 49's cab were the hum of the wheels on the road and the whoosh of passing cars. I wondered what lay beyond the Chariot. Would it

300

take us to Bork and Diacos? How could Cavanaugh have known where they were going to be?

I planned to travel through it. There was no other way to determine where it went. Whether it was a place that would help us or not was something I would discover.

"Well?" Aliena said. "Who wants to take a trip into the unknown?"

Chapter 41

Monday, January 26, 9:12 p.m.

We were back at my place, the three of us standing on the patio. Marcus had called with the intention of stopping by but changed his mind when he heard Hamilton was with us.

We were still deciding the question of who would go through the portal.

"I want to go," Aliena said.

"Not a chance," I said. "That is out of the question."

"You might need me."

"No."

"Why can't Aliena go?" Hamilton asked.

"She just . . . can't. I do not want to place her in danger," I said, staring at her. "She can't take the risk. *We* can't take the risk."

"I agree," Hamilton said.

Aliena opened her mouth, but I interrupted her.

"No, Aliena." I said it softly with a pleading note in my voice. We could not take the chance that the portal led to the other side of the earth, where the sun blazed in the sky. We would not be able to get back fast enough to save her.

She finally nodded. "Yes, I agree, I will stay here."

"Thank you. That leaves you and me," I said to Hamilton. "I am definitely going."

"You can count me in," he said. "If there's any chance that thing will take us to Bork, I'm going. I have something for that mutha."

That decided, we walked into the living room. "What are you going to do?" I asked Aliena.

"I will wait here."

"If we don't get back by, um, too late, you may want to stay someplace else. They know this location."

"Yes." She came to me, put her arms around my neck. "Please be careful. I could not stand to lose you."

I kissed her. "I will. I promise."

"How do we get back?" Hamilton asked.

"Well, if we end up a long way from home, we'll come back the old-fashioned way: by plane."

He looked at the archon. "Flying seems archaic now."

"We don't have a star card, so it's not possible to return through the cards."

We both checked our guns, replaced them in their holsters.

"Do we have to go through the card together?"

"Yes."

He grunted. "We don't have to hold hands or anything, do we?"

Our preparations completed, Aliena gave me the Chariot.

"What's the password?" I asked.

"All invitation cards have the same one. Say, 'I am a guest' in any language, and the card will transport you."

"Is that what you said in Parmalee's armoire?"

"No. I was not traveling through it."

"So you know the actual code word as well."

"For the star card, yes."

I decided not to ask her what it was. She might not want to say in front of others.

I looked at Hamilton. "Ready?"

"Yes. Should we go with our guns drawn?"

"No. We'll just have to risk it. When we get through, just be alert. And quiet. Our priority will be to discover where we are."

"Okay."

"Take my hand."

He looked at me.

"Just kidding." I held the card up. "I am a guest."

The card began to expand immediately. I let go of it. When it was as big as a doorway, Hamilton and I stepped inside.

Chapter 42

Tuesday, January 27, 6:30 a.m. Eastern European Time

After the blast of air, the quick freeze, and the starscape, Hamilton and I exited next to a couple of trees on the side of a road. A light rain fell, and the temperature was at least forty degrees colder.

"Okay?" I asked Hamilton in a low voice.

"Yeah. That was a rush." He rubbed his hands together. "It's damned cold," he said, a cloud billowing from his mouth.

I looked around. "Yes. Let's figure out where we are."

The temperature made it obvious we had traveled to a different place on the map. The sun had apparently risen not long ago. Across the street sat an inn. The building looked to have been constructed in the sixteenth century. The name over the front door when translated was The Moon and Shadow. The language confirmed our location.

"We're in Turkey," I said, setting my watch. "We have traveled into the future."

"What do you mean?"

"Turkey is ten hours ahead of Pacific time. It looks to be about six thirty in the morning. Tuesday."

"Why here? Did Cavanaugh just expect us to know what to do?"

"We know we have to find Diacos. Cavanaugh was a Magistine. He would have picked this place carefully." I put my hands on my hips and stared across the road. "I think we should start there." I gestured at the inn. "We came out facing it."

He looked, nodded. "Let's do it."

We jogged across to the hotel.

Once we stepped inside, dark wood paneling dominated. A large coat closet sat to the right of the front desk. On the wall to our left were hooks for jackets. At the end of the room, a brick fireplace containing a small mountain of kindling soaked the scene in amber light. Positioned in front of it was a big, round oak table surrounded by six low-backed leather chairs. The place exuded Old World serenity, beautiful in its details.

"May I help you?" The woman behind the desk watched us.

"Yes, thank you," I replied in Turkish as we walked up to her. She wore a tag on the left side of her dress that said Sevil. No last name. "We are here for breakfast."

"Of course." Deep red hair hung to her shoulders. She regarded us with calm gray eyes while she pushed a stray lock off her forehead. Quite good-looking. Her gray eyes mesmerized above a sculpted nose. "Sally?" she called. We heard shuffling. A girl came running from the hallway to our right. She looked to be about twelve or thirteen years old and wore a red-and-black gingham dress like Sevil's.

"Yes, mama?" She had red hair with a hint of blonde, and green eyes.

"Show these men to a table, honey. See if they want something to drink." She had a nice soft voice. Circles smudged her eyes.

"Yes, mama," Sally said. "If you will follow me, please?"

"Thank you," I told Sevil. She nodded.

Hamilton and I followed our diminutive hostess across the lobby and into the restaurant portion of the inn. Five other parties dined in the large room. Sally led us to a window table looking out at the trees where we had appeared.

"Is this fine?"

"Yes, thank you, Sally."

"I will bring you tea and water."

"Thank you."

She wound her way through the dining room to my left until she stood in front of the bar. Three patrons sat next to her, clearly needing refills, but when the bartender saw her, he went over to her.

"Well?" Hamilton said. "Have you learned anything?"

"Patience. I have not yet asked any questions."

"You did see the woman behind the desk had red hair and gray eyes?"

Hamilton couldn't understand the language, so he would have watched her face even more carefully than usual. And he had seen what I had seen.

"Yes, I noticed."

"Well, what do you think? Niece? Sister?" He casually turned and watched her. "She's related to Diacos somehow and based on the resemblance, fairly close. I would guess sister. No matter what, she's hot."

"Yes. But her name is not Salomé."

"I know, I saw the tag, too. Sevil?" He sounded it out.

"Not bad," I said. I pronounced it for him and he tried again. "Very good."

"How many languages do you know?"

"I have lost count." That was true.

"Come on, Sebastian. Don't give me that crap. You know what I mean."

Time for a lie. "Fourteen or fifteen." I actually knew more than a hundred languages and dialects.

"How did you learn so many? I didn't see any traveling in your background."

"I have an aptitude for languages and studied them on my own," I said.

He looked toward the bar. "Is that her daughter?"

"It would appear so. Sally."

The bartender handed the drinks to her on a round tray. She took it and wove through the tables and chairs, heading back in our direction. She had a pleasant gait and carried herself well for her age.

Walking carefully, she came up to our table. "Here you are." She set the tray down and put the glasses in front of us. We waited while she poured the tea.

"What city are we in, Sally?" I asked.

"You don't know?"

"We got mixed up changing planes."

She gave me a lingering look as she set the teapot on the table. Not suspicious. Excited. "This is Ankara."

"Thank you."

"Tea?" Hamilton raised the cup to his nose, sniffed.

"Would you rather have a coffee?" I asked him.

"No, I guess this is okay."

"Are you from America?" Sally asked in English.

"You understand us?" Hamilton asked.

"Oh, yes. I speak five languages." She turned to me. "Your Turkish is very good."

"So is your English."

She flushed with happiness. "Would you like to order something to eat?"

"Eggs and sausage?" I asked.

"Of course," she replied. "*Sucuklu yumurta.*"

"Perfect," I told her.

"That sounds fine with me," Hamilton said.

"Thank you," she said. "I'll bring bread and cheese."

After she had deposited the bread, cheese, olives, sliced tomatoes, butter, and marmalade, she headed toward the back and through a swinging door.

"If Sevil is Diacos's sister, does she know what her brother is doing?"

"I doubt it," I said. I took a sip of tea. "If she does, she couldn't do anything to stop him." She was younger than he was, too, not older. It seemed Diacos's lies made no sense. He apparently used them for his private amusement.

Sally came out of the kitchen and walked by us, humming a lilting tune.

Watching her, my eyes grew wide when the final piece of the puzzle I had been trying to build slid into place.

"Diacos is a liar," I said to Hamilton, "but he told enough of the truth that I think I know how he intends to resurrect these people."

"How?"

"The cards are based not only on sounds, but on words, even sentences."

"So?"

"So we know the cards are capable of fine discrimination, recognizing words in many languages."

He leaned forward now. "Yes, that's true."

"When it comes to a song that produces awesome magical effects, the cards would require precision. And in a song, pitch may be as important as pronunciation."

"What are you saying?"

"It may matter whether the singer is a man or a woman. Or an adult."

He stared at me. I knew he would process the information the same way I did. "A child?" He turned to the girl. She stood next to her mother, probably telling her about us. "Sally? Christ. Salomé?"

"Bingo."

"Are you saying she's the one to sing the song?"

"Yes."

He stared at the duo. "How is Diacos going to get her to do it?"

"That I don't know. Did you notice anything about her mother?"

"Yeah, she looked exhausted."

"He's putting pressure on them somehow. And if it's anything to do with Bork and Diacos, I'm sure it involves violence."

"But they're family—Sally's his niece." He stopped, thought about it. "Bork. He can use Bork as the bad guy. That way he doesn't seem involved." Then, with what sounded like grudging admiration, "He does cover all the bases."

"Yes. He's probably helping Salomé, telling her he will be with her every step of the way. And he will be—to make sure she does it."

"But, if he's done that, won't she be on his side?"

"Very likely."

"What do we do?"

"I'm thinking." Did I really want to try to ask for her help? Not now. Why would she believe a stranger when her uncle Erol said something different?

"Isn't this procedure going to be very dangerous?" Hamilton asked.

"Yes."

"He probably told her it was a game."

"Something like that," I agreed. "And whatever pressure he is applying to them will be sufficiently high that he can depend on Salomé and Sevil's complete attention."

"The bastard."

"We need to get out of here."

"Right now?" he said. "What about our food?"

"Do you want to ask for a doggy bag?"

He hesitated. I watched him, amused. He glanced at Sally and her mom. He shook his head. "No. Do we just walk out?"

I stood up. "Yes." I pulled out my wallet and unzipped a back pocket. It contained two thousand British pounds and five hundred in Euros. I selected a hundred-pound note, dropped it on the table. "Let's go."

"Wasn't that exorbitant? Now everyone will definitely remember us."

"My friend," I said. "There probably isn't another pair of men speaking English within fifty miles. Uh-oh, they've seen us."

Sally hurried toward us, and her mother began to come out from behind the counter. I tried to wave and leave. The girl broke into a run and shouted in English, "Wait! I want to talk to you!"

I pushed the door open and had one foot outside when I realized Hamilton was no longer behind me. I turned and saw him watching Sally approach. "Come on, Steve."

"Just a minute," he said. "We could be wrong about her. I want to hear what she has to say."

"The longer we stay here, the greater the chance we run into Diacos."

"I know."

I could not make up my mind. Then I went back inside and let the door fall shut.

Sally ran up to us. "Thank you," she said to Hamilton. He nodded. Sevil joined us as well. Sally took Hamilton's hand and led us back to our table. I followed, palming the hundred-pound note as we sat.

Sally took a chair across from me, next to Hamilton. Sevil remained standing.

"Did you come here for a vacation?" Sally asked me.

"Not exactly."

"I knew it! You came here to help us, didn't you?"

"Help you with what?" Hamilton asked.

"To stop my Uncle Erol from bringing those dead people back to life."

Chapter 43

Tuesday, January 27, 6:51 a.m. EET

I looked from Sally to Sevil to Hamilton. "Did I hear that right?"

"I did," Hamilton said.

"I will bring your breakfasts," Sevil said. She walked to the kitchen.

"So you know what your uncle is planning to do?" I asked.

"Yes. He wants to bring some of our ancestors back to life."

"He told you?"

"No. I heard him arguing with my mom."

"What exactly does Erol want you to do?" Hamilton asked.

"He wants me to sing an old family song."

There it was again, that germ of truth within the lie. He had said Salomé knew the correct song because it had been passed down through her ancestors.

"Here?"

"No. He's taking me to the forest."

"You don't want to go?" I asked.

She shook her head and looked at her mom as she walked up with our plates and set them down. "Mother doesn't want me to do it, either."

"Then why are you going to help him?"

Tears filled her eyes. "This big man will kill Giray if I don't."

"Her—her brother," Sevil added.

Speechless with rage, I knew if either of those miserable bastards were here right now, I would crush them into tiny little Magistine bits. Sally stared at my hands. They had curled into

312

fists. I relaxed them. "How do you know?" I said it in a voice barely under control.

Sevil said, "They sent us a video."

"It shows your son?" Hamilton asked.

"Yes. He is tied to a chair with a hood over his face. They pulled the hood up long enough so we could see it was Giray."

Hamilton glanced at Sally and Sevil, his jaw tight as he surveyed their distress.

"Where is this part of the forest?" I asked. "How far?"

"It's about a kilometer up the road and a half kilometer or so into the forest on your right. There is a big rock you can see from the road in the middle of two trees. Walk between the rocks and you will come to the ancestral burial grounds of the Diacos family."

I had known it would be something like that. "When?"

"After sunset."

"So about eleven hours from now."

"Yes."

"Do you have a place where we could stay until this evening?" I asked.

"Yes, the two rooms next to ours are empty," Sevil said.

I turned to Salomé. "He's going to pick you up here?"

She nodded.

"Good. Well, this food looks delicious, so give us a little time to think about what to do." Hamilton had already spread his napkin on his lap. "Do you still have the video?"

"It's a DVD. I have a portable player," Salomé said. "I could bring it down here."

I unfolded my napkin into my lap. "That would be perfect Sally." She ran off. I looked up at Sevil. "Don't worry. We'll be there somehow. You will not do this alone."

"That's right," Hamilton said. "We'll take care of Mr. Diacos, I promise."

Sevil picked up his hand, kissed it, and held it to her cheek.

"No, no, that's not necessary," Hamilton protested.

She held on to him. "Thank you," she said to us. She kissed his hand one more time, then released him and returned to her station in the lobby.

Hamilton watched her go, a bemused expression on his face.

"She is lovely," I said. "Makes you feel like a knight saving the damsel in distress, doesn't it?"

He gave me a sour look. "You know, sometimes you can be too smart. Be quiet and eat your eggs."

"Well, excuuuuuuuuse me."

The *sucuklu yumurta* tasted so good, Hamilton and I had nearly finished by the time Sally returned with her portable DVD player. I took a last bite and set my plate aside. We had decided the only good course of action was to get to the burial grounds before Diacos arrived.

"I already put the DVD in," she said. She sat and put the player in the middle of the table so all three of us could see it and started the video.

There was snow at first and the two flashes of aborted scenes that seem to precede all amateur work. The image steadied and became clear. It showed a boy wearing khaki pants and black sneakers sitting in a chair with a cloth sack hiding his head, his legs dangling over the edge. His chest, wrists, and ankles were fastened to his seat with a thin wire I recognized.

"Giray," Sally said.

We could hear someone moving about, and now a man came into view from the left. A very big man.

"Bork," Hamilton said in a tight voice.

"Do you know him?" Sally asked.

"Oh, yes. He visited my town and . . . made an impression. I must talk to him about that."

Bork stood next to the chair, grabbed the top of the hood, and pulled it up. The boy underneath was sweating, and his eyes blinked at the light.

"Oh, Giray."

"Sally, you should help your mother," I told her.

"No. I'm okay."

Bork pushed the sack back down. He moved out of the frame, we heard him fumbling with the camera, and the screen went blank.

"No demands," I said. "What about your father?"

"Papa died three years ago. He got sick."

"Sally, I am sorry."

"It's something that happens," she replied, not looking at us.

"Did your uncle give you this DVD?" Hamilton asked.

"Yes, he gave it to my mom."

"Of course. And he said this man was forcing him to participate in this, uh, ceremony, too. Or the man would kill your brother."

"Yes. After his argument with my mother, I was sure he was lying. I could tell he wanted to do this ritual so he could reanimate our old relatives."

"You're a sharp young lady." Hamilton did not speak in the patronizing voice adults often use with kids. "We should make you a detective when you're older."

"Is that what you are? A detective?"

"Yes, that's right."

"Really? Like on TV?"

Hamilton said, "Yes, just like on TV."

Sally still looked unconvinced. "Then you should have a badge."

Hamilton pulled out his LAPD detective's shield and handed it to her.

Sally took it from him as if she were receiving some rare and fragile treasure. Once she held it in her hands, she looked at

315

it closely—she read all the words, turned it left and right, traced a finger over the center of it. Then she handed it back to him. He replaced it in his jacket. She looked at me expectantly.

"I'm not a detective. I'm just his assistant."

"Oh."

"Do you have a plan yet, Mr. Assistant?"

"As a matter of fact . . . no, not a complete one. I only know we want to catch Diacos off his guard. And that will most likely be during the ceremony."

"You're saying we should let him start it?"

I nodded. "And Sally, you're going to have to start singing."

"But that's what makes them come alive."

"Only if you finish it. Sing the first half of it and stop."

"But won't the big man kill Giray if I do that?"

"Ah, yes, your brother." I pulled my cell, dialed an international number. Aliena answered on the third ring.

"Sebastian? Is everything okay? Where are you?"

"We're in Turkey, near the Diacos ancestral graveyard. So far everything's fine. You remember the caves where you found me?"

"Yes?"

"Bork is holding a young boy there. He's very important to us."

I heard Marcus's voice in the background. "Marcus says he will be happy to take this boy away from him. He was planning on finding Bork later anyway."

"The big guy's a popular man. Tell Marcus I am indebted to him. Could you text me when you have him?"

"Yes. How long will you be there?"

"At least twelve hours. Diacos plans to bring his ancestors back to life just after sunset, local time."

"Be safe, darling."

"You too." I replaced my phone.

"You know where her brother is?" Hamilton asked.

"Yes." I had recognized the chair and the rough walls. "He's being held in a dungeon somewhere around here."

"Marcus knows how to get there?"

"I know Aliena does."

"Are you sending someone to bring Giray home?" Sally asked.

"Yes, I am."

"Sebastian," Hamilton said, shaking his head. "A civilian against that maniac?"

"Civilian, yes. Civil, no. Besides, Aliena's friend Marcus has crossed Bork's path before."

"Who is this Marcus? *What* is he? A commando?"

"He's much worse than that. Trust me; Bork will have his hands full with Marcus and Aliena."

"Are you nuts? You're not letting Aliena go, are you?"

"As I have told you before, Steve, nobody 'lets' Aliena do anything. She does what she likes, and she never asks for advice. At least, I've never heard her ask for any. I also told you Bork tried to hurt Kismet, a dear friend of hers. She has a personal grudge against him, same as you."

"It's just crazy."

"Don't worry," I said to Sally. "My girlfriend is very special and so is her friend Marcus. I think they will be able to take Giray away from Bork."

She watched Hamilton (who was shaking his head), and I could tell she believed him more than she believed me. I did a mental shrug. I could only hope Marcus and Aliena were successful. It might be easier than we thought. Diacos probably wouldn't expect anyone to recognize the location, so there might be no one guarding Giray.

"We should probably get out of sight," Hamilton said.

"Follow me," Sally said.

She led us back to the lobby, where her mother handed her two keys. We followed her to a wide staircase and climbed to the second floor. She turned right, walked past two rooms, and stopped halfway down the hall in front of the third, number 27.

"Here you are," she said. She handed Hamilton a key. "The other room is there," she told us, pointing farther down the hall. She handed me a key. "And Mama and I are in the room after that."

"Try to get some sleep," I told Hamilton.

He yawned. "Good idea."

"We'll see you later, Salomé," I said. "Please thank your mother."

"'Kay."

"And tell her everything will be fine," Hamilton said.

Chapter 44

Tuesday, January 27, 5:17 p.m. EET

An hour before sunset I met Hamilton in his room, where we had a light dinner, discussing our strategy. When the sky began to darken, we left, after assuring Sevil we would protect her daughter from harm.

    We had been walking on the hard-packed road for fifteen minutes. It had turned full dark. We both remained silent and even our steps on the dirt sounded muted. A full moon shone above us. That helped. Again, Diacos demonstrated excellent forethought and planning. Dark in the country is not like dark in the city. Without the moon, we would have had trouble seeing anything that wasn't right in front of our eyes.

    We stayed to the right as Sevil had instructed. Hamilton stopped, pointed. A big rock more than a meter high shaped like a potato sat between two tall trees just off the road to our right. I nodded, and we proceeded past it, both of us dragging a hand along the rock as we went by. After we had walked for ten minutes, we came to a small clearing.

    There were no grave markers standing up or placed in the ground. In the middle was a collection of long, low rocks. When we approached from the side, I could see this was not a loose collection but more like a diamond on the end of a string. Four rocks shaped vaguely like coffee tables formed the closed shape and three extended in a line away from it.

    "Seven rocks," I said in a low voice. Even then, I felt every creature in the forest could hear me.

    "Isn't that how many cards are in that combination?"

    "Yes."

    When we came to the rocks, I stepped up on one. From this vantage point, I could see each block of stone had a tarot card etched on top. I jumped into the middle of the diamond. The grass sprang beneath my feet, the air lightly scented. Hamilton stayed on the outside, watching me. I crossed back over.

"What now?" he asked.

"We hide." I started toward a densely packed group of trees. They stood about four meters high on the outskirts of the glade. From there, we would be looking from the right side of the rock configuration.

"That's what I figured. What do we do after that? We're both armed, so if he's not packing, we just take him, right?"

I had to tell him about Diacos's abilities. "He doesn't need a gun. He has special command over sounds and can use it to assault us. He will not be easy to take."

We had come to the trees. We walked around and behind them. Their slim trunks fragmented our view of the clearing, but it was enough for now.

"Do you have a plan?"

"I'm thinking." And I was but nothing was coming.

We heard the electric ripping sound. A shining card appeared on the trunk of a big tree to our right. It wasn't facing us so I couldn't see which card it was, only the light radiating from it. It pulsed twice and Diacos stepped out, holding hands with Sally. He stopped just to our right. We were in full view if he only turned. I hoped Hamilton knew our best chance was to remain unmoving so Diacos wouldn't detect us with his peripheral vision.

We stayed frozen. Finally, Diacos walked off, never glancing our way. He strode toward the rock formation, pulling Sally along so fast she had to jog next to him.

"In you go," he told her as they came up to the rocks arranged in a four-sided diamond shape. She stepped up as I had, crossed the top of the smooth stone, and jumped into the center, exactly where I had stood.

Diacos looked toward the outside of the clearing. He had his hand curled like a megaphone in front of his mouth. We could not hear anything—I couldn't even see his lips move. As he turned in a circle, small dots of light appeared in the air at the edges of the glade, softly glowing over the grassy scene like hanging lamps.

"He's doing that with sound?" Hamilton said.

"Yes."

"Is he going to wait for Bork?"

"I don't know. It doesn't look like it."

Diacos pulled some tarot cards out of his back pocket. He began to arrange them in the center of each rock. From my memory of the rock formation, he set his card, the Emperor, at the top of the chain, above the Empress and the Ten of Pentacles. Sally was at the bottom. The Devil, Death, the Tower, and the Ten of Swords surrounded her. The little girl had grim company.

As soon as Diacos set the Emperor down, a loud crack rang out. Hamilton ducked instinctively. Beams of green light connected all the cards, and the rocks glowed whitely as if they had a thin outer layer with lightbulbs inside.

Diacos steepled his hands in front of his chest. He nodded at Sally. She looked around fearfully. Then she started singing.

From her first note, the cards began to pulse, the gold borders lighting up. They went in sequence from the Emperor at the top to the Devil on the bottom. The blinking continued.

The rocks began to turn red—first pale-rose, then cinnamon, and finally scarlet. Even this far away we could feel the heat they radiated. It must have been unbearable where Sally stood. Now the glade was easily visible, with different-colored lights bouncing off the leaves in the trees along its perimeter.

Hamilton pulled his piece. "Fuck this." He pushed the safety up and started edging around to the left so he could get behind Diacos.

I stayed put. From this position I remained closer to Sally, about fifty meters away.

Diacos brought his hands down to belt level and turned to his right. He held them thumbs together, palms out, and made a pushing motion away from his body while his lips moved. The trees on that side blew backward as if a bomb had been set off close to them. The sound of wood and branches tipping and breaking was so loud I could not tell if Hamilton yelled or not.

Sally stopped singing.

"Why are you stopping, Salomé?" Diacos asked in Turkish. "You're already halfway there."

"Why are we doing this? We shouldn't be doing this. It feels wrong."

"We have to, remember? Or that big man will hurt our Giray." Diacos did use a patronizing tone, talking to her as if she were a little kid.

"I don't think so. I think you want to do it."

The cards began to cycle more slowly, and now Death turned solid red like the rock underneath it. Sally shrunk away from it. "It hurts, Uncle Erol."

Diacos looked around, plainly impatient. "Salomé, just finish the song. Then we can get out of here. Come on, keep singing." The ceremony was not going as he had planned. Good girl.

But it was a dangerous tactic.

"Did you take my brother?"

Diacos didn't answer right away. Then he said, "Yes. And if you don't finish singing, I swear I will kill him. You believe me, don't you, Salomé?" He turned toward my side of the glen and made the same gesture as before.

I ducked as a huge wave of wind rushed over the area. The blast lifted me off my feet and hurled me into the trees behind. I hit a hard trunk headfirst and fell straight down, a limp bag.

I came to consciousness on my back with leaves and bark draped over me like a blanket. I sat up cautiously and looked in the direction of the clearing. A mound of debris shielded me from sight of the stones. The blast had tipped the thin trees backward, and now they looked as if they were bowing in my direction. I crawled to the dirt mound and peered around.

Salomé was singing again. That was okay as long as she didn't finish.

The Devil and Death were no longer solid red. They were back to blinking in turn with the others. Diacos's gaze darted all over, but he seemed satisfied with the way everything was proceeding. I saw he had blasted another section of trees directly opposite me. I did not think he knew that Hamilton and I were here. He was taking no chances.

Wispy gray figures began to rise from the ground around the rocks. Eleven of them.

"Yes!" Diacos shouted. "Yes!"

The ghostly shapes came to a stop two meters up, taking on a human form at the torso and above. I could see what looked like a woman's head, shoulders, and hips just a few meters from where I stood. She had her arms crossed over her chest and, like all the other etheric entities, faced the formation of rocks, watching Salomé.

The girl saw them. She stopped singing again.

"No!" Diacos yelled. "Keep singing!" Immediately, Death turned solid red and after a few seconds so did the Devil.

This was my chance. I came out of hiding and began sprinting toward Salomé, flashing past the ghostly woman. Diacos's lips moved, and he pushed his hands toward me. My left leg jerked backward as if pulled by an invisible wire. It twisted me around, and I passed through a man cloud and hit the ground on my side. I ended up staring at one of the boulders—it was, literally, under my nose. I flinched back from the heat. This close I could hear a sound coming from it, a straining hum, as of something operating beyond its capabilities.

The sound a device makes right before it blows up.

Diacos turned on the girl. "Keep singing!"

"No!"

I stood up. Diacos looked at me but jerked his head around as Hamilton came into view from behind, weapon pointed. I thought he should have come out shooting.

Before Diacos gestured at him, Hamilton dove to his right, rolled, and started firing from the ground. Diacos went down. It looked like Hamilton got him in the arm.

"Sally!" She turned to me, standing inside the diamond, trapped. The cards were now sizzling hot, shooting electricity into the air. One thin, crooked bolt hit her on the arm, and she screamed.

I took off my jacket. One of the flaming tendrils hit me in the stomach, and I doubled over automatically, the electricity forcing my muscles to contract. I fought it off and straightened up.

The heat was terrific. Sweat poured down my face. Sally seemed to flicker on the other side of the Devil as the baking waves rising from the rocks distorted the air between us.

"I'm going to jump in," I shouted to her.

"You'll be killed!"

There was no time. An ounce of demonstration was worth a pound of explanation. I pulled the jacket over my head and face, took a couple of steps back. Then I rushed forward and leaped over the Devil and the rock upon which it sat.

I was reminded immediately of the time Diacos kicked me in the sack. The flow of energy came from the ground up. Too late I realized that vaulting with my legs spread would put my jewels right in the line of fire. So to speak.

My mouth opened in a silent scream as the electric fire shot into me and ripped through the top of my head. Then I soared clear of the flux, crumpling at Sally's feet.

She came over, fell on her knees next to me. "Please," she said. "Please don't be dead." I felt her touching me hesitantly on the elbow. "Are you okay?"

I couldn't answer. I shook my head at her.

My eyes were scrunched closed, my body on fire. Were my clothes burning? I couldn't open my eyes. Sally was not screaming or beating on me, so I was sure I was not aflame.

Good. Only my flesh burned. Somehow, that did not make me feel better.

I bit back a scream as I exhaled. The electric charges had even hurt my teeth. Over my groans, I could hear my eternal engine roaring in my ears, and I felt my cramped muscles begin to loosen. Physical control came back to me slowly.

"Can I help you up?" Sally asked.

I grunted a negative. When I could move, I looked at my clothes. My pants were scorched in the middle and my shirt had holes in it. Both garments smoked. I lifted my head. My jacket lay under it like a pillow. It took me half a minute, but I finally staggered up, Sally hanging on to my elbow. I stopped with my hands on my knees.

"I'm okay," I told her. My voice didn't sound like it was coming from me. I was still pretty far from okay, but we had to move soon. Already, strength poured through my body, and I could feel the itch that told me I was repairing broken skin.

The heat on this side of the cards was blistering. Sweat and tears streaked Sally's face. Her skin shone red, her hair matted. She watched me anxiously.

"We have to hurry," she said.

I took a deep breath, stood up straight. The electric heat around us was worse than ever, and all four cards pulsed faster than strobe lights. My eyes began to water.

"What are we going to do?"

"I want you to put my jacket on," I said, holding it out.

Two lines of electricity passed between us. One of them hit a sleeve, and Sally snatched the jacket down with a cry. She started putting it on, her face puzzled.

"It will give you some protection," I explained. As soon as she finished, I turned away from her and knelt. "Climb on my back. Hurry now!"

Her arms encircled my neck.

"Pull the jacket over your head so your hair and face are protected." One of her arms let go of me and I could hear her struggling with the coat. Then her arm came around again and she grabbed her right wrist.

"I'm ready," she said, her voice muffled. I felt her lay her head against the back of my neck.

I stood. The crackling electric heat seemed equally bad whichever way I looked. No time to think about it. I took one big step, reached up and grabbed Sally's hands, then launched myself over the maelstrom, trying to stay as horizontal as I could so she would not take the direct charge.

The electricity ripped through me and burned my consciousness to a flicker. The pain stabbed everywhere at once—my cheeks were on fire, my ears were burned to cinders, and it felt like there were hot pins under my fingernails.

I felt the ground when I landed, but the impact seemed distant. My clothes and hair were aflame. My mind silently shrieked with unholy misery. Mercifully, I blacked out.

Chapter 45

Tuesday, January 27, 5:54 p.m. EET

I awoke moaning in agony. Someone had dipped me into a vat of burning oil, dunking my head under the surface. Then they had deposited my carcass in a field.

It took me several moments to have enough sense to determine my orientation. I had ended up on my side. The soft blades of grass under my cheek stabbed like wickedly pointed stilettos against my flayed flesh. My spirit sagged as I realized I had to accept that torment. I could not yet move.

I tried to force my eyes open. I succeeded but only for a blurry moment. If you have ever gotten soap in your eyes, you know how difficult it is to open them right away. This was magnitudes worse. My eyelids would not obey my command to stay up.

I kept trying. Now I could hear things around me. A shout. Sounded like Hamilton's voice. That snapped me to attention.

I forced my eyes open and kept them that way, although I blinked rapidly to clear them. My immortal machinery growled in my ears as my body underwent a massive renovation.

"Sebastian?" Sally's voice. "How could you be alive?"

I could feel itching all over my body, including the top of my head. The electrical flux had apparently burned my hair off. That had happened a couple of times before, and I knew it was not going to grow back right away to the length that I liked. My whole head, including my face, seethed with activity. If my hair had gone, probably my skin had, too. No wonder I hurt like the dickens.

"Oh!"

I looked down at my body. My clothes were toast. Literally. Where there were gaping holes, I could see my flesh underneath turning from a bloody burned mess into wholly healthy, unmarked human flesh. Sally was not looking at that. She stared into my eyes.

I wondered what I must look like to her now. I could feel the skin on my face as it covered my bones again. Did my head look like a bloody demonic skull regenerating itself? Probably.

Lifting my cheek off those sharp spikes, I reached up and scratched my nose, rubbing hard. God, it itched! I stopped and looked at my hands. They already appeared normal. I sat all the way up, groaning.

Sally fell on her knees in front of me, still wearing my jacket. Her gaze continually strayed below my belt line. I suddenly realized I was naked from the lower abdominals to the tops of my thighs. Only the waistband and belt remained of my pants.

I covered myself with my left hand. "Sorry."

"I don't mind," she said, blushing furiously. Her left eye had swelled up and the skin around it shaded toward purple.

"Be a good girl and hand me my coat." I gestured with my right hand. She took it off and passed it to me. I covered myself. "Thank you."

"What are you?"

She had just watched me reskin myself, so I couldn't deny much. "I honestly am not sure," I told her. "I am different from everyone else in this matter of dying, but otherwise I'm just like you." I became aware of how hot it was. The air sizzled with a buzzing hum and sparks rose over Salomé's shoulders. I stood and tied the arms of the jacket around my waist. My jeans remained connected in back. I took Sally's hand. "Let's get out of here."

We ran along the outside of the arrangement of stones toward the Emperor at its head. The cards burned red, spewing sparks and blue electricity into the air. The rocks beneath them glowed white-hot. Looking in that direction hurt. When I did, all I could see was a wavering picture distorted by rising heat.

On our left, Hamilton came into view in close combat with Diacos. With an underhanded movement, Diacos lifted him into the air and tossed him. When Hamilton hit the ground, Diacos pushed his right hand at the inert body. I saw the grass next to Hamilton's feet flatten. Diacos was not using his left arm. It hung limply, covered with blood. Apparently, his aim was not so good with one hand.

"Wait here," I told Sally. I released her and sprinted at Diacos. He was preparing to take another shot at Hamilton when I shouted, warning him off. He turned to me, astonished, and pushed his right hand at me. I jigged and felt the blast of air pass by my left arm. Looking frantic, he pulled a card from his back pocket and held it to his mouth. As the card began to expand, I launched myself through the air. He lifted his good arm protectively.

I crashed into him and we tipped into the widening rip.

Chapter 46

Tuesday, January 27, 6:07 p.m. EET

Something hit me so hard when we exited the card that I staggered to my left and fell awkwardly, scraping my cheek on cool rock. I couldn't believe I was already down again.

A strangled yell of fear echoed off the walls. I wearily climbed to my feet, noting we had journeyed to the Bork ancestral dungeons. Or were they really the Diacos family dungeons?

A wave of heat blasted over me, and I immediately took several steps in the opposite direction, holding my arm up for protection. I saw my clothes had begun to smoke. Again. The pain was considerable. I looked up as another yell rang down the corridor.

The shrieks came from Diacos. I could see his problem.

Aliena held him in a crushing embrace, her mouth at his throat. It looked as if she had broken both of his arms at the elbows—his hands lifted off his sides, unnaturally pointing out. Even as I watched, she gripped him tighter, as if trying to squeeze him dry like a bottle of ketchup. Her head jerked as she dug her canines in. This time he screamed, a cry high-pitched with terror, the mouse realizing its neck is in the jaws of the cat.

Aliena's clothes began to smoke. Diacos had said anyone too close to him when he activated his shield would catch on fire. If that began to happen to Aliena, it would burn him as well. I don't think he ever considered an attacker might actually be attached to him when he employed his defensive screen.

I started toward the two of them. Five steps later my feet stopped automatically as my skin encountered broiling air. My body would not move toward the heat. It was as if I stood in a thick atmosphere—one more substantial than water. My posture was that of a man leaning against a strong wind.

I was now about two meters away from the entangled pair, my face dripping sweat. Only the back of Aliena's head was visible from my angle. Diacos's face showed clearly. His eyes fluttered. The air cooled. He was either depleted of blood or burning from his own heat.

His shield fell. When I reached the entwined pair, the air turned fresh and the sweat on my body chilled.

Diacos stared at me, mortal fright in his eyes. His mouth moved, but he made no sound. His light-colored irises rolled up and out of sight as Aliena took every drop of his life away. His body sagged, limbs going slack.

Aliena finally pulled her mouth off his flesh with a pop and let his corpse drop to the floor. She leaned over and spat on it, her clothes smoking, her canines still extended, eyes fiery. The lupine expression on her normally gorgeous face unsettled me as always. "I have wanted to do that since our first meeting," she growled.

I thought she might have forgotten me, but suddenly her arms were around my chest, the vestiges of her vampire leer giving way to her gorgeous face. "Are you okay?"

"I don't know."

She looked up at me.

"Yes, I'm okay," I said, kissing the tip of her delicate nose. "How did you know he would come here?"

"I didn't. But since his prisoner was here, it seemed he'd have to come back sooner or later."

"What about Bork?"

"I am not sure. He was activating his star card when we got to the cell. Marcus moved toward him, and they both disappeared."

"Where is the boy they were holding?"

"He's at your place. Unharmed."

"Good."

She stood back a bit, looked down, and pushed my jacket aside. I felt a breeze. She reached under. I gasped as she closed

331

her warm hand on me. "What's the meaning of this?" She came closer, staring up into my face.

"My clothes got fried and some pieces burned off when I was saving Salomé."

She squeezed, causing me to stand on tiptoes.

"You must tell me all about her."

"Of course, my darling. How about the fact that she's thirteen?"

"What does that matter?"

I thought about Sally's face when she looked at my nudity. Her expression had been curious, even excited—not repulsed. "Nothing, I guess. Except I don't like women that young. I never have."

"Are you saying I'm old?"

Chapter 47

Tuesday, January 27, 5:17 a.m.

Before we left the dungeons, I patted Diacos's body down and found the card he had used to escape from the forest. The Wheel of Fortune. Then Aliena took us home using the portal below my fireplace's mantle.

Salomé's little brother sat on the patio when we appeared in the living room, so he did not see our entrance through the card. He had many questions, but I avoided them, telling him that he needed to go home immediately—his mother and sister were very frightened. With one phone call, a limousine cruised to my door in eight minutes and Giray was off to Los Angeles International Airport, traveling first class to Turkey. Preston would arrange for one of our men to meet Giray at LAX and help him get on the plane.

I cleaned up and changed into a new pair of jeans with a white shirt and a light jacket. For the second time this week, all the clothes I had been wearing were in the garage trash can. At this rate, I would be out of casual pants by the end of the month.

As soon as I returned to the living room, I made an international call to Hamilton's number. It took nearly a minute to start ringing.

"Hey, Sebastian," he said. "Where are you?"

I sighed with relief. "Thank God you're okay."

"I'm fine, bro-mo, thanks."

"I'm at home with Aliena."

"What about Diacos?"

"He's dead."

"Good. Did you do it?"

"Of course not."

"That's it? That's all you're going to tell me?"

"On an open line, yes."

"Yeah, okay. But I want some real answers when I get back."

"Of course."

"How about Bork?" I could hear bells, whistles, and shouts behind his voice.

"Unknown," I told him.

"That stinks, man. We have got to get that mutha."

"I know. What happened there? How's Salomé?"

"She's fine. That part of the forest is on fire. As soon as you and Diacos disappeared into the card, those rocks started shooting flames into the trees and, whoosh, the whole place started to go up. I grabbed Sally and streaked out of there. My ass got pretty hot, but we made it."

"What happened to the cards?"

"No idea. No one can get near that area right now."

"What are you doing?"

"I'm having dinner with Sally and Sevil. Sevil said I could have the room upstairs next to hers and stay the night."

"Oh ho."

"Yeah, well, since I brought Sally back unharmed, she looks at me like I'm a hero."

"And you, of course, will play the part to the hilt."

"Until I'm neck deep in it."

"And tomorrow?"

"I'll look around and see if I can find out what happened to the cards."

"Good," I said. "I'll have your passport and a credit card delivered to you in the morning. Is first class okay for your air travel?"

"Never done it. And listen, I may want to stay a few days."

"Your ticket is good anytime. Want me to send two more?"

A hesitation. "I might."

"Okay. Have fun."

"Hold on, Sally wants to talk to you."

I heard him passing the phone. "Sebastian?"

"Hi, sweetie," I said in Turkish. Aliena also spoke the language and gave me eyes like daggers. I held the phone away. "Stop that now! She's a child!" I whispered loudly. I put the phone back to my ear. "How are you feeling?" I remembered she had the beginnings of a black eye when I last saw her. It was probably swollen shut.

"My left eye hurts, but otherwise I'm okay."

"What happened?"

"When you jumped over the electricity, your body went limp before we hit the ground and your head bounced up and hit me in the face. It hurt a lot."

"I'm sorry, dear."

"Don't be silly. You saved me. I wanted to thank you."

"You're very welcome. You were brave out there, standing up to your uncle."

"Thanks."

I waited. I knew what was coming.

"Sebastian?"

"I know, but don't say anything to Detective Hamilton about my repairs, please. In fact, I would like it to be our secret. He has never seen me, um, recover from wounds the way you saw. Did I look dead?" As long as we stayed with Turkish, she could talk freely in front of him.

"Yes. I think you were for a little while."

"It probably scared you to see me fix myself."

"It surprised me, but I wasn't scared. Your repairs were fascinating. Although it looked like you were in a lot of pain for a long time."

"I was."

"But you were okay a few minutes later. I thought only people in movies could do that."

I smiled. "How do you know you're not in one?"

"I wish! Will I ever see you again?"

I considered. "Probably not."

"That's what I thought." She was quiet for a few seconds. "I want you to come back. Please."

"I can't, honey."

"Just once." She did not conceal the longing in her voice, a desire infused with teenage intensity. "We didn't have a chance to say good-bye."

"I know." I waited.

"Mama said you would probably do this. Is it because your life is really complicated?"

"That is it exactly."

"She said that, too." I could still hear sirens in the background. "Okay. I'm really going to miss you, Sebastian."

"And I you, my dear."

Chapter 48

Tuesday, January 27, 11:44 p.m.

Aliena had retired to her room for the day shortly after we returned, and I relaxed until she woke. She had gone out for a bite to eat but now stood impatiently in the center of the living room.

"Come on, we have to get to Kismet's place." Aliena paced the living room. "It's almost midnight."

"Okay, okay." I drank a second bottle of ice-cold Stoli, tossed the dead soldier into the recycle can, and walked to Aliena. She held the Moon to her lips, and it began to expand. She released the star card and reached her hand out. I clasped it, and we stepped through the portal.

As soon as we arrived, the sounds of a roaring party surrounded us. Balloons popped, and someone tooted a toy horn. Streamers hung from the walls and the glass floor blinked with different-colored lights. We took our shoes off and left them with the twenty or so pairs already there.

Kismet had lit the inside of her house even more elaborately than usual, including adding a disco ball that turned slowly above the pool. Streamers of every color created a rainbow on the walls, and helium balloons floated in the air and on the water. The living room and indoor pool boiled with the conversations of many guests.

I saw Marcus talking to Echo. She reclined on her side on one of the lounge chairs. She reached out to him. Her tiny white bikini barely contained her considerable curves. It looked like her hand rested on his belt buckle.

Remembering Diacos's infatuation with her, I imagined Echo as a potential mate. Incredibly beautiful, she had exotic eyes, light brown skin, and a long body. Glancing at her cautiously so Aliena did not notice, I could see intellectually that she was the stuff of men's dreams. For some reason, she did nothing for me. It had to be because I was in love with another.

I looked for Kismet, spied her in the pool. She smiled and talked, surrounded by three handsome young mermen. The men bobbed very close to her, swishing their tails back and forth languidly. She looked over and saw us approaching. She stopped in midsentence.

"Allie!" She left the men immediately and sped to our side of the pool and, jumped out of the water onto one of her lounges. She had been a little too excited, just like the last time. "Oh, dear," she said as she crested the back and began to vault off the top.

Aliena got there in a blink and steadied her before she fell. They really were a complementary couple, with Kismet's clumsiness offset by Aliena's quickness.

"Oh, thank you, darling." She wrapped her arms around Aliena and kissed her on the mouth. Aliena rested her hands on the mermaid's hips. After a few seconds, she pulled back and gave Kismet a scolding look.

"Behave yourself."

The mermaid reluctantly let her go, looked at me, and then lowered her eyes. "I'm sorry," she said to the floor. "I can't help how I feel."

"I know," I said. My heart went out to her. I could not imagine the pain of being a former lover of Aliena's. It had to be especially difficult for Kismet: she knew she was Aliena's *only* lover, past or present.

I looked around. It was a lively party, with several humans in attendance. I saw we had attracted some attention. The three men with whom Kismet had been chatting looked at Aliena with thinly disguised contempt. Based on their expressions and low laughter, I was sure they were making unsavory comments about her. If so, they had better not state them within my hearing. I had killed men in the water before.

I looked to the left, at the part of the pool that tapered into one of the channels leading to the back rooms. Two beautiful girls sat in the curve watching me. When I looked at them, they twitched their flukes above the water. They floated close to each other, their arms touching. I couldn't help but wonder if that meant they had come together. The one on the left sent me a kiss. About a meter from them, two mermen, their arms crossed over their chests and their faces scowling, also stared at me.

Aliena appeared at my elbow. "Switch it off, Sebastian."

"I don't even know what I'm doing." That earned me a pinch. "Ow!"

"You could at least not look at them."

"Jealous? Ouch! Stop that!"

We sat in the chairs facing Kismet's lounge, me rubbing my side. I scooted my chair a bit so I was out of Aliena's range. She saw it and scooted her chair, too. I knew it would be a waste to continue.

A table stood to my right with two bottles of champagne on ice and a dozen crystal glasses. I poured two flutes, handed one to Kismet. We toasted.

"Can you feel the effects of alcohol?" I asked her. Vampires did not consume anything but blood, but merpeople seemed to be closer to human beings—except for the tails.

"Oh, yes." She took another sip and giggled. "I love it." She finished and handed me the empty. I refilled it and handed it back to her. Her expression turned solemn. "You killed Diacos but not Bork?"

"Yes."

"You have nothing to worry about," Aliena assured her. "We'll take care of that big beast."

Kismet shivered. "Oooh, that animal, How I hated his hands on my tail! Why did he try to take me?"

"Divide and conquer. Diacos was sure Aliena would stay here and protect you, thus taking her out of the equation. He did not realize she was a vampire and could not remain during the day anyway."

"That monster," Kismet said softly. "I told him—I told him about my love for you," she said to Aliena. "He—he acted like he cared." Tears seeped out of her eyes at this unimagined betrayal. Kismet, for all her age, remained remarkably innocent.

Aliena patted her hand. "He doesn't care about anything anymore, dear," she said seriously. It took a moment. Then we were all laughing.

I finished my champagne and poured another glass. "Does the feeling of the alcohol last very long?"

She stared at me blankly. "Compared to what?"

"Well, compared to human beings." Since merpeople are immortal, they should have a metabolism similar to mine—alcohol should have a limited impact on their bodies. There might be slight differences for size and weight, but the overall effect should be short-lived.

"Oh. I have never noticed. May I have more?"

I filled her glass again. "You've had two glasses of champagne," I said, wanting to know. "How do you feel now?" I passed her the flute.

"Now you're making me nervous."

"Sebastian," Aliena said.

"Okay, I'm sorry." I pulled on the reins of my curiosity. "I apologize, Kismet." I drank the rest of my champagne in a gulp and filled the glass again, knowing I would have to use observation to find the answers I sought.

I watched the two of them as they talked. Good conmen read people as well as any detective and can identify a person's weaknesses in moments. Diacos had recognized a perfect mark in Kismet, a soul who could never conceive of a friend lying to her. In an important way, the filthy pestilence had raped her.

I was jealous of Aliena. I wish I could have killed the bugger. I hoped I would find Bork first. After all that had happened, I wanted to kill *some*body.

"We have to be going, Kiz," Aliena said.

I came out of my reverie, glanced at my watch. Five minutes before midnight. She really never missed her accursed fights. I glanced at Marcus. He kissed Echo's hand. She did not look at him and appeared very put out. He turned from her and headed our way, a small smile on his face. Marcus never missed the damned bouts, either.

"It's almost midnight," Kismet said. "Do you still watch your fights?"

"Yes." I thought Aliena sounded a little defiant. I guessed 49 had been a sore spot for them, too. My poor dear. Everybody disliked her favorite entertainment.

"They're not so bad," I said. I remembered Gary Yu and the way Lourdes had sucked his life through his wrist. That had been bad. But the fights didn't usually play out like that. The end was nearly always swift.

Kismet gave me a sad smile. I felt a rush of tender affection for her. "I know," she said. She set her glass down and reached her hands out to me. I stood, took them, and leaned down so we could embrace. "Thank you, Sebastian."

The smell of her intoxicated this close. I felt a yearning stronger than ordinary friendship. "You're welcome."

"Please watch over her."

"I will." I straightened up, a fog of sultry emotion enveloping me.

Aliena also stood and kissed the mermaid on the cheek. "I'll come back soon."

"You won't," Kismet said. "But I understand."

As we moved to go, Marcus walked up and joined us. "Going to 49?" he asked.

"Wouldn't miss it. Not tonight."

They exchanged a secret smile. What the hell?

"Okay," I said as we put our shoes on, "now what are you two not telling me?"

"Whatever do you mean?" Marcus said. He held the Hanged Man to his mouth.

"Oh, never mind."

Aliena removed her star card and whispered to it. It began to expand. "I suppose I will find out later."

"Maybe sooner than you think," she said. She took my hand.

And with that, we stepped together into the black opening that transported us through space and time.

Chapter 49

Wednesday, January 28, 12:32 a.m.

I could not believe my eyes.

We sat in our usual ringside seats. I had received my customary fang-bearing reception, including a lip-licking smile from the leather-clad young man who always sat to my right.

"How did you get him to fight?" I asked, astonished.

Bork stepped into the ring, a massive figure in shorts, his black Magistine tattoo sharply delineated against his pale skin. He had his hands and ankles taped. No gloves and no shoes. This was apparently going to be a mixed martial arts event. When he saw Mario standing in the other corner, bare-chested and wearing his voluminous red trunks, Bork hesitated with his right leg halfway through the ropes, looking like a dog about to tinkle on the azaleas.

"We offered him one hundred thousand dollars to fight to the death," Marcus answered.

"And he took it?"

"He's violent by nature, so it really wasn't that difficult persuading him."

Bork stepped the rest of the way through and took his place in the blue corner, bouncing lightly on the balls of his feet and throwing rapid shadow combinations. The emcee entered the ring wearing his moth-eaten black tux, his black-and-white hair sticking up like a backward waterfall.

"Let's get ready to drink uuuuuuuppppppp!"

Cheers filled the auditorium.

"In the red corner, wearing the red trunks with the red trim," he shouted, "fighting for the fourteenth century, with a record of two thousand forty-eight and oh, with two thousand forty-eight coming by way of bite-out, is Mario de la Francisco Mejia!"

"I *love* Mario," Aliena yelled, jumping up, clapping and shouting. "Woo-hoo, Mario!"

I had to laugh. Mario pranced over the canvas doing his usual girly pirouettes, waving to the crowd, the baggy boxing shorts swaying loosely past his skinny knees. He appeared as thin as an ex-husband's alibi and had a mustache so threadlike it looked to be drawn on with eyeliner. Over his slicked-back black hair, he wore a fine hairnet. He could not have weighed more than one twenty, or so. As a jockey, I could see him—not a fighter.

The crowd cheered lustily.

"And in the blue corner, fighting for the city of Magisty, wearing the blue trunks with white trim, is Detrit "the Destroyer" Bork!"

Now came the boos and shouts of "Pop his neck!" and "Give him a fang for me!"

Bork must have taken issue with something the emcee had said, for now he advanced on the little vampire, pointing at him. The emcee darted left and hustled right. Bork turned to follow, but Mario suddenly blocked his path, holding his hand up, wagging his index finger back and forth in a no-no gesture.

Clearly enraged, Bork brought his right hand up and smashed it down on top of Mario's head. The vampire sagged, his skinny legs wobbling. Bork pounded him again. Mario hit the deck.

Bork straddled him and began teeing off on his face, landing one crushing punch after another. The vampire's head bounced off the mat after each blow. Mario finally blocked one and slid between Bork's legs.

Both men got up. Mario smiled and waved to the crowd. Cheers washed over him as Bork approached from behind. The big man took two steps, leaped into the air, and delivered a crushing kick to the side of the vampire's head. From behind.

What did you expect from a fight to the death? Sportsmanship?

Mario dropped like a bag of grapefruit. He rolled over and slowly came up on all fours. Bork stepped up and kicked him in the face. The blow was violent enough to catapult his diminutive opponent out of the ring. Soaring over the ropes, Mario somersaulted three times before crashing headfirst into the third row of spectators.

Four men in the crowd helped him to his feet and back to the ring. The skinny fighter jumped over the ropes. His hairnet remained perfectly positioned, and he did not have a mark on him.

Bork did not charge this time. He may have been slow, but he knew his opponent should show some damage. After those two kicks to the head, no one should have been able to get up, let alone remain unmarked.

Mario walked back to the center of the ring and assumed a fighting pose. He looked ridiculous challenging a man the size of the Magistine to a bare-fisted fight, yet Bork was the one who hesitated.

The crowd—and Aliena—loved it. As Bork began to close in, the noise in the room reached a boisterous pitch, and Aliena bounced up and down on the balls of her feet. "Go Marioooooo," she said. I stood, too.

Bork threw a right that connected with Mario's temple. He was following it with a left cross when a sticklike leg shot up and banged into his groin. Bork didn't go down, but he did cover himself with both hands and let out a bellow of pain.

Mario danced back and forth in front of him, shadowboxing.

Bork let out another roar, this one of rage. He leaped toward Mario. He collided with nothing but air and hit the ground on his stomach. The vampire jumped on him and began pounding the back of his head with a pistonlike movement of his clenched fist. After the third blow, every time Bork's head bounced up, blood sprayed over the mat underneath him.

Mario grabbed the big man's hair and yanked his head back hard enough to break his neck. The vampire's head flashed to the Magistine's throat. Bork's arms jerked when Mario bit him. He moved sluggishly for a few moments. Then the muscles of his body sagged, and he fell still.

Aliena clapped and whistled. She jumped into my arms and kissed me on the mouth. "Did you enjoy that one?"

"Yes, I did." Looking at the smile on her face, I could tell she did want to share 49 with someone important in her life. Her question proved that. She cared whether or not I had fun here.

She laughed delightedly, kissed me again, and turned back to the ring.

From past remarks I had made, she knew I did not like the fights. Watching her cheer as Mario drained the killer Bork, I swore to try harder to enjoy the bouts and made a vow never to complain about coming here again. For her. She was worth that and more.

I leaned past her. "Marcus, could you make sure his body is found tomorrow and that the police will be able to identify him?"

"I have already made the arrangements."

"Thank you."

The little emcee approached the ring. Mario patted his stomach, then locked his arms around Bork's limp body, lifted him off the mat and into the air, and carried him behind one of the rows of seats. Ten vampires turned as he lowered the Magistine to the ground. They all leaned over and fastened themselves onto the big body.

So the man who killed Gonzales was dead and that account was now paid. That reminded me. I pulled out my phone, contacted my lawyer, and told him to arrange the payment of $10 million to the detective's family, as I had promised him I would.

"Put it through the department. They can't know it's coming from me. Use the alternate insurance story and explain that the large amount is due his heirs because he gave his life in the performance of his duties."

As I slipped my phone into my pocket, I noticed Aliena had remained standing.

"Okay, we can go," she said.

"No, let's stay for at least one more." I sat down and pulled her onto my lap. The leather-clad vampire to my right said something under his breath. Similar to most of the vampires here (male and female), he probably hated that Aliena had chosen me for a mate. As if that were not bad enough, it undoubtedly galled him to sit next to me when he could not rip my jugular open.

She played with my ear. "You really want to?"

"I really do. We're in no hurry tonight." I kissed her neck. "We can do whatever we want."

She squeezed me, tipped my chin up, and kissed me hard on the mouth.

We watched two more fights before we left. Neither bout generated the same crowd response as the first match, but that was not surprising. After all, Mario de la Francisco Mejia was a famous world champion.

Chapter 50

Wednesday, January 28, 4:32 a.m.

Aliena and I reclined on the patio, holding hands and watching the cosmos spin, when she made an announcement.

"I want to go to bed."

I glanced at my watch. "It's more than two hours to sunrise."

"Yes, I know. Would you like to tuck me in?"

My heart beat faster. "Every night."

"Carry me."

I picked her up. She laid her head on my shoulder, her lustrous hair pressed against my cheek. The door to her room stood open, so I walked through and set her down on her feet.

She wrapped her arms around my neck and kissed me long and lovingly. "I have wanted you for a long time," she said, fingers stroking the back of my neck. She released me and began taking her clothes off. Now my heart beat like a snare drum . . . until she reached for her pajamas and put them on. She climbed under the covers and pulled them to her neck. I sat on the edge and leaned down, running my hand through her hair.

"The pleasure of love has become something I am accustomed to denying myself," she said. Her eyes shone, luminous, and I thought I had never seen her look more beautiful. "And after a hundred years, it seemed more important than it probably should have."

"Yes, I felt that when reading your diary." I kissed her cheek. "I understand."

She took my hand and held it against her cheek. "When you kiss me, I feel weak, almost delirious, and when you run your hands over my derrière, it makes me feel hot and cold all over. And this Christmas, I knew you were the one."

"Your dear Maman told you more than a century ago," I said.

She giggled. "Yes, she did." She pulled me close, kissed the tip of my nose. "That's how I knew you loved me enough to wait for me to make up my mind."

"Well, I waited but not in chastity, as you know. There—"

She pressed her fingers against my lips. "Don't, Sebastian, please. I cannot bear the thought of you with someone else. Not anymore."

I kissed her fingertips. "I apologize."

"Are you all mine now?" she asked, her dark eyes wide.

"For as long as you want me."

"Promise?"

"It is not up to me, my darling. My heart tells me what to do when it comes to you. I love you. I could never leave you."

She closed her eyes and sighed, a smile on her face. "That makes me feel so wonderful, I can't even describe it." She sat up again, clapping her hands gleefully. "I don't think I have ever been this happy in my life."

Now I could see it. My darling Aliena was in love with me. Finally, romantically, infatuated. I felt that thrilling, full-body rush that happens when you realize you are not separate anymore: you are two becoming one. It's as simple and elemental as that, yet breathtaking in its possibilities.

I let my feelings off the short leash on which I had kept them these many years, and my spirit exulted, releasing all the emotion and spiritual joy that is love. I remembered how I had felt when I thought I had gone to Heaven. This felt the same.

"I know I have never been happier," I told her.

She pulled me down, crushing me to her, and kissed me with fiery passion. When she released me, she reached under the blankets. She squirmed around and came up with her Bugs Bunny pajama bottoms, tossed them on the floor. She pulled the top over her head. She leaned back against the pillows, the blankets at her hips, her skin cream in the lamp's glow. Her eyes shone, vulnerable and excited, trusting me with something she had not given out in almost150 years.

Her heart.

"I have waited so long," she said with a tremor in her voice. "I love you, Sebastian. Please love me."

"My darling," I whispered. With shaking fingers, I took my clothes off and climbed in next to her. We slid on our sides until we pressed our naked bodies together, our hands exploring. Her breath came in gasps as I caressed her nipples with my lips.

"Sebastian," she said in a long sigh.

When I gently parted her legs, I explored with fingertips and tongue and lips, drawing a low murmur from her as she dragged her nails leisurely along my shoulders.

I came up and clasped both of her wrists, pushed her onto her back, and forced her arms above her head, holding them there. I moved between her legs and we looked into each other's eyes as I slowly eased myself inside.

Our groans of ecstasy were simultaneous as we became one. Once her hips were in position, I leaned down and kissed her, moving rhythmically, both our mouths open, me occasionally groaning as she whimpered and shuddered beneath me. For uncountable minutes we floated on an ever-building tide. I felt the crest approaching as if from light-years away, and my body tingled from head to toe.

Aliena pulled her mouth away from mine and began panting against my throat. "Sebastiannnnn . . ." Her hips bucked beneath me as I lost control and became one with the Gods. I released her wrists and lowered my hand to her behind, pulling her tightly to me.

She wound her arms around my neck, gripped my hair, and said very softly, "Ohhhhhhhhh . . ." as she melted beneath me. Her rising hips slowed in de-escalatory rhythm until she was still.

We stayed like that, breathing heavily together for a long, comfortable time. Aliena finally broke the silence.

"Oh my God, Sebastian. No wonder people talk about making love the way they do. I never dreamed it could feel so good."

I leaned up to gaze at her, and she dropped her hands to my butt, pulling hard. "Stay with me," she said.

"Oh, yes. I just wanted to look at you." While we stared at each other, I felt a connection click inside, as if some unfinished part of me was now complete. When she smiled, she was more beautiful than a sunset. I rejoiced that we were finally together. For me, life on Earth could not be better.

I pressed atop her again, taking handfuls of her hair and pulling as I brought my mouth against hers. While our tongues fenced playfully, I felt myself responding. I began a slow tempo.

"Mmmmmmm." I don't know which of us had sighed. For more than an hour we murmured and kissed, our bodies and souls melting into each other, our spirits singing a deliriously blissful duet.

Too happy to write, Diary. Sebastian and I are together. Last night still vibrates my being, surrounding me with a sensation more euphoric than I ever imagined possible. I may not be back for a while. The time for recording has passed. I want to live more than ever now, with Sebastian. Because being in love is the most wonderful feeling in the world.

Sebastian Montero
Malibu, California
March 9, 2010

Acknowledgments

Once again, my humble thanks to Mia Turner for her tireless review of *Tarot of the Archons*. She investigated anomalies and corrected factual errors just as she did for book one. The first two books in this series are extremely clean as a result of her efforts. Thank you, Miafraulein, for helping me appear knowledgeable.

Thank you to the Kindle Scouts who nominated the book, and to my Kindle editor, Ruth, for her many improvements to the manuscript.

Thanks to my daughter Lauren and Kristi Cha, my target readers, for their enthusiastic praise. As with all my works, I owe a debt to everyone who read my stories along the way and provided me with important feedback.

Thank you to Leo and Barbara Mongrain for encouraging me to read when I was young, thereby creating my dream of being an author.

Made in the USA
Charleston, SC
03 October 2016